DARKER
THAN
DESIRE

DARKER THAN DESIRE

SHILOH WALKER

St. Martin's Paperbacks

This is a work of fiction. All of the characters, organizations, and events portrayed in this novel are either products of the author's imagination or are used fictitiously.

DARKER THAN DESIRE

Copyright © 2015 by Shiloh Walker.

For information address St. Martin's Press, 175 Fifth Avenue, New York, NY 10010.

ISBN: 978-1-250-03242-3

Printed in the United States of America

St. Martin's Paperbacks edition / March 2015

St. Martin's Paperbacks are published by St. Martin's Press, 175 Fifth Avenue, New York, NY 10010.

10 9 8 7 6 5 4 3 2 1

To my family, always. I thank God for you.

By special request . . .

*Dedicated to Cassie & Derrick, Shane & Melissa,
Tiffany & Dane . . . love you.*

A huge thank you to my readers. You are all wonderful.

CHAPTER ONE

He was a man who understood pain.

That's all there was to it.

The boy he'd been, David Sutter, had been groomed to understand it, and although it hadn't gone as planned, he'd been groomed to *need* pain. To want it, then to inflict it.

Now, more than twenty years gone from the broken child he'd been, he thought he knew everything there was to know about pain. But he'd never felt anything quite like this. There was a hollow, empty ache in his chest where his heart should be, a knot in his throat that felt like it would strangle him, and he could barely breathe.

For too long, he'd thought he'd forgotten *how* to really feel. Anger, yeah. He could feel that. He *liked* feeling that. But he existed on the two As. Anger and apathy.

Not pain.

The people around him didn't grieve quite the way he did. After all, death was part of life and Abraham was gone because God had willed it. They would miss him, David knew that, and he could see their grief in the damp eyes of the women across from him, the solemn set of the men's faces.

But while he sat there, furious in a way that he couldn't

explain and hurting like a son of a bitch, they all had a peace about them. Yet another reminder of why he didn't belong here.

Abraham had lived a full life and he was gone because God had willed it—David had heard that more times than he could count today. If he heard it again, he thought he might do something violent. God—he'd stopped believing in any such being so long ago.

David couldn't even remember the last time he'd prayed. It might have been the second time, or the third, maybe the fifth time he'd been dragged down into a dark, bloody hell, gagged and tied, left to the vices of whatever monster wanted to break him next.

What sort of God let that evil happen?

David didn't know.

The voices around him rose in song again, but he just stared at the wooden box, the still, peaceful face of the man lying inside it.

Abraham Yoder, the man who'd been David's rock for years, was gone.

The air inside the church was hot and tight. He felt like he was choking, smothering inside his own skin. How long had it been since the service had started?

David—known to these people as Caine Yoder—was all but desperate to escape.

The service dragged on. It felt like hours. Experience told him it was probably roughly just one before they filed past Abraham's coffin one final time and then he helped load it into the buggy that would take the old man on his final journey.

David barely remembered doing it. Barely remembered helping Sarah over at the house over the past few days, barely remembered anything since he'd received the call.

He hadn't even been here.

The entirety of this day was just a blur, save for this moment, clear and brutally harsh, as he stood alone at Abraham's grave.

Everybody else was gone. Thomas had quietly come to guide Sarah away. People must have seen something in David's face, because not one approached him; not one of them said a single word.

Minutes ticked away into hours as he stood there and he couldn't drag himself away.

Once he did, once he turned his back, this final connection to Abraham would be gone.

He'd died in his bed, quietly in his sleep. A heart attack, most likely. David couldn't have picked a better way for him to pass from the world. But David was a selfish son of a bitch and he hadn't wanted the man to leave at all.

There would be no more gentle advice, no more calm talks when David thought he was really going to step over that edge into rage-fueled oblivion.

Abraham had pulled David back from the brink so many times. And the few times Abraham hadn't been there to stop David from slipping over, he'd been there after and helped pull him back up.

Abraham had never known, not really, just how much hell David carried inside him. Maybe it was good that he'd gone now, before it all came out.

That was what David told himself.

And he lied.

He was pretty damn good at that. He should be, though.

He'd lived a lie for twenty years.

A soft sound caught his attention and slowly he lifted his head.

As she came toward him, in a simple black dress, deceptively simple, deceptively sexy, David turned his head away. "You didn't have to come," he said, his voice a monotone. It was easier, better, to cut things between them now.

But Sybil Chalmers didn't do easy and she didn't do simple.

Perhaps if he had truly let himself join this world, become part of the community here and left the outside world to itself, he could have cut her out of his mind, out of his soul.

It would have been easier to will himself to stop breathing.

She picked her way through the simple grave markers until she could stand at his side. "He was your family." She reached down, caught David's hand.

Her skin was shockingly hot.

Or maybe he was just cold.

Clamping his fingers tight around hers, wished he could send her away.

"He wasn't my family," he said, biting the words off. "He was an old man who took me in when I was a kid. I stayed because I felt like it. He kept me here because I was useful."

"Hmmm." She didn't look away from the grave. "If that's all it was, then why are you still here when everybody else is gone?"

Instead of answering, he just closed his eyes.

She didn't know where they were.

He'd pulled her up into the buggy, leaving her car behind on the narrow little strip of a road that led to the cemetery.

Now they were moving down a quiet little bit of road while the moon shone down on them and the night creatures sounded in the distance.

They were completely alone.

Very few ever drove a car out here. Thanks to David, she knew a little more about the community here than most.

There was a larger Amish community—the Old Order, with all the strict rules, rejecting modern technology and the way the English dressed—but then there was the smaller group that David had been with the past twenty years. Abraham had never gone into much detail about it, but apparently the two communities had been one at some point in the past, but something drove them apart.

Abraham, the man David refused to admit he'd loved, had been part of that smaller group. She'd once asked David why they hadn't left and David had just shrugged. "Abraham is kind, gentle . . . patient. They'd have to outwait him to get him out of here, and that's not going to happen."

She guessed not. Abraham had been eighty-nine when he died.

Next to her, David sat rigid, so stiff she thought he might break if she touched him. She thought he might break if she didn't. After an internal war that seemed to last forever, she reached over, touched his hand. "I wish I could make this better for you."

A second later, he pulled up on the reins and the horse obediently stopped.

Her breath caught in her lungs, but he didn't look at her, didn't say anything.

Instead, he climbed down from the buggy and was lost to her sight.

Closing her eyes, she blew out a soft breath and caught the long skirt of her dress in one fist as she started to figure out the process of climbing out of a buggy. In the dark. In heeled boots.

Before she'd managed to figure out where to so much

as put the first boot, a pair of hard hands closed around her waist. She jerked her head up, but he wasn't looking at her as he set her down.

As soon as her feet touched the ground, he turned away and started to pace.

"Why are you here?" he finally asked.

"Where else would I be?" She stood with her hands loose at her sides, resisting the urge to fold them over her middle, tuck herself away, hide away. Protect herself from the hurt she suspected was coming. Maybe not tonight. Maybe not next week, or even this month, but David was pulling away from her. She could feel it.

A bitter curse escaped him and he reached up to shove a hand through his hair only to encounter the simple hat. He tore it off and threw it to the ground.

She tensed as he drove his booted foot down on it, all but grinding his heel through the stiffened fabric.

When he was done, she licked her lips and then looked back up. All she could see was his stiff shoulders as he faced away from her. "Feel better?"

He spun around, his mouth open.

She inclined her head. *You don't scare me, tough guy.*

His eyes narrowed.

She closed the distance between them, each step slow and precise—she was terrified she'd trip over something on the dark, uneven ground and fall on her ass.

She didn't stop until she was close enough that his heat seemed to reach out, taunt her skin. Then she leaned in, pressed her mouth to his. She didn't give him a sweet, soft kiss, though. David was well past the *I'll kiss it and make it better* point. That never would have worked for him anyway. Instead, she sank her teeth into his lower lip. Hard.

He stiffened against her.

Slowly, she drew back, dragging her tongue along her

lip, staring at his mouth for a long second before looking up to meet his gaze. "You're hurting. You're feeling mean. I want to help, if I can. If you'll let me."

She went to turn away, but a hard arm banded around her waist, hauled her back against him. "And how are you going to help? How can you make any of this better?" he demanded, his words a harsh rasp against her ear. His chest was an iron wall against her back, and tucked against her bottom she felt the hot, heavy length of his cock.

She suppressed the urge to shudder, barely.

But then a wide, warm palm came up to rest on her thigh, fingers catching the material of her skirt, dragging upward. "Maybe that's a stupid question." His fingers dipped inside her panties and she gasped as he started to stroke. "This always makes me feel better."

For a little while, at least, she thought, breaking inside. But it wasn't like she could pull away. Already she could feel her muscles clamping around him and she knew in just a matter of time she'd be riding his hand, practically desperate for him.

"You want to make me feel better, Sybil?"

David tangled his fingers in her hair. She'd tamed it into a somewhat reserved twist, but he dislodged the clip and pins, impatient, sending the curls spilling down over her shoulder with his free hand while he continued to stroke her with the other hand.

She hadn't answered him, though.

He had to hear the words.

With another taunting, slow twist of his fingers, he stopped touching her and forced her to turn. A soft, sexy little cry escaped her and then a ragged breath as he stroked his fingers, from her sex, across her lips.

"Make me feel better."

She went to lick her lips and he caught her chin in his hands. "Don't," he growled, angling her face up. There was another ragged breath, a broken moan as he licked the sweet/tart taste of her away and then proceeded to slip his tongue inside her mouth, another slow, teasing slide of his body into hers. "I'm the one who gets to taste. I'm the one who gets to lick . . . feel . . . touch. . . ."

He gripped her ass in his hand and dragged her against him. "Like this."

Lust burned, roared inside him, and he pulled away. He had to be inside her. Had to.

His eyes, used to the dark and these fields, searched the area and found what he needed before he caught her hand and laced their fingers together.

Her face was pale, her eyes dark and wild in her face, as she and David reached the fence just fifteen yards from the buggy. He pulled off his jacket and draped it over the top, a barrier between the rough wood and Sybil's back. Then he urged her up against it, his mouth crushing up against hers as he slid his hands down her back, along the curves of her hips to grasp her butt and pull her in tight.

"Make me feel better, Sybil," he rasped in between one breathless, soul-stealing kiss and another.

She slid a hand between them and he groaned as she started to stroke him. He pulsed in her hand and he felt something wet seep out. Forcing distance between them, he braced his hands on the long, sturdy boards that made up the fence's rails. "Take off your panties," he ordered, his voice harder, harsher.

Sybil's lashes swept down in a slow blink, a faint smile curving up the corners of her mouth. He wanted to fist his hands in her hair, haul her back up against him and feast on that mouth. Every day. Always.

Instead, he curled his hands tighter into the old, weathered boards and watched as she dragged up the sleek column of material that made up the skirt of her dress. Starved, he watched, barely able to see anything over the pool of fabric, but imagination served him well. Soft thighs, round and smooth and strong. Her hips, lush and female. The neat patch of curls between her thighs, covering the heat of her, where she was already wet for him.

Once she had the panties off, she held them in her hand and he reached over, pushed them into his pocket. "Take me out. I want to feel your hands on me."

A harsh breath stuttered out of her, and while it soothed some of the raw, jagged edges inside him, it also made the burning need worsen. She needed this, needed *him* just as much as he needed her.

But this was poison . . . or addiction. Both. Something he'd started to crave so long ago, he couldn't imagine *not* wanting her, not needing her, not needing to feel her under him. She was inside him, in every way that counted . . . just another sign that he wasn't as closed off as he wanted to be, needed to be.

Don't think about it now.

Easy enough, because Sybil had his trousers open and her fingers closed around the heavy ache of his erection and his head fell back, bliss spreading through him as she started to stroke. Firm, tight strokes, her thumb occasionally brushing over his cockhead in a maddening little caress that went straight to his balls.

That sensation raced through him, drew him tighter, tighter—

His cock jerked and for a second he thought . . . *maybe* . . .

The thought of coming on her, in her hands, losing control just like that, burned inside his brain, something he wanted, he needed.

You need the pain—

He swore and all but tore her hands away.

"Rubber," he said, forcing the words through his teeth.

Like a magician, she produced one. Where she'd had it, he didn't know and he didn't care. "Put it on me."

Her lashes swept down low and he used those brief seconds away from her gaze to try and regain control, but it was impossible. Her fingers smoothed over him as she dealt with the condom, turning the task into a seduction. When she was finished, he boosted her up and drove into her with savage hunger. Sybil cried out, hooking one hand around his shoulders.

Her eyes stared into his with naked hunger, naked shock, as he slammed into her, hard and deep, little care for finesse or control. He just *wanted*. He just *needed*.

And she met him stroke for stroke, touch for touch.

He pressed his face to her neck and sank his teeth into the supple curve there, felt her tighten around him like glory, and he grunted, felt the warning spasms in her sex. She pressed a line of kisses to his jawline, his ear.

Blind, he turned his face to hers, fusing their mouths together.

That need drove him on, still hard, still demanding.

Sybil cried out into his mouth and he shuddered in agonized pleasure as she clamped down and came around him. He *could* feel the release, feel it hovering just on the edge—

Her teeth sank into his lower lip, exactly where she'd bitten him earlier, harder this time. At the same time, her hand gripped the shorter strands of his hair and twisted.

The line between pain and pleasure blurred and he felt it collapse, that unseen wall inside him. With a groan, he climaxed, his cock jerking, pulsing inside her as he emptied himself.

* * *

"What are you going to do now?"

She asked the question softly as he took her back to her car.

His body was sated, his brain dull, from the release and the exhaustion of the day.

Her question took more thought than he liked, even though he didn't really have to think very hard. He'd been thinking about this for . . . well. Maybe ever since the day he'd run away from home.

He'd always known, David realized.

Sooner or later, he'd have to go home and face his demons.

Turning his head, he met her eyes from under his lashes.

"I'm leaving here."

Her eyes went wide, her mouth falling open.

Before she could say anything, he focused his gaze on the dark road. The moon was full, giving them more light, but they had to go slow and he needed to get Sybil away so he could think, start to figure things out. He never could think clearly when she was there.

"Leaving . . . ?" she whispered.

"Abraham is gone. He left the farm to his daughter and I could stay in my house on the hill, but it isn't right." He looked around the quiet darkness surrounding them, felt an odd tug in the region of his heart. He'd miss it, he realized. Some of it, at least. "I don't belong here."

"Where—" She cut herself off, but from the corner of his eye he could see the strain on her face.

"I'll find a place in town." He shrugged. He'd already looked around, checked a few things out. Money wasn't an issue. He had money. The issue was everything else.

"Town. You're moving to Madison," she said, her voice ragged.

From the corner of his eye he watched her for a moment. "Did you really see me going anywhere else?"

Her gaze flicked away. "I don't know. You . . ." She heaved out a sigh. "But I don't see you being happy in town."

"Happy." He snorted. "Happy . . . ? Yeah, sure. I can be happy there with half the town staring at me like I'm a freak and the other half like I'm a monster."

"You're *not* a monster." Her gaze cut to him. "And you're no more a freak than I am."

Faint amusement worked through him. "At least you don't lie and tell me I'm normal."

"What is normal?" she asked, reaching up to touch his cheek.

This . . . part of him wanted to believe this was normal. That this could *be* normal. "Normal . . . not me." He shrugged. "People in town know. Unless they've been living under a rock, they know who I am and the ones who aren't idiots are already figuring out . . ."

He stopped, unable to continue. Unable to voice that shame in front of her.

"Figure out what?" she asked, her voice gentle. "That your father was a monster? Good. People *should* know he was a monster."

Fury pulsed in her voice. "It's made me *sick* the past twenty years, watching people mourn him and your mother."

Her gaze came to his. "You know . . ." She hesitated.

He jerked a shoulder. "You knew he was abusive back then. You were one of a few." His heart thudded hard against his chest. "One of a very few."

"I'm sorry."

"Why?" His laugh sounded like jagged bits of glass. "Because people know? Don't be. You're right. Everybody should know he was a monster." Shaking his head, he murmured, "Yeah. They should know."

Her hand smoothed up his back while secrets and shame slithered through him, but for once, it all wanted to come spilling out. Clenching his jaw against the words tearing up his throat like bile, he said, "I can't leave. There's too much left undone, unanswered."

Sybil's hand, soft and strong, smoothed up his back. "Some questions won't ever be answered."

Nobody knew that better than him.

But he had some of those answers himself, tucked away inside his head. And if he'd look deeper, he could probably find a few more.

Sybil watched from the road as he turned the buggy off the main road. She would have liked to follow him, but it was weird enough coming out here just to offer him comfort he clearly hadn't wanted.

He hadn't wanted it, no. But the pain in him was wild. The need enough to take her breath away.

She'd probably have bruises on her hips in the morning, and although her body felt bruised in that wonderful, blissful way that could only happen when you have good, hard sex, she knew he'd just done the same thing he always did.

Used her body to avoid looking at his own pain too deeply.

Used her so he wouldn't have to think about the fact that he needed her.

He did need her. She'd seen it in his eyes, on his face, in the way he clung to her as their breathing calmed and their hearts slowed. He needed her, and because he did, he would push her away.

He'd been doing it for weeks.

To be honest, she'd been half-expecting this anyway.

Hell. She was actually shocked David Sutter had ever let her get close to him at all. One look in his dark, tortured eyes and she'd realized that he had demons living inside him. All the truths were coming to light now and she understood more about those demons than she really ever wanted to know.

She wanted to hunt down the people who'd hurt him as a child.

She wanted to put herself at his side so he never had to go through anything alone again.

But David—Caine, whatever he called himself—only wanted to be alone, except on the rare occasions he didn't. Then he turned to her. When he left in the quiet hours before dawn, she was exhausted, aching, and the need for him was like a drug in her system. *More, more, more . . .* that was all she wanted.

But he gave her less and less.

Sybil was stupid enough, desperate enough, needy enough, to accept whatever he was willing to give her, to give him as much as he was willing to take.

And all the while, she hid some truths from him that she'd likely never reveal to him.

Sighing, she did a three-point turn and headed back into town. She needed to get out of her boots, get into her bed and crash. Alone. Thankfully, she had that option.

She'd left her nephew, Drew, with her best friend. Taneisha Oakes had a boy about Drew's age and the two had become almost inseparable. It was a good fit, in more ways than one.

Taneisha wasn't going to be intimidated or freaked out if Drew's mother, and Sybil's sister, showed up looking for him. It wasn't likely to happen, because Layla didn't have a maternal bone in her body and the few times she'd actually tried to get involved with her son she'd been doing it to get something from Sybil.

But if she tried to square off with Taneisha, Layla would find herself in for a rude awakening. Taneisha might leave a few shards of bone when she was done, but that was it.

Someday Sybil wanted to think her little sister would get her act together, stop the drinking, the drugs, and kick the revolving-door habit thing she had with men.

Until that day, though? Sybil's goal was simple—keep Drew out of his mother's destructive orbit.

He'd be safer. Happier.

And if Sybil knew what was good for her, she'd pull out of David's orbit before it was too late.

But that point had already come and gone.

*　*　*

Within minutes of his leaving her, that raw, edgy energy returned.

David knew he should be doing better than this—it shouldn't hit him so hard that he'd lost Abraham, shouldn't hit him so hard that he was alone in the quiet, again. Without Sybil.

He'd been alone in the quiet for most of the past twenty years and this was how he'd wanted it, why he'd deliberately set out to shut himself down, shut himself off, so he couldn't feel, so he *didn't* feel.

Maybe it had all been a lie, though.

Brooding, he stared out into the night. It was past midnight. It was quiet, the air in the house cool and still. And his brain wouldn't shut down. He'd wanted to collapse and just sleep, but he couldn't.

There was too *much* inside him. The grief for Abraham, the need to leave here—*now*—and find Sybil, wrap himself around her so the nightmares wouldn't find him. They never did, not when he was with her.

He'd told himself that was why he let this go on so long.

Except it was a lie.

He knew it now, just like he'd known it then. The escape from the nightmares was a plus, but the reason he couldn't pull back was because it was Sybil. Because he enjoyed the way she felt, the way she smelled, the way she moved against him in her sleep and the way she looked him dead in the eye with that unflinching way she had.

Some part of him might think he loved her, but he knew that wasn't right. David was too flawed, too fucked-up, to love. He didn't buy into the shit that he'd done something to make his father hurt him, or that it had happened because of something David was—that wasn't why he couldn't love.

David couldn't love simply because he'd spent the past twenty years smothering those emotions inside him. He'd killed those urges until he might as well have destroyed the part of his soul that made him able to feel. Even with Abraham, a man David *wanted* to love, a man who had him grieving and hurting inside, he knew it wasn't love that he felt.

He did care, though. Because he did, and because he cared too much, he knew he needed to end things. Too much of the ugliness in his past was about ready to come spilling out, ready to stain and ruin everything he touched.

Once she really understood all of that—

His hands started to shake and he made a deliberate effort to block everything out. If he just didn't think about it, it was easier. That slow crawl of red didn't creep in on his vision and he didn't think about slipping out of the house, taking the old truck or even just making the hours-long walk into town and trying to find one of them.

Were there any left?

David didn't know, but there were times when he'd been ready to paint the town with swaths of murderous blood-red just to find one of them. Especially over the past few months. Because it hadn't stopped.

That, he knew, was what had him so close to the edge now.

Why he woke up choking and clawing his way out of the nightmares, still hearing their voices. Voices that echoed, lingered, a stain on his soul.

"Stop." He swiped the back of his hand over his mouth and spun away from the window so he could pace.

The shaking would stop. The rage would ease.

Then he'd be able to think again, as long as he didn't give in to that rage.

He'd given in to it before. Just a couple of times. He'd never killed anybody . . . yet. But he'd taken back some of the blood, and he'd reveled in it as agonized cries managed to break through gags or muffling hands.

David didn't regret it. If he stood before a judge one day over it, they'd probably lock him away or send him to a home for the mentally unfit. He'd smile and say, *I'd do it again.*

Two men. Two men who'd never be able to tear into a boy the way they'd torn into him. Maybe he should be sorry for it, but regret was another emotion he couldn't feel.

As the edgy, broken rage spun inside him, he started to pace, the four walls of the plain home he'd built for himself closing in around him. Suffocating him. The silence beyond these walls was doing the same. Abruptly he turned and headed toward the closet where he'd been stowing boxes. Not many, just a few. But he didn't need more than that.

He grabbed them and hauled them out, dumped them on the bed.

There was duct tape in the truck and he went outside, the cool air washing over his overheated flesh. It brought little relief. He found the tape and a utility knife and headed back inside.

Within five minutes, all of the boxes were ready to be filled, and he went about do just that.

It took an hour for that red haze to melt back.

Having a task, a chore, something to accomplish, helped him focus, helped to center him.

Everything at the farm down at the bottom of the hill was quiet. A few days ago, during a family meal—the last he'd ever share with Abraham and Sarah—David had told them the truth he'd been keeping to himself over the past few weeks. It was time to leave here, time to return to the life he'd run from years ago.

Sarah had looked at him as though he'd slapped her. *Go back to the English? Why?*

Abraham had simply studied him, but in the back of his eyes David had seen understanding. Abraham, unlike Sarah, had known the truth: David had never belonged here.

Now that Abraham was gone, there was nothing to hold David here and it would be better if he left before the mess in town followed him.

He couldn't let it happen.

Sarah would never understand that.

As he looked around the small house, he realized the entirety of his life had been packed away into five boxes. Twenty years of living and he'd tucked everything that mattered into a few boxes.

There was the furniture. He'd have to come back for it. Abraham had helped him build it and each piece mattered. Aside from those pieces they had built together, nothing else had any value.

This place had been for Caine, or the person Caine had pretended to be.

Caine was gone, buried under an explosion of ash the day the Frampton house burned down. Or maybe even the day those bones were revealed, under that rotting floor, when Trinity Ewing fell through the floorboards.

Caine was gone. David was back and David didn't belong here.

There was a quiet sound behind him as the door opened. She didn't knock, but then she never had. He'd gotten over being irritated by it a long time ago. Sarah was who she was and she wasn't going to change. Like her father, she loved David. Unlike her father, she thought loving David would somehow change him, make him fit in here, somehow. As if she prayed enough, it would somehow smooth out all the rough edges, fill in the void inside him.

That wouldn't happen.

She insisted it would, if he gave it time.

He had stopped fighting her a long time ago. Her words rolled over him and sank into the ground around him like rain. They meant nothing. And he suspected there was another watering to come.

"It's late, Sarah. You should be home asleep."

"I buried my father today. I don't need you telling me what to do." She looked around, stared at the boxes, her mouth pinched, her eyes dark and unhappy.

"I'm not trying to tell you what to do. But it's been a hard day. We could all use our rest."

She flung out a hand. "That's what you are doing? Resting?" Nudging a box with the toe of a plain black shoe, she glared at him. "How can you leave me now? We've just buried my father. I need help. I need you here."

He thought about just ignoring that simply spoken, soft statement but instead met Sarah's stark blue-grey eyes. She'd been pretty once. Time and unhappiness had worn that gentle beauty away. It wasn't right and he wondered how much of her unhappiness could be laid at his feet. "I don't belong here, Sarah. I always knew that. Your father knew it. And you don't need me. Your cousins are ready to help you. They've already told you that. Thomas will be here at dawn. He'll always be here for you."

"*You* should be here. This is your home."

"No. It's not."

"It could be, if you would simply let it." Sarah set her jaw and squared her shoulders under the plain blue dress she wore.

Was it as simple as that? He didn't waste more than a minute on it. If it were as simple as that, he would have found the peace that Abraham tried to offer him a hundred, no, a thousand times over the past twenty years.

"Then I guess I've chosen not to." He shrugged and tucked the flaps of the boxes in, closing them up.

"Everything will change for you if you return to that life," Sarah said, her voice stiff. "Nothing but trouble will be there. How will you explain the past twenty years?"

He jerked a shoulder in a shrug. "That's my concern."

"You have—" She stopped, her mouth puckering with distaste. "It's been twenty years since you used that name. You've worked. You've made money. Under another name. Won't that cause problems?"

He saw what she was getting at, especially considering how he had just been thinking about some of those complications. Shrugging it off, he said, "I've always been aware it could be a problem. There was never any guarantee things from back then wouldn't come back to bite me. They have. Now I deal with it."

That seemed to catch her off-guard. "So people already know."

"By now?" He pretended to think it over. "Probably half the town, if not more."

He had slipped into the hospital twice, but each time he'd gone in quietly, left the same way. There for one reason, to check on old Max. His condition was no longer critical, and the last time he'd opened his eyes they met David's. Max had recognized him. But other than Max and the handful of nurses who'd done their best to chase David out, nobody had seen him for long enough to say a word. Toot Jenkins had almost wrecked his truck when they'd passed each other at a four-way stop. All up and down Main Street, David had felt the eyes on him. He wasn't a fool. People knew.

Right now, Lana was in town facing the heat all on her own.

He'd planned to be there, dealing with it as well, but then Thomas had found him, told him about Abraham. So for four days David had been here.

He couldn't continue to linger, though. The longer he was here, the more likely it was that Sorenson was going to hunt him down. That was one thing he'd promised he'd never allow. David didn't want that evil to come here, taint this quiet, peaceful place.

"Why?"

He whipped his head up at the low, angry thread he heard in Sarah's voice. Narrowing his eyes, he studied her. "That's hardly your concern."

"You're part of the family." She paused, her head cocking as though she was thinking something through. "If you leave, people are going to want to know why.

What made you run. You'll have to talk about it. Those are your secrets, secrets that should stay within the family. We always protected you. Stay here, and we'll continue to protect you."

"Abraham was the closest thing to a father I'll ever have." It was nothing but the truth. There was no way in hell he'd claim the monster who'd spawned him. He turned his back on her. "And yes, he spent a long time protecting me, but that time is over. I haven't needed protection for a long time, Sarah. And I'm not part of this family. I don't belong here. If I choose to talk about all those secrets, then that is my concern."

He was quiet for a moment and then said, "But people already know."

Sarah's lids flickered. "What do they know?"

"Who I really am." He tried not to think about what *else* they might know, what they might be thinking— guessing. All the speculation . . . would it even come *close* to the reality?

"How do they know?"

At the soft, almost scared question, he looked up. "Because I stopped hiding."

He'd only told the sheriff, the night Max was shot, but there were others around when he did it and in a town like Madison, news spread like wildfire.

"Why . . ." Sarah stopped and licked her lips, looking away. Her gaze roamed around the room and she stared at everything *but* him. Finally, she shook her head. "I don't understand why you would do that, Caine. We worked so hard to protect you, to give you peace here. Why would you *tell*?"

"It wasn't going to stay buried forever, Sarah."

A static, almost heavy silence fell through the room and David stood there as Sarah stared at him, her gaze flat, blank as a mirror. He couldn't see a thing behind that gaze, had no idea what she was thinking. Not that he really cared. He knew what she wanted. For him to settle down here, stay here, probably take over the farm.

Abruptly she sighed and looked away. "Of course. I just don't know why you wanted to bring it all back up. You would be so much happier if you'd just let those troubles die."

Her words haunted him.

He lay in his bedroom for probably the last time, staring up at the ceiling until his lids were too heavy, and when he slid into dreams they were anything but pleasant.

But then, his dreams never were.

Let those troubles die. . . .

In his dreams, those words echoed mockingly around him. Die. How could you let something die when it was a demon that lived inside you? He was facedown, tied to the bench again, while a whip cut into him.

Let those troubles die! She screamed it this time, watching from the side, her hair falling from her prim white *kapp*—the little bonnet Amish women wore. And as she screamed, somebody came up behind him. He swore, jerking against the ropes. They couldn't do this to him again. Not now. He was bigger. Stronger. Stronger than they were.

There's always somebody stronger, boy.

He jerked his head up, found himself looking at Sorenson.

Next to him stood Peter and one of the faceless monsters who'd joined in on the many, many times David had been dragged down into hell. *It's your turn now, boy. In time, you'll be a man and it will be your turn to join the brotherhood. Be ready to receive the honor we give you. In time, you'll pass it on to others. Just as we pass it on to you now.*

The words echoed in his ears, repeating, louder and louder, and when a hand touched his spine he jerked against the ropes. This time, they snapped like threads and he came up, spun around, grabbed the neck of the person behind him, slammed him—

No.

Her.

It was Sybil.

Her eyes were wide on his face.

Caine . . .

That was all she said before he killed her.

CHAPTER TWO

Caine jerked upright in the bed, staring out the window at the dull grey of a predawn morning.

"Shit." He shoved the heels of his hands against his eyes. That didn't help. Like an afterimage, her face was seared in his brain, pale and lifeless.

He moved out of the bed, feeling too old, awkward in his skin as he stumbled to the foot of the bed and snagged the trousers. Drawing them on, he moved to the window and absently dug into the pocket, looking for one of the cigars he'd developed a taste for.

They weren't there, though, and he had to remind himself why—he'd been cutting back, so the smell of smoke wouldn't be on his skin, wouldn't bother Sybil or the kid.

"Might as well pick the habit back up," he muttered, bracing his hands on the windowsill. Since he couldn't kill himself on the nicotine, he sucked in a slow, steady breath of the cool dawn air.

The nightmare lingered in his mind, all too vivid.

They usually started to fade almost the minute he woke up, but not this one.

It clung to him like a greasy, sticky film and the worst

of it was Sybil. Her wide eyes dull and sightless, her mouth slack.

He saw the way she'd looked as she stood at his side in the cemetery. The way her eyes held his as he drove into her, clinging to her like she was all that mattered in the world. All that mattered to him.

He remembered the way she'd looked at him before climbing back into her car, the sympathy, the sadness.

If he'd gone with her, if he'd brought her back here, the nightmare wouldn't have happened. When she was with him, the chaos in his mind faded away.

He could lose himself in her body. Silence the screams. Or better yet . . . he could make *her* scream as he brought her to one breathless orgasm after another. That was the one time he could forget. Forget everything. Forget the pain, forget the shame, forget the misery.

Only with her. It had only ever been with her.

One hand curled into a fist, braced on the wall next to the window.

He was desperate, almost painfully so, to see her, to touch her. But he had to stay away. He had to cut Caine out of him, and if he didn't want the ugliness inside him to touch her it was best if he cut her out of his life as well.

It wasn't like he could ever give what she deserved anyway.

She deserved somebody *whole*.

David had so many broken, jagged pieces of himself missing, it was a wonder he could touch her without slicing her to ribbons.

Shoving away from the window, he put his back against the wall and closed his eyes.

He should have gone back there. To that house, dug up those bones and hidden them somewhere else.

Of course, to do that, he would have had to know they were there.

He'd never thought to ask.

Max had kept his secrets well.

Maybe it was time he figured out what other secrets the old man had kept.

* * *

He looked old and tired, lying in that bed. Wearing a pair of jeans that fit too close and felt scratchy against his skin, David rested his elbows on his knees and studied Max's face.

A few weeks ago, David had stood with the man on the edge of the river, staring out over the water while they spoke of old, ugly secrets. David had needed names. Max had just smiled, a serene, peaceful sort of smile that hadn't made much sense, at the time.

Of course it hadn't, although it should have.

Max had set about quietly cleaning up messes, just as he'd done twenty years ago. David had stupidly thought if they cut off the dragon's head—by taking down his father—everything would stop. Max had known better and he'd gone about dealing with it in his own way.

At the time, David hadn't really understood just what was going on, even though he'd breathed out a sigh of relief each time one of them had died.

Why wouldn't he?

He'd been just a kid, a skinny teenage boy barely kissing puberty, the first night his father had woken him up. *You're old enough now. Come on, boy. There's something you need to see.*

He hadn't known, hadn't had any idea.

Are you my son? Do you want to be part of the family?

Part of something important? Are you willing to do what it takes to really be a man?

Insidious words, softly spoken to a vulnerable boy. *Yes.*

The next thing he knew, he was pressed against something hard and flat and hands were grabbing at him.

He hadn't been raped the first time. Or even the second.

But each time, when he was dragged out there, crying and scared, his father had told him, *Remember. This is part of being my son. You'll learn what that means. This is who you are . . . part of you knew it, or you wouldn't have said yes.*

Two years of pure hell stretched out before him and he came to know the names of a few others, but not all. He knew about Abel Blue, the Sims brothers.

Some of the others David had suspected, but he hadn't known for sure. Not until one by one they turned up dead.

Keith Andrews, the chief of police.

Abel Blue—one of the men who'd loved to take the whip to David.

Billy Sutter, David's own uncle.

Luis Sims and then the final one, Garth Sims, Jeb's father.

David's father had been the dragon's head, and he thought if his father was stopped, everything else would stop, too. It hadn't stopped the way they'd planned, but in the end it had stopped. One by one, the men who'd torn his life apart had died. It wasn't until the final one— Garth Sims, Jeb's father—that David realized just what had been going on. Andrews died in a hunting accident— his partner found him dead at the bottom of a rocky incline, his neck broken from the fall, face smashed in. Abel Blue's heart attack, the car crash that had killed

Billy Sutter, all of them David could just write off as karma getting her pound of flesh.

But Garth . . . that hadn't been quite so easy to overlook.

Everybody saw it as a tragic accident, but David knew better.

There were likely only two—no, make that three people who knew the truth. David, possibly Garth's son, Jeb, and the man who'd killed him.

Max.

Garth had been found bare-ass naked on the bottom of his pool, his blood alcohol level sky-high. All around the pool there had been scattered skin mags. It had painted a picture of a man who'd gotten plastered while getting his rocks off, then tumbled face-first into the water, too drunk to stop himself. Maybe he'd passed out.

That was what Max had wanted people to think, totally destroying Garth's image.

Just as Garth had destroyed David so many times.

The man to break David, as they called it, had been Peter, his own father.

But the next one, and David's most frequent abuser, was Garth Sims.

Max had made sure Garth's name was ruined.

Those little details were what clued David in. Because he knew certain things about Garth. Garth didn't drink. And David couldn't see the cold, controlling bastard who'd terrorized him doing something like getting plastered while sitting naked and jacking off beside the pool.

By the time it was all done, the boy called David hadn't been seen in town for more than three years. He'd taken the name Caine. At twenty, he was bigger and stronger but still scared, still broken. He'd faced

Max across the width of the porch, refusing to look at the house where he had tried to flee from hell.

Why? he'd asked.

Max had just smiled and shrugged. *You get on back to the farm, Caine. Abraham needs you.*

But he hadn't gone. Not right away.

He'd done a quick walk through town, shoulders hunched, waiting for somebody to recognize him. Nobody had.

After the first ten minutes, he'd slowly lifted his head, started to watch others from under the brim of his hat. How many others were there? He'd known the four, but sometimes people had come at him masked and sometimes the men had just watched. Watched as he was humiliated, watched as he was broken, watched as he bled and begged.

It was that night that he realized he couldn't leave the pain or the trouble behind. He couldn't just let it die. It would always follow him.

Unless they managed to cut this cancer out, it would eat at this town and it would eat at him.

So he made himself go back, look at the memories. Through a disconnect of three years, he started to remember things, details. It was precious little, though. Some of that information might be inside the head of the old man lying on the hospital bed just two feet away.

A weak, tired sigh escaped Max and then the man lifted his lids, eyed David narrowly. "An old man can't even sleep without having people staring at him," he grumbled.

"You get a lot of people in here staring at you?"

Max just watched him.

David looked away, leaning back in his seat. The T-shirt he'd picked up with the jeans rode up and he scowled down at it, tugged it back into place. He'd left the plain clothes behind, back at the farm, taking only the clothes on his back because he'd planned to buy the sort of clothing he would have worn if he'd never left town.

But everything still felt weird, the jeans too tight, the sleeves of the T-shirt too short. For reasons he didn't quite understand, he felt exposed in these clothes and part of him wished he'd brought his plain clothes with him. He hadn't ever joined that world, but bits and pieces had worked their way into his thoughts and those things would take a while, maybe even a lifetime, to unlearn.

Feeling Max's eyes on him, he stopped plucking at the shirt and met the older man's gaze. "I can relate to the staring. I had to go buy clothes. I need a place to stay. People look at me like I'm a ghost."

"To them, you are." Max reached out and pushed a button on the bed rail, raising the head of the bed until he was in an upright position. From there, he pinned his blue eyes on David. "They saw you for years, knew you— or so they thought. You were Caine Yoder, an Amish man. But under it all, that was never who you were. And now . . ."

The old man went to shrug but stopped, grimacing in pain. "To some of them, it's like you're back from the dead, even though you never even left."

David curled his lip. "If people had *looked*, they might have figured that out a long time ago."

"Well." Max smiled sourly. "People are very often stupid."

"Yeah." David scowled down at his hands. Of course, he couldn't be surprised that nobody had seen him—the *real* him. Sarah, Thomas, all of them had known *who* he was, even under the mask he'd worn when he was in town, and they had seen only the mask.

Many of them had thought that in time he'd find peace, that he'd join the community. He'd never been baptized

into it, and if they'd belonged to the larger, more traditional community miles away things would have gone
very differently. Old Order Amish believed very strongly
in the church, the community. But the smaller community that Abraham and his family belonged to was less
traditional, with a more modern view on things. They
allowed vehicles for the purpose of jobs outside the community, and while David—or Caine, as they'd known
him—had never joined the church, they'd continued to
accept him, work with him, talk to him.

They'd accepted the broken, bleeding boy Abraham
had brought into his home. They'd given David the one
thing he'd never really known—a real home.

That was another thing he would miss.

Pushing those thoughts aside, he focused on the pres-
ent, and on Max.

"You look like a man with grim thoughts."

David skimmed a hand back over his hair, the shorter
cut unfamiliar to him. Just like everything else around
him right now. "I left." He flicked his eyes to Max's, saw
that he understood. "I'm not going back."

"That was always your choice," Max said softly.
"Abraham was there for as long as you needed him,
needed a haven."

"Abraham's gone."

Max closed his eyes, but not before David caught sight
of something sad there. "Yes. He's gone now.

"And what do you expect to do now?"

David wasn't sure how to answer that, what to say.

So he just shrugged. "Have you been able to remember anything?"

The attack that had landed Max Shepherd here was
still very much a mystery. It had left his wife of more
than five decades dead and he'd almost died himself.

Nobody knew why.

David had to fight not to show any of the anger that pulsed inside him as he thought of that sweet old lady he'd seen so many times over the years. He'd kept his distance at first, not wanting her to recognize him when he'd first started to sneak into town and try to get answers from Max, answers about where Lana was, answers about what had happened that night. He'd stopped after a while, because the old man had never given him answers and he'd realized the truth on his own—if Lana had come home, she'd come home to a whole hell of a lot of trouble. That hadn't stopped him from going by the judge's house, though. Or the Frampton place. David had been drawn back, always, like a moth to a flame. And there had been Max, and his Mary.

Now Mary was dead, Max was wounded and David wanted answers.

Feeling the weight of Max's gaze, David shifted his eyes back to the bed.

Faded blue eyes studied him. "No." Max sighed, his chest thinner than David remembered. Even for a man in his eighties, Max had always seemed bigger than life, strong enough to take on the world. Not anymore. "I have bits and pieces of the last few days, but that's it."

He smiled a little. "Mary tried to make breakfast—burned the eggs. The smell. I'll never forget that smell. And I had to eat them, too." He closed his eyes, turned his head. "Now she's gone."

"I'm sorry, sir."

One hand tightened into a rawboned fist on the tan hospital blanket. "You and me both, son. Who would go and shoot an old woman like that? She never hurt anybody. Not once in her whole life."

David looked down at his hands. Big hands. Strong. Just then they felt useless. *He* felt useless. Here he was, twenty years later, and he felt helpless all over again. "It wasn't about her, old man. You already know that."

Max's blue eyes slid his way.

Outside in the hallway a squeaking cart wheeled by, and they both lapsed into silence.

Moments passed before either of them spoke again.

"You remember calling me to come out to your place that day?"

"Did I?" Max shook his head. "I can't say as I do."

He could have been lying. The judge had a talent for lies, something David knew better than most. Eyes narrowing, he studied the man's face, looked for some sign, some hint, but he saw nothing more than a tired old man lying in a hospital bed.

"What are you going to do now? Got a place where you plan to live?" Max said. "I know it's got to be hard leaving home. Have you thought—"

He stopped as David leaned forward. "I don't have a home. I haven't had one in years—I don't think I ever did. And quit trying to distract me. You called me to your house. For some reason, that day, the day you were shot. Do you remember why?"

"I just said I don't."

"No, you said you don't remember calling me. Not the same as not knowing why you'd want to talk to me," David pointed out.

"Same thing in my mind." Max sighed and shifted on the bed. "Damn miserable place. Can't get comfortable." He flicked his gaze to the open door and then back to David. In a low voice, he said, "Bits and pieces are loose in my head. It's like a puzzle. I don't see the picture yet. Don't push me, boy."

David opened his mouth, but the sound of voices outside had him biting back the words.

An aide came in and David lapsed into silence as she checked on Max. "I need to check your vitals. Would you like your guest—"

"The boy is fine," Max said, his voice sour.

The woman's sunny smile didn't dim one bit, although her gaze seemed to bounce right off David. Like he wasn't even there.

Something else he'd gotten used to. He'd been the object of too much study over the past week or so. Although any time he went to meet a person's gaze, too many would just look away.

It had been just a little over a week ago when Max was shot, when David finally opened up about the secrets he'd kept hidden all these years. One week—and if there was a damn soul in town who hadn't heard the news, David had yet to meet him.

He could see it in their eyes, in the way they looked through him, around him . . . but rarely *at* him.

Just like the pretty young aide taking Max's blood pressure. "Looking good there, Max," she said, her voice cheerful. She put two fingers on his wrist, counting his pulse and looked up. Once more, her gaze bounced right away from David.

"Now . . . can I get you anything? More water? Another blanket? It's getting cooler out."

"Only thing I want is some peace and quiet," Max said, scowling at the wall. "Can't find it nowhere."

"Just let me know if you need anything, Judge." She nodded at him and then, for one brief moment, her gaze connected with David's. "He'll be needing some rest soon."

"I can damn well tell people when I need rest." Max glared at her back as she headed out.

"Wouldn't hurt to get a little," David said mildly.

Max slid him a look that was faintly amused. "Unless I want people in and out of my door all day, I have to play the grouchy son of a bitch."

"It's not a part you play if that's who you are."

Max wheezed out a laugh only to groan and press a hand to his chest, his face tightening in pain.

David didn't ask him if he was okay. It was clear by the look on his face that Max was hurting. David waited until Max's breathing leveled, until his hand lowered.

Max was the one to break the silence. "I guess it's safe to say you've given up on that old life altogether, judging by your clothes."

"It was never my life," David replied, rising and moving to the window. The peace of it had been what he'd needed, for a very long time. Long, dark nights when he'd lain in a bed with absolutely no sound—no cars, no music, no sounds of the TV drifting in from somewhere else. He'd been able to listen to nothing, absolutely nothing. He'd fallen asleep to the sound of nothing . . . eventually.

When there was utter silence, it made it that much easier to listen for the sound of footsteps. He'd hear them again. He'd believed that. For the longest time, he'd thought he'd hear somebody coming to drag him out of the bed. Even when he was no longer a skinny, scared kid, he'd still felt broken inside.

He wondered if he'd ever stop listening in the night.

The mornings had been bright and early, and loud.

The opposite of mornings that he'd been used to. Diane Sutter had been a stringent supporter of the *children are to be seen, not heard,* rule and Peter had often been out of the house by the time David was up and moving. Breakfast had been a grim, quiet affair, where she had eaten a half a grapefruit and he had the other half along with a bowl of oatmeal. Never any deviation. In the

Yoder house, he'd been fed so much food, he'd thought he'd explode from it—bacon, eggs, biscuits, homemade jams and gravies. And there was noise—prayers said over the morning food and people talking, laughing, discussing the jobs of the day and other things going on.

"Is that why you're running away from there so fast all of a sudden? You could have left at any time, but you chose now."

"I didn't choose the time. The time was just . . ." He reached for the words and failed. "The time chose itself. I can't hide away there while Lana deals with everything on her own. I can't wait for Sorenson to come out there and bring his ugly questions. I owe Abraham more than that."

"He didn't want you to feel like you owed him anything." Max closed his eyes, his voice thick with weariness. A minute passed before he dragged his eyes open again. "You're going to deal with some trouble now, boy. People know who you are now. I've had too many in and out of here, talking about you . . . and Lana."

"Fuck," he muttered. Then he scowled. "I'm sorry, sir."

"Quit *sirring* me," Max muttered.

David looked back at him and their eyes met. Eyes, the same blue eyes.

"Is that all they're talking about?" he asked, almost dreading the answer.

"For now. It'll get worse before it gets better."

"I'm used to worse." David braced a hand on the wall, staring out the square of a window instead of at the man behind him.

"I guess you are. If you need a place to stay, you can take my house. Noah, he's got the keys to the place. You ask him, tell him I said to give them to you. I won't be going back there. No, I won't." His lids jerked around like he couldn't stand to let them rest on any one thing. There was a picture of his Mary on the bedside table, and he took great care not to look there for even a second.

Something pricked in David's heart. It might have been sympathy. It had been so long since he'd felt anything *real*, anything beyond the burn of anger, beyond that endless apathy—other than the soul-stealing lust he felt for Sybil. But even without having the experience to really cue in on the emotion, he was almost certain it was sympathy. He'd bring the old woman back for Max, if he could.

But there was nothing to be done for it and he had no words of comfort to offer. Instead, he just stared hard at Mary's picture. He wondered what it would be like to love somebody that much, so that even the thought of returning to the home you'd shared was painful, all because that person would no longer be there.

"She didn't suffer," he said, the words slipping out of him. He hadn't realized he'd even intended to say anything. Turning his head, he met Max's eyes. "The doctors said it was fast, that she felt no pain."

A halfhearted smile lit the old man's face now. "I feel enough for us both, but that's good. I . . . yeah, I know she went fast. I just wish I knew who did it so I could make them suffer, too, before I pass on."

"You're out of danger." David felt himself going cold as he sat there, listening to yet another who had always been there talking about death. So easy, so casual. "The doctors said you are strong. Strong enough to get through this."

"But do I care enough?"

"You need to. I'm not done with you yet. I still need you." More words that he hadn't realized he was going to say. Floundering, he shoved up from the chair and started to pace.

"You know things I need to know," he said into the silence. "You have answers. I have questions. I want their names—"

There was no sound, but something urged David into silence and he turned, once more looking at Max.

Max said nothing, his gaze resting on David's face, and after a moment he muttered, "I just wish all of you would leave me alone. You hear me? You let them kill my Mary; why can't you—"

There was a knock at the door.

"Am I interrupting?"

David turned his head and met Chief Sorenson's placid eyes. "Actually, yes. You are. Why don't you come back in, oh, say . . . fifty years?"

He was a sly piece of work.

Just like the old man in the bed lying just beyond him.

Max put on a good act, but that's all it was, an act. He lay in that bed, putting up a frail, fretful face, and any time Sorenson or his top detective, Jensen Bell, pushed for more than a minute or two he started talking about his wife. Asking if they had any idea who had shot her, why she was dead.

Sorenson couldn't even say it was a stalling tactic or misdirection.

The old woman had been helpless, confused. Advanced Alzheimer's had made her one of the most vulnerable victims Sorenson had ever had to stand for and it pissed him off.

It pissed him off even more because he knew, as sure as he knew his own name, that Max *knew* something. Or he had answers. Not about Mary—he'd pull hell apart to find who had killed his wife—but there was information he withheld, nonetheless.

"I'm afraid fifty years from now isn't a good time for me," Sorenson said easily, slipping into the room and pushing the door shut behind him. "I plan on having my butt tucked into a beach chair, somewhere down on Maui, and getting sunburnt every day. That's my retirement plan, in . . . oh, maybe twenty-some years. Before that happens, though, I'd like to deal with whoever is terrorizing people in my town. That's why I'd like to talk to Max, and you, Cai—I mean David."

David just smiled at him, but the smile was dead, just like his eyes.

That man creeped him the hell out. Did David Sutter feel *anything*? Or had the ability *to* feel been destroyed, just like the boy he'd been had been destroyed?

"I'm not much help, Chief," David said, his eyes still empty. "I wasn't there when Max or Miss Mary was shot. I didn't show up until later. I promise you, if I had any idea who'd shoot a sweet old lady like Miss Mary, you wouldn't have to look for me to help you out—I'd drag the motherfucker to you."

"Hmmm." *Assuming you didn't finish the person off.* Sorenson kept that behind his teeth, but he doubted he was far off. How he, or anybody else, had looked at this man and seen anybody remotely mild mannered or even tempered was a mystery.

Shifting his attention from David to Max, Sorenson moved around the foot of the bed.

Max glared at him, already settling into his ornery old codger routine. He did it well, too; Sorenson had to give him credit.

"Why do I got to put up with this horseshit?" Max grumbled. "Nurses coming and going all hours of the night. People knocking on the damn door all day. All I want to do is sleep and you people keep showing up."

"Would you like us to find who shot you? Who shot Mary?"

Max's thick white brows dropped low over his eyes, the vivid blue gaze snapping. "You think you're any closer than you were two days ago? If you are, then spill it. If you're just here to nag me, then get your ass out."

"You don't pull punches, do you, sir?"

"At my age, I don't see the point."

Running his tongue around the inside of his teeth, Sorenson debated. The old man just wouldn't give. Wouldn't back down. It was odd, Sorenson thought, looking from one to the other. He felt like he was staring at one big, impenetrable wall. Max was older but just as solid, just as unbreakable.

He was likely fishing in the dark here, but hell. Sometimes that was what it took.

"I did come down here to discuss a thing or two with you, sir. Things of a sensitive nature." He flicked his gaze to David. "If you'd step outside . . . ?"

David went to rise.

"Sit down, boy," Max grumbled. "Whatever he has to say can't be worth shit."

Sorenson rocked back on his heels. "I don't think you want to discuss this with anybody else in here."

"Not like David's going to tell people. If anybody can keep his mouth shut, it's him. He's done gone and proven that." Something glittered in Max's eyes. "Why don't you just say what you want to say?"

Ornery? Hell. Max wasn't *ornery*. He was stubborn as the day was fucking long. Crossing his arms over his chest, Sorenson tried one more time. "Are you certain? Some things, even just rumors, can leave a mark."

"Why don't you just get it done?" David said, his voice slapping at the air, hard and heavy. He shoved up and paced over to the window, staring outside at the steady flow of small-town traffic. "If you haven't figured it out by now, once he's made his mind up there's no moving him."

"Is that a family trait?"

Well, if Sorenson expected shock, he was destined to be disappointed.

Max was staring at David, like his reaction was crucial.

No. *Necessary*. Like he'd live or die, depending on how David reacted.

David?

As he turned and leaned against the window ledge, there was something of amusement on his face, the faintest grin lurking on his lips as he crossed his arms over his chest.

"Is that what you call *getting it done*, Chief? If it is, I feel sorry for any female you might date. You probably hump her leg and call that a wild party." He shoved off the ledge then and prowled across the floor, stopping five feet away, dark hair spilling into his eyes, his blue eyes bright, glinting, almost a mirror of the man lying on the bed. "Do you not know how to just ask what you're asking or is it a cop thing?"

"Fine. I'll ask. I heard a . . . well, I can't call it a rumor as it's not really flying around town. But one of the women I spoke to, trying to nail down the events of twenty years ago, was Elsie Darby. Owns the B and B outside of town."

David just lifted a brow.

Sorenson looked away from David, then, focusing on Max. "Elsie seems to recall a time, right before you and Miss Mary hooked up. You spent a few weekends with

Hilda Pritchard. She left town not long after, came back while you were off serving in the army."

"Yes. That sounds about right." Max just watched him.

Damn the both of them. Neither of them was going to make it easy, were they?

"She came back with a little girl, ended up having to move in with her father. He didn't exactly make her life easy. Her life, or her daughter's life. Word has it that Diane had a rough time of it."

"Yes." Max sighed now, turning his head. "Yes, she did." He looked back then, but not at Sorenson. His entire focus was locked on David. "I didn't know. Not at first. Mary and I saw a preacher the summer I enlisted. Sometimes, I think the only thing that brought me back was knowing that she waited. Then I get back here and I see that little girl with my eyes . . . my eyes, and her granddaddy was so mean to her." He ran a shaking hand across his eyes. "I told Miss Mary. We had no secrets. She was upset, as you can imagine. Then I talked to Hilda. Tried to see if we couldn't just adopt Diane, but she wouldn't hear of it. That little girl was the only happiness she had, she told me. She did let me give her money, but she banked it. All for Diane, keeping it away from her daddy, not telling anybody. She didn't want anybody to know, though. I was a fool, not pushing harder, not trying harder. It took me years, though, to realize how much of a mistake it was, letting it go as I had."

David's face was like stone, his gaze staring at nothing.

"You knew," Sorenson said softly.

Slowly, the younger man lifted his head to meet Sorenson's gaze. "I've got his eyes. I've got his hands. I've been in his house and I've seen pictures. As I got older, the resemblance got stronger. Figured it out a while back." There were words unspoken in the back of his eyes, but no amount of pushing would get him to reveal any secret he wasn't willing to share.

Sorenson hadn't even been sure. Just how this was connected to the mess he was trying to unravel he didn't know, but he'd reached out, taking that blind stroke, hoping to catch something.

Well. He had the truth.

But not much else.

Looking away from David, he said to Max, "It must have been hard on you, all of these years. Not knowing where your grandson was. Even as a boy, seeing him, but not being able to reach out to him the way you wanted, especially seeing as how you and Miss Mary couldn't have kids. And it turns out he was here all along. Did you see it? He saw you in him, but didn't you see him in you?"

"I guess we all see what we expect to see." Max met Sorenson's eyes levelly. He didn't bat a lash and his gaze was dead-on.

He also lied through his teeth. Sorenson would bet his badge on it. But what proof did he have?

"I guess it burns some, looking back now. Seeing as how you lost twenty years with him. You never really had him for any time, but the past twenty years—"

"You want to know what burns?" Max asked, his voice going hard as a diamond. "Want to know what hurts?"

He shoved the blanket back, grimacing as he pulled himself up farther in the bed, shoving skinny legs ropy with muscle over the side so he could face Sorenson. "What *burns* is the fact that my daughter, a girl I helped bring into this world, grew up so twisted that she turned a blind eye to what was happening to her own son. *My* blood. What burns is that that the man who was supposed to protect *my* grandson was nothing more than a monster. What *burns* is that fact that all of that time, I didn't know a thing. None of us did, because those snakes in the grass hid it. If I had known, no force on this earth could have kept me from helping my grandson, or any of those boys. But I didn't know. Not until it was too late."

He paused to take a breath. "And now I—"

David stepped forward, rested a hand on the old man's shoulder while silently Sorenson cursed. *Now you what? What had he been going to say?*

David crouched in front of his grandfather and the two of them stared at each other for a long, taut moment. "This is pointless," David finally said. "Neither of us can undo what's done. You can blame yourself. I can blame you. But it's all wrong and we know it."

"Do we?" Max watched David. "If I'd fought Hilda harder, when I saw how she struggled, how bad her daddy was to her and Diane, could I have had that little girl with me? Maybe she would have had a chance to be . . . something better. She would have done better by you then."

Sorenson cleared his throat, awkward now, caught in a moment where he knew he didn't belong.

David rose, turning to look at him, arms crossing over a chest heavy with muscle, strong from years of hard labor. He looked nothing like the pictures of the skinny boy that had been passed around this town over the years. The resemblance to Max wasn't overpowering—they had the same eyes, they had the same hands, and if somebody knew what Max had looked like fifty years ago they might see a similarity, but then again, maybe not.

Max had been robust, full of life, full of love for his Mary.

David was more than half-dead inside. Too hard. Too cold.

"Did you get whatever you were hoping to get?" David asked, his voice just a step above a whisper.

"I wasn't hoping to get anything," Sorenson said. But he lied. He hated that this big, cold man could make him feel nervous inside his skin. David hadn't even done anything, hadn't moved toward him.

But David had a way of looking at you that made you realize that you didn't even exist. Not to him.

It was . . . unsettling. Eerie.

"You don't tell lies as well as you need to," David said. "Not if you want me to believe them. I grew up on lies and I've survived on them for longer than you can imagine."

"How long is that, David?" he asked.

"All my life." He moved now, taking one step away from Max's bed. "You want to push at me, do it. I can handle it. You got questions you want to ask Max about Miss Mary or the day he was shot? I can't stop you. But don't come hammering at him. He's got nothing that will help you."

"I'm afraid you don't get to dictate how I do my job there, son." He looked past David then, met Max's tired blue eyes. "I'm sorry if I brought . . ." *any inconvenience?* This was more than that. *Unhappiness?* That didn't touch it. Floundering for a word, he finally said, "I'm sorry for this. But I've got crimes to solve, some of them going back for twenty or more years, and I can't do it without asking questions. Feelings will be bruised when I'm done, but there are dark, ugly secrets and they need to be exposed, and the criminals need to be brought before a court of law."

David turned away. "Too bad you're too late for the worst of them. That would be my father and his lackeys. Too bad you didn't come along in time to get them."

"They can get theirs in hell," Max murmured. "The devil can torture them from now until eternity."

A humorless laugh escaped David. "Hell is here on earth, Max. The devil? He was every man who took a child into that room."

Then he looked back at Sorenson, and for a minute the cop was left to wonder if maybe David wasn't right. Maybe hell was here on earth, and maybe the devil did dwell inside men—perhaps even inside the man standing across the room from him.

CHAPTER THREE

"No visitors," Max said again to the nurse David had hunted down.

Melanie Hawkins nodded. "Got it, Judge Max. It's noted in the book, I've got a sign up and you're right by the desk, so I'll be keeping an eye out myself." She paused and then asked, "Are you okay?"

Max didn't respond, just shifted around in the bed. After a minute, he said, "Tell that damn doctor I can't sleep. I want something so I can sleep. Every time I close my eyes . . ."

He didn't finish his sentence, but David imagined he knew the problem. He'd close his eyes and see Mary. Lifeless. Gone. Everything he'd lived for.

Within another minute, Melanie was gone and David moved to stand by the bed, pulling a chair up so Max could see him.

"You got any idea how many are left?" David studied him.

Max flicked a look at him. "Don't know what you're talking about."

"Don't give me that, Max."

"You know, for once in your life, wouldn't hurt you to call me Grandpa."

Sighing, David bowed his head, hair falling to shield his eyes. Slowly, he reached up and caught one of Max's hands in his, squeezed. "I don't know if you really want that. I think of family and I think ugly things. I don't have that connection with you." Breaking the contact, he looked away. "I wish I could tell you the sort of things a man should be able to say to his grandfather. I do owe you; I know that—"

"The fuck you do." The words ripped out of Max, ugly and full of poison. "You don't owe me shit. I never should have—"

"Please don't. You didn't know." Because David did wish he could give the man something, he decided to give what little he could. Rising, he made his way to the window. "Back before things got bad, I used to dream, you know. My father's parents were dead. Mother never spoke of hers. Now I know why. But kids would talk about their grandparents and sometimes, I'd make up my own. In my head, my grandpa always looked like you. Big and strong, not afraid of anything—tough. That was how you looked to me. And my grandmother would look like Miss Mary. Sweet, with a voice pretty and soft."

He looked back at Max, but Max had his eyes closed.

"I need to know who else is left," David said softly. "Don't tell me you don't know. I know what you've been doing. I need their names."

A moment passed, then another. David counted the beats of his heart, it had grown so quiet.

"There is a journal," Max finally said, his voice barely more than a whisper. "It was in Harlan's study. I got it now. You want it, you'll find it at my house."

"Where is it?"

A faint smile came and went on Max's face. "Look around my house. I've got the journals there. I . . ." His gaze moved to the door, and his voice dropped. "Just you look. But there's not much left. Most of them are either dead or in jail."

A band wrapped around David's chest. "Most. Not all?"

"Don't start down this trail, David. There's nothing down it but death for you if you take even the first step."

"I took the first step years ago. I can't undo it."

"You can. You're not too far gone." Max blew out a heavy sigh. "I was willing to take those steps, because I'd made a promise. It was a risky, fool thing to do, and if I'd messed up it would have hurt Miss Mary something awful. But every time I thought of what had been done . . ." He shook his head. "I had to do it. You don't. The cops here, now, they care. The men I know about are gone. You can let it go. Take the journal to them. Let them do their job. Don't go chasing death down. After all this time, boy, you deserve a life. . . . Don't let them take anything else from you. Not even because you want vengeance."

David didn't answer.

A life. He wouldn't know how to make one even if he wanted one. He didn't understand the concept. Vengeance, though . . . *that* was something he understood.

He went to slip outside and a quiet question made him pause.

"Will you come back?"

He gripped the door frame, stared straight ahead. He wanted to say no. Wanted to pretend he hadn't heard. But it wasn't possible. There weren't many in this world he felt he owed much of anything to. But Max was definitely one of the few he did owe. "Yeah. I'll be back."

* * *

"Come on, you icy bitch. All I need is a grand. Five hundred would do it."

Sybil blocked out the anger, blocked out the insults and just said, "No."

Layla reached out. With the ease born of years of practice, Sybil sidestepped her younger sister's hand—and those half-inch-long nails—and avoided being scratched or grabbed for what was probably the dozenth time in just the past ten minutes. "It's not like you're hurting for money," Layla said, her tone snide. "Look at this place."

She picked up a Nikon that had cost Sybil over five thousand—*not* including the accessories. Pursing her lips, Layla held it up. "I bet you could put this on pawn and get a few hundred easy."

"Put my equipment down."

Hearing the threat in her sister's voice, Layla looked up. "Shit, what crawled up your ass and died?"

"I told you the last time I gave you money, it wouldn't happen again." Since Layla was still carelessly holding a very expensive camera, Sybil stepped forward and took it, returning it to its place. "And before you even start to consider it—all my equipment is registered *to* me. The pawnshop here would call me if you even tried. If one of my cameras goes missing, I'll file a report. I'll let Sorenson know you were here looking for money and I'll call every pawnshop within a day's drive of here. If you take one of my cameras, I'll have you arrested for breaking and entering, and theft. I'd also like to point out—there's not a camera in here worth less than three grand. Keep that in mind before you think about trying anything. I've got one worth three times that. If I can get you arrested on grand theft? I'll do it."

Layla's mouth went pinched and tight. "You'll spend

that kind of money on a fucking *camera*, but you can't spare a few hundred on your own blood?"

Any guilt she could have once felt for Layla had long since died. Crossing her arms over her chest, she stared the younger woman down. "And what about last year when I asked you if you'd like to go buy your son some Christmas presents? You didn't have the money. You had the money, though, to haul your worthless ass to the liquor store twenty minutes later. You can't spend your money on presents for your *own blood,* but you can buy booze?" As Layla opened her mouth, Sybil stepped forward. "I *have* expensive equipment because *I* am the one who has to care for that boy and I need the equipment to do my job. I'm the one who buys him toys and food and clothes. *I* am the one who pays for his medical bills—I can't *get* him insurance because he's not my son. I can't get him on Medicaid because you never show up for the appointments. Right now? I'm paying off a thirty-two-hundred dollar hospital visit to the emergency department from the last time his asthma flared up. You want to talk about *blood*?" The words came out in a fury of pent-up rage. "Where in the hell have *you* been every time your son needed you? When he was sick, when he was hurting, when he just *needed* you?"

Layla's face was white, but as the words lingered, then died in the air, blood slowly crept across her face. "Don't you dare go laying it at my feet when he gets sick. I can't help that the kid has those breathing problems. He's healthier around you, at least."

"That's because I don't smoke around him. I don't parade a line of boyfriends through the house that chainsmoke around him. I don't drag him around when he's sick just because I'm *bored* and I have to get out and do something," Sybil said, sneering. She backed away before she gave in to the fury and did something violent, something desperate. She wanted to shake her sister, make her see what she was doing, what she was losing, what she'd already lost.

Drew looked at his mother with something just a step away from disgust in his eyes. It wasn't that he didn't *know* her. It was that he didn't *want* to know her.

"It ain't my fault," Layla said, her voice shaking. Shaking with the need to believe it. "He was always sick like that. I tried, Syb. I did. I'm just not—"

A wave of weariness crashed into her and Sybil looked away. "You tried. Yeah, I've heard this before. You tried. And when it got hard, you dumped him on Mama. Then she wasn't there and I was. It's fine. I love the boy. You know that. But you don't get to come here, demanding money from me, sneering at the things I do to take care of him and getting pissy with me when I tell you no. I'm not your moneybag, Layla. You're on your own now. I told you that once. It hasn't changed."

Layla opened her mouth, closed it.

Then she just slumped against the wall, slid down it. Drawing her knees to her chest, she tucked her face against them. "I don't know where to go. I got kicked out of my apartment. I've been crashing with guys I know, but I'm running out of places to go. Nobody . . ." She sniffled and when she looked back at Sybil there were real tears in her eyes. "Nobody wants me, Syb. Nobody at all."

Even as her heart twisted inside, Sybil had to bite back the unspoken question: *Do you blame them?*

Shoving her hair back, Sybil moved to the window. "Why did you get kicked out?"

"I can't pay the rent." Layla thunked her head back against the wall. "Adam . . . I . . ." She licked her lips and slid Sybil an embarrassed glance. "You know Adam fired me. Nobody else around here will give me a chance.

It was just him. Now I have no job, no money. I—" She started to shake.

Those tremors were telling.

"How long has it been since you used?"

Layla clamped her lips shut.

"Truth, Layla."

The younger woman averted her face, staring down the mellow golden hallway that led to the front door and out to Main Street. "I haven't been using that much. I—" She stopped and blew out a breath. "Booze was easier. I could swipe it from the bar, take a bottle from the back. Guys never minded buying me a drink. I was doing some speed some nights. Smoked weed or swiped whatever pills I could if I was crashing with somebody who had them. But the shakes are from the drinking. It's getting bad, too."

"I'm not going to give you money so you can go buy yourself another bottle."

Layla shoved herself upright. "You've already established that," she said, her voice mocking. She set her shoulders, managed to pull the scattered threads of her pride around her. "I'll figure—"

Sybil ignored her and pulled out her phone. "I'm calling Noah. He's got the number of a rehab place in Kentucky. You want help? Go in there. Dry out. Then maybe you and I can talk."

Layla went red.

Sybil narrowed her eyes. "You've got one last chance, Layla, and something tells me you know it. It's staring you right in the face. It's either this or you're going to end up dead on a slab somewhere."

"Does it even matter?" Layla whispered as something dark and haunted passed across her face. "Would anybody care?"

"I would. Drew would." Sybil hoped she wasn't lying.

Layla averted her face. "The kid is better off with you. Everybody knows that. I don't even know how to take care of him."

"That's because you never bothered to learn. I didn't know how to do it, either." Her heart ripped in two, even thinking about it. "But I figured it out. You can do the same."

She gripped the phone, stared at Layla. "Do I make the call?"

"I'm sorry." She stared at Noah as he loaded Layla's bag into the back of his trunk.

He crooked a grin Sybil's way. "Why? You didn't do anything."

Sybil crossed her arms over her chest. "I can't help but feel this is a waste of time. That . . . well, I read about that place in Kentucky a while back."

One of the teens—well, Brittany was grown now, married, with a baby on the way, but she'd been in a bad way for a while. Noah had met her through the forum, but everybody in town knew who she was. He'd helped get her into a program and she'd come home more than a year later a different person. People looked at Noah like he'd turned wine into water, but he'd just shrugged. *It wasn't me. I just gave her the tools. A lot of prayer and hard work on Brittany's part did the rest.*

Sybil didn't think all the prayers in the world could help her sister, but she was ready to try anything right then.

"It helped Brittany," she said quietly. "Can it help her?"

They looked through the window at Layla's bowed head, resting on her fisted hand.

"That's up to Layla. She's been cruising along rock bottom for a while, but whether or not she wants to get out of the hole is up to her. Plenty of people can give her the tools. Can offer her a hand up. She has to decide if she wants to reach out and accept."

Sybil just nodded, thought about going to say something.

In the end, she just backed away.

As Noah drove off, she dropped down onto the bench and watched until even the taillights were lost to her sight.

"Man, Trinity has got to be a trusting girl to let him go off with that."

Slowly, Sybil lifted her head, turned to look at Leslie Mayer. Leslie had cut her long, heavily layered curls to chin length. It was slightly—only slightly—more flattering to her round face. Her skin was ruddy and her expression was that of one who rarely smiled. "Excuse me?"

"Oh, I don't mean anything by it." Leslie shrugged. "You know how your sister is. She chases after anything with a dick. Where is she off to with Noah, anyway?"

"Off to a new store in Louisville," Sybil said blandly. "Shopping for a new attitude—for you and her. Seeing as how yours sucks just as bad as hers."

Sybil rose just as Leslie whipped her head around.

"What the—" Leslie stopped mid-sentence as somebody came striding across the street.

Sybil's heart rolled, heavy and hard, in her chest and heat gathered inside her.

"Who is that?" Leslie murmured.

Sybil managed to choke back the snort of laughter, although it took some effort. Leslie couldn't stop herself from ragging on Layla and how she came on to anybody with a dick, but Leslie was just as bad. But really, when a man looked like that it was hard not to notice. Sybil had the added distraction of knowing just how wonderful it felt to have that strong, hard body moving over hers, under hers, to feel his voice, just this side of cruel, rasping in her ear—

"I wonder who he is," Leslie said, her voice an unwelcome grating against Sybil's nerves.

"Oh, for crying out loud. You've seen him two thousand times," Sybil said. The image of him was burned on the inside of her, just like the feel of him was imprinted on her skin. She didn't let herself stare at him, as much as she wanted to.

"I've never seen that man," Leslie said, licking her lips.

"Man, a guy gets a haircut and changes his clothes," Sybil muttered. He had gotten his hair trimmed, the longish strands now almost brutally short and the clothes he wore highlighted a body she knew as well as her own. Did he look different? Maybe a little. But she'd know him in the dark. Shooting a look at Leslie, she said, "That's David—or you might recognize the name *Caine* better."

Leslie snapped her mouth shut. And the heat in her eyes went cool as disgust danced across her face. "Oh. *Oh,* he was one—"

Sybil put herself between them. "Say it," she warned. "Say it and you'll find yourself an ugly, messy smear on the ground."

Leslie was still gaping at her in shock as Sybil turned on her heel and strode back toward her office. Away from David. Away from Leslie.

Sybil and David hadn't talked since the night of Abraham's funeral. Once, she'd tried to call David. He'd answered with a cool, *Now's not a good time.*

Fine. If he was pulling back, just let him. But she'd

be damned if she listened to the bile Leslie had been
about ready to spill from her noxious mouth.

Just as she'd be damned if she stood around staring
at him soulfully and hoping he'd look at her. Just
once.

CHAPTER FOUR

For a moment, David almost went after her.

Sanity intruded, reminding him of his decision to put distance between them.

The sight of the woman lingering where Sybil had been reaffirmed that decision. Her eyes lingered on him, skittered away, then returned, something that was revulsion and curiosity and disgust dancing in her gaze before she finally made a quick retreat, moving in the opposite direction.

He'd never expected to be able to hide what had happened if he had to come forward. He'd never planned to, not really. He was tired of living behind masks and secrets. The shame, a familiar, ugly burr under his skin, would never fade, but the logical part of him understood that the shame didn't really belong to *him*. If a bitch like Leslie Mayer wanted to look at him like that, that was her problem. Although it pissed him off that she'd upset Sybil.

All the more reason to stay away from her. All the more reason.

It would make it easier for her, in the end.

That nebulous end . . .

Lately, he'd been thinking about it, like there really

was an end for him. He'd focused on an *end*, thought about it. Lately, the idea of an *end* obsessed him. Probably because he was so tired.

"Think about that later," he muttered as he came around the corner, eyeing the sign above Benningfield and Son. He was still twenty feet away when the pint-sized blond tornado came speeding down the sidewalk. He stayed where he was, watching as Noah's new wife appeared around the corner. They'd been married for two weeks now.

David had been at the wedding, watching and waiting, half-expecting something else to go wrong, but nothing had.

Now they were back from their quick trip to Florida. Disney World, if he'd heard right, because Noah, being Noah, had wanted his new stepson along for the trip. Typical Noah.

David stood there, watching the boy and his mother as they came to a halt. Trinity noticed him almost immediately, her calm grey eyes studying him as he closed the distance between them. He went to tip his hat at her and remembered he hadn't worn it. He looked like he was part of this world again. Not that he'd ever been part of that other world.

"Hi," she said as he reached the two of them.

Micah looked up at David and David shoved his hands into the front pockets of his jeans. Kids made him feel . . . awkward. Useless. This one watched him with avid eyes, and the longer David watched him, the wider the boy smiled. "You're big," the boy said, his voice firm, like he'd come to an important decision.

"You're not." The response surprised him.

"I will be." Micah puffed up his chest. "One day, I'll be as big as Noah—I mean, my dad. I get to call Noah my dad."

Something just this side of adulation shone in Micah's eyes and David couldn't help but smile at it. "That doesn't sound like a bad thing. Noah's a good guy."

"He's the best."

"Micah, why don't you put your stuff in the car?" Trinity said, cutting in.

"But—"

"No buts, Micah," she said, her voice firm. "Now go."

As the boy dragged his feet across the busted sidewalk, Trinity turned to look at David.

"Hi." Her gaze was unreadable. He might as well be looking into a mirror for all the reaction he saw there. "Ah . . . I'm at a loss. Do I call you David or Caine?"

He shrugged. "I'll answer to either." Running his tongue across his teeth, he deliberated a minute and then added, "Although I suspect it's going to be easier in the long run to just go with 'David.' 'Caine' was just . . ."

A mask.

Those words didn't want to come and he just shrugged.

Trinity just nodded. "David, then. Noah had to leave. Something urgent . . ." She sighed and pushed her hair back. "I guess this is one of those things where I'm not supposed to discuss it. He won't be back in town for a few hours. Is there anything I can help you with?"

"I need the keys to Max's place."

"Max's?"

"Max said Noah had them." David continued to stare at her, realized it was probably bothering her. People were used to him looking away, down, anywhere but at their face. He'd developed the habit of not really *looking* at people a long time ago, after Abraham had pointed out to him that he looked at people like they just weren't even there. He tried to focus, made himself see Trinity. A pretty woman, married to a man he didn't really hate. She still didn't look entirely comfortable around him, but he didn't see any reason why she *should* look comfortable.

"Yes, he does." She blew out a breath and looked away. "We were over there a few days ago, cleaning up. It's awful, what happened."

David didn't say anything. It was awful. Everybody knew it. No point in him adding his two cents'. Besides, the only thing he could offer was that if he found out who'd killed Miss Mary he would like to kill the son of a bitch himself.

"Do you know where the keys are?"

Trinity frowned. "Why?"

"Because Max is going to let me stay there." He bit back a sigh. This conversation thing was a pain in the ass. Even before he'd taken off, he hadn't cared for talking to people. When you talked to people, they acted like they had a right to *ask* you things, know things about you. He hadn't ever been able to tell people shit for fear of being punished, a lesson he'd learned early on. Now, even though that wasn't an issue, he just didn't see the point in . . . talking. "Can I have the keys?"

"I think I need to check with Noah first."

David arched a brow. "Can you do that then?"

Trinity crossed her arms over her chest, her nails, painted a vivid blue-green color, tapping against her arm. "Anybody ever tell you that you're not exactly a people person, David?"

That startled a smile out of him. "I really haven't ever had a reason to be a people person." Sighing, he looked away, staring past her shoulder to the narrow slice of river he could see through the gaps in the trees. "I'd just like to get those keys."

"Fine. Just give me a minute."

* * *

Noah hadn't quite made it through Hanover when the call came through.

He pulled the phone from his ear, frowned a little, then said, "Run that by me again?"

"David is here. Caine, David. Whoever he is. He said that Max told him he could have the keys to his house and stay there. Wanted you to give him the keys. Should I?"

Next to Noah, Layla was chain-smoking, going through the pack of cigarettes she had so fast, it would be a miracle if she had any left by the time they reached Jeffersonville. "Well, yeah. It won't hurt anything."

"I just—it seemed weird, to me."

"Weird to me, too, angel," he said softly, checking the traffic before pulling through the stoplight. "But David wouldn't lie about it."

Layla's gaze slid to Noah, then jerked away again.

"Okay." On the other end of the line, Trinity paused, then asked, "How long you think this will take?"

"I'm not sure." He wished he could have passed this on to somebody else. Anybody else. He'd looked at Layla, though, and seen a look that was too familiar. She'd finally hit that point. That point he'd hit when he'd woken up in a hospital bed, convinced he'd killed somebody, and he'd been desperate, ready to do anything and everything to crawl out of the hole he'd put himself in. His dad had helped him find the rope he needed. He couldn't turn away from somebody else looking for a rope. Even if the woman was Layla.

"You think she's actually going to see this through?"

"Nobody can decide that." Before she could ask anything else he said, "The keys are in the desk in my office at home."

Trinity snorted. "I know that. *I* am the one who organized that disaster you call an office. I'll get them.

You're sure I shouldn't check with Max about this? I can have one of the nurses ask him."

"It's not necessary. It will be okay." His skin felt tight, oddly itchy at the thought of David settling into that house where Max had been shot, where Miss Mary had died. But he'd think on that later. "I'll call you once I know when I'll be headed home, okay?"

"Okay. We love you."

We . . . the thought of it sent a rush of warmth through him and he smiled. "Love you guys, too. Give Rocket-boy a hug for me."

The line went dead and he dropped the phone into the cup holder, focused back on the road.

The past twenty minutes had passed in an odd, strained silence. If the rest of the drive could be like that—

"Is it hard, raising a kid that ain't yours?"

He glanced over to see Layla staring outside. The wind tore at her hair, messing it up, but she hadn't complained, something that told him more about her distracted state of mind than she'd probably like.

"Micah feels like he's mine," he said softly.

"But he's not."

"Doesn't mean I don't love him." He shrugged. "I'm going to adopt him, give him my name. It's all a formalization, though. In my heart, in my head, he is mine. He has been for a while."

Maybe even from the very first time Noah laid eyes on him.

"Do you think he loves you more than his real dad?"

Her voice was husky now, husky and soft.

Sympathy stirred in him and Noah, not for the first time, wished he could find it in him to offer something false and empty that wouldn't hurt as much as the truth.

She had enough hard stuff in front of her. Offering her some sort of hope could make it easier.

But false hopes, empty hopes, weren't going to help. Not in the long run.

He'd been silent too long and she turned her head, glaring at him, the lenses of her purple contacts looking odd with her swollen red eyes. "Well?"

"Micah's dad wasn't much of a father," he finally said. "Micah barely remembers him. Doesn't talk much about him."

"I . . ." She licked her lips, shrugged. She took a final drag off the cigarette and then put it out in the Coke can she'd been using in lieu of an ashtray. "Maybe things can change. People can make themselves better, right? You did. And you really did change. Sometimes I hate you for it."

"I don't know what you want me to say to that, Layla." Slowing at the stoplight, he looked over at her.

She stared stonily out the windshield. "I want you to tell me I can change."

"That's up to you, though. Do you *want* to change?"

"If I didn't, I wouldn't be in here with you, Preach. That's for damn sure." She scraped her nails down the front of her jeans, her hands shaking slightly. "I don't want any damn thing, not from you. But look where I am."

Silence ticked away; the light changed. Pushing down on the gas, he pondered his response another few seconds and then finally said, "I think, if you really want to, you can change."

"How?" she said, her voice the faintest whisper.

"The same way I did. By focusing on one day at a day. At first, you focus on one second at a time. One minute. And you never lose sight of what matters to you the most."

She slanted him a quick look.

"You've got something that matters, Layla. We both know who it is."

"He doesn't care about me." She plucked at a thread coming loose from her jeans. "I didn't really give him much reason. And he's happier with Sybil, you know. She knows how to take care of him. I don't."

"So learn."

Keys clutched in his fist, David stood in the driveway, but he had yet to move toward Max's house.

Instead, like a moth drawn to a flame, David found himself walking toward the skeletal framework of the Frampton house. That hellhole where he'd had been broken, where he had bled and screamed behind a gag. Where he had prayed, begged for help. Where he had finally realized that prayers wouldn't be answered. Devils might exist, might walk on this earth, but God wasn't real.

Ducking under the yellow *caution* tape, he moved closer and closer, circling around the back, remembering.

She'd seen.

Once.

Lana didn't know *what* she'd seen, but she'd seen something.

They'd been finishing up. She'd been out doing whatever in the world supergirls did in their world where determination could right everything that was wrong in the world. He'd never even thought to ask her what had her out that late.

Past midnight, certainly, because they never finished early.

He had been stumbling, barely able to walk, but he'd forced himself to because the thought of somebody touching him had made him sick. He'd half-fallen against one of the trees and that was when he saw her, pressed half against the stone wall, lost in the darkness, save for the pale circle of her face. In the next second, even that was gone.

He'd thought maybe he'd imagined her. He'd imagined a hundred times that somebody would see. Somebody would realize what was going on and just *help*.

The next day, though, she'd looked at him, those grey eyes of hers stark and solemn.

And he'd realized. She'd known.

He hadn't been trapped alone in the pit of hell anymore.

He'd dragged her down with him and she'd suffered for it.

Broken glass, splintered wood, crunched under his foot as he moved across the ruin of the house. It would be demolished. Nothing here was worth saving. It might have made him smile if he could find it in him. But even as he muscled a ruined door out of the way, he just kept looking for another horror.

How long did it go back?

Caleb Sims, one of the boys who'd tried to destroy this place, had been being abused by his father. Blue, another boy, had almost been brought in. Abel had been back in the old ring.

There was a sound behind David and he turned, slowly. Some part of him expected to see his father there—whispering those words to him, all over again.

Be ready to receive the honor we give you. In time, you'll pass it on to others. Just as we pass it on to you now.

It wasn't his father, though.

Hank Redding stood there, his round, ruddy face oddly pale, his hands clenched into fists gone white at the knuckles. Slowly, David nodded.

"Hank."

Hank didn't even seem to see him. Instead, Hank stared past him, looking toward the mostly intact cellar door.

"This whole place could come down around us," Hank murmured.

David looked around. It wasn't likely. The worst of the damage was from smoke and water. Still, he kind of liked the idea of the place falling down, timber by timber, brick by brick.

"They dragged you down there, didn't they?"

David tensed. *So, yeah.* People would find out, already had, it seemed. But he'd be damned—

"It was an *honor*," Hank said, spitting the word out like it tasted foul. "That's what he told me."

He might as well have hit David with a two-handed fist.

Son of a bitch . . .

David had known there had been others, but this was the first time . . .

He sucked in a breath but Hank didn't even seem to notice as he moved forward, as though drawn by a string. "An honor . . . and he was so fucking disappointed when I told my parents. They thought I was sick, thought I needed help."

"Hank."

The other man turned his head, stared at David with a ghastly smile. "You know who they thought I should talk to, David? You know who they thought was the best person to offer advice to a troubled young boy?"

Fuck—

"They took me to your dad. Explained to him, while I sat in a room with your mother, just why they were worried, what had them concerned."

Hank started to laugh then, laughter that went on and

on, bleeding away in what sounded almost like jagged, cutting sobs. He went to his knees, slammed a hand into the soot-stained floor. Blood streaked it when he lifted it, but that didn't stop the man. He struck again and again.

"Stop." David moved to him, caught Hank's fist. Glass glittered on the ground and David had no doubt there was some of it embedded in Hank's knuckles now.

The fight went out of him and Hank sat back on his knees, with David still gripping one fist. They stared at each other. "They call them *counseling sessions*. They had no fucking clue what they'd done. One time, they even brought my grandfather along."

His words trailed off and abruptly Hank surged upright with a roar.

David didn't do anything but watch as Hank raced for the pantry, kicking the door down and staring down into the open, gaping pit. His hands clutched at the doorjamb, his shoulders rising, falling.

"How many?"

Slowly, David uncoiled and came to his feet, staring at the other man's back.

Hank whirled around, his eyes half-wild.

"How fucking many? How many of us did they drag down there? How many of us did they break?"

"I don't know," David said starkly.

Sagging against the wood, Hank lifted his head and stared upward. "I kept quiet. All this time. I was so ashamed, and those sons of bitches passed it on to their kids. I didn't even know. I thought it was just me. I . . . I thought there was something in me that made them do it. But they were doing it to others. All those other boys, and then they grew up and started it all over again. We let them."

"We didn't *let* them," David half-snarled.

"Didn't we?" Hank's laugh was wild, full of pain and

fury and misery. "We didn't say nothing. We kept it quiet because . . . because . . ."

David thought of the one time he'd *not* been quiet. He'd gone to the cops, thought he could try to tell. And the cop had been one of them. David hadn't been able to walk for days. The whip had peeled skin from his back. He'd been left pissing blood, tasting blood. Everything had turned to a haze of pain for him.

He hadn't tried to tell anybody what had been done to him because he'd known the next beating would kill him. Yes, he'd been quiet after that. He'd never seen anybody else, but as he got older, stronger, he'd fought more and more, while the rage inside him grew hotter, brighter.

He'd have to get out or kill himself trying.

And he'd rather get out, because that was the only way to make sure his father paid for what he'd done.

All because of those words, words that haunted David, even now.

You're old enough now. . . . Are you my son?

You go in there a boy. You come out a man. . . .

Be ready to receive the honor we give you. In time, you'll pass it on to others. Just as we pass it on to you now.

The honor.

They'd expected *him* to play their evil, awful games.

He would have died first, but he'd rather see them all suffer.

"It stopped," he said softly, looking out the empty frame where there had once been a window. "For a while, it stopped. They rebuilt it. That's on them. Not us."

"Is it easier to sleep at night? Telling yourself that?" Hank shook his head.

"I haven't sleep well in over twenty-four years." He'd stopped sleeping well the first time his father had woken him from a dead sleep, promising him that he'd show him the path to manhood.

The path to manhood was via pain, according to Peter Sutter.

David had spent nearly a quarter of a century on that path. It was a one-way road to nowhere.

Hank straightened and looked around, the fury in his eyes clearing, a frown on his face. When he looked at David, it was almost like it was a different man looking at him.

"I've been thinking about going to the cops," Hank said, his voice soft.

David cocked his head. "Have you now?"

"Yes." Not looking up, Hank just nodded. "It eats at me now. Tears into my brain and I can't sleep. If . . . if I do go, I won't mention you."

David snorted and turned away. "Plenty of people already know I was dragged into this and those that don't? Hell, they'll figure it out soon enough. My father was the head of it." He shrugged. "Don't know why you'd try to keep me out of it. I'm about as neck deep in this shithole as you can get."

"I just didn't want you . . ." His words trailed off and he sighed. "I don't blame you, you know. I tried to kill myself after one of those *sessions.* Your parents used to pick me up, drop me off. After the last one, I got . . . well, violent. Told my parents they weren't listening, they weren't hearing me. Your dad just kept staring at me, so sad, so serious. And your mom . . . fuck, she was a cold bitch."

He shot David a look. David had nothing to add. *Cold* barely even *touched* on what Diane had been.

"That night . . . that night, I snuck into the basement. That's where Dad kept his guns. Grabbed one. My mom had seen me, though. She came down right when I was putting it in my mouth—she screamed."

"Shit, Hank." The word ripped from him as another one of those emotions he'd thought he couldn't feel cut into him. Shock. And the fury. His father, evil bastard, however he'd left this world, hadn't suffered enough.

Hank swiped the back of his hand over his mouth. "They panicked. I dropped the gun and Dad came running down, grabbed me. I went crazy. Told them I had to do it, I had to. Told them if they ever made me see Pete again, I'd kill the bastard, I'd kill myself and I'd kill my grandpa, too."

"Did they . . ."

Hank shook his head. "No. I think they realized something was wrong. Pete tried to make them give in, but Mom wouldn't hear of it. Not after that. We stopped going to church where he preached. Stopped being anywhere where we might see him, or even my grandfather."

"If they believed you, why didn't they go to the cops?" David asked, his voice tight.

Hank was quiet for a moment and then he shook his head. "They didn't believe *me*. They just knew something was wrong. They'd make sure nothing bad happened anymore, and I guess that was better than nothing. But my mother couldn't believe that her father had done what he'd done."

He nodded, like he had answered some long-held question, and then some of the lines smoothed away from his face. "I hated them, for a long, long while. Maybe I still should. But I'm tired of letting this control me. I *want* to go to the cops. I just . . ."

He looked away, his face slowly turning red, then white.

He didn't say it, but David knew.

That ugly shame was something few could understand.

"If you need to do it, then do it. That poison may not stop eating at you until you do," David said. "I won't say anything to stop you. We all handle this as we need to."

Hank jerked his head in a slow nod and then turned, walking away in silence.

CHAPTER FIVE

Sybil sat across the table from Drew, holding her cards, studying his solemn face.

He had her face—Layla's face. And big green eyes. Those big green eyes were probably the only thing his father, whoever the man had been, had passed on to him. Well, that and a face for playing cards.

Sybil tapped a finger against the ones she held and then glanced down, sighed. "Go fish."

Drew did just that. She couldn't tell a thing by looking at his face, but ten seconds later he put his cards down, grinning like a loon. "I win again, Aunt Syb."

"That you do. Card shark." She went to say something, but the words froze in her mouth, for just a moment. Movement, in the backyard. It was late, too late, really for Drew to be up, but he'd had a rough day. Somebody had told him about Layla and he'd been broody, moody all day.

It looked like Sybil had another broody, moody man flying under her radar now.

David was out there.

"Why don't you go pick out a movie for us?" she suggested.

Drew's eyes popped wide. "Really? It's already ten. You gonna let me stay up that late?"

"Why not? It's Friday, right? Let's party." Never mind her headache or the gritty itch of her eyes. If it kept the boy from thinking about his mom, then he could stay up until two. She doubted he'd make it past midnight, though. "You go on in. I'm going to slip out back for a minute."

She did just that and found David in his normal spot, leaning against the big oak, lost in the shadows. He didn't have one of the slim little cigars she'd half grown accustomed to seeing him with and the sight of him in a dark T-shirt, one that clung tight to hard, heavy muscle, made her heart stutter in her chest.

"Look what the cat dragged in," she said, keeping her voice steady. She curled her hands into fists to keep from reaching for him. "Decide you have time to talk now?"

He didn't say anything.

She sighed and averted her gaze. "Drew's had a rough day. He's inside waiting for me, so if you're just looking to brood, I'll leave you to it."

But as she went to turn away, a hand came out, closed over the back of her neck.

"The way I hear it, you had a rough one, too."

Her heart jumped up in her throat as he moved, his heat coming up to warm her back as he tucked her up against him. She wanted to just sink right into him, let him take her weight, take *her* if he wanted. Instead, she just stood there, lifting her hands to cover his. Moonlight filtered down through the trees.

"You know, for a man who doesn't much show his face in town, you pick up on a lot of gossip."

He rubbed his cheek along hers. "I hear what I want to hear." Silence fell, like a blade.

She pulled away from him and turned to stare at him once she'd put some critical distance between them. She felt each inch, and they all hurt. "And why would something like this matter to you?" she asked, hearing the caustic edge to her tone and hating herself for it. She sounded like a whiny bitch.

David lifted a brow. In the silvery, shadowy light, he looked even more beautiful, more dangerous, than normal. He'd cut his hair. He was no longer even remotely pretending to be one of the Amish—and that was all it had ever been. She'd known it then, but he'd needed the mask, so she'd ignored it.

Even that was gone. His hair, dark and silken, was cut short, almost brutally so, leaving the harsh lines of his face unframed. His gaze locked on hers and she had nowhere to hide from his focus as he said softly, "It matters to me because it affects you. Do you really think she'll change this time when she never did before?"

It was one of those ugly truths Sybil had been avoiding all day. One she'd face when and if she had to. Shrugging, she looked back at the house. "In the long run, this has more effect on her and Drew than me. I just want to make sure *he* isn't hurt from it."

There was no sound, but she tensed nonetheless and when he reached out, touched her cheek, she flinched. "You are affected. Don't lie."

Closing her eyes, she lifted a hand and caught his wrist, nudged it down. "David, why do you care?"

I don't.

The words formed on his tongue and he tried to say them. Wanted to say them.

The problem was they wouldn't be true.

He could give lies, easily. He'd told lie after lie for twenty years. To everybody, to strangers on the street, to people he'd known all of his life, although they hadn't even realized who he was. He'd even given *her* lies. Lies as they spoke on the street, as she lay next to him in bed, her body still damp from sweat and him.

Why couldn't he give her a lie now?

I don't care. Three little words should be so easy to say and it would help add to the distance he needed to put between them. That distance would make it easier.

But he couldn't force the words out.

He'd gotten his hair cut earlier, tired of yet another part of the mask he'd worn. Cutting his hair had been like peeling away yet another layer of the deceptively simple disguise he'd worn for so much of his life.

While he was in there, he heard a couple of the guys talking, talking—and mocking. *You hear the news? Layla actually thinks she can get clean. I heard she had Noah take her to some residential rehab in Louisville. I saw them getting in a car myself.*

Layla can't get clean. She don't wanna *be clean.*

David had no care one way or the other, save for how it affected Sybil and the boy.

And that, he realized, was the problem. He did care, as much as he could. Because he didn't like to see the bruised, defeated look in Sybil's eyes and he knew when Layla failed—and she would—this would just put another bruise on Sybil.

Yet none of that had anything to do with why he was here, why he'd waited in the backyard, watching the house and waiting for the lights to go out.

Nine o'clock had come and gone and the lights still burned bright. He should have left, but he hadn't.

He hadn't planned to leave, either.

He was here. He was bruised.

He'd walked out of that house, all but staggered over

to Max's, wandered those empty halls and felt like he was going to come apart.

Come out of his skin.

Minutes ticked away into hours and then he found himself striding down the sidewalk. His feet had led him to town, wandering around, and it was no surprise that he'd found himself here. All roads led him here. Sooner or later.

Which was why he was having so much trouble cutting this piece of himself out. Here, with Sybil, was the only place he'd ever found *real* peace. Not a temporary respite from the noise inside him, some solace from the demons that chased him.

When he was *here*, with her, it was like he was just . . . himself.

Slowly, he reached up, pushed a hand into the soft, tumbled curls that fell past Sybil's shoulders.

But when he tried to tug her closer, she averted her head. "Drew is still awake. We can't do this right now."

It was enough to make him go still. Aching, he dropped his head onto her shoulder, half-expecting her to push him away. He'd ignored her or pushed her away for the past week. Now it was her turn.

Instead, she slid a hand up his back, curved it over his neck. "Come inside, David. Watch a movie with us."

The feel of her lips moving against his skin was a distracting torture and he had to think those words through twice before they made sense. "I can't do that, Sybil."

"Why not?"

Why not . . .

It sounded so easy. Go inside, watch a movie. He tried to remember the last time he'd seen a movie. It didn't count, really, the brainless shows that had come on while he sat in the hospital waiting for news about Max. It had been twenty years, he thought. Back when he'd still been that other David. Weaker, scared, broken.

He was still broken. No longer weak. Not scared anymore, either. You had to care to really be scared and David didn't give a shit if he lived or died.

Broken, though . . .

Yes, he was broken.

Fisting a hand in the material of Sybil's shirt, he lifted his head, looked down at her face in the pale moonlight.

She waited for him to answer. "Why can't you come inside and just watch a movie? Is there something stopping you?"

You, he wanted to say.

He needed to stop this. Needed to push her away.

He'd come out here thinking about losing himself inside her, one more time. It was always one more time, but the kid wasn't asleep. If he couldn't have that one last time now . . .

"A movie," he murmured.

*   *   *

Dawn rolled around.

David lay in the guest bedroom of Max's house, a small room tucked under the stairs, and he listened to the quiet. Always the quiet, so he could hear those footsteps that would never come.

He'd watched a movie.

Sybil had fallen asleep on his chest and Drew had fallen asleep on her leg.

In the end, he'd left them both there and tucked a blanket around each of them before he left.

He'd gone there hoping to bury himself in Sybil's body. Sex was never a peaceful thing for him, but he didn't need it to be peaceful; he just needed it—with her.

He'd find *peace* anyway, just by being with her. The hot bliss of driving his dick inside her, feeling her nails dig into him, the bite of her teeth, all of that was just a drug, something he needed from her—craved.

Last night, though, he'd discovered a different sort of bliss and he wanted to damn himself for it.

He didn't even know what movie they'd watched. A boy named Harry, some sort of stone, a school. It had managed to catch his attention a few times and Drew had loved it, but the magic of the night had been just . . . the night.

He'd sat in a house, with a woman curled up next to him and a boy sprawled on the floor in front of them for half the movie. Sybil and Drew had laughed, teased each other while they quoted bits and pieces of the movie, and to David it had felt like he was caught in some bizarre spell.

Was that what *normal* was? Sitting down and just existing like that? Laughing and teasing and eating popcorn with too much salt and butter and just . . . *being*?

Sybil's hand on his thigh, her head on his shoulder, a soft, gentle tease that should have called up that monstrous lust inside of him. Then Drew had curled up on the couch and both of them had fallen asleep.

How could they do that? Didn't they know what he was? What had been done to him and what *he* had done?

It was like they trusted him, and the very idea had left him shaken.

Trust was for people who actually had something in them *worthy* of trust. David was too . . . broken, with sharp, jagged edges left raw and exposed. Sometimes he imagined people could get too close and they'd draw back bloody all because of those jagged edges.

Not that it was much of an issue. Back on the farm, nobody but Abraham or Sarah had bothered trying to get too close. There had been casual friendships, established later, with men like Thomas who'd realized that there would always be a wall between David and everybody else.

They'd seen that wall and kept a safe distance. He'd let Abraham in. Sarah had tried, pushed for more, tried to pull David into that safer, peaceful world, and each time he pulled further and further away.

Sarah had tried and suffered for it. She'd thought she could pull him into their world, and each time she'd done so she'd gotten a harsh reminder that he—whether he went by "Caine" or "David"—didn't belong in that peaceful, gentle place.

Even when he'd moved in the town, under that disguise, people had kept their distance. Noah, one of the few who'd actually managed to establish even the most circumstantial relationship, had known enough to keep his distance.

Sybil was the only one who'd never bothered.

She'd seen the edges—he knew that—but she'd ignored them. She felt the scrapes, but she never let it show.

That trust that he never wanted was there, regardless.

And the boy seemed to share it.

Now, because of that fragile, undeserved trust, he had the memory of something he'd carry always. Just a simple night, in front of the TV, watching a movie about a boy named Harry, while they all ate popcorn. Sybil and Drew had watched the movie and David had watched them. If he was honest, he might even admit, he'd wished he could really have that. Have nights like that.

But they weren't for him.

Now, in the still, quiet morning, he let himself acknowledge that maybe that night should be it. He should let go. If they ever started to look at Sybil as they looked at *him*, the fractured hold he had on control would break.

If they looked at the boy, then at him, and wondered—

One big hand curled into a fist and he had to breathe through his teeth just to calm the red crawl of rage.

It's your turn now, boy. In time, you'll be a man and it will be your turn to join the brotherhood. Be ready to receive the honor we give you. In time, you'll pass it on to others. Just as we pass it on to you now.

Every secret would come out.

People were already looking at him, but soon, they'd *really* start to look. At him, at everything he did. Everything he touched.

If it was only him affected, he wouldn't care.

But it would spill over and touch anybody he allowed around him and that just wasn't acceptable. The dead surface of his soul might not be concerned with how others viewed *him,* but even he wasn't going to let their thoughts slide down that path as they looked from him to those around him.

And he didn't want her sympathy. Didn't want that hard, desperate hunger of hers to ever turn to anything else. A pity fuck was about as pathetic as they came.

He stared at nothing, gazing through the open window into the coming dawn without seeing. Curtains fluttered gently in the window. He'd spent too many years without air-conditioning, and the unnatural feeling of cool air circulating against his skin annoyed him. The first thing he'd done when he opened up the house was open up half the windows. It had chased out most of the stink of death and stale air. Now he could smell the river, the scent of morning, and the chill of a mid-fall morning felt good on his naked chest.

Rising, he moved to a window and stared out. The outline of the house—*that* house—loomed in front of him, larger than life, larger than he knew it truly was.

I hate you. The words were like a child's foolish taunt

in the back of his head. It caught him off-guard, the venom building inside his chest. That absolute loathing he felt for a pile of rubble and rock. One hand curled into a fist and he had a hot, vivid image of him finding a sledgehammer, taking it to the walls, tearing the rest of that place down until nothing lingered.

It was such a potent image that he had to turn away before he gave in to the urge.

It wasn't like anybody would really miss the place. He'd be doing the world a favor.

But he had something else to do today.

Find that journal.

CHAPTER SIX

She wasn't surprised when she woke alone.

Sad, yes.

Surprised, no.

He'd stayed, though, through the whole movie. That he'd even come inside had surprised her, and if she'd let herself think past the next hour, or even the first cup of coffee, it might have given her hope.

Sybil didn't like to think about things like hope. Hope could be such a disappointing bitch, though. Her mother had died of cancer and she'd told Sybil through the whole thing, *We have to hope for the best*. As Layla spiraled more and more out of control, Mom had always said, *We have to pray for her, be there. If she ever hits rock bottom, we'll be there for her. Until then, we hope for the best*. Then Layla had a kid and Sybil and her mother both *hoped* that Layla would get her act together.

Hope was a fickle, useless bitch.

Sybil dealt in reality.

But it had done something to her heart, made something burn hard and bright to see him sitting there on her couch as they watched *Harry Potter and the Sorcerer's Stone*. He'd even cracked a smile or two, and for David that was borderline miraculous. She'd planned on staying awake until the end of the movie, getting Drew to his room.

The past few weeks had been rough, though, and the exhaustion had dropped down on her like a sledge-hammer.

She'd see David in town, though. Maybe she could even *hunt* him down. Drew was going to the Louisville Zoo with a friend of his, then having a sleepover—something they'd been planning on for over a month, so it wasn't like she didn't have the day pretty open.

All she had to do was find David.

Well, get Drew up and moving. Get coffee. Shower. A few other things, including the hygiene things. She probably resembled a brown-haired medusa at this point. But later on, she could definitely hunt him down.

Her good mood evaporated in Louisa's coffee shop.

Sibyl had made plans to meet with Taneisha and her son, Darnell, at ten. It was 9:51 and if she had just waited, she could have avoided this. But no, she had to have her damn latte, didn't she?

"I just don't know what to think," Louisa nattered on as she put a lid on Sybil's coffee, completely unaware that Sybil wanted to commit bloody, brutal mayhem. "I mean, it's *awful* what was done to those boys. And . . ."

She paused and looked around.

Then, leaning in closer, she said, "Rumors are flying, saying the Sutter family was involved—that *David* was involved. He got caught up in that ugly, vile mess."

She paused again, a dramatic sigh escaping her. "If that's true, then his daddy abused him and his daddy was abused by *his* dad . . . it just keeps going! It would be best, really, if David just left and never came back. We can't break a cycle if any of them are here."

Louisa *finally* came to the end of her ugly little mono-
logue and smiled at Sybil. "That will be three eighty."

"I've changed my mind," Sybil said. She looked at the
caffeine, pursed her lips. "I get these awful headaches
when I don't have caffeine. Then I have caffeine and it
goes away for a while. But the headache just comes back
and I'm better if I have another . . . I think if I just stop
the coffee altogether, I'll do better."

"But caffeine is fuel," Louisa said, smiling proudly.

"And abuse is abuse," Sybil snapped. "Whatever was
done to those boys was *abuse*. They didn't ask for it and
just because *they* were abused doesn't mean they'll turn
around and abuse somebody else. Does a rape victim
turn around and abuse everybody she comes across?"

Louisa opened her mouth, shut it, looking oddly like
a fish as she did just that several times over. Finally, she
pressed a hand to her chest. "Why, Sybil. Surely you understand that I have nothing *but* sympathy for those who
were injured by this. It's just that I—"

"It's just that it's easier for you to spout shit out and
talk about horrors you can't *comprehend*. You don't have
sympathy. You want to gossip and add to the misery."
She leaned in, held Louisa's eyes. "You want to tell those
young boys who had the courage to come forward that
they will grow up and be monsters? They stood up; they
fought. What do you have to stay about them?"

The coffee shop had gone silent.

"Nothing to say, Louisa?"

"You're making a scene in my place, Sybil." Louisa
looked around furiously, her face going from white to
red. "I don't appreciate it."

"You made the scene. It's okay to gossip like an old
hen, but if people call you out on it, there's a problem?"

"Of course there's a problem when people call a rude
person out. Nobody likes to have the truth thrown at

them—it's too ugly, too blunt . . . too honest. That's the way it is." Doug Bell, his voice low and tired, stood, his chair scraping across the floor. "Personally, I'm tired of all of the backstabbing and then the smiles and cooing to your face. I had to listen to it fifteen years ago, and again at my wife's funeral. I think I'm done now. As to those boys . . . ? Louisa, if you lack the words, I can give you a word for them. I call them brave. You probably aren't familiar with the concept."

Doug smiled at Sybil and nodded on his way out.

In an oddly silent fashion, a family in the corner rose and followed. Followed by Jensen Bell, who'd been leaning against the counter, waiting to place an order. Vernon Driscoll vacated the table where he'd been, as did three more people.

Sybil looked at Louisa through her lashes.

The bell over the door rang and Drew came in, looking for her. He came up to her side and said, "Darnell is here. Did you get your drink yet, Aunt Sybil?"

"Oddly enough, I don't need it anymore, honey."

Without another word, she headed out.

"If this is your idea of cleaning, we need to talk."

David tensed instinctively, whirling around and already on the verge of attack even before recognition hit him. The adrenaline drained out of him as he saw Lana leaning against the open door of the little woodshop tucked in the backyard of Judge Max's yard.

Breath sawed in and out of David's lungs. It took a concentrated effort to calm down.

Lana lifted a brow and he had the disconcerting feeling she knew exactly what he was thinking, what he was feeling and how close he'd been to coming after her.

She probably did.

She'd kept a good twenty feet between them, and

although she kept her stance easily enough, he couldn't help but notice the odd . . . tension about her. Like he wasn't the only one braced for attack. The idea pissed him off, made him mad enough to tear something apart.

There were shadows on her soul now, too, and that was his fault.

"That . . ." He blew out a breath, waited another beat because his voice was hoarse. "That was damn fucking stupid coming up behind me like that."

"Thus the reason I'm a good twenty feet away, darlin'." She winked at him. "Besides, I haven't spent the past twenty years getting pampered and babied. I can handle myself."

He had no doubt of that, but he didn't want to think about himself losing it like that, going after one of the few he could actually call friend.

Lana lifted a brow at him as she shoved off the wall. She had a faint smile on her face as she wandered around. "Man, I don't miss this place."

"What?"

She shrugged.

"This is where Max had me hide."

He blinked and then abruptly spun around. "Lana, I'm already walking a hair trigger. Don't add to it."

"Or what? Are you going to turn into the Hulk or something?"

He turned his head, stared at her. "You act like this is a joke. You should be more careful." He left the words *around me* unsaid.

"Nah." She lifted a shoulder. "If you honestly think I need to be *careful* around you, then you need a swift kick in the ass. Probably a dozen of them."

He swiped a hand across his face and swore under his breath. He kept waiting for that red crawl to roll across his vision, the shakes to grab him—a sure sign that his temper was going to slip away and he'd find himself on the verge of violence. When that had happened, he'd always just lost himself up on the hills, wandered for hours until he thought he was steady again.

Somehow, he didn't see Lana letting him just disappear.

But red didn't slip in to obscure his vision and his hands stayed steady.

For a minute, he stared, took a moment to just wonder at that.

Then he looked back at her.

She had a glint in her eyes, something that spoke of challenge and temper like she was just dying to push at him, poke at him. "What are you doing?" he asked softly.

"Waiting to see you." A strange little smile lit her face, one that didn't make sense, not at all.

"What?"

She shrugged and turned away, started to roam around the four walls of the barn. "You heard me. You spent twenty years trapping yourself behind a mask. I trapped myself in a box miles away from here. I'm done with it. I'd think you'd be about the same." One shoulder rose, fell, as she stopped in front of a dusty set of shelves.

There were books, a lot of them. Notebooks, some DIY type of books. David had already looked through them with little interest, but Lana seemed to be intent. She reached up and touched one. "This one," she murmured. "Huh. Kingsolver. I don't see Max reading her. *Prodigal Summer.*"

She slid David a narrow look over her shoulder. "Just what are you doing out here anyway?"

"What does it matter?"

"Call me curious. That's one thing that never did change." She eyed the tools he'd moved around, shelves he hadn't put back into place. "It almost seems like you're looking for something. Me, I can't help but think maybe you should look at this."

She reached up and pulled down that large-print edition of *Prodigal Summer*. Unlike every other book on the shelf, this one only had a fine layer of dust. She flipped it open and then pursed her lips. "Well, I'm pretty sure this wasn't in the copy *I* read," she murmured. She eyed the hollowed-out pages for a moment and then reached in, pulled out two slim leather journals. "You wouldn't be looking for these, would you?"

He started with the older one first. Written by Harlan Troyer in an elegant, neat hand, the journals detailed meetings—and to David's unending disgust and fury, more names. His, Hank's, Jeb's.

This was his nightmare. That it had involved others. According to the journal, there had been three going through it along with him and he had never known their names. Initiates, they were called.

Three of them going through the same hell he'd gone through while another was formally accepted into the club. Jeb. Garth's son. "Son of a bitch," David said softly. Now that red crawl that he had expected all day rolled across his vision and his gut twisted in fury.

Sitting on the porch as the sun made a slow trek through the sky, David read through the first journal, flipping through the pages until he reached the halfway point. There it detailed what Harlan knew about those final days and the months that came after.

Things had changed after the disappearance of Peter Sutter—David's father. Some of the older members had talked about trying to keep it going, but others thought it was too risky. Those higher up in the food chain, the Sims brothers, Andrews, Troyer, had ended up making the call and Cronus, as it had been, ended.

Without knowing what had happened, where David had gone, they didn't want to take the risk.

The last journal entry was six weeks after David and Lana had disappeared from Madison. No other notes. Nothing.

He reached for the next journal and flipped it open. A note fell out. He recognized the scrawl on it immediately:

Hopefully the right person is reading this—the prodigal son.

Of course, if you are, that means I never had the chance to turn these over to you. A part of me wonders what might have happened. We talked about the lines you cross—I crossed those lines so long ago, I can't even remember who I was before I crossed them, and once it was done I had to draw new lines. I lived by them, for a good long time.

I crossed them again, after what happened to you, and I don't regret it, but it changed me, each time. Changed me from the man I wanted to be.

I don't want to see that happen with you, boy.

You carry too much darkness in you. If I could keep any of this from you, I would. But secrets won't help you heal. Secrets put you on this path to begin with.

I'm not showing them to you so you can burn the town with them. Town is already burning. I haven't helped any, but then again, I made a promise and didn't keep it. I wanted to fix things, and those sons of bitches wouldn't have paid.

But you have more right to know than anybody who they were. That it did stop for a while. It's not good enough and I'm sorry I didn't keep my word to you, boy.

It should stop now. Pete was always the leader of the pack and the ones who tried to pull it back together had no idea what they were doing. He had his own personal hell where he reigned as king. The rest of them didn't even have a third of his brains. It's a good thing, that. It made it easier to bring it down this time.

Easier.

If anything about this can be called easy.

Max's name was scrawled at the bottom.

Down below that, in tight print, like he had decided to squeeze it in, were a few final lines:

I loved you the minute I saw you. Tried to talk her into letting me spend time with you, but she wouldn't have it. I never hated anything in my life as much as that.

Not until I saw you that night. I should have done better by you. It's a regret I'll carry the rest of my life. Forgive me.

Carefully, David folded the paper. Then he tucked it inside the journal, keeping it closed.

He couldn't look at the second journal, not just yet.

It was strange.

For so many years he'd felt little. Except the rage. Rage could always cut through. The past few weeks more and more managed to cut through, but as he sat there, it was like something inside him started to crack.

I don't want this, he thought, heart and soul aching even as he tried to push it all away.

The fucking letter. Should have shoved it back inside. Shouldn't have read it. Shouldn't have looked for the journals.

Max had warned him, hadn't he?

Sucking in a breath, David tensed his muscles, torn between locking the journals up, out of sight, and taking them to the river and hurling them into the slow-moving waters.

Before he could decide, the world shifted and moved sideways on him. The hairs on the nape of his neck stood up.

His blood started to pump.

Slowly, he shifted his gaze and found himself staring across the neat, tidy little lawn.

There. That was the other thing he felt, a bizarre mix of need, longing and a twist in his heart that he couldn't fully understand. It only happened around one person.

It wasn't a surprise that she'd found him here.

Nor was it a surprise when his heart did that odd little twist.

These feelings he was familiar with, and because he'd rather deal with this torrent than the confusion that had been raging inside, he focused on what thrummed inside him when he was with Sybil.

She made him want.

She made him *need*.

And, he realized, she made him feel regret. He *could* feel it.

That pang, that tug in his heart, because he knew he needed to push her away, because he couldn't reach for her the way he wanted.

Regret that he wasn't as strong as he should be, because even as he told himself to push her away she started up the walk, the short skirt she wore barely clinging to her thighs, and all he could think about was pulling her into his lap so that the skirt rode higher and he could cup her hips, pull her down to straddle him.

Vivid, overbright starbursts seemed to explode behind his eyes as that fantasy played out in his mind.

This was a secluded street and people had finally given up on the rubbernecking. Hardly anybody drove down the street to check out the burned-out wreck of the Frampton house. He could pull that stretchy bit of fabric up and be inside her in two minutes. It would be so easy to just lose himself to her.

She came to a halt in front of him. His blood pounded in slow, steady waves while need clenched inside him like a fist.

Tell her to leave, common sense dictated. He'd already made the decision he needed to make.

But his head, his heart, his cock, didn't want to listen.

"Hey," she said, her red-slicked lips curving up.

He stared at her mouth, thought about seeing that mouth open, seeing it glide down his chest.

Blinking, he managed, barely, to look away. "Hey back."

This was yet another thing he lacked, the ability to talk, even to her, about anything that didn't involve getting her naked and fucking her. Naked wasn't even necessary as long as he could be inside her, lose himself to her, hide away from the demons that chased him.

But if he kept doing that, all those demons were going to start chasing her, too.

David wasn't worth a whole hell of a lot and he didn't care about a whole hell of a lot. But he'd burn this whole damn town to the ground before he let anything from his past start to haunt her. Every moment of peace he'd ever known had come from her. She mattered, more than anything or anybody else in his miserable world.

So instead of reaching for her, he stared out at the water, acutely aware as she sat down at his side. The journals sat at the other and he resisted the urge to grab them, disappear inside the house, hide them away from her. Hide them away, hide their secrets, as if that would make the truth any less than true.

"I don't blame that kid," Sybil said out of the blue.

Caught up in his own head, he barely understood what she meant. Looking over at her, he tracked her gaze, and then, as a shiver of cold raced up his spine, he looked back over the water.

"Plenty of people don't. Too bad he couldn't find a way to trap his dad and uncle in there, too."

Sybil murmured, "His uncle's brains splattered all over the chief's wall."

"He went too easy."

"True. But Jeb's is still gone." Her gaze came over to David. "We fell asleep on you. What did you think about the movie?"

David frowned, tried to remember something about it. The boy. Wands. A rock. Then he shrugged. "What sort of name is Snape?"

Sybil laughed. "An interesting one. For an interesting character. Is he a good guy or a bad guy?"

The question caught David off-guard. Then he looked down. "What does it matter?"

"Well, if you want to watch more of the series with us, it would be kind of fun for me to know now, what you think of him. He plays a big part in it."

I'm not watching more. That was what he should tell her. Sighing, he looked away. Everything he should do, he couldn't do. It had been like that for most of his life. He should have found a better way to make people listen. He should have fought harder. He should have run sooner.

Then there were the things he *shouldn't* have done. He shouldn't have involved Lana. He shouldn't have stayed in town. He shouldn't have reached for Sybil that first night.

A hand reached up, touched his cheek. "You're always so serious, David."

"Little reason to be otherwise."

"True." She moved then and he didn't even have time to brace himself before she had settled herself in his lap, one leg planted on either side of his hips. Her hands came up, cupped his face. "How much longer until you decide to tell me?"

His hands moved of their own volition, fingers splayed wide across satiny soft thighs. "Tell you what, Sybil?"

"Don't play games with me." She dipped her head so that her hair fell around them like a curtain. "You've never done it before. Don't start now."

Noise clamored in the back of his head, all that chaos rising to a roar as he stared into those beautiful eyes. They slid between gold and green, and right now they all but glowed as she watched him.

Send her away. Tell her.

He slid his hands up, cupping her ass. And he groaned when he found her naked under that sorry excuse for a skirt. "I keep thinking it's time to tell you to just go. To stay away from me."

"That's what I thought." She rubbed her mouth against his. "Why don't you do it, then? So I can ignore you and we can fight it out?"

The cool silk of her hair brushed against his cheek. He tangled one hand in it. "This isn't a game anymore."

"It never was." She eased back, watching him with knowing eyes.

He curled his lip. "It was one thing when you were fucking some Amish builder. It's another thing when it's David Sutter, possible murder suspect, sick degenerate. It's just a matter of time before the cops decide to start pulling me in, demanding answers about what happened the night I disappeared. Just a matter of time before everything comes out in the open. When nobody knew—"

She lifted a hand and pressed her finger to his lips. "I always knew."

He flinched.

Sybil watched as his face went tight, watched as his eyes went blank.

The hand on her hip tightened reflexively while the one fisted in her hair fell away.

He surged to his feet, moving so fast, she would have tumbled to the ground if it hadn't been for his holding her tight against him.

But then he let her go and she had to hold on to the railing for balance.

"What?"

He had his back to her, those strong shoulders straining against the cloth of his T-shirt. He looked so different now. Those simple clothes he'd worn for years had been a mask. He wore a dark T-shirt and black jeans and he looked like a fallen angel—sent by Lucifer to taunt and tempt and destroy.

He could destroy *her*. So easily. She'd been in love with him for years and nobody had as much power over her as he did. "I've always known," she said again, refusing to allow her voice to shake, refusing to let herself look away when he turned to face her.

It had been his eyes.

How anybody had ever looked into those eyes and not known she couldn't understand.

Those eyes now cut into her and she tried not to tense as he closed the distance between them. His hands came up, bracketing her in as he grabbed the railing on either side of her hips. "Explain that, Sybil," he said, his words short, bitten off like it was a chore just to talk.

For him, it was. She knew that. She knew more about him than he'd probably like. She knew so much about him that there were times when she'd lie in bed and cry.

"What's there to explain?" she asked softly, lifting a brow and meeting that searing blue gaze. "That first time you came in town—fifteen years ago, five years since the night you disappeared. You were there for that damn candlelight vigil. I heard you introduce yourself as Caine, but even then, I knew who you were."

CHAPTER SEVEN

The glow from a few hundred candles might strike some people as pretty. The somber atmosphere was probably poignant to others.

To Sybil, it was just a sham.

She'd seen the blown-up pictures placed on easels and the sight of them had sickened her. The people of Madison hadn't just made one *set of images, but five, and from her position she could see all but one set. There was a set on the steps and then the others were spread through the crowd so everybody could gaze upon the faces of the Sutter family.*

Diane. Peter. David.

Of the three of them, only one was really worth mourning over.

Sybil had met the boy—younger than her by two years, but he had old eyes, even then.

Of course, if she had parents like Diane and Peter, she'd probably have old eyes, too.

Her mother used to clean for Diane, but then she'd been fired.

At the time, Sybil had wanted to be pissed—at the kid.

It was something they'd found in his room that had

led to her mother being fired. Maybe Sybil shouldn't have said anything, but that wouldn't have helped.

How could she keep quiet about it anyway? Blood on the sheets wasn't exactly a normal thing. Well, if David had been a girl on the rag, maybe. But that wasn't the issue. She'd told her mom. They'd looked at the sheets and they'd mentioned it to Diane. Diane was a bitchy thing and Sybil had never liked her, but she had to care about her kid, right?

She'd looked at the sheets. Looked at them. Then she took the sheets, folded them neatly. "David plays a lot of sports. He hunts with his father and is the typical boy. He gets injured sometimes. He is also a restless sleeper. He has some scrapes on his back. I cannot believe you would imply something like this. I'll send your final check to your house. Now please leave and do not ever let me see you again."

Karen Chalmers might have been a broke woman who hustled to pay her bills, working every odd job she could find, including cleaning houses, offices and any other place that would pay, but she had a spine of steel. Standing by Sybil, Karen had seemed to grow three inches as she faced Diane Sutter. "I wasn't implying anything, Mrs. Sutter. I just wanted you aware that your son had some sort of injury. I know how teenagers are. Clearly, you are more concerned about your image than you are about the fact that I was just concerned. I expect the check within the next two weeks, as discussed when I started working for you."

She'd turned to go, nodding at Sybil.

"You will be paid when I see fit."

Karen had then looked at her daughter. "You will cut the check within two weeks of service unless you want it known that you don't pay for services rendered. You see, unlike you, I don't give a rat's ass what people say about me. *I'll make sure tongues wag in this town. If you don't want that happening, then cut my damn check."*

Once they left, instead of going home, they had gone to the cops, spoken with Chief Andrews.

But nothing ever came of it.

David, and his parents, had disappeared a few months later. Along with a girl who lived a few blocks away from Sybil. Sybil had liked the girl—a lot. Her name had been Lana Rossi and she was one of the few people who didn't back down from anybody, including Sybil's bitchy little sister.

And Layla was *a bitch. Sybil didn't know why, didn't understand what had gone wrong inside Layla's head, but the wires were all crossed.*

A song started to ring through the night and Sybil sighed, lifted her face to the night sky. " 'Amazing Grace.' Please."

Turning away, she started down the street but hadn't gone more than a few feet before she crashed into Vernon. He caught her arms, steadied her. Distracted, ready to be distracted even more, she met his wide, wicked smile with one of her own.

"Why aren't you down there singing 'Kum Ba Yah' with everybody else?" he teased.

Shoving her hair back, she cocked a hip and planted a hand on it. "First, I had to work. Helping Lancaster in his studio, and it was my night to close things up. Second, they are singing 'Amazing Grace.' Third, I'm not going to a vigil when I couldn't stand two of the people they are weeping and wailing about."

Vernon's brows shot up. "Yeah? Which two?"

"Mommy and Daddy Sutter. She was a bitch and he was just as bad. The whole town is blind, too busy adoring them, but I know better." She sighed and looked over at the church. From there, she could still see one of the *pictures of David. He'd been a nice-looking kid. Sullen, quiet. But who could blame him?* "Anyway, I don't want to talk about them."

"Me, neither." *He moved in closer.* "How about we go grab a bite to eat instead?"

Exactly seventy-two minutes later, she all but fell out of his truck, desperate to get away.

"A bite to eat doesn't mean I'm going to spread my legs, you son of a bitch," *she snarled as he came around the truck, rubbing his jaw where she'd elbowed him.*

"You are such a little cock tease."

Planting her feet, she steadied herself. She was tired of this. Layla fucked everybody with a dick and people seemed to think Sybil was the same. She liked sex just fine—more than just fine—but she was rather selective about her partners and it took a lot more than just one or two dates before she decided if she was going to sleep with somebody.

Curling her lip as he drew closer, she raked him up and down with a look. "Please, Vernon. Don't flatter yourself. You'd have to have a cock worth teasing before I'd bother with you."

He tried to cage her in up against the shop window, but she dashed to the side.

Her heels were going to be problematic here, she realized. But as she went to kick them off, a shadow peeled itself off the wall.

As he moved in between her and Vernon, her heart stuttered for a few beats before it settled back into a normal rhythm.

"I think the lady is done with you."

His voice was rich, deep. Sinful, seductive as chocolate. Something in her belly clenched just at the sound of it. As his words connected in her brain, she arched a brow.

A white knight.

She hadn't ever had a guy rush to her rescue before. It was . . . sweet. She'd never really needed it, either. She could handle Vernon—she'd handled worse. Regardless, it was still very sweet.

Vernon sneered at him and she had a moment to catch her breath, debate about how to handle the change in circumstances.

"Go back to the farm, boy," Vernon said, his voice mocking.

Sybil flicked a look over his clothes, saw the simple blue shirt, the sturdy, plain brown pants. The dark bowl of a haircut and the hat he held clenched in one big hand completed the picture.

An Amish *white knight?*

Weirder and weirder.

Vernon moved in closer, his face in a scowl, but all the man did was stand there.

Then Vernon reached out and the man moved, caught Vernon's hand in his.

It was done, then. Sybil's mind was still processing it and she couldn't believe what she'd seen. Vernon was on the ground, facedown, his voice high, pinched from pain, while the man still held his wrist, twisted and wrenched up in the air.

"I told you that it was time to leave the lady alone." His voice was as steady as if he'd been discussing the weather.

"All right, all right, I get it, I get it!" Vernon was whimpering by the time the final words left him. "I'm sorry, fuck—Sybil, I'm sorry. Tell him to—"

A moment later, the man let go.

He turned to look at her.

She staggered back against the window as those eyes connected with hers.

His face—harshly hewn, darkened by stubble, the face of a man who'd looked into hell. It didn't fit that rich as chocolate voice. But it fit those eyes. She knew those eyes.

She'd looked into them once before.

"Are you well?" he asked, his voice oddly formal.

"You . . ." She licked her lips. "You're . . ."

"My name is Caine," he said, dipping his head. "I saw what was happening and wanted to help. Are you well?"

Caine. She blinked and passed a hand over her eyes. Caine? She sucked in a slow breath, let her brain process that as she thought about the circus, draped in somber clothing, going on behind her.

Then, as understanding dawned, she met David Sutter's eyes. Caine. So he'd remade himself. Good for you, she mused. Meeting his gaze, she nodded. "I'm fine, thank you . . . Caine."

The memories of that night, as clear to her as if it had just happened, spun away. Blinking, Sybil turned her head and looked over David. His gaze bored into hers.

"How did you know?"

"Your eyes." She shrugged. "Like I told you, anybody who looked into your eyes and didn't see it, they were just blind."

A little like him, she supposed. He looked at her now and didn't see. He'd looked at her for all these years and didn't realize it. They hadn't become lovers until a few years later. He hadn't even trusted her at first—she knew he didn't really *want* to trust her now, but in some way he did. Otherwise she couldn't do what she was doing.

Lifting a hand, she laid it on his chest. Under her palm, she felt that rapid-fire beat of his heart.

"I was never *just fucking* anybody," she murmured, pressing her hand tight against him and relishing the heat of his skin, the strength of him, and that steady, soothing beat of his heart. "I knew who you were, but none of the things that concern you worried me. You could have spent your life on a construction crew, working in the circus or hiding out from the law. All I need to know is this. . . ."

She rose on her toes and pressed her lips to his. "I want you. I've always wanted you. I always will."

His hands gripped her hips, tugged her closer. "When things get ugly? What then?"

"You've met my sister, right? I'm already familiar with ugly." She caught his lower lip between her teeth and tugged. "I want you. Nothing is going to change that. Now . . . come on. Or are you still under the impression you can foolishly protect me from whatever?"

He wanted to deny that. He didn't want her thinking that he was *protecting* her. Even if that was the case. If she believed that, though, she might realize that he did care. That she did matter.

That wouldn't turn out well, because he knew her. She'd wrap herself around him even tighter, refuse to let go. And if she really fought, fought for *him*, could he make himself do what he needed to do?

This added complication was one he didn't need. His life had gone from the simple act of just getting through one day at a time to having to think about the others in his life.

When had he started to *care* about the fact that there were others who mattered?

Although—

His hands tightened on her waist and he pressed his face into her neck to keep her from seeing the turmoil on his face. Although, even the first time he'd seen her, she'd mattered.

On the street, glaring at the dickhead Driscoll. She'd sneered at him with nothing but defiance and determination on her face, and David had no doubt that even if he hadn't intervened Sybil would have put the other man on his back, all but begging for mercy.

But fury, unlike anything David had known, had splintered inside him when he'd seen the man moving on her.

He could explain it away, if he wanted to: He'd been a victim. The thought of seeing a man prey on somebody else lit the short fuse of his temper, but even that felt like the lie he knew it was. Yes, predators infuriated him, but when it came to Sybil anything that left a mark on her would piss him off.

Even when he hadn't known her.

She was the one weakness he'd never been able to afford.

Which was why he needed to move past this. Move past *her* so he could deal with the nightmares he'd have to face in the coming months. So he wouldn't have to look at her and see the misery he'd no doubt bring into her life.

He didn't want to ever see those lovely eyes fill with disappointment, disgust, disillusion. But it would happen. How could it not?

"You think so very hard," Sybil murmured, rising onto her toes and pressing her lips to his. Just that light, soft kiss, barely more than a brush of her mouth against his own.

And he knew he'd have to deal with thoughts, doubts, regrets later. Much later.

Her fingers slid under the hem of his shirt, and as she started to stroke up along his spine, control shattered, flying apart like a million shards of glass.

Hauling her up against him, he boosted her up into his arms. Blind desperate hunger drove him as she twined her legs around his waist. She didn't say a word. Good. That was good. If she didn't say anything, then he wouldn't have to worry about answering, thinking.

Just then, he barely had the state of mind to get them inside the door. Barely even managed to get them down the hallway. If it had been his home, he wouldn't have cared, but Max's home . . . no. His room, they had to go to his room.

But once he got there, it was all done. Grabbing the hem of her skirt, he yanked it up and turned her around.

She groaned as he forced her to bend. There was a chair and she braced her hands on it.

The sight of her, bent and willing and ready for him, was practically his undoing. Naked under that sorry excuse of a skirt, and when he touched her he found her already wet.

But that wasn't enough. He needed to brand her, mark himself on her body in a way she'd never forget. Just as she'd branded him. Sliding a hand up her rump, he teased the dark crevice between her cheeks.

Brand her . . .

Going to his knees, he pressed a kiss to one rounded cheek. Memories—of himself, bound and helpless—tried to work free.

"David . . ."

He trailed his fingers along the seam of her buttocks, seeking her out with the most intimate of touches.

She made him so weak.

So vulnerable.

As he pressed against her, she gasped.

He needed to see *her* vulnerable, needed to know he wasn't the only one weakened and overwhelmed.

"Did you remember?" he asked, his voice a rasp in his throat.

Something small and black fell on the chair. Her purse. Everything in it fell out, and there wasn't much inside, making it easy to see the tube of lubricant there. He grabbed it in one hand, fisted his other one in her hair. "Can I make you scream? Can I make you beg?"

"You can do whatever you want to do with me."

With a harsh groan, he jerked her up and covered her mouth with his. He wanted things from her that should send him screaming into the night, but instead, it was like the need sent him screaming . . . to her.

He wanted her in more ways than he could even begin to describe, more ways than he could begin to imagine. All of them had to do with her coming apart for him. All of them had to do with her sobbing out his name—*his* name. He wanted her to know *him*. Fuck the secrets, fuck the shadows, fuck the scars.

He needed to have her in the most intimate way possible and he needed to hear her break for him as he took her. Needed to hear her moaning out his name.

Sinking his teeth into her lip, he said, "Say my name, Sybil. Say it."

"David."

Her voice was steady and low, and need bloomed in her eyes.

The sound of his name on her lips had something clenching in his heart an emotion he couldn't even begin to look at, and it only grew more painful when she reached up and back, curling an arm around his neck. Her fingers slid through his hair and she murmured his name again, this time on a sigh. "David . . ."

Fuck—

Shoving everything down inside, he urged her forward again and tore at his jeans, his hands half-fumbling with the unfamiliar zipper, the button. The clothes seemed too tight, clinging to him, and just then they pissed him off. Shoving the jeans and shorts down, he freed his cock and tucked the head against her core; he hissed at the slick, naked feel of her.

"Condom," he gritted.

"No." She rocked back on him.

David groaned as she closed around his cockhead, clamping his hands tighter to keep her from taking him deeper. "We need a rubber, Syb."

"No. We don't. I'm on the pill. I haven't been with anybody else since we got together. Have you . . . ?"

He stared at the elegant line of her spine, wondered what she would say if she knew. "No." He dragged her farther down, relishing the silky wet. "We shouldn't do this."

"Yes, we should. We absolutely should." She rolled her hips and he snarled, set his feet and drove deep, deep inside.

She cried out. The sound was the sweetest he'd ever heard. "Again. Scream for me again," he demanded as he seated himself inside her again, hard and fast.

But she didn't. She wouldn't. Not until he dragged it out of her. It was a challenge—everything with her was. Lids lowered, he stared at the shadowed crevice just above where he shafted her. Stroking one thumb up along the sensitive skin there, he murmured, "There. If I fuck you there, you'll scream. You'll moan. You'll beg . . . won't you, Sybil?"

Did she need him that much? As much as he needed her? It was a terrifying thought, one that should have him tearing away from her and putting distance between them, but he couldn't. He'd never been able to turn away from her.

She shivered, her only answer a low whimper. He'd dropped the lube without noticing, but now he grabbed it, flipped open the cap. It was cool and slick in his hand and he almost welcomed the relief of it as he pulled out and started to slick it over his cock.

This here, the pleasure, was almost too much. The pleasure of taking her, sliding his cock inside her, of feeling her skin naked against his own. If anybody else touched him, even in the most casual of ways, it was akin to torture. With her, the sweetest of pains and the darkest of pleasures. Every touch of her hand, every brush of her body against his helped smooth away some jagged, rough edge.

He got more lubricant and smeared it across her entrance, bending over her to murmur in her ear as he pushed first one finger, than a second, inside. "I want to feel you squeezing my dick like that, Sybil," he whispered.

Wanted? No. He *needed* to feel it. Needed to feel her yield to him as the hunger tore them apart.

She turned her head and caught his mouth. Her teeth nipped his lower lip, hard. Pain flared and the rush of it went straight to his balls, making them ache. "Stop teasing me," she said.

"Is it teasing?" He twisted his wrist, felt her shudder. A moan caught on her lips.

"David—"

That hit him, like a punch in the gut. The sound of his name on her lips was still new, still a delight.

His name, not the name of the man he'd pretended to be. A man who wasn't real.

Swearing, he tossed the lubricant down and straightened. He wrapped his hand around his cock and steadied it. His flesh was darker than hers, all over, and she was pale, smooth and soft, so soft, as he pressed the head against vulnerable flesh.

Voices, chaos, rose inside him, vying for control, trying to tug him back to the past.

"David . . . stay with me," she said, her voice a rasp.

His vision narrowed down to nothing, locked on the sight of her flowering open around his shaft as he pressed inside. A whimper escaped as he gave her one inch, then withdrew. Slow and steady, two inches, then back out.

The shadows fell away and all he could see was her, all he could hear was her. All he could *feel* was her.

Sybil was shaking and sobbing, her limbs trembling by the time he seated his length within her and his balls were drawn tight against him.

He'd never gone skin to skin. Never, and *this*—the molten, satiny feel of her wrapping around him, tighter and hotter than her pussy—was a pleasure he didn't think he could stand.

"Tell me you're ready," he said, forcing the words out.

"Make me scream."

He swore and pulled out, drove back in.

The sound of her voice bouncing off the walls was enough to drag a shaky curse from him. Again, and again, his fingers digging into her hips, holding her steady for each hard, deep thrust. She arched her back, undulating, as broken whimpers and words fell from her lips.

She came—hard and fast—and still he moved. Couldn't stop.

It was there, a brutal climax burning inside, but he couldn't reach—

Desperate, he hauled her back against him without breaking their connection and spun them around, taking her to the floor. A breathless gasp came from her, but he barely noticed, locked on the ache in his balls, the need to come, so fucking elusive.

Her weight shifted and he felt her pressing against him. Letting her shift, he eased back onto his heels, pulling her with him. She took his hand, brought it up.

Sharp teeth sank into his wrist and pain streaked through him.

Head falling back, David felt the dam break. And that, too, was another form of pain, jagged and intense, his release ripping out of him like she'd torn it from his soul.

And maybe she had.

Sometimes he thought she might own it anyway.

Sybil should be used to it. The raw, guttural power that was David. She'd all but drawn blood when she bit him and he'd called bruises from her skin.

She'd loved it all.

But her heart hurt. Even now as he slid into the shower with her, she had to blink back the tears before she could smile at him. She hurt because she needed him, because he needed her. And he wanted to push her away.

"You still think you can protect me?" she murmured.

He stood beneath one of the angled showerheads, eyes closed. He slid his hands over his face, through his hair, before he turned his head to look at her. "Sometimes I think I need to protect *me* from you."

"That boat's long sailed, sugar." She lifted a brow and moved forward, grabbing a bar of soap. She lathered it up and started to soap up his chest. "I've got you in my sights. I don't plan on letting you get away."

He sighed and sagged back against the wall. "You're thinking the wrong sort of thoughts. This . . ." He moved a hand back and forth between them. "This is all we have, all we can have."

The ache in her heart grew. She thought maybe she

heard something crack, a narrow fissure forming in her heart. "This?" she asked, sliding a hand down the hard muscles of his abdomen before she closed her fingers around his cock. He was hard already, heavy in her hand, and as she slicked the soap over his cock, he started to pulse. "You mean sex?"

"You know that's what I mean."

"Hmmm." She pumped her hand, using the rhythm that worked for him, her hand tight, her strokes almost brutal. His eyes glittered as he stared at her. Glittered with lust, glittered with need, glittered with emotions she couldn't describe.

"This is sex. We have this." She stepped back and let the water rinse him off and then she went to her knees, taking him in her mouth. When she bit him, he swore and grabbed her head, started to fuck her mouth. It was fast and desperate and he came almost immediately. She rose, stared him in the eyes. "We have that . . . and that's trust."

She lifted a hand and placed it on his cheek. "You know as well as I do that there's more between us. You can deny it all you want, but denying it doesn't make it any less true. I'll wait until you're ready to stop fighting it."

Then she turned back to the shower to wash up.

Whether he'd let her stay or not, she didn't know.

But she'd put the thoughts in his head and she did know one thing—he'd have to think about it now.

CHAPTER EIGHT

The face in the mirror looked harmless.

Most people never looked more than once.

As it should be.

It was particularly handy now.

Moving through the hospital was easy. Getting inside Max's room wasn't. The cop at the door didn't move. Waiting for him to take a break proved tedious.

Patience, though, was a virtue.

The one who watched knew how to wait. It was, after all, something long practiced. This had started more than twenty years ago. What was a few minutes? A few hours?

Finally, that patience paid off.

There was a fight down the hall, between an irate father and a stepfather. When the fight went from verbal to physical the opportunity arose.

Moving inside the room, the one who watched looked around, eyed Maxwell Shepherd. He was still, looked almost small under the bedclothes, and he was asleep.

That made it even easier.

A pillow, held over the face.

He fought, but in addition to being patient, the one who watched was strong. It took very little time.

In just under moments, the one who watched returned to the door and checked outside. The cop was still struggling with a man on the floor. People were focused on them.

It was that easy to slip in, then slip out.

That easy to take a life.

"Where do we stand?"

Jensen Bell didn't sit in the police department with the chief. They also hadn't met in the coffee shop the way they had more than once in the past.

They each had a cup of coffee, but they'd picked it up from a nearby gas station, meeting at the little gazebo down on the river. "Missy Sutter came in to talk. Finally."

Sorenson didn't speak. He knew Missy Sutter, the widow to one Charles Sutter, Jr., had been in to see Jensen. Sorenson didn't know the particulars of that conversation, yet.

"She still insisting that Charlie was too good, too sweet, to be connected to Cronus?" Sorenson's voice was sardonic, his lip curling on a sneer.

Jensen looked down at her feet, her heart twisting as she remembered the battered, bruised look on Missy's face. "No," she said on a sigh. Then she reached into her bag and pulled something out, turning it over to Sorenson without a word.

The evidence bag did nothing to limit his view of the top picture.

"Her parents apparently left her a cabin down at Rough River in Kentucky. It was still in her name. Missy isn't from around here, so we didn't know about it." Jensen grimaced, the cop in her pissed off that she hadn't unearthed that detail—yet—but her focus hadn't really been on Missy but on her dead scumbag, child-molesting husband.

He hadn't died hard enough.

"She found these there?" Sorenson asked, his voice neutral.

"Yep." She slanted him a look. That neutral tone was even more dangerous than if he'd been yelling. "She didn't know, Chief. She really didn't. She didn't even drive herself home. She had a friend with her and that friend ended up driving her home. The woman—her name is Denita Albi—is the one who packed up all the pictures, talked her into coming to the police department."

"She didn't want to come?"

"It's not that." Jensen thought of the pale, quiet zombie of a woman she'd spoken with earlier that day. "She was almost completely shutdown when we spoke. I asked her questions and she answered in this monotone, but when she looked at me, she was looking through me. That son of a bitch managed to break her, even from his fucking grave."

"You really believe she didn't know?"

"No." Jensen took a sip from her coffee, more to wash away the taste of gorge that kept trying to crawl up her throat than anything else. "Look at the pictures, Chief."

He blew out a breath and then tugged out a pair of thin gloves from his pocket, donning them before he started to flip through the pictures. When he reached the very last one, he stopped.

It was a picture of a smiling boy, maybe nine. He had Missy's eyes. That was the one thing Jensen had noticed on her own, before asking Missy about him.

Missy hadn't been able to answer.

It had been her friend Denita who'd responded.

That's her baby brother, Tyler. He lives with her twin, Mitchell. He still lives here, in her parents' home. He got custody of Ty after her folks died.

Sorenson stared at the picture for a long, long time before he looked up at Jensen.

"Who is this?" he asked softly.

"It's Missy's little brother." Jensen barely managed to resist the impulse to hurl her coffee at something. Resisted, barely, the urge to scream, to pummel something. Violence pumped hard and heavy in her veins. "She didn't want kids, something they fought about, a lot, but mental illness ran in her side of the family—her mother was bipolar and Missy had issues with depression. Then her parents died, and Charlie started to fixate on her brother."

"Fixate."

Jensen took another sip from her coffee. "Yes. That's what she told me. Tyler is what made her really come out of that dazed state. She's furious now. Charlie and her fought, over and over, about that kid. Now she finally understands why."

"That son of a bitch."

"Yeah." She pulled out the other evidence bag and handed it over. "He did one useful thing, though."

Sorenson frowned as he gingerly pulled out the faded brown journal, flipping through it. The details noted in it had his face going white, lines bracketing his face.

"How is this useful?" he asked grimly.

"Well. Missy says she didn't look at it, said she couldn't. Neither did the friend." She slid him a grim smile. "The way *I* see it, there's a good chance nobody knows about this. It's possible we could let it slip that we found key evidence that will likely lead to the arrest of the rest of Cronus. Anybody willing to testify against the others will get a more lenient deal."

"You want us to bluff them into turning on each other."

Jensen arched a brow. "You got a better idea?"

"No." He smoothed a finger across his left eyebrow. "No, I do not. Let me think this through, Bell."

"Okay. If there's nothing else, I think I'm going to head out to the judge's place. I hear David Sutter is staying there, and it's about time we pin him down and ask those questions that need to be asked."

She turned to go, but the chief's voice made her pause.

"Use care, Detective. We've got lots of questions, but that's not a man who'll respond well under too much pressure. Too much of it, and he'll go nuclear on us."

She nodded and then continued down the sidewalk to her car.

* * *

Trust.

David brooded over it, hours after she left.

He was still brooding over it when Jensen Bell pulled into his driveway.

He eyed her narrowly over the long, slim cigar he'd been trying to enjoy.

He didn't offer to put it out as she came toward him, just continued to puff on it as she came to a stop in front of him.

"You do realize we've been trying to get you to come in and give your statement," she said bluntly.

David lifted his face to the sky, studied the endless blue. "You do realize I have little use for statements. Even less for cops."

"You have good reason."

That had him looking back at her.

She arched a brow. "Surprised? I know some of the slime who have been wearing a badge. I want to beat them bloody. I'm waiting for the day they stand before the judge and end up getting slapped with a *guilty* verdict and they end up in the general population. However . . . I still need your statement."

"About what exactly?"

The man was beautiful, Jensen had to admit. A woman would have to be blind not to notice it.

He was also either deliberately obtuse or an idiot.

The cool blue eyes—a surreal shade of pale blue surrounded by a darker rim of near indigo—weren't the eyes of an idiot, though. Jensen had tangled with this man before, the night of the fire, and she knew when she was talking to somebody with less than average intelligence.

That wasn't David Sutter. Caine Yoder. Whatever the hell he called himself. He could be Peter Pan and leading a merry little band of Lost Boys and she wouldn't give a damn.

She wanted his fucking statement. Once she could eliminate him—from *all* of the cases linked to him, and hell, did she have a lot of cases she could link to him— then she could move on to the others. But she couldn't do shit until he stopped fighting her.

Hooking a thumb in her belt loop, she tapped her nails against her thigh and studied him.

He stared right back.

Typically, people didn't like it when a cop just stared.

Actually, in her experience, people didn't like it when anybody just stared.

David didn't seem to give a shit.

She suspected he would sit there for the next hour and let her stare and he'd stare right back. His face would never yield a damn thing. While interesting to contemplate, it wouldn't get her anything.

"Look. I don't have time to dick around with you," she said abruptly. "You don't like cops. You don't trust us, and that's understandable. I won't go into detail about how much I'd like to go back in time and stop Sims from putting a bullet through his brain—he should have gone to court and he should have gone to jail. But he won't answer for his crimes."

Taking a step forward, she held David's gaze. "There are others who are going to get away with it if we can't build a case against Cronus. Not to mention that both you and Lana Rossi are going to have a hell of a lot of trouble in your lives if we don't get some answers about the night you two disappeared. There is information *you* know about the night your mother died, information you know about every fucking dirty secret in this town, and I know it. I can see it on you."

"Can you really?" His tone was bored.

But flames burned in his gaze.

Something subtle, and lethal.

"Do you *want* them to get away with what they've done?"

He lifted a heavily muscled shoulder. "Seems to me that somebody has been busy lately. Dealing out their own form of justice."

A dark, ugly smile curled his lips as he looked back at her. "I don't think there will be as many skating by without answering this time, Detective Bell."

He knows. The realization hit her, hard. The cop in her wanted to demand he tell her, and now. If he didn't, she could just haul him in. But that same part of her held back—David was too smart. Too sly. And too angry.

She understood that anger. The man who'd killed her mother was currently sucking down painkillers and getting a book or two a week as cancer ate away at him. He hadn't been tried for her death. He might answer to God, but he wouldn't answer here and the injustice of it all sucked.

Frankly, justice sometimes *sucked*, but Jensen believed in her job, at the heart of it.

Which was why she didn't make that demand. The man in front of her would shut down. She knew, without a doubt, he would rather go to jail than tell her any damn thing. He might, eventually, tell her on his own timetable, but that was a maybe.

Refocusing, she blew out a controlled breath.

"Let's put all of that to the side. I didn't even come here, specifically, to discuss any of that. We need to talk about that body that was found over there." She nodded to the Frampton house. Trinity Benningfield's place. It was going to be torn down. Noah had passed the news on to Adam and Jensen had heard it from her sister— Chris worked at the bar Adam owned. The small-town grapevine made sure everybody in town would hear about it in no time flat.

David didn't look at the house. He continued to stare at her. A few weeks ago, he'd worn his hair in that bowl-like haircut she was used to seeing on the Amish who came into town. It was cut shorter now, almost brutally so, with nothing to detract from the harsh, beautiful lines of his face. Nothing to protect a person from the unyielding power of his gaze, either.

Now, as he continued to study her, Jensen realized she had to fight the urge to look away. That made her mentally square her shoulders. *The jackass.* She wasn't going to play these games with him.

A few more seconds passed and then he said, "The body. You mean my mother."

"Your mother," she prodded. "Yeah. Let's talk about her."

"I don't see the point. She's been dead twenty years, give or take."

Blowing out a breath, Jensen did a silent count of ten.

"That is just *what* we need to discuss. How she came to *be* dead, why she was put down there, why the authorities weren't notified, why you disappeared. All of that. That's why I need your statement."

Jensen Bell, he'd heard, was like a dog with a bone.

It looked like they'd given him to her for a chew toy.

Settling his weight back on his hands, David tried to decide whether or not he wanted to talk to her. He had no desire to tell her anything, but sooner or later he supposed he'd have to give them something. If he didn't, they'd just keep at it; plus, they'd also keep hassling Lana.

Lana was going to have to deal with them on some level, anyway. But if he gave them enough to satisfy them, maybe they'd leave her alone.

He'd already ruined enough of her life. Now that she was finally trying to put it back together, he sure as hell didn't want the past to interfere. Not if he could stop it.

And he didn't want it messing with Max, either.

What if they decide to mess with you? It was a quiet voice, one that murmured from the back of his mind, but he brushed it aside. If they decided to place the blame for all of that on him, it was no more than he'd expected and far less than he deserved.

He'd deal with that when and if it came to it.

He debated a few more seconds and then shrugged. It was going to come out. Sooner or later. Much better, he figured, if he controlled the circumstances. "I was going to run away. I reckon you can imagine why."

Something that might have been surprise briefly lit Jensen's eyes, but then it was gone. "You wanted to get away from your father."

"Yes. It was that, or kill myself. Lana . . ." He paused, searching for the words. "She'd figured out what was going on. She had planned to give me money, knew of a place where I could go. We'd gone there to meet. My mother heard of it somehow and followed us. We got into a fight—physical. My mother had a gun, called my father." His lip curled as he thought of it. "She told him there was a *problem*. She would deal with the problem, but he had to come and get me."

He watched as Jensen reached into her pocket and pulled out a small, black notebook. She made notes as she started to fire off questions. "She had a gun? You saw it?"

"Clear as I see you now," he said softly, the image settling in his mind. "She had it pointed at Lana."

"Was Lana this problem?"

With a tight smile, he said, "Of a sort. Ol' Pete was coming to get *me*. She didn't call Jimmy Rossi and tell him to do something about his recalcitrant daughter. My *mother* was going to handle that particular problem."

"What happened?"

"We tried to run." That wasn't the exact truth. He remembered how he'd felt. The fear and how, not for the first time, it had bled into rage. Anger had grabbed him before that—grabbed him and held him in a choke hold, one that blinded him to anything and everything else. But in that moment, he'd been clearheaded. Clearheaded and ready to kill. Diane had looked at him, really *looked,* and he'd seen the shock in her eyes. It had felt good. He remembered that, too.

"What then?"

Blinking, he turned his head. The sight of Jensen standing there threw him for a moment. He'd felt lost to those memories. To *that* memory. Seeing his mother go down. Hearing the crack, the shatter of glass. He'd lunged for her and she'd brought up her feet, kicked him. He'd gone down and she'd moved, grabbed one of the shards of glass from the floor.

He could still remember how it had felt when it went in. How it had felt to look into her eyes as she did it.

It had been almost a relief.

She hadn't ever loved him, and he knew that.

But in that moment, he'd been able to let go of any idea that he should love *her*. As blood spilled out of him, he'd almost felt free. But then Diane had turned on Lana and he lunged for her.

Diane was dead.

Somebody would probably have to answer for that.

If they tried to go after Max . . .

No.

Decision made, he studied Jensen from under his lashes. Everything he said here could be proven in one way or the other. The scar he had was old, but it didn't look like anything he'd done shaving or working on the farm.

Lana didn't remember much and she'd been out of it after hitting her head.

And Max . . .

Grimly, David focused on the river.

Maybe if he did this, it would help lift some of the weight he dragged around. He felt no guilt over what had happened to his parents, didn't wonder how much his dad might have suffered before Max put him out of his misery. He didn't regret their loss at all.

But he had almost choked over the guilt about what he'd done to Lana's life. Now he had a chance to fix some of it, he hoped. By just telling the truth he'd hidden for so long.

Averting his gaze, he focused on the river, the way sun glinted off of it, so bright it almost blinded him. "She had the gun pointed at Lana. She was going to shoot her. I ran at her, knocked her down. She dropped the gun. I would have done more—attacked her, I guess. But she kicked me and I was on the ground, bleeding. There was glass—a window. I guess a window busted, a bullet went through it or something. Broken glass, everywhere. She had a big shard of it and got up, shoved it in me. I couldn't move, couldn't breathe for a minute, it hurt so bad. Then she got up, went after Lana, cut her with that glass. I was trying to get up. Lana hit her. She went down. We got out. Tried to run."

He'd let it go at that for now. It was all the truth, and if he was going to do what he planned to do he wanted to take his time, make sure he gave everything in one piece, had it all together in his head.

Aware of the intense scrutiny, he looked up and met Jensen's eyes. One dark brow arched. "Just like that."

"Excuse me?"

"Both of you injured, and you run. Just like that."

"We sure as hell tried." He shrugged easily enough, went back to studying the river. He thought of the rusted-out wreck that still tucked in one of the barns over on Abraham's land. By now, David couldn't even get the engine to turn over. He'd tried, once, a few years ago. Out of everything he'd owned, that car was the one thing he'd valued. Because every now and then he'd thought about the freedom it offered.

Not that he'd ever thought of running—not until Lana. He'd get caught; he knew that. If he ran, they'd find him, bring him back. But there were other kinds of freedom. Taking that car, speeding down those winding roads that ran through southern Indiana. Pressing on the gas, at just the right moment. Ignoring the brakes. He could have flown. Free, for the first time in his life. And it would have all ended.

He'd never done it, of course. His sorry ass was still here.

But the car had promised freedom. Then it was a reminder.

One he hadn't been able to let go of.

The backpack and everything he had tucked in it that
night were still secure in the trunk. He'd thrown the keys
in the river one night, desperate, half-ready to throw
himself into the water as well. But he didn't need keys
to pop open a trunk.

"Yeah," he murmured, half lost in the memories. "I
would have run. Just like that. I had my car, had the
money. Thought of finding a hotel. But Lana was hurt.
I was hurt. We needed to find help. Get off the road."

"This isn't coming together for me," Jensen mused,
tapping her pen on the notebook. "Didn't the judge hear
any of that noise?"

"You'd have to ask him," David said levelly.

"He never said anything to you?" She shook her head.
"That's another thing that's not coming together. I think
there's something between the two of you. Seeing as how
you're here, at his place."

Something between the two of you . . . David narrowed his eyes. The chief hadn't told her. "Meaning . . . ?"

"You get my meaning. You and the judge have some
sort of connection. What is it? I've seen the two of you
together. More than once. Seen you out here, in hundred-
degree weather even, dealing with those flower beds, cutting the grass. The flower beds are a real puzzle. Both
of you do it and then Miss Mary—that poor soul—she'd
be out here within a week, whistling up a tune as she
pulled up every single flower. Then either you or him
would be planting the damn flowers all over again.
Sometimes it was almost a race to see who'd do it first.
I always passed it off as a kindness on your part, but

then . . . well. If you have a kind bone in you, you hide
it. It goes deeper than that. What is it, David?"

"Maybe I just have a green thumb." David bared his
teeth in a mockery of his old friendly smile.

"Now you see, I'd like to buy that. But I can't. You
two have a history and I'm thinking it's a long one. Like
twenty years long." She ran her tongue across her teeth,
her brows drawn low over her eyes. "I think he knew.
About that night. About your mother—was she—"

Her phone rang. She pulled it from the case at her belt
and gave it a distracted look, her gaze coming back to
him for only a second before it went back. She frowned
and took the call.

As she answered, he heard a phone inside the house
ringing. Frowning, he turned his head, looked over his
shoulder. Now who in the hell was calling—

"Sir, what did you say—" She cut the words off
abruptly, but her tone sent an icy shiver down David's
spine and he slid his gaze to her. She was staring at him,
her expression oddly stiff and her eyes flat.

Noises, chaos, rose in his head. Climbing to his feet,
he turned and headed into the house.

"A minute, sir," she said.

David heard her dimly over that noise, but it was disconnected.

"David, just a minute, okay? Something has—"

He reached out a hand, closed it over the handset of
the old-fashioned phone, thought about how many times
Judge Max—his grandfather, all the decency he'd ever
seen in his family—must have picked up this phone. He
thought about Miss Mary, that sweet old lady, and how
many times he'd wished *she* had been his family.

A kindness? Jensen thought he'd been here out of
kindness.

No. It was because it was one of the few *connections* he was capable of feeling. One of the few he'd allow himself.

Everything slid into slow motion as he lifted the phone to his ear. He didn't say anything. He just held it there and waited.

"Ca—Sorry. David, are you there?" Noah asked, his voice agitated.

"What happened?" he asked.

"Max," Noah said softly.

David closed his eyes before the red rush of rage descended on him. "Tell me."

"I don't know," Noah said. "I just heard he was found dead. I . . . *damn* it, I'm sorry. I don't know what's going on, but I didn't want you to hear it, be unprepared."

Slowly, while Noah was still talking, David lowered the phone down in the cradle and lifted his head, staring at the picture in front of him. That picture was the one he'd seen when he'd figured it out. Carefully, he took it down and because he could look at Max and Mary's face, because he could *see* that connection, he placed the portrait facedown on the table and then he turned and looked at Jensen.

Her face was pale, tight with strain.

"What happened?" he said gently.

"I don't know."

Without looking away, he grabbed the phone, yanked it out of the wall and hurled it. It crashed into the mirror on the far wall, shattering glass. As mirrored shards rained down onto the floor, he asked again. "What happened?"

"Look, big guy, you can throw things around all you want, but it's not going to turn me into a mind reader." Jensen's instincts screamed for her to draw her weapon. Everything inside her was telling her one crucial fact—

the man in front of her was dangerous, and he was this close to slipping over an edge.

His eyes were half-wild. There was rage, yes. But there was more grief than she'd ever seen in a man before.

She was no stranger to grief. She'd experienced more than her share. Her lover had lost a child. She'd watched her father, her brother and sister, slowly come apart after Mom had disappeared.

She knew grief.

But she'd never seen anything like she saw in David's eyes. She thought maybe this was what a man looked like when you ripped away the one and only thing he'd ever cared about.

Then, just like that, it was gone.

He looked down. Wide shoulders rose and fell on a sigh, and when he looked up his face was smooth and blank. His blue eyes were clear, empty. It was like gazing out over the unbroken surface of a lake. She saw nothing.

It was just about one of the freakiest things she'd ever seen.

"I'm going to the hospital," he said, his voice stark.

"I can't stop you." She had a feeling it would be like trying to hold back a tank. "But you have to understand, you're not family. There's nothing they'll be able to tell you."

He paused, reached over and picked up the picture he'd taken from the wall.

On his way out the door, he shoved the picture at her.

Jensen recognized the judge. Not because he looked the same, but because of those eyes. Piercing eyes. Penetrating eyes. He stood with his Mary, in front of this very house, his arm around her, a smile on his normally stern face.

But for the first time Jensen saw something else, and it was a punch in the gut.

That face . . . it wasn't identical, but whoa.

"Son of a bitch," she breathed out, turning to look at David's broad back.

Pieces of a puzzle started to settle into places, bumping into an uncomfortable fit. She didn't like the overall picture, but it made an awful, beautiful sort of sense.

That realization frightened her, more than a little.

Just what did you say to a man who'd just lost the only real connection he had to a world he had every reason to hate?

CHAPTER NINE

Sometimes her gut told her things she just didn't want to hear.

This was one of those things. Sybil was coming out of her studio, where she did her absolute *best* brooding, when she crashed into Ali from the pizzeria. Ali looked distracted and upset—totally not the normal for the easy-going, laid-back woman.

Going by the grim look in Ali's eyes, part of Sybil wished she'd just coast on by with an easy wave.

But over the past few weeks they'd been talking wedding photos and Sybil had grown to like the younger woman. Plus, that was a look of sadness she just couldn't ignore.

"You okay, Ali?" she asked, hoping it didn't have anything to do with Tate.

"Hell, no." Ali gave her a weak smile as she dashed away a tear that had escaped to roll down her pale face. "You didn't hear, did you?"

Her belly went icy and cold. "Hear what?"

"Max."

Dread grabbed her. She knew Max—hard not to, since her sister had been one of the ones who got in trouble out at his old place, more than once. He and Sybil had talked, more than she liked, and she had a grudging respect for him. But that wasn't the reason for the dread.

Clenching a hand into a fist, she asked softly, "What about him?"

"He's dead." Ali shifted from one foot to the other while she fought a valiant effort with the tears. Her voice wobbled a little. "Chris was up there delivering flowers and she heard the news, saw the cops outside his door. It's going around town fast. He's gone."

"Did he . . ." Sybil cleared her throat, thinking of the arrogant old bastard she'd had to deal with more than once. Arrogant. And then he'd look at his wife and his face would light up, like the sun coming out after a cold, bleak day. Sybil had seen that love on his face so many times. "Was it because of the injury?"

"Nobody seems to know. But if it was, why would they have called the cops?" Ali shrugged. "My parents are covering the place for a while. I used to be in Miss Mary's Sunday school class and I loved her something awful. This is just killing me."

"Oh, honey." Moving in, she caught Ali in a hug, stroked a hand down her hair while Ali squeezed her tight. "I hate to say it, and it's awful, but Max would rather be with her than here anyway. We all know that."

"I know." Ali pulled back and nodded, but this time her face was cold. "I just—it's messed up. He was getting *stronger*. He was getting better. I don't think something just *happened* after . . . what, it's been a couple of weeks. It doesn't feel right, and after everything that's going on it pisses me off."

"I know." That was part of the reason she felt so cold inside. Part of it. But not all of it. "Listen, I need to go. I have to . . ." she hedged, unwilling to go into detail about that.

But Ali was already nodding. "I better get back anyway. I just needed to walk. I called Tate. He was shutting down his studio and heading over. I told him not to, but I kind of hoped he'd do it anyway." She grinned sheepishly. "Should I feel bad about that?"

"Ali, if I had a guy like Tate coming to comfort me, I wouldn't feel bad about wanting to have him there. At all." She squeezed Ali's shoulder and watched as the woman headed off down the street.

Five seconds later, she headed for her car.

She had to get to the hospital.

Inside her head, she could practically *hear* the words, *hurry, hurry, hurry*. . . .

There was a man standing between him and the place he wanted to be.

Normally, that wouldn't deter David. Very little deterred him when he had a focus. But he had respect for very few people, and because he did respect Noah—and regretted the misery he'd helped bring into his life—he tried once more.

"You want to get out of my way," he said quietly.

"You're not wrong," Noah agreed, his blue eyes unreadable. "The problem is that I can't. You don't need to be going in there, interfering. If something happened here, don't you want answers?"

"If?" He curled his lip and shifted his gaze away to the men standing at the door. Two of them had their hands resting lightly on the weapons they wore strapped to their sides. "You think there's any *if* here, Noah?"

Noah ran his tongue along his teeth. Fleetingly, David hoped it didn't come to the point that he had to shove those teeth down the man's throat.

"To be honest, I *hope* I'm wrong. But no. I don't think there's an *if*. And that's why if you go another step, you'll be going through me." Now Noah took a step forward and his eyes went cold and hard. "I see the mean in you, David. I see it and I recognize it. But I'll be damned if I let you interfere with what those cops are doing. If somebody took Judge Max away before his time, then I want to know. You're not going to mess that up."

"You think you can stop me?"

"I've got a better chance than most." Noah cocked his head. "Including those two cops over there. They both looked scared to death of you." He flashed David a wide smile. "Guess what? I'm not."

"That's enough."

The sound of Lana's voice cutting between them might have thrown a bucket of ice on his anger, at any other time. But with the red roar of rage pulsing through him, clawing at his mind like a beast, David didn't even look at her. "Stay out of this, Supergirl."

"The hell I will." She wedged herself between them, and when they wouldn't give her room she demanded it, driving an elbow into David's gut. He managed to ignore that. It was harder to ignore when she lifted a combat-booted foot and drove it down onto his—or tried to. He moved out of the way, still glaring at Noah.

Lana had accomplished her mission, though, putting a few—just a few—more feet between him and Noah.

"You two need to stop," she said, swinging her gaze from one to the other. "You really think this is *helping*?"

"Right now, I don't *care* about helping. I want to know what happened." *Then I want to find the son of a bitch who did this and kill him.* He kept those words behind his teeth, figuring it wouldn't help the matter any.

"Noah."

At the sound of a new voice—belonging to a man David had never really cared for—Noah shifted his gaze to the left, but only for a minute. "Yeah, Adam?"

"Why don't you see if you can get somebody to talk

to you? They'll open up to you quicker than they will for the hothead here," Adam said, moving into David's line of sight. Then he flashed a determined smile at David. "If he keeps trying to push his luck, Lana and I will just keep trying to talk sense into him."

Lana snorted. "Baby, you have no sense."

David lowered his lids, staring at Adam from under his lashes. "The only reason I haven't gone through Noah is because I consider him a friend—of sorts. Can't say the same for you. If you end up a bloody smear on the floor, I won't lose any sleep over it."

"You'd have a harder time than you think," Adam said, his voice low.

Lana blew out a breath. "Save me from testosterone overload. Are you *determined* to beat the shit out of somebody tonight, David?" she asked. "And are you determined to pick a fight with one of the few guys I care about?"

Something knotted in him as he turned his head and looked at her. In that moment, Noah slipped away. David almost went after him, but Lana moved to block him. "People talk to him. You know that, better than I do probably. You've been here. I haven't. Give him a chance."

"I *have* to know—" He stopped, closing his eyes. All the reasons he needed to know burned inside him. He didn't want to share this, didn't want to tell others. If people knew, for certain knew, they'd start looking at Max differently, and now that he was gone it seemed . . .

Wrong.

Opening his eyes, he straightened his shoulders.

Tension knotted his muscles, holding him tight as a spring. He could have let it go. Maybe. He could have done it.

But somebody passed by. He didn't know the name.

Recognized the man's face, but only just because he'd seen him on the streets. The man gave him a look and then looked at Lana.

For a moment he held still, and then he shook his head. He muttered it, his voice low.

Just not low enough.

David heard him, clear as day, as he said, "This fucking town would have been better off if the two of you had never shown your sorry faces here again."

Lana heard it as well, close-cropped hair swinging as she whipped it around. "What?" she asked.

Her voice barely penetrated the fury.

The man, built like a tree trunk, solid through and through, paused to look at her. His lip curled and he shook his head. "I wasn't talking to you."

"Maybe not, but I think you wanted me to hear." She took a step forward. "The town would have been better? You didn't want us stepping up and talking about what happened twenty years ago? How it's connected to what's happening now?"

"What you *say* is happening." He jerked a finger toward the cops. "All this crazy shit started with you-all."

Noah appeared around the corner, his face tight. He stopped at the sight of the man squaring off with Lana and David and then he sighed. "Zeke, you don't need to be doing this. Not here. Not now."

"Then when? After somebody else ends up dead? Did they accuse Max, too? *Max?*"

"You son of a bitch," David snarled. That red haze didn't crawl across his vision, didn't creep into his brain. It just rose up and grabbed him, almost the way he found himself snaking out a hand to grab the older, pale man by the front of the shirt. He didn't even remember moving, but he had. He had the faded flannel shirt in his hand and the other was fisted and closed, ready to strike.

"Don't."

Noah caught his wrist.

David growled under his breath.

Sybil panted up the last level of the steps, her lungs tight, her airway feeling like somebody had wrapped a fist around it and just kept *squeezing* and *squeezing*.

Stupid asthma. It was like she had an elephant on her chest. But it wasn't just sitting there—it *danced*. At the same time, her throat viced up, making breathing feel impossible. She could run three miles easily, but put a flight of steps in front of her and she was a goner. But the damn elevators were too slow here. In the back of her mind, she still heard that voice chiding her, *Hurry hurry hurry . . .*

Hitting the floor where Max had been for the past few weeks, she shoved the door open and then, for just a bare moment, she stood, her mouth open.

Then she surged forward.

It was probably a stupid thing.

If there was anybody else who knew about the rages that David fought most of his life, he'd never told her.

But she knew about them.

On top of everything else, the last thing he needed was to get arrested for what he was planning to do to Zeke Kenner, even if the tactless son of a bitch deserved it. She saw Noah grab his fist and she grimaced, because Noah wouldn't deserve shit.

Shoving Zeke back, she planted herself in front of David and reached up.

His head swung around at her touch.

Holding his eyes with hers, she cupped his face. "Don't."

For a taut, long moment, he held still. Noah still held his wrist. Sybil could feel the tension shrieking inside

David, feel everything inside him, it seemed. Leaning in, she pressed her mouth to his. It didn't matter that everybody around them saw, didn't matter that his chest had started to rise and fall raggedly against her own.

"Don't do this, David. It won't help; you know that."

Abruptly he twisted and jerked away from Noah, and she half-expected him to do the same to her.

To her shock, what he did was wrap his arms around her waist and in the next moment her feet left the floor as he buried his face against her neck.

"He's . . . Sybil, he's gone."

Staring at the wall over his shoulder, she slid her arms around him. One gripped him, her hand tangling in the faded material of his shirt. She smoothed her other hand across his hair, down his neck. "I know. I'm so sorry, David. I'm so sorry."

His chest shuddered against hers and then he went to his knees, right there in the middle of the hall. He still clutched her to him, his arms wrapped around her waist like she was the only thing anchoring him there. "He's gone."

CHAPTER TEN

A security guard shifted and Sorenson reached up, pressing his hand to the middle of his chest as he eyed Sybil Chalmers and David Sutter. Sorenson had been a step away from interfering. The reason he hadn't was Noah. He'd expected Noah would talk David down—Noah Benningfield could talk anybody down, just about. Sorenson had seen it. During his tenure here as the chief of the Madison Police Department, he'd seen that man bring comfort to widows and peace to the dying and just the other day he'd actually managed to talk *Layla*, of all people, into going into residential treatment. If he up and walked on water, it wouldn't have surprised the chief.

But it hadn't been Noah who'd broken through the ugly layers of rage gripping David.

Sybil curled a protective arm around him, using her body as a shield. There was a fierce look on her face and Sorenson had no doubt that if anybody moved toward them she'd tear them apart.

Everybody around her and David had either developed a fascination in the floor or managed to find something terribly important to tell the person they were with.

Well, maybe Lana and Noah and Adam and the two nurses out in the hall were that polite, but Sorenson was anything but polite. Besides, in his job *polite* had its place, but it only got him so far. Nosiness did a lot more than courtesy ever could. Reaching up, he stroked a hand down his beard and continued to watch them as curiosity grew.

They were comfortable with each other.

Too comfortable. This wasn't just something that had sprouted over the past few weeks, since David had come out of his hand-crafted Amish closet. Sorenson smirked at bit, amused with himself as he continued to ruminate. They'd been together awhile. Quite a while.

Hmmmm.

Now, Sorenson hadn't had a steady lady in his life since his divorce. His ex had taken him for a ride and a half, not that he blamed her. Being married to a cop, even a small-town cop, was a lousy deal and she'd found that out the hard way.

Too many nights alone, too many missed dinners, and she'd gotten colder and colder. He'd gotten lonelier and lonelier. A pretty young woman who'd been working dispatch had made a move and he hadn't backed away, a fact he regretted to this day.

He still stung from the way his wife had torn into him. For the betrayal, for the lies, for the humiliation.

He knew all about how a woman hated the lies. It was *more* than the betrayal. A woman hated being misled, hated the dishonesty.

Would a woman like Sybil be so fast to cozy back up to a man who'd misled her for years?

Now that was a question.

David didn't remember moving into a waiting room, but he looked around and realized that was where they were. With little interest, he studied the carpet, the walls, the news on the small, wall-mounted TV.

The noise from it was too loud and the light was too bright. Turning his head away, he found Sybil next to him, watching him.

He closed his eyes, feeling too exposed.

She reached down and caught his hand.

Convulsively he squeezed.

She squeezed back.

"Has anybody told you what happened?"

He lifted his lids, stared at her from under his lashes. "Nobody will tell me shit, even if I ask," he muttered. "I'm not *family*."

Her eyes held his. He saw something flicker there, and he wondered, as he had so many times, if she could see right through him. It was an ugly, miserable thought, because there were so many things inside him that he wanted nobody to see, nobody to know.

"I found somebody to talk to."

David swung his head up, looked at Noah.

He stood in the doorway, his features shadowed by the bright lights shining in around him.

Then, with a quick look behind him, he ducked inside, shut the door behind him. He came over, eyed David narrowly.

David saw the assessing look in the other man's eyes. He met that gaze levelly. He didn't care enough to be pissed at Noah and he suspected that probably showed in his eyes. After a few more seconds, the other man just looked away. "One of the nurses had checked on him around two forty. The guards were at the door. Then a couple of visitors got violent, roughly two forty-five. They had that cleared up and under control within five minutes. The cop returned to his door, but got distracted by the patient's kids—it's an older guy, from someplace across the river. I don't know them. It was a few more minutes before he looked in on Max—the nurses were switching shifts then and they opened the door. . . ."

Noah stopped, looking away. He had his arms crossed over his chest and David saw the way the muscles in his arms clenched and went tight. Then, slowly, Noah looked back at him, holding his eyes. "There was a pillow over his face. Somebody killed him."

The only thing that kept David in that seat was the way Sybil's hand tightened on his.

Blood thudded dully in his ears as he gazed at Noah.

But he wasn't seeing the man.

He was seeing old Max.

Standing on his porch.

He heard his voice, the way the judge had sounded when he called him that last day, before somebody had shot him. The endless ringing of the phone. The way Max had sounded when he'd answered.

"I need to speak with you."

"I don't want to speak with you." David never really wanted to speak to the old man. It wasn't easy facing the man he knew was family, knowing he wouldn't ever claim him. But at the same time, he'd wanted to be around Max, as much as he could. Even though he was well into his thirties, far past the age of boyhood, he'd needed that connection.

"I don't give a damn, boy."

For years, David had convinced himself that *he* hadn't given a damn.

He'd told himself that lie for so many years.

It was too late, now.

A hard shudder wracked him as he surged up and strode out the door.

Too late . . . just like always.

Sybil called out his name, but he ignored her.

He'd taken too much comfort just from her being there. But really, what right did he have?

Shoving to her feet, Sybil went to go after him.

Noah caught her arm. "Maybe you should leave him alone for a while. The judge and him were a lot closer than people realized."

"Gee, I never would have noticed, Preach," she said deadpan, staring up at him. She rolled her eyes when he started to try again. "I hate to tell you this, big guy, but I know that man out there better than anybody else *here*. Just move out of my way already."

She shoved past him and looked around.

David was already gone.

Stubborn son of a bitch. Grabbing a fistful of her hair, she tugged at it, hoping it would clear her head and let her think.

Would he go back to Max's?

Heavy, solid footsteps caught her ears and she looked up, found Chief Sorenson in front of her. And he just stood there. Watching her.

Dread crept through her and she lowered her hand to her side. A few years back, when Layla still lived at the house and Sybil had to deal with cops showing up at the door—or, worse, searching the damn house because of Layla's drug issues—she'd had to deal with Sorenson and other cops. She knew how to do it, but she sure as hell didn't like it.

There was a way to handle it, though. At least for her. She didn't try to blank her features, because it was already obvious she was upset. Instead, she made sure to keep just *how* upset she was tucked down inside and settled on frustration. She had years and years of experience at masking her emotions. She could thank her sister for that. Nobody could work your emotions like an addict could.

Huffing out an impatient breath, Sybil penned him with her eyes. "You need something, Chief?"

"Just curious about a few things," he mused, cocking his head.

"It's a bad day for curiosity," she bit off.

Max was dead. David was hurting. And now, thanks to Noah, David was probably also *pissed*. That was a very, very dangerous combination.

"Seems the two of you have some sort of connection."

She arched a brow. "Who?" she asked, folding her arms over her chest and glaring at him.

"You and Sutter." Calm blue eyes watched her as he reached up to stroke a brow. He waited a minute and then moved in closer. "I saw the two of you. He was pretty pissed there, thought he might haul off and hit Preach. Then in you walk and all you do is touch him. Now that is something I've already noticed is a dangerous thing. He holds it in, but you can tell that man does not like being touched."

Sybil bared her teeth at Sorenson. "Can you blame him?"

"No." He shook his head and said again, "No, ma'am, I cannot. But that's neither here nor there. You lay one hand on him and everything about him changes. Just why is that?"

"I got the magic touch." She shrugged flippantly. "Just ask Drew."

"I'm more interested in talking to you. Just how long have you known David?"

Well, hell. She fought the urge to heave out a sigh. *Just where are you going with this, Chief?* Holding his gaze, she said levelly, "He's lived here for years. Maybe not as David, but he's still been here. Maybe you haven't noticed, but Madison's a small town."

"And you knew him as Caine?"

"That's the name he gave me." She gave an abbreviated version of the night they'd met, how he'd come across her and Vernon and played the knight in shining armor, even if he was somewhat dour about it. "When it was all said and done, he told me his name was Caine, and that's all she wrote. Since then, yes, we've become friends."

"Friends." Sorenson drew the word out slowly, like he wasn't quite sure what it meant. Then he shook his head. "Somehow I don't look at the two of you and see bowling buddies, Sybil."

"Well, that's because I don't bowl." She shrugged again.

"You want me to think there's nothing between you two."

"I never said that." Then she went to go around him. "But what's between us is our business, not yours."

Feeling like his demons chased him, David all but ran out of the hospital, unable to move fast enough, focusing on the ground underneath him and nothing else.

Which explained why he crashed into Taneisha Oakes.

He moved reflexively to keep her from falling, his hands going to her arms. The feel of skin against his own had him clenching his teeth and he wanted to jump back as though she'd burned him, but he'd all but barreled over her, so he remained there, waiting until she was steady.

"Sorry," he said, gritting the word out.

She sniffed and dashed a hand over her cheeks.

Aw, hell.

Then she looked up at him, the elegant lines of her dark face softening into a faint smile. "It's okay. I wasn't really watching where I was going. I'm . . ." She paused and then blew out a sigh. "You . . . you're David, right?"

He uncurled his hands and took a slow step back. He was tired of the questions, the stares, the looks. "Yeah. I need—"

Her soft comment stopped him: "I'm sorry."

He looked back at her.

"Max was . . ." She shook her head. "That's why I was lost in my own world, thinking about him." She moved a little closer, apparently unaware of the way he stiffened. "He was a mean old grouch sometimes, but I owed him a lot."

Frozen, David watched as she reached up and worried the necklace she wore. "He's the reason I was able to graduate high school, go to college. He's probably the reason I didn't end up dead or in jail," she murmured, sliding David a look. "I was one of the kids he mentored. Don't know if you knew about that, but he meant a lot to me."

David looked away.

"I'm sorry. I just . . . I saw you sneaking in to visit him in ICU, saw you coming in three or four times to visit him the past few weeks. Figured you were close." Her dark eyes held his.

Slowly, having to force the words out, he said, "We were."

Then he had to force himself not to move as she moved in and pressed a kiss to his cheek.

"He was a unique man. I can't believe he's gone. I . . ." She moved back, a soft blush rising under the warm, smooth brown of her skin. "I just wanted to tell you I'm sorry."

Then she was gone.

That uneasy feeling crawled through his skin, and because he didn't trust himself just yet David waited there, gave himself a minute to just . . . stand. Do nothing.

The red had pulled back from his vision, but now the only thing inside him was misery.

Why had he left Sybil?

If he were with her, he could pull her up against him and just lose himself inside her, in the soft strength of her arms, and forget about everything else.

Sucking in one slow, steady breath, he turned to go back.

That was when he felt it.

Eyes.

Crawling all over him.

It was a hard, stinging impact like he'd fallen into a pit full of hornets, and he held still for a moment. Everything in him wanted to swing his head around, look for whoever it was that watched him.

There was hate in that glare.

Hate, and anger.

David knew the feel of malevolence, how it could rip the air and burn the skin. It didn't much worry him, but since the few people who mattered to him were all inside the hospital behind him, he started to walk, away from the hospital, each footstep slow and measured.

In the back of his mind, he thought, *Come on. Follow me. I'm feeling mean enough to take on an army.*

He walked the distance from the hospital to Max's house, barely able to think about being inside the walls again.

Each step of the way, he felt those eyes.

Each step of the way, he felt like whirling to attack.

But as aware as he was of being watched, he had no idea where it was coming from.

* * *

This wasn't done.

The old man was dead.

But it wasn't done.

It had been so easy, though, to break that fragile grip the man had on life, send him off.

Anger brewed inside, made it almost impossible to think.

There had been all the insanity after.

People talking, prattling on.

Cops swarming the hospital. Perhaps that should have been a consideration. It was so hard to think. This had been necessary, but to plan for everything . . .

It had been easier last time, but now there were others around, more who could see. Taking the pillow away—should that have been done? Would that have helped?

Too late now.

I don't know what to do. A walk to the river might help. A clear mind made everything easier, and it wasn't possible to think when one was angry, after all. *Anger* was an ugly, evil thing, but it had a tight, firm grip. Time to let that pass. Time to be calm.

Time to think.

This wasn't done.

The old man was dead.

But there were still others.

Others who had to be stopped, eliminated.

It had been easier a few weeks ago, but now it seemed like the list was growing, and growing and growing.

Stay calm. Just think.

The only ones who had to die were the ones who mattered.

The ones who could get in the way.

They were the concern.

Once they were gone, things would go back to how they should be.

"Who would do this?"

Standing over the lifeless, frail body of Max Shepherd, Jensen blinked, once, hard, before she looked up at her boss. "Sorry," she said, swallowing. "This one is hitting me hard. I loved the old grouch."

"A lot of people did." He nodded and glanced up at the county coroner. "Doc."

Dr. Liz Pittenger blew out a breath, shadows visible on her face, despite the light makeup. Her lightly greying hair was pulled back into an elegant coif and her gaze was sad. "I can honestly tell you this—I never once thought I'd have to do this. Judge Max, murdered. The man is so damn mean, you'd think people around here would be too scared to touch him. He'll be slapping that gavel down when they meet up with him before God, I'll tell you that."

"You're certain it's murder." Sorenson didn't touch on the fact that the pillow had been shoved down on the old man's face. He was here for facts, nothing else.

"I can't conclusively say *yes* until I do the autopsy, but if I had to make a call here and now? Yes. It was murder." Pittenger started at the head. "His eyes, for example."

They had already seen the broken blood vessels, but always playing devil's advocate, Sorenson said, "No way he could have pulled the pillow over his face, maybe to block out the light, and just . . . smothered?"

Pittenger gave Sorenson a look that made him feel like he'd fallen off the back of the turnip truck. "No. Those pillows, even a couple of them, wouldn't have had the weight to keep him from breathing. Somebody held them down, with force. I imagine when I—" She stopped, looking away for a moment. She took a deep breath and then looked back at them. "This is hard. I've known Max for more than thirty years. It's never easy in a town this small, but we . . . were friends. I had to perform the autopsy on Mary. Now on him. I'm sorry."

"I understand." And he did. He couldn't imagine being a big-city cop, not knowing the names, the faces, the people who owned the businesses you'd sworn to protect. He'd protect, no matter where he was—serve and protect, that's what he did. But he belonged here, in Small Town, U.S.A. It came with costs, though, and this was one of them.

"Once I perform the autopsy, I may well see other signs. His lungs may be swollen." She moved to Sorenson's side and closed a gloved hand around Max's lifeless one. Normally, she'd do this once she'd started the exam, but this was Max. Judge Max. Champion for the children in this town. Max. Her friend. Lifting his bagged hand, she studied it through the clear plastic, turned it upward to study his bloodied nails. "He fought. There's blood. We'll find skin."

As she looked at Sorenson, he nodded. "We'll find skin. Blood. Maybe luck will be with us and we'll get a DNA match."

"Luck hasn't exactly been our friend lately," Jensen said grimly.

"All the more reason that it's time for it to change."

"I can't believe people are going to link *Max* to those monsters," Jensen growled under her breath as they left the hospital. Upon leaving Max's room, she'd heard the first of the whispers, but they were just the first. When she'd all but cut a person in two with her glare the whispers went abruptly silent, but only until she was gone.

And still, people watched.

She wanted to look around, see who it was staring at her. The angry bitch inside her wanted to shriek, *Got a problem? Huh? Huh?*

Under most circumstances, she'd be irritated, but she'd deal.

Under *this* circumstance, it pissed her off in ways she couldn't begin to list.

"People very often only see what's on the surface." Sorenson shrugged, but his eyes were grim, just as flat as her own. "The best thing we can do—and will do—for Max is find out who did kill him and why."

Sorenson stopped then and turned to look at her. "You're a good cop, Bell. Now go out there and help me figure this out."

Then he turned and walked off.

Scowling at his back, she resisted the urge to stick out her tongue. *Figure this out.* She planned to do just that. *Thanks.*

She turned and crashed straight in the hard chest of the one man who managed to make everything in her world better, just by existing.

"Dean."

Maybe it was because she'd just stood over the dead body of the man who'd helped her focus all the anger and grief she'd felt as a child, but she did something she rarely did when she was working. She moved up against Dean and wrapped her arms around him.

He did the same, one strong hand sliding up her back to cup her nape. His breath tickled her skin as he murmured into her hair, "You've had a rough day already."

"The worst." Blinking back the sting of tears, she said, "Judge Max was the one who helped me figure out how to fight all the . . . anger. The grief. Everything. I was a mess after Mom died. Tate was just . . . angry. But he had his art. Even then, he could lose himself for a little while by grabbing a sketchbook. Even reading helped him. Chris would go outside and yank up weeds, plant roses. Every house near us had free gardening service for the next couple of years. It was how she coped. I just . . . existed. I was angry, got into a couple fights in school, and that was how I ended up meeting Max. I knew him, yeah, but . . . that's not the same thing."

Tipping her head back, she said softly, "I became a cop because of my mom. But he's the one who made me realize that was what I needed. And now somebody took him away."

Dean's dark, velvety eyes stared into hers. Everything around them slowed down, and although the ache in her heart was massive, in that moment she felt like she could breathe. "So it's certain?" he murmured, stroking his thumb across her skin. "It's murder?"

"Suffocation." She nodded. "It sounds like they were watching for the opportunity. Max still had cops, some guys with military experience, volunteering to watch his door since we don't know who shot him. Today it was Braxton, works with county, newer guy, just trying to help out. There was a problem with some visitors, a *physical altercation*." She curled her lip as she said it, the words bitter on her tongue. "He got involved. Whoever did this, he went in while Braxton was distracted, shoved a pillow over Max's face and in those few minutes killed him. Slid out just as quiet as you please and left. It's like a ghost did it. Nobody noticed anything, saw anything."

Dean was quiet a moment. "It's somebody who is used to being seen there, in town. Invisible."

Ice spread through her and she nodded. There were a lot of people in town who could move around without being noticed. But just *who* could slip unnoticed into a hospital?

A doctor?

A nurse?

A preacher?

CHAPTER ELEVEN

The day of Max's funeral dawned cold, hard and bright. The sun shone harshly done from a sky so blue it hurt to look at it. David thought the day suited the man they were burying. It was a hard-edged day but still somehow beautiful, the sun shining through the fiery maple leaves, the air heavy with the scents of fall. Wind whipped through those trees, sending the leaves swirling around in little storms as the mourners gathered.

David stood at the back.

Noah had briefly left Trinity's side to urge him to the front, and there was a look in his eyes that made David suspect that Noah knew something.

But David didn't want to be around others.

The only thing that brought him here was the fact that he'd loved Max.

Yeah. He'd loved him. An emotion he'd never wanted to claim. In the weeks since Abraham's death, the wall David had kept around him had gotten weaker and now it was so full of holes, it was a miracle that wall even remained.

Now, as he struggled to rebuild the wall around himself, emotions stormed inside him. Too many emotions, all of them unwanted, unfamiliar, *unwelcome*.

He couldn't shut them down. The pain was a monster in his gut. He'd grieve over Max every day for the rest of his life.

"Why, David . . . I didn't expect to see you here."

Slowly, he lifted his head.

Something spasmed in his jaw and he had to fight the urge to snarl. Respect for the man in the casket kept him silent and he just stared as Louisa made her way over to him.

She held out a hand and he flicked it with a dismissive gaze before looking back up at her.

She gave a nervous laugh before looking around again. "Well. Max did make some unusual friends, didn't he?"

Go away, he thought. The black suit she wore was fussy with lace and beads that reflected the light and she wore too much perfume. Under the perfume, he could smell the coffee from the coffee shop, like she'd just thrown the suit on in her office and doused herself with the cloying scent to cover the smell from the shop.

The effect was nauseating.

"Well. I guess you're not much for talking, are you?" Something glinted in her eyes and she lowered her voice; although her tone remained sweet with sympathy, he saw the vulture that lurked in her gaze. "I guess I can imagine why. People are talking . . . well, I mean, we *all* know by now. After everything you went through, poor boy, it's hard for you to talk—"

"Don't touch me," he warned, catching the hand she'd been reaching up with. "Not ever."

She squeaked in shock, although he kept his grip easy. Her skin was almost papery under his hand and everything in him screamed, *Back away! Back away!* He wanted to wash his hands, wanted to get the stink of too much perfume and coffee off him, but people were staring and Louisa was babbling and the funeral was about to start.

"Why, I *never*—"

"David."

He let her hand go at the familiar voice, backing away one step, then another, before turning his head to look at Noah.

Dressed in a solemn suit of black, Noah looked between him and Louisa and then back. "There's a seat up front," he said quietly.

Louisa perked up. "Why, thank—"

"I'm sorry," Noah said gently, moving to cut her off. "Those seats are reserved for family and close friends. We held it for David."

Louisa's mouth fell open, and for a moment she was stunned into speechlessness. Although he didn't expect that to last, David took advantage of it to turn and walk away. He didn't want to sit up front where people could gawk at him, try to talk to him—or worse.

But if he had to even look at that viper another moment, he thought he'd lose it.

"Are you okay?" Noah asked.

David didn't answer.

There was no point.

Okay?

When had he ever been okay?

He didn't remember sinking onto the open seat next to Trinity. She gave him a small smile and then looked back up front. Noah was already up there, a fact that didn't surprise David. He'd been the one to speak at Miss Mary's funeral as well. Knowing the old man, he'd probably arranged it all.

Had to control just about everything—

David cut the thoughts off. Thinking about him hurt. Thinking about *anything* hurt. This had done it, David realized. The ice that he'd wrapped himself in was gone, smashed by the old man's death, and he was drowning now, drowning in a storm of emotion that was more he could handle. Drowning in loss, misery, despair, rage. Even the emotions he was used to feeling—rage and disgust—were spiraling higher and tighter than normal.

Just don't think. Closing his eyes, he kept that mantra up, ignoring everything else.

If he could manage that, for however long this took, he could get the hell out of here. Get in his truck. Drive for however long it took him to get away from here, and then he could . . .

Do what?

What was it going to take to exhaust the eruption he could feel building inside?

There was a movement next to him and he tensed as somebody sank onto the sole remaining seat. A hand slid over his.

And just like that, some of the chaos in him eased.

The pain was still there. It would probably always be.

But Sybil was there.

He didn't even have to look. He knew her touch. He could be lost in an unending dark hell and he'd know her touch, her scent, the brush of her skin against his own. Even in death, he'd know her.

After a few more seconds, he opened his eyes and looked over at her.

She was staring straight ahead.

The music came to a close and he forced himself to look back as Noah started to speak.

It was all a blur, almost everything Noah said.

A few times, David managed to drag his thoughts to the here and now when Noah would tell a story about the old man or mention something that Judge Max had been known to say.

One in particular jabbed a dull, rusty knife into David's heart. Noah, his gaze roaming over the crowd, said, "I remember once, when my father was dying, how Judge Max came to me: *In the end, son, we all look back. Some of us will look back with regret and quite a few probably do. The lucky ones look back with pleasure at a life well lived. I imagine that's your dad.*" Noah paused and David tensed as his eyes lingered on him. And it wasn't his imagination the way that penetrating stare cut through him.

The man knew.

Somehow, Noah knew.

"I'd imagine Judge Max could look back on a life well lived."

Blood started to roar in David's ears.

And a knot settled in his throat.

He hadn't cried in more years than he could remember, not even when Abraham had died. He'd lost the ability, he'd thought, after that awful, brutal beating that left him in his bed for days while the long, thin slices on his back slowly healed.

But he wanted to weep.

"I never knew the two of you were such good friends."

Sybil walked at his side, and when Louisa cut them off she was the one to speak while David stared at the older woman coldly. "Who, David and I?" Sybil asked, her voice bright, her smile sharp edged.

Louisa gave her a look that might have made some other women wither, but Sybil just cocked a brow.

"Hardly." Louisa racked Sybil with a look. Although she wore a slim-fitting coat, the long, slim black column of a dress, sedate as it was, did nothing to hide the body beneath. "I imagine everybody knows what David is looking for with you, after how many years of living a restrained lifestyle with the Amish."

David's lips peeled back from his teeth. Sybil squeezed his hand tightly. It was the only thing that kept him quiet. That and the memory of the grave behind him. But it was a fight to control the anger building up in his throat.

"I *meant* you and Max," Louisa said, pasting a false smile on her face. "This must be even *harder* for you then. After everything you went through, losing somebody close to you. How awful you must feel."

This time, not even that tight grip from Sybil could do it. Taking a step forward, David leaned in, studying Louisa's face. "Which one was it, Louisa? Your mom or your dad?"

She blinked, confusion heavy on her features. "Excuse me?"

"One of them went and fucked a hyena, to come up with a piece of work like you." She went white and then red. Her hand came up and he caught her wrist before she could strike him. "You're out for blood, but you won't find it here. So just tuck your tail between your legs and get away from me. And *stay* away." He flung her hand down like it was dirty and then led Sybil away while Louisa glared at him. He could feel the heat of that stare cutting between his shoulder blades. Uncaring, he kept walking until Noah's voice cut him off.

Blowing out a sigh, he looked at Sybil.

She reached up a hand. "If you don't want to stay, don't."

"If it was anybody else, I wouldn't." He shrugged and turned his head before looking back as a familiar figure caught his eyes. Was that—

Then he shook his head. *No.* Probably just the lack of sleep and everything else catching up with him.

Noah drew even with him, but his eyes didn't meet David's. Not right away. Noah was looking at Louisa, who had cut through the cemetery a different way and was standing there, waving her hands angrily as she talked to Chief Sorenson. Her voice was loud, the words carrying over the crowd.

"You brutalized her, huh? In broad daylight with all of us watching on?" Noah asked, lifting a brow.

"Oh, for f—" Sybil snapped her mouth shut and made a face at Noah. "That's utter crap. She went to slap him and he kept her from doing it. *I* ought to go assault her and show her the difference."

Trinity arched her brows. "Can I watch?"

Noah ran his tongue across his teeth and looked at David.

If he expected any help from David's corner, he was looking in the wrong direction. The thought of seeing Sybil pissed was actually rather appealing.

"Not necessary," Noah said, nodding to Sorenson. The chief had a hand on Louisa's shoulders and was leading her away. Already the strident tone of Louisa's voice was dying.

If he never had to hear her again, see her again, it would be too damn soon.

"The chief isn't going to listen to her, is he?" Trinity asked, moving in closer, keeping her voice low as she glanced around.

David didn't really give a damn. Noah was the one to answer and David looked up, skimming the crowd again, looking for that familiar figure in black. But he didn't catch a single glimpse.

"He's got too much sense to listen to Louisa's rambling," Noah said, shrugging it off.

Or seeming to. David could feel his speculative study and knew if he looked over there Noah would be watching him like he could piece together everything just by staring at him long enough. Both him and Max, and the way they looked at people. Noah should have been the one related to that old man, not David, fucked-up mess that he was.

"There's a dinner—" Noah started to say.

David turned his head, stared into Noah's eyes and shook his head. "Don't bother."

A faint smile tilted up one corner of the other man's mouth. "And here I was thinking you'd be jumping for joy at the idea." He shrugged and looked away. "Just wanted to let you know you're welcome."

Yeah, Noah might feel that way. Most others wouldn't. How many knew, he wondered. How many knew that he was Max's grandson?

Sorenson and Detective Bell knew. He'd told the detective and Sorenson had figured it out. Had others?

Somehow he doubted it. If people had known, it would have gotten around.

Aware that Noah was still watching him, he looked away. The thought of sitting around, listening while people speculated or gossiped made his gut churn. Worse, the thought of being around the people who'd loved the old man and *could* talk freely about their memories . . .

No. The last thing David wanted right then was to be around people.

Sybil stroked one thumb down his hand and instinctively he squeezed. She returned the gesture and he had to amend his thought. There was one person he wanted to be around just then. Only one. Turning his head, he studied her face. If she wanted to go, he'd go, just because the thought of not being around her was even worse than the thought of being around others. "Were you going to go?" he asked quietly.

"I came for you." She reached up with her free hand and stroked his cheek. "I go where you go."

Those words, so easily stated, sent another rush of emotion through him. With a short nod, he glanced at Noah. "I'm done here, then." He started to walk and then stopped. Without looking back at the man behind him, he said quietly, "You did good by him. Thanks for that."

It was a slow, mostly silent walk, especially the first twenty minutes. They stopped at a cross street and David looked at Sybil for the first time when she pulled her hand from his.

She gave him a rueful grin as she tugged something from her coat pocket. "It's a good thing I know you."

That didn't click until he saw her pull out a narrow pair of slipper-like shoes from a pouch and swap them out in place of her heels. She put the stilt-like shoes in one hand and then took his hand, sighing a little in relief.

"We could have taken your car," he said as something he recognized as guilt worked through him.

"Difficult." She slid him a sideways smile. "I caught a ride with Trinity and Noah. I . . ." Her words trailed off and she shrugged. "Well, I figured you'd be there and I wanted to be with you in case you needed me."

This time, he was the one to stop.

In case you needed me.

Words rose in him, trapping in his throat as he turned to face her.

They were still close to two miles from the little house where Max had lived all these years. Brilliant streams of sunlight shone down around them and cars passed by, but all David saw was her. Reaching up, he threaded his fingers through her hair, cupped her face.

He opened his mouth, trying to figure out the way to

say everything pent up inside. He wasn't a man who *cared* about words—they meant little, in his mind. Except what she'd just done proved him wrong. A few gentle words could somehow slash into him and yet flood him with something . . . *indescribable.*

Leaning in, he pressed his mouth to her forehead while a war waged inside him. He thought back to the first time he'd seen her, the fury that had lit inside him when he realized what he'd come across. The defiance and fear and anger he'd seen reflected in her eyes. The way she'd smiled at him the next time they met. Then, the third time, when he'd thought he was being casual about it and she gave him that slow, *I see what you did there* look.

It started then, he realized.

When he started to feel again he'd thought it was just lust and he'd welcomed it. Lust was a *normal* thing. He hadn't felt it, not really, until she'd given him that slow, sure smile of hers and he'd thought about covering that red-slicked mouth with his own, fantasies that he hadn't entertained in . . . ever. He'd never had them.

He'd fed that hot, hungry feeling then, let it consume him, but he'd never really noticed everything that grew along with it. The obsession. The *need.*

"You're in my blood, in my soul. I can't remember a time anymore when I didn't need you," he whispered, the words slipping from him without him even realizing it.

Sybil tensed, a startled sound slipping from her.

He lifted his head and watched her from under his lashes. "I made Samuel put in that bid on your studio," he said.

Well, well, well. Sybil walked into the studio and all but dropped her jaw. Okay, yes, she'd known the group the contractor had gotten for most of the construction was one of the Amish families out of Switzerland County, but Caine was with the crew?

What were the odds?

He hadn't so much as looked at her, but she recognized him—would recognize him, no matter what, whether it was a dimly lit street and he was striding down the street with more confidence than any man should have or he was here, among the rest of the quiet, soft-spoken men, like a wolf among sheep.

In that very moment, he looked up and, as if he was surprised to see her, he blinked and cocked his head, then just nodded.

But she saw it, in just that moment, that he wasn't surprised.

He'd known this was her place. Once they were done, it would be her studio, and she planned on making something of it.

She smiled back and lifted a brow.

He kept his face blank, a shutter falling across his features, but she didn't let it get to her.

He was here.

What to do about that?

That memory, more than a dozen years old, slammed into her and she reached up, curling one hand into the thick woven material of the black sweater he wore. It was scratchy soft under her hand, the heat of his skin like a furnace.

"Samuel?"

He shrugged restlessly, a gesture that was out of place on him. "He was Thom's father. Used to head up the crew before I took over. Thom is going to be taking over now, I guess. I asked Sam to take the job. Actually, I convinced Abraham to talk him into it."

"And why did you do that?"

He pressed his face into her hair and she shivered at the feel of his breath teasing her skin. He mistook it for cold and wrapped his arms around her, pulling her close. "Because I wanted to be around you. It was a weird thing for me. I never cared if I was around anybody or not— no. That's not right. I preferred *not* to be around people, but on that job, I tried to get the inside work as much as I could. Abraham heard about it, thought maybe I was . . ."

Sybil turned her head slightly toward him, rubbing her cheek against his when she felt the rasping brush of his stubble. "Getting better," she murmured. "But there's no getting better. It's not like you had a cold, is it?"

"More like cancer."

"They're the cancer." She stiffened and lifted her hands to his face, forcing him to meet her eyes. "*Them.* Not you."

Volatile emotion sparked in her eyes, but for the first time in he didn't know how long he had a hard time meeting her eyes. *Them. . . .*

Sometimes he deliberately fooled himself, especially lately. Always with her. She'd known—always known. He'd tried so hard to keep those broken pieces of himself hidden, but she'd seen them anyway. Now, aware of her vivid stare, as he let himself fully acknowledge that, he let some of the bitterness he felt spill out.

"Yeah. They were a cancer. And they spread it around." He caught one of her wrists, dragged it down as he continued to watch her, stroking a finger across the inside of her skin. "You see so much, Syb. You always did. When did you figure everything out? How long have you known?"

She blinked, looking confused.

He advanced on her, moving his hands to her waist and urging her back, back, back until she bumped up against the brick wall of the building behind her. "Did you just look at me that first time, the second time, or was it the third time when you realized how completely fucked-up I was inside?"

"Exactly where are you going with this?" she asked, her voice level.

"When did you know?" Bracing a forearm on the wall by her head, he dipped his head until their eyes were on the same level. He'd never been able to figure it out, why she could stand to be around him, put up with him. He'd never figured it out.

Her gaze met his. Then she angled her chin up and narrowed her eyes. "I figured something pretty shitty had happened to you the first time we had sex. Those scars all over your back didn't exactly happen because *boys will be boys*, right?"

Something twisted inside him and he swallowed in his throat. "You didn't know. . . ."

Sybil heaved out a breath, the motion causing her breasts to rise and fall. "Hell, David. What did you think was going on here? Some sort of marathon session of pity fucks?" She curled her lip as she said the words and they fell distastefully from her lips.

One hand clenched into a fist. "It's occurred to me."

Sybil reached up, slid her fingers inside the neckline of his sweater, the tips splaying out until she could trail them over the topmost edges of the scars. She never once moved away. "I don't *pity* you. Something in me breaks knowing what was done to the boy you were. You're not him anymore. Either they killed him or you did. But you're *not* him. You're you and I wake up every day wanting you, needing you. Don't think otherwise, not for one minute."

Some of the tension he felt drained out of him and he dipped his head, buried his face in her hair.

"I'm sorry," he said, his voice hoarse.

Sybil hooked an arm around his neck as she turned in to him. "We've established the fact that you're fucked-up. I figured that out a while ago, but I don't think you're fucked-up so much as . . . pulled in. You only let pieces of yourself out in small doses."

Eyes closed, he listened to the rhythm and cadence of her voice as he let the words sink in slowly. *Not fucked-up. Oh, hell.* Yes, he was.

If he was smart, he'd pull free of her and stay away.

But that was one thing he couldn't seem to do.

After a moment, Sybil nudged him with her hands and he eased back, staring down at her. A car went blasting down the street, stopping at the stop sign with just a squeal of the brakes before speeding off down the street like a bullet. Neither of them even looked away from each other.

"I don't pity you," she said again. "That doesn't mean I can't hurt for what was done. To you, to God only knows how many others."

He let his hands fall away as a torrent of bitter anger rose inside him. He fought to keep it trapped. Letting it explode out of him wouldn't hurt anybody but Sybil.

"God." He spat it out as more bitterness, more rage leaked free. Spinning away, he stared down the street. He laughed and even that felt like acid boiling up his throat.

The sound of that laughter, ugly and broken, was like jagged glass on her skin. Sybil stared at his averted back, every line of his body rigid. "God knows how many?" he echoed. Then he turned and looked at her. "There is no God, Sybil. God wouldn't allow the things that happened here *to* happen. So not even *He* knows."

A wave of sadness rolled through her.

Sighing, she moved up and stroked a hand down his back. She might not have the kind of faith that somebody like Noah did—his could probably move mountains. That was the saying, right? But she did believe in something higher than herself. It seemed kind of sad to think this was it, that there was nothing else.

"David," she said, sliding her arm around his body. "This isn't about the things God *allows*. He gave us life, free will. That means the sons of bitches who choose to act in evil ways are going to do it. At the end of it all, they'll answer for it."

"Fuck," he muttered, his voice thick with scorn, the word all but lost in a derisive snort. "You know how many times I cried? Prayed? Begged for help? It never came. I was alone. I've always been alone."

Sybil moved around him, then cupped his face in her hands. "You're not. I'm here. I've been here a long time. I won't go away unless you make me, and even then you'll have a fight on your hands."

His lids flickered. "That's not—"

She rose up on her toes. "Shhhh. I know. This isn't anything I'm trying to change your mind about. You have to decide for yourself anyway. I just don't care to believe that it all ends here. And regardless of any of that, you're not alone. You've got me."

"Do I?" His arms came around her, banded tight, sliding yet again under the heavy, long material of her coat. One fist tangled in the material of her dress while he buried his face against her neck.

"Always." The words she really wanted to say remained trapped.

Somehow, she knew this wasn't the time. The place.

But one day soon, she'd tell him. Whether he wanted to hear it or not.

She stood there, holding him close while he practically clutched her to him. Every line of his body was tense, so tense, she could almost imagine him vibrating. After a moment, his lips rubbed against her neck, the slight movement sending an electric thrill racing through her. How many years had she been with him? Not enough. She could spend a century, taking as many of these stolen moments as she could, and it wouldn't be enough.

His lips found her ear and she shivered as his breath ghosted over her skin. "Where's Drew?"

"Staying with his friend Darnell." She forced a smile and shrugged. "I called Taneisha—you met her at the hospital, I think. She took care of Max. Anyway, I wanted to be here—"

He lifted his head, pinning her with an intent stare as her words trailed off.

"I wanted to be there if you needed me. Going to . . ." She trailed off, uncertain what to say. *Your place? Max's place?*

"It's too far." He dipped his head and rubbed his lips across her neck. "Your studio."

She caught her breath as he slid his hand up her torso, cupping her breast in one palm. Her coat shielded the action from view, but it still felt so very . . .

Wicked.

Wonderful.

And not enough.

"Let's get there, then."

CHAPTER TWELVE

It was unpleasant when outside influences forced changes to the plan.

But after witnessing the debacle earlier, the plan, indeed, had to be changed.

Again, it was easy, to slide inside, barely catching any attention. Eyes glanced, then moved away.

They never notice me. The thought echoed until it was forcibly cut off. None of that mattered.

The noise and muted chatter in there didn't matter, either.

Just getting to the back, inside that little office.

Madison, such a small town. Where people loved to talk. *Gossip.* That was what it was.

And the woman standing at the register, taking in the money she made hand over fist in this place, was one of the worst.

"The chief didn't even *listen* to me," Louisa said, her voice rising in cadence. She'd already repeated the tale out on the street, and here she was doing it again. "Told me that he'd seen it with his own eyes and Caine—David, what*ever* he calls himself—was merely acting in his own defense. A man striking a *woman*—"

"Ah, horseshit." A voice rose up in the back.

Who is this . . . A pause, a thorough study, and the name came to mind. Hank. His name was Hank.

"I saw it well enough," Hank said, eying Louisa with disgust. "If he'd hit you, I'd have to side with you. But you went to slap him and he stopped you from doing it. You don't like that? Don't try to slap the man next time."

"Hank, you are a bald-faced *liar!*"

The Lord should strike you down for your lies. Such lies.

But there was no time to waste. The risk of being noticed was too great.

A few short minutes later, the door to Louisa's office was closed, the lights off. So easy. It was just so easy. Tucked away inside the bathroom, the door closed, save for a slit. Now it was just a matter of time.

"Bunch of pathetic ingrates."

Louisa's head pounded.

She should have just gone home. If she had, she wouldn't have had to deal with everybody implying she'd gotten what she deserved from that degenerate abuser.

Rubbing at her wrist, she made her way over to the ergonomic chair she'd bought a few months ago. It didn't help. Her back still hurt; her hip still hurt; her shoulders ached. Why shouldn't they when she spent so much time hunched over a desk, wearing herself down to provide a nice service to the community?

"Nobody here even appreciates it, either," she muttered. She sniffed and reached down, pulling on the knob of the desk. It stuck and she sighed, reaching into her pocket for the key. She'd had to start locking her desk lately. She just had a little nip every now and then, but the bottle went emptier quicker and quicker these days. Somebody was getting into her desk, but how could she point that out to the cops when the only thing missing was her Maker's Mark?

She pulled out the bottle and took off the cap, reaching for the little glass she kept tucked into the drawer as well. She splashed some whiskey into the glass and then reached for it, some of the stress of the day already melting away.

A drink.

If she'd had one of these before she went to that funeral, she could have handled David so much easier. All she'd wanted to do was pay her respects. She didn't see *why* David had to be up with the closer friends anyway. Wasn't like David was family. And she was stuck in the back, hardly able to see anything. How could she—

Something creaked over in the corner.

She lowered her glass, frowning.

Then, shaking her head, she tossed the amber liquid back, relishing the burn down her throat. *Oh.* That was bliss. More. She needed just a bit more to smooth out the rough edges.

Refilling, she stood and moved around the desk, her gaze flicking to the corner where the bathroom was. The door was cracked. "Fuck it all. I'm going to fire people if I keep finding out they have been in here," she muttered, storming over to the door and slamming it shut.

Swearing, she turned around and strode back over to her desk. Beyond the door, out in the main area, she could still hear the muffled chatter of voices. Normally that sound made her smile because it meant there were a lot of people. Many, many people. Which meant money.

But she didn't want to hear voices. How many of *them* would have sided with Chief Sorensen? Noah would have. He'd proven that. Proving his stripes after all this time, just like she'd expected he would. He'd always been a perverted son of a bitch. She'd bet David was, too.

"Bunch of animals, all of them." Shaking her head, she went to stand in front of the sound system she'd had put in. She hit a button and smiled, swaying a little as the cool, soothing sound of cello and piano filled the room. She turned it up louder until it completely drowned out the sound of the voices.

The door outside opened and she saw the pale oval of the assistant manager's face, her eyes wide. "Get out," Louisa snapped, raising her voice to be heard over the music. Carina's eyes went wide and dark in her pale face, but she jerked the door closed.

Better. Much better. Much better. Irritation burned in Louisa and she wondered if Carina was the one slipping into her office. Using her bathroom? There was an employee bathroom. Taking her whiskey? *The little bitch.*

Louisa edged up the music a bit more. *Better. Much better.* She could think now. Tomorrow she'd find out who'd been coming into her office.

For now, she'd have another drink. And listen to the music. She locked the door and then headed over to the desk. Blissfully unaware.

Behind her, the door to the bathroom creaked as it opened, but the sound was lost as the music swelled and crashed through the air.

She was bent over, pulling the bottle out of the drawer, when the first blow came.

Her cry was muffled and a fist shot into her hair, jerking her up and then slamming her face into the desk.

The sound of haunting cello and piano drowned out a choked sob as something wrapped around her throat and jerked, dragging her across the floor. Louisa tried to fight, tried to scream.

But there was no air.

No air . . .

Darkness edged in ever closer.

She sagged and her attacker let go.

Air rushed back into Louisa's lungs and some part of her thought, *He's not going to kill me!*

Then solid, ugly black shoes moved around, cutting across the field of her vision as she lay there, unable to move, her head pounding. A hand came up, caught her hair and jerked her up.

Louisa gaped, shock rolling through her.

"You . . ."

She tried to say it. Fire burned in her throat and nothing recognizable escaped her.

Flat eyes stared back at her. Then a hand covered her face and she was slammed back against the floor. Once. She tried to fight. The pain exploded. Another strike of her head against the hard floor. She went limp, barely able to move.

There was a third strike and then nothing.

There was nothing now except the pain radiating through her. If she could have puked from it, she would have. But other than the whiskey in her belly, she hadn't eaten or drunk anything all day. The whiskey burned its way up her throat and she started to gag.

Choking on it, she tried to roll on her side. Darkness swarmed in. Did she pass out? She didn't know. There was so much pain. Her mouth tasted sour, like blood and Maker's and . . . fear.

But there was so much silence. She couldn't see anything, her eyes swollen shut.

She went to say something, but terror glued her mouth shut.

Some dim part of her hoped—

Hope died a second later as she was shoved onto her back. She fought, but her movements were sluggish, her hands barely moving as she was forced to her back. Then panic lurched as something hard and unyielding pressed against her throat.

No!

Fighting was useless. A solid, heavy body pinned her body down simply by sitting on her.

And still the sound of cello and piano filled the room.

Beyond the panic, the fear, Louisa had one odd, disconnected thought. *This is what dying sounds like. . . .*

Sybil opened the door and hit a light.

Instantly music wailed. Cello and piano filled the air, the haunting sounds of Adam Hurst wrapping around her. She went to move across the floor to turn it off, but before she took one step, David caught her arm and she was spun around, up against the shut door.

"The music—"

"I don't care," he muttered, his mouth at her throat as his hands went to her shoulders. One quick yank and her coat was on the floor. "Need you."

The stark, rough hunger in his voice sent a rush of desire racing through her and she wrapped her arms around him, turning her face to his just as he lifted his head to kiss her. "Then have me."

He caught the long, simple fall of her skirt starting to drag upward, drawn by his hand. His gaze never moved from hers. Her heart started to race. Her breath was already ragged. Need was a beast inside her belly, ready to attack.

The skirt cleared her hips and he slid his hands inside her panties and smoothed them down. "Here . . . ?" The questioning lilt in his voice had her smoothing her hands up his neck.

"Here. There." Her lids dropped as the underwear fell to the floor, tangling around her ankles. "Anywhere."

"Hmmm." His hands cupped her hips. It had been a long walk and he was chilly, making her shiver as he drew her closer. "Anywhere, Sybil?"

She smiled against his lips. "Anywhere. Anytime."

"You're all but daring me now," he muttered, catching her lower lip and biting her gently.

Heat blistered through her. Such a simple thing and it turned her on. Of course, David just had to *look* at her and she wanted him. Had to exist and she wanted him.

Sliding a hand down, she stroked him through his trousers. They were black and fit him close, clung to long, hard thighs and showcased his ass so very well. "You look so different wearing this kind of clothes," she teased as he arched into her hand. She squeezed tight, watching as his pupils dilated. "I saw women checking your ass out and part of me wanted to tell you to go back to the other clothes."

"I will." He pressed a hot, openmouthed kiss to the center of her chest, just above the swell of her breasts. Her skin prickled from the sensation and she groaned as need twisted inside her. "I don't care what I'm wearing."

She flicked him a look, saw nothing but sincerity in his eyes. She smiled as she started to tug at his zipper. "No. You're you now. Be you." Then she shoved his pants and shorts down far enough that she could wrap her hand around his cock.

A harsh flush settled on his cheeks and he reached down, covered her hand with his. "Sybil." It was a hungry, demanding groan and he started to pump against her hand, using his own to make her squeeze tighter and tighter.

She twisted her wrist. "Stop."

He did, not even a heartbeat after the word had left her lips.

"Did I—"

She cut the words off with a press of her lips to his. "Inside me now. Please," she said, all too aware of the near-desperate plea inside her voice.

The ragged, desperate whisper in her voice nearly put him on his knees even as it flooded him with more delight than he thought it was possible to feel. He could make her feel that way. Make her want him like this.

It was a feeling that he couldn't describe.

He wanted to go to his knees and press his mouth to her, spread her open and taste her. Except the hunger that rode her was pushing him, too. He could take his time once he'd made her come, once he'd eased that vicious ache he saw in her eyes.

Boosting her up, he caught her ass in his hands as she clung to him.

"Now," he muttered.

He pressed against her, felt the soft, swollen tissues of her pussy yielding to him. It was almost reluctant, the way her slick heat accepted him, bit by bit, slowly, and even as she wrapped around him she squeezed down on him, so tight and sweet, he felt like he was fucking his way into a silk-gloved fist. Except only Sybil felt this sweet. Only Sybil made him wish he could be more, give her more.

He pulled out slowly, surged back in and listened as she gasped out his name, her nails sinking into his flesh to leave tiny little darts of pain as she tightened her grip. He shuddered as that sensation raced down to his cock, drew his balls tighter.

He wanted—

Even as he went to push away from the door, though, he stopped.

No. This was what he wanted. Dragging his eyes

open, he focused on her, on the splayed length of her thighs as he drove into her, the soft pink flesh stretched around his cock as he plunged deep. Shifting his grip, he slid a hand down the satin of her leg until he could reach her clit.

There she was swollen. So swollen and hot, just a light touch had her jolting, bucking and grinding against him.

He gritted his teeth at the sensation, driving into her harder, deeper.

She whimpered, a broken sound that had him tensing.

Then her eyes flew open and she sought him out blindly. "Do it again—"

He did, driving into her hard as he started to tug on her clit, feeling the rhythmic pulsing deep in her sex.

Her hands tangled in his hair. "David . . . please . . . please . . ." she said, her voice a mindless chant in his ear.

Lost in the sound of her voice, he felt her tighten around him. Soon. She'd come soon, and then he could—

She tangled her hands in his hair. Tugged his head gently to the side. Then she set her teeth in his neck and bit.

Everything went black and he snarled as his hips bucked against hers.

His climax exploded from him before he even realized he was coming.

Sybil managed to hide her smug smile against his chest.

Right up until he moved.

They'd slid down to the floor, then he went to his back, her body draped over him, but that had been ten minutes ago, easy. Maybe more. The only thing that she was sure of was that she hurt in the best way possible.

Well, that and David had just rolled her onto her back and was kissing his way down her neck.

"David . . ."

He didn't even look up.

Oh, well. Wasn't like she'd expected him to discuss it. They'd never really talked about it anyway, but she knew things were different with them.

But this had *really* been different.

His mouth touched her hip bone and she squirmed. Her skin broke out in goose bumps at the caress of his breath, but she tried to force her body under her control.

Not that her body—or her libido—wanted to listen. "I need to shower," she whispered, self-conscious.

He paused; then a soft sigh skittered across her belly. "Am I invited?"

"Hmmm." She slid a hand down his back and then tangled her fingers in his hair. "Always."

A moment later, she was shrieking in surprise as he tossed her over his shoulder, her ass up in the air. "Damn it, you idiot. Put me down."

"I like you this way." His hand curved up over her rump and she shuddered as his fingers dipped between the crevice of her cheeks. "Got to be honest, Syb. There aren't many ways I don't like you."

"Clearly, you haven't seen me when I'm raging with PMS."

He lowered her to the floor once he crossed the floor into the bathroom. "Can't be any worse than me seven days a week, for the past twenty years." He cupped her face and arched her head back. "But you're still here. Why are you still here?"

"Why are you having such a hard time figuring that one out?"

His blue eyes held hers for a long moment, and

then finally he eased back without answering, turning to the shower to turn on the water, waiting until it warmed before he came back to her. "I want you wet and naked, under the water. Then I'm going to fuck you again."

Her breath hitched in her throat. "Promises, promises . . . I hope you plan on keeping them."

It was something he tried not to think about. He'd climaxed, all from being inside her and the way she'd bitten him.

He usually needed a lot more than that, but it had happened again in the shower.

Unwilling to chance it a third time, he'd just held her when they fell onto the little daybed she had in her office. She'd mentioned that sometimes she had to get up for early-morning shoots and there were other times she ended up with a cranky toddler who needed a short nap. The bed was proving to be handy now, too, although it was a tight fit, his frame almost too long for it, and they didn't fit unless they were on their sides, his body tucked around hers.

Not that he had a problem at all, lying there with his cock cuddled up against her ass, her back smooth and soft against his chest. It wasn't late, that soft, pearly light of the coming evening just settling across the sky.

But he was exhausted.

Her hand stroked his.

As he drifted closer and closer to sleep, the only thing on his mind was that he was glad she was here.

He kept meaning to pull away, to push her away.

But he just didn't know how.

It was dark out when the knock came.

Hard and firm, like whoever was knocking knew she was there and wasn't taking *no* for an answer.

Sybil sat up, or tried to, as much as she could with David's arm half-locked around her waist.

She glanced down at him and saw him staring up at her in the dim light. "I need to get up."

"No, you don't. You're not open."

He pressed his lips to her hip, his teeth scraping her skin lightly.

Shuddering, she broke his hold and stood. "If I don't get up, they'll just keep battering."

Besides, she'd rather be close to the alarm in case somebody was trying to—

"Sybil, if you're in there, open the door. It's Detectives Bell and Thorpe, from the Madison Police Department."

"Well, hell." Grimacing, Sybil hit the light and moved into the main room, pausing only long enough to grab her dress and pull it on. Behind her she heard David moving around, and she glanced back to see him zipping up his pants as he came in.

Looking down at her braless breasts, well aware of what she looked like, she moved to the door and opened it a crack just as Jensen went to knock again. "What in the hell do you want?" Sybil asked sourly.

Jensen stared at her, her face flat, eyes unreadable. "Is David Sutter in there with you?"

"Why?" A cold chill raced down her back.

"Just answer the question."

Sybil gave them a cool smile and shrugged. "I've got no reason to. Private place, after hours, yadda yadda yadda. Unless of course you give me a—damn it, David!" She glared at him as he caught the door and forced it open, despite her attempts not to let him.

Jensen eyed her for a moment and then looked at David, her gaze taking in his bare chest before returning to linger on Sybil. Sybil had no doubt she was noting the bare feet, mussed hair, lack of a bra and other details that Sybil hadn't yet thought about. "I've got questions and it will go a lot easier on David if you two would just be forthcoming," Jensen said bluntly.

"Yeah, I hear that all the time," Sybil said. "David, call your damn lawyer."

Jensen opened her mouth, but David cut her off. "What do you want?"

Sybil hissed and rounded on him, but he wasn't even sparing her a glance.

"How long have you two been here?" Jensen asked, her voice sharp, impatient.

Cocking his head, David was quiet a moment and then shrugged. "Probably since two thirty or so. Sybil has a security system. It's got video feed and can verify the exact time, I'd imagine."

Was it just Sybil or did Jensen seem to relax a little? "And you didn't leave? Not even once?"

Sybil was the one to cut in this time. "If he'd tried to leave, I'd have hit him over the head with a tree branch or something. I'm in a cavewoman sort of mood lately."

Thorpe went red, but Jensen just arched a brow. "So you dragged him off to your cave the day of his . . . friend's funeral?"

Sybil stared at Jensen without flinching. "There are different types of comfort."

David's hand came up, curved over the back of her neck.

"Funeral aside, my sex life aside . . . Jensen, why are you here?"

The cop slid her partner a look and then blew out a breath. As her hazel eyes came back to them, Sybil felt her gut draw up into a tight, cold knot. "I need you both to get dressed. Sybil, if you need a few more minutes, that's fine, but we need to wait inside. The two of you need to come down to the station and give us a statement."

"Why?" David demanded, his voice flat.

"You had an altercation with Louisa Mueller earlier today," Jensen said, her tone an echo of David's. "We had a call from her coffee shop a short while ago."

Sybil felt that knot drawing tighter, colder, as Jensen's eyes passed back and forth between them.

Softly Jensen said, "Louisa Mueller was murdered today. Not long after the funeral."

CHAPTER THIRTEEN

Stubborn, cold son of a bitch.

Sorenson studied David Sutter from across the table and tried to think of some way to crack the man's icy exterior. So far, Sorenson hadn't yet been able to so much as put even one small chip in it, much less crack it.

"You sure you don't want some coffee?" Sorenson had been forced to stop drinking it thirty minutes ago, but if something didn't give soon he'd have to step out of the room, and damned if he wanted that to happen. This was the first time he'd managed to get the bastard in the station and he planned on taking advantage of it.

Maybe he was skirting the line here—there didn't seem to be a connection between Louisa's vicious murder and the calm, methodical executions that had taken place here in town over the past few weeks. The only reason he had for bringing David in was the incident between them in the cemetery, and if Sutter had anything to do with her murder Sorensen would eat his hat.

Although the man had made his feelings about Louisa clear. *She is—well, she was a vindictive bitch. That isn't any reason for me to kill her.*

He'd made that statement in a cool, flat voice, all the while staring Sorenson dead in the eyes.

David hadn't asked for a lawyer, but at the moment he hadn't said shit-all anybody could use, and he hadn't said a damn thing to implicate himself or anybody else.

Of course, he hadn't said much of anything that didn't need to be pried from him with a crowbar.

When he remained silent over the offer of coffee, again, Sorenson just sighed and leaned back in his chair. A quick glance at the clock on the wall told him they'd been at this for over three hours, but only the first hour and a half had been going over the events of the past few days.

Then David had talked. In clear, concise sentences, he'd detailed what he'd been doing for the day, right up until the part where he and Sybil went inside her apartment.

Something had flickered in his eyes then.

And as much as Sorenson didn't care to poke around in somebody's private business, he decided that was what he needed to do. Poke around there, right there. Not because he gave a damn about what David and Sybil did, but if he hit the one area where David seemed to have a weakness maybe he'd lose that iron grip he had on his control.

With a casualness Sorenson didn't really feel, he flipped back through his notes. "Let's get back to talking about today," he said easily.

"And here I was thinking that's what this was all about," David said mockingly. "Since Louisa died *to-day*. Not a few weeks ago, not twenty years ago. But thanks for the walk down memory lane."

Sorenson shot David a look, but his eyes showed nothing. It was like staring at a pond frozen over. Icy blue. The chief just nodded absently. "You never know when the dots will connect, though. Sometimes that connection is right there, but we all walk right past it, look right past it, even though the clues are pretty simple. So, about today. I need to know more about just what happened once you and Sybil got to her studio. Why you went there, instead of home."

David ran a thumb down his cheek, his gaze boring into Sorenson's. "One thing my psychotic mother did do was make sure I had some manners. I don't kiss and tell, Chief."

"The two of you were there just for . . . personal reasons."

David lifted a brow. "Personal reasons?" He snorted and shrugged. "I guess I can go with that. Yes, it got pretty damn personal."

"All afternoon."

David's lids dropped and he tipped his head back, staring up at the ceiling as he slumped on the hard ladder-backed seat. He lounged in it like it was a La-Z-Boy recliner. After a few seconds, he shrugged. "We slept a little. She's got a bed in her office. One of those daybeds. We were in there when Jensen showed up."

"So between . . . personal activities and sleeping, you two were busy all afternoon and well into the evening."

David straightened and focused his unnerving gaze on Sorenson once more. A smile curled David's lips ever so slightly. "Yeah. All afternoon. Well into the evening. I'd have been happy to spend the rest of the night there, if y'all hadn't shown up."

"Where was her nephew in all of this?"

A vein ticked in David's brow. "Drew spent the day with a friend."

"Convenient." Sorenson tapped his pen on his notepad, never taking his eyes from David's face.

"Convenient?" David's voice dropped, and for the first time that ice finally cracked. It wasn't the heat of anger that bled through, though. It was cold, deadly menace.

"I don't think you can describe anything about this day as *convenient*. The man we buried was the closest thing I had to a father. Sybil was there because she wanted to be there for me. She didn't think it was the best place for Drew—it's not like he's had the easiest life with his junkie mother who only shows up in his life when she wants to beg for money or bitch at Sybil. Then Louisa decides she's going to make a scene at the judge's funeral, screeching like a harpy. Sybil and I came *here,* because we wanted to be alone and it was the closest place. Louisa ended up dead somehow, and while she was a harpy, she didn't need to die for it. Then the cops show up and drag Sybil and me to the police station although she didn't have shit to do with anything. You had no reason to bother her even if you do have a hard-on for me. Three hours later, I'm still stuck in here and you want to say anything about this is convenient?"

Sorenson blinked as David came to a stop, his voice biting and cold. He'd never once raised his voice and his fury was that much more menacing for it. That much more cold. Sorenson had always been of the mind that a man who controlled his rage could be more dangerous than the one who acted in the heat of passion.

As he sat there looking at David, he knew a few things. To the bone.

David hadn't killed Louisa. Even if he hadn't had an ironclad alibi, Sorenson didn't think he would have been looking to charge him. Whoever had killed her had done so in a fit of rage.

David damn well had the capacity to kill the men who'd died in this town over the past few months. Yet somehow Sorenson didn't see him being the kind of man who'd shove a bagful of M&M's down one guy's throat or spike another's man whiskey with Benadryl so he could slip a knife in, nice and easy.

No. If David wanted a man dead, he'd do it. Up close, personal. Because that's what all of this was for him.

Personal.

"Did Troyer abuse you?" Sorenson asked, keeping a close watch on the man's face. Every last line.

David's flinch was so minute, if Sorenson hadn't been watching for it he wouldn't have seen it. Then, finally, David looked away. "I don't know."

"You don't know?"

David's eyes slanted his way, glittering like frozen bits of ice under an arctic sun. "Unsure of the meaning, Chief? Let me break this down for you and I'll be clear, because it's the only time I'll speak of it. Ever. I only knew a few names, and the men I *did* know you can't do shit about because they died during a span of five years, starting with the hunting accident Chief Keith Andrews had. Abel Blue was the next to die—he had a heart attack. Luis and Garth Sims both died within a month of each other. Those are the names of the men I knew about, in addition to my father. Other than that?" David shook his head. "I don't know."

"If you did?"

David leaned forward, his eyes vivid, lethal. "If I knew, there would be more blood spilled in this town than you could handle."

"You realize that's not exactly a wise thing to say to a cop."

"Maybe I'm not a smart man." David showed no emotion as he said it.

"Did you have anything to do with the deaths of Harlan Troyer, Willie T. Merchant or Gary Quimby?" Sorenson asked, well aware he might not get another chance to ask that question.

A sneer twisted David's mouth. "No. I didn't know they were involved, but if I had known? I would have killed them, but they would have died a far bloodier, more painful death than you can imagine. Spiked whiskey and M & M's aren't the weapons I'd choose. The only one who suffered at all, from what the papers are saying, was Willie T." He lifted a brow, paused a moment. "Gut shot, right?"

"Yes. He had a bullet wound that perforated his large intestine. Without immediate emergency surgery, he had no chance."

David's smile widened. "I wouldn't have used a gun. It wouldn't make him hurt enough. I never even bothered to learn how to shoot, because if I'm going to kill somebody, I'll do it with my bare hands. *If* I ever killed one of them, I'd want the man to look me in the eyes . . . and know who I was, and why he was dying."

"You really think anything you've just said has put my mind at ease, son?" Sorenson asked softly.

"You aren't going to be at ease around me anyway." David shrugged, his lack of concern obvious. "I can tell by looking in your eyes. You already suspect I could, and would, kill if it came down to it. What you want to know is if I killed any of the men who've died here in town." He stood up, towering over Sorenson now. "I didn't kill them. I can't tell you who did. Now unless I'm under arrest, I'm going to leave."

He stood in the hall for five minutes, waiting for the anger to fade, trying to ease the ugly, slimy feel of shame that once more saturated every thread of his being.

It wasn't possible, but he had to be able to walk out there and look at Sybil.

Had to find a way to get himself level before he looked at her.

This was a fuck of a time to realize just how much, how desperately, he needed her with him. He'd always known he needed her. From the very time he'd touched her and felt the way the noise and chaos inside him seemed to calm.

And now, more than ever, she needed to be *away* from him.

Some of him had hoped that if he just kept his mouth shut the cops would realize he had nothing to tell them and they'd let it go. They knew it was Diane Sutter who had been found.

But they didn't know what had happened to Peter. David didn't know, and he didn't care. But they had an unsolved disappearance, they had numerous murders, all things that tied back to him.

He was a fool for thinking he could keep this from spilling out onto her. Onto Drew.

But he wasn't going to stay a fool.

It was time to bring this all to an end.

Tonight, while he still had this ugliness of the past few hours harsh in his head. They'd brought her in, questioned her. Louisa never would have confronted him if it weren't for the ugliness in his past and he wouldn't have been questioned over her death. All of this was because of him.

Hearing a soft, tired sigh out in the lobby area, he lifted his head.

He had absolutely no fucking idea how he was going to walk away from her.

It was the most painful thing he'd done in twenty years. Maybe ever.

He had been on the receiving end of pain more times than he knew, but once he'd found it in him to leave he'd wrapped that shell of ice around him, letting next to nobody in, and it had been safe. Leaving without knowing what was going on with Lana, that had hurt, but he'd been half out of it with pain. Realizing that his mother had been waiting for them and he'd put Lana in danger, that had hurt, but the shock of it all had dulled everything but the fear.

This time, though, there was no danger to dull anything.

No jagged wound in his side spilling out his blood to cloud his thinking.

No fear for his life, or somebody else's, to push him on.

Just the knowledge that he had to do this. He had to go out there, look at Sybil, take her out of here. He had to get her home. Had to find a way to look her in the eye and tell her it was done.

And then he had to walk away.

For the first time in decades, he wanted to go to his knees and pray for some other way.

But there wasn't anybody up there to answer anyway.

So he didn't bother.

Sometimes the only way was the painful one. This was the best thing for Sybil. And for Drew.

"You don't need to wait," Jensen said softly as she gave Sybil a cup of coffee. Sybil's statement had been brief.

David, though, he'd been back there for more than three hours.

Rotating her head to eye Jensen narrowly, she let the silence draw out before she finally said, "I'm betting you'd just run off and leave your guy here alone, right?"

Jensen looked away without response.

"That's what I thought." Closing her eyes, she went back to brooding.

Louisa was dead.

Mean, backstabbing gossip.

Oh, there were other gossips in town. Meg Hampton cut Sybil's hair, and you couldn't trust that woman with a secret to save a life. But she didn't have any mean in her. Louisa was—no. Louisa *had* little room for anything but mean. Mean and petty.

And somebody had killed her.

Then the cops came to the door looking for David.

Hasn't he had enough trouble in his life? Sybil asked silently, shifting her gaze to stare upward.

There wasn't an answer, though. Sybil hadn't really expected one.

"You've got Drew to think about," Jensen said.

"Drew is with a friend." *Until noon.* She'd have to leave before that. Leave, think of something to say. Think of some way to explain this to the kid. Especially if they didn't let David leave.

A quiet sigh drifted toward her. "Look, Syb—"

"Don't," she said, her voice low and angry. Rising from the seat, she started to pace while a hundred angry words crowded in her head. She stopped halfway across the room and whirled around to glare at Jensen. "I don't care what *you* or any fucking cop here thinks. Never mind the fact that he was with me, all day long. If we weren't at the funeral then he was either under me or on top of me, and yes, I can paint you a picture if you need it. But forget that. That man wouldn't kill a helpless woman and that's what Louisa was. She was no threat to him."

"She made him angry earlier," Jensen said, her voice level.

Sybil snorted. "If *anger* alone was all it took to make him kill, half the people in this town would be dead. *I* would be dead, because I can guarantee that I've pissed him off. David isn't going to go kill somebody just because he's pissed off."

"So why would he kill?"

A soft sound caught her attention, but even if she

hadn't looked up, hadn't seen David standing there, she wouldn't have answered that. His blue eyes, blank as a doll's, stared into hers for a long moment and then he glanced at Jensen.

Slowly, Sybil turned her head and looked at the other woman, quirked a brow. "I don't know. Why would *you* kill, Jensen?"

"This isn't about me." Jensen rose, staring at them both.

"Well, it's not about us then, either. Because neither of us killed her." Sybil shrugged and turned, heading toward David. He just stood there as she rested a hand on his arm. Something in her heart cracked a little when he didn't look down at her, didn't take her hand. Too much had happened, she told herself.

That was all.

Too much had happened.

She kept right on telling herself that, even as he followed her into the house. He'd gotten his truck to take her home.

Normally, that would have filled her with pleasure—and heat.

But once the door shut and she caught sight of the look on his face, she knew she wasn't going to like how this went. A hollow ache spread through her chest.

If you play with fire . . .

She wondered if the same could be said of ice.

David had heat in him, although it only came out on rare occasions. She'd played with him to try to crack that icy sarcophagus he'd buried himself inside and oh, man, the heat that had come whipping out to tease her.

The ice was back, though, and thicker than ever, swathing him like a cocoon that left her shivering even though she hadn't touched him.

Settling down on one of the lounge pillows she kept

piled in front of her gas fireplace, she used the remote to turn it on. Staring into the flames, she wrapped her arms around her knees.

He still stood by the door. She could see his reflection in the protective glass and her heart bled one slow, bitter tear. Clearing her throat, she managed to say, "Well, today was memorable."

His boots echoed on the floor as he moved to stand next to her, staring down, not at the fire, but at her.

She felt the way his gaze traced over her and it only added to the ache inside. It was like he was memorizing every last thing about her. And in the very bottom of her soul, she knew he was doing just that. Right before he told her good-bye.

"*Memorable* is one word," he finally said, his voice gruff.

Slowly, he sank down, keeping a good two feet between them as he looked into the flames.

Firelight danced off his skin and the sight of it hit her in the heart. The artist in her wanted to grab her camera, tell him not to move. It would be a beautiful shot, a way to keep him frozen like this forever.

And it was a memory she couldn't bear to memorialize.

Unable to sit there another minute, she rose to her feet and headed to the kitchen door. Pausing by the counter, she pulled her skirt up to her knees so she could unzip her boots. Feeling his eyes on her, she suppressed a shiver and continued to remove the boots, leaving them to fall where they were as she reached into the fridge for a bottle of the Mill Street White she'd opened a few days ago. She could use a whole damn bottle, but there was only a glass or so left. She found the biggest wineglass she had and poured out every last drop.

"I'm assuming since you didn't jump me the minute

we got inside, you have something else on the mind other than sex," she said after she'd taken one deep drink. Over the rim of the glass, she stared at him. "So why don't you say whatever you need to say? I'm tired."

Scared. Sad. Missing you already. But suddenly, despite her threats to fight him if he walked, despite her determination to do just that, she was . . . tired.

And she *hurt*. Realizing that he'd just walk, now, hurt like he'd just ripped her heart out.

Maybe he had.

She'd chased him all these years. If he didn't want to be with her, then she couldn't change that.

His blue eyes bored into hers.

Sybil lifted a brow. "What? Cat got your tongue, David? Or did you decide you wanted a quickie before you left? You'll have to be quick. I'm tired."

When there was no response, she tossed back the wine and put the glass down, went to go around him. He caught her arm and whirled her around. She barely managed to stop herself from crashing into his chest and then she brought up her hand, balled into a fist, punching him.

His head snapped back and she jerked away.

Blue eyes flew to her face as he wiped the blood away from the corner of his mouth. "You going to give me some clue what that was about?" he asked calmly.

"If you're going to dump me, just get on with it," she said, furious. Misery and fury swamped her, and her entire body trembled. "Don't think I can't see it. You've been dancing around this for weeks and I told you that I'd fight you, but . . ." She trailed off, the words dying.

"Sybil—"

She slashed a hand through the air. "I don't want to hear the excuses and the reasons and the lies. The bottom line is you don't want me enough. So fine. It's over."

He grabbed her and hauled her against him. "You

think I don't want you?" The words were rasped against her lips and she tasted his blood, but she didn't care.

His tongue pushed between her teeth as she gasped. All the rage he felt, and the pain he always covered, was poured into that kiss. She didn't hold any of hers back, either. Because this was the last time, she realized. The very last time.

Curling her hand into the front of his shirt, she sagged between him and the wall as his tongue slid along hers, tasting her everywhere. And it was like the way he'd stared at her earlier—as though he was memorizing everything about the kiss, the way she tasted, the way she felt against him, the curves and hollows inside her mouth, as well as the curves of her body as he slid his hand down her back and grasped her hip to pull her closer.

They couldn't be any closer unless they each dissolved into the other. She felt his erection grinding into her belly, his chest crushing against her breasts as she twined her arms around his neck.

And then . . .

Nothing.

Her legs wobbled with the speed with which he put her down.

He was three feet away and standing in the middle of the floor, staring out the back window.

"You think this is because I don't want you." His voice was flat, level even. She'd heard him talk to a cop, his adopted father, Abraham, and total strangers in that same tone of voice. But when he turned his head to finally meet her eyes, that blue gaze was vivid, all but burning. "Is that what you think?"

"You seem to make a habit of trying to walk away." She wished she could sound as uninvolved. But her legs were shaking, her heart pounding, and just staying upright—without crying—took all of her energy.

He turned to face her. "The key word there is *trying*. I've been *trying* to walk away for years. I always knew things from my past would come back to bite me on the ass and I wanted you out of the way before it happened. It's not because I don't *want* you, Sybil. I want you too much. And I won't let everything *I* am stain what you are."

"Everything you are . . ." she echoed, shaking her head. As the words spun around and around inside her head, she found the strength—and the fury—she needed to shove off the wall. Glaring at him, she strode across the floor. There was still a smear of blood on his face and Sybil was tempted to hit him again. Her hand was starting to throb, but that didn't much matter at this point. She was going to feel like a walking, bleeding wound here in a bit anyway.

"Everything you are." She lifted a hand and covered his chest, staring at her widespread fingers. "What's in *here* determines who you are." She moved her hand up, pushed it into his hair so that her fingers now spread over his skull. "And what's in here. The monsters in your past didn't *define* you. They tried to break you and they failed. They tried to make you into a monster, but you made yourself into a man. You've defined yourself, not the past, as awful as it was. Not the monsters, not your evil father and not that bitch who whelped you. *You* did it, from the time you took the first step to leave right up until now, and you'll keep on defining it."

She moved back. "Are you really going to choose the past over *me*? Over *us*?"

Her eyes, so big and beautiful, cut into him. Every emotion she felt was right there. Anger, misery, resignation, hunger and pain. It was all right there and it laid him open. He'd take just about anything over this, including that fucking whip again.

"I wouldn't choose *anything* over you." Curling his hands into fists, he focused on some point past her face, because if he looked at her too much he'd lose his resolve. "It's because of *you*, how much you matter, that I have to do this. I can't let all of this spill over onto you. I won't let it."

"Believe it or not, David, I'm a big girl. I can handle it and you're not the only one who's been ready for shit to hit the fan. I've been expecting this for years."

The rough sound of her voice stroked over him, inflamed him, tormented him, but he didn't let himself look. "And what about Drew? You ready for this to hit him? Hasn't he had enough just having Layla toy with him?"

"Oh, for fuck's sake." The words flew from her like stones, crashing into him. "You're reaching now. How can *you* hurt Drew?"

Slowly, he lowered his gaze and stared at her. "People are going to look at him, and wonder. They'll wonder if I'm carrying on what my father did."

"Then people are fucked-*up*. You think I'm teaching Drew a good lesson in life to tuck tail and run because of what people *might* say?" Color flooded her face now and her eyes danced, snapping with the force of her fury. "You arrogant son of a bitch. That boy is *my* concern and has been almost from day one. Layla sure as hell doesn't care. You don't get to make decisions that affect him. Not unless you decide you want to be in his life— in mine."

"You're right." He nodded. "But this decision affects my life, too. And I won't let any of my troubles spill onto either of you. I—" He stopped, uncertain of even what he'd been going to say.

She stared at him, bright eyed, her jaw clenched. "You what?" she countered gently.

When he remained quiet, she laughed gently. "You can't say it. Even now." She sighed, slid her hands up and hooked them behind her neck. "It's really over. Ten years, all coming down to this . . ." Her lashes drifted down over her eyes.

For a long moment, they both stood there. Then, unable to remain so close with this chasm separating them, David turned to go.

"You won't say it," she said, freezing him at the door. "And I won't keep it inside, not anymore. I love you, David. I've loved you for a long time. And it might take a long time, but I'll find a way to stop loving you. You choose to walk away now and it's done."

The words stabbed him in the heart, sharp as a blade. If only they'd managed to kill him.

"Be happy, Sybil."

CHAPTER FOURTEEN

Be happy.

Three days later, the words still rang in her head.

Not a pretty set of bells, though.

More like a death knell.

Happy.

She curled her lip as she huddled over the coffeemaker and waited for it to squeeze out enough coffee to wake her sleep-addled, miserable brain. Yeah, *happy* was a long time coming.

Behind her, she heard a familiar cough and the shuffling of feet on the floor. Pasting a smile she didn't feel on her face, she turned to watch as Drew came into the kitchen.

"There's my morning bird," she said softly. "We'll never need an alarm clock with you in the house."

He eyed her through bleary eyes. "You were up before I was yesterday, too. What's wrong?"

"Nothing." She gave him a bright, false smile even though the action felt like it might split her head open. "I'm just not sleeping too well lately."

"You're sad, too." Drew flopped down in the chair and watched her with old eyes. He was all of eight, but he had old eyes. Sometimes she wondered how he could have come from Layla. He shouldered responsibility, looked life right in the eye and never backed away from hard things. Layla was the exact opposite and always had been. "Why are you sad?"

She shrugged. "Just got the blues, Drew. Why don't you tell me what you want for breakfast?" Turning away, she poked into the cabinets, although she already knew the answer.

"Peanut butter toast, I guess." He sighed and she heard a thud as he propped his elbows on the table. "You never tell me anything."

"Sure I do. I tell you when it affects you and I tell you things you need to know." Pulling out the jar of peanut butter, she turned back to look at him. "Right now, this is a thing that affects me and it bothers me and I'm trying to deal with it. When I get a little more steady with it, I'll tell you. But it's not your concern and it's not going to affect you, okay?"

A tension she hadn't realized he had eased and he heaved out a heavy sigh. "So it's not about Mom?"

"No." As guilt hit her like a fist, she put the peanut butter down and moved to drop onto the seat across from his. "You talked to her the same day I did. She sounded pretty good, right?"

He nodded. She almost hated to see the hope in his young eyes, but she'd felt the same thing. Layla had sounded stronger somehow. Steadier than she'd sounded in years.

"Then stop worrying about your mom, okay?" She leaned in and pressed a kiss to his forehead.

"I'll try." He squirmed a little as she pulled away, staring at the tabletop. "I . . . I was kind of wondering. What if she gets better? That means I have to go live with her, right?"

Sybil's heart started to crack. But she kept her voice level. "She is your mom, Drew."

"But she can't take care of me. She barely manages to take care of herself. If she gets mad or scared or worried, she'll start drinking again. Or doing drugs." He hunched his shoulders. "I don't think she could stop. I . . . I don't want to live with her."

His words finished in a whisper and then he looked up at Sybil, his eyes bright with tears. "I love Mom and I want to see her. But this is home. I want to be with you."

Sybil moved in and grabbed him, hefting his weight into her arms. "Oh, Drew." She breathed in the scent of him, Irish Spring soap and the Jergens lotion she had to force him to use. "Baby, I want you with me, too. But you are Layla's boy. We'll have to work this out, if and when the time comes. But I'll always be a part of your life and I'll always be there to take care of you. Promise."

He sighed, his head on her shoulder.

It wasn't what he wanted.

It wasn't what she wanted.

But it might be what they had to live with.

Life kind of sucked that way sometimes.

David was helping Noah gut the empty building across from Louisa's when he saw her.

He didn't even *see* her, not at first.

His heart was pumping, his skin went tight and that was how he knew.

Slowly, he lifted his head and over Noah's shoulder he saw her coming up the sidewalk. Her eyes met his, and just like that she looked away.

"Come on, David; this is heavy," Noah said, his voice rough with strain.

David glanced back at him, something ugly springing to his lips, and he stopped it only a split second before it left his lips. Tearing into Noah wasn't going to do anything to lighten his black mood. *Black. Bleak.* That pretty much described everything since the night he'd walked away from Sybil. The sun came up and went down, but it didn't shed any light on the shadows that seemed to fill his every waking moment.

Once they dumped their load, Noah dropped down on the ground and pulled a bandana from his pocket to wipe the sweat from his brow. "You going to tell me what your malfunction is lately?"

"Well, gee, Preach." David gave him a sharp-edged smile as he picked up a bottle of water. "I get hauled in over Louisa's death because naturally, everybody thinks I snapped all because she jumped down my throat. She's done it to everybody, but naturally I'm the one who is going to lose it and kill her. People all are looking at me sideways and muttering as I walk by. You had somebody call and tell you to find somebody else to help finish a job if Thomas planned on keeping me with his group. I wonder why on earth I might be a little grouchy."

"Grouchy." Noah snorted. "*I* am grouchy. You're like a bear who just had his foot caught in a trap. So just get the trap off or chew your way free, whatever. Deal with it, before it gets worse."

Deal with it.

He curled his lip and looked away. "Mind your own business, Preach," he said softly.

"You're my friend. That makes this . . . whatever . . . my business."

Noah's voice was closer now and he turned his head, watched as Noah took another step closer.

"I can't help but notice that Sybil looks about as happy lately as you do. Also can't help but wonder why."

David just stared at him.

"She's stood by you a long time," Noah murmured. "I can't say I really noticed it, but looking back, I can think of a lot of times the two of you were together. Really together. If I'd actually been looking, I'd have seen it before now. All that time together and now, when things are rough, you're suddenly not. Why'd you push her away?"

"What makes you think I did the pushing?" David could have hit himself the second the words left him. He knew better, knew how Noah had a way of making people open up, spilling the words they had inside. He couldn't do that. Couldn't do this.

"Because I see how Sybil looks at you. Very little would make her walk. But I can see you pushing her away . . . probably because you want to protect her." Noah shrugged. "I can't make you change your mind, but I can say that's a misguided sense of chivalry. I can't think of anybody who needs your protection less. She's handled Layla all her life. She can handle any bullshit the town might throw at her for a few weeks as things settle down about you."

He opened his mouth, went to close it. Shaking his head, he just turned away, and that was when he saw Hank Redding standing in the doorway.

David's spine went rigid.

The look on Hank's face flooded him with tension and suddenly something wet splashed down the side of his leg. Looking down, he realized he'd crushed the water bottle he'd been holding, spilling all the water out.

"Hank."

Hank didn't even look at Noah, just stared at David with a wide, unfocused look. "I . . . I need to talk to you, David."

A hand came up, caught his arm. David turned his head and looked at Noah.

David just shook his head and moved forward.

He already knew what was going on. There was no avoiding this.

Without saying anything to Noah, David followed Hank out in the cool, bright light of the November morning. A few minutes ago David had been dripping with the sweat, and the brisk morning air should have felt good.

But he was chilled to the bone, and when Hank turned to look at him it only made it worse.

"I think it's time," Hank said softly.

"Time?" David lifted a brow.

He'd been putting this off for too long, Hank realized. At first, he hadn't understood why he felt the need to speak so badly. But then he started to understand.

David had been right. It *was* poison, one that had eaten at him, damn near destroyed him and his marriage, his family. It had to be purged.

"I'm going to talk to Jensen Bell." The words tumbled out of him, hard and fast like he'd change his mind if he didn't say them, but he knew he wasn't going to. He had to do this. Mostly because he'd seen the way his cousin, Clay Brumley, had been eying him the past few days.

Like he wanted to say something to him but wasn't sure how.

And he was almost certain things had happened to Clay.

If Clay was one of them, then things had to be done.

Clay had a six-year-old son.

This ugly, vicious circle would end. It would end now

and it would never be formed again, even if Hank had to die to find a way to end it.

Feeling the weight of David's eyes on him, he looked up.

"Okay." That was all David said. Simple and understanding acceptance.

"I—" He stopped, cleared his throat. "This sounds fucking weird and I know it, and you can say no, but I'd appreciate it if you came with me."

David closed his eyes and tipped his head back to the sky. A vein pulsed in his neck and Hank was two seconds away from yanking the words back, saying, *Never mind, forget it*, when finally David slowly shifted his gaze back to him and then just gave a short nod. "Let me tell Noah."

Not trusting himself to not lose his nerve, Hank ducked inside the building. In a few months he'd be helping with the new roof here, but for now it was up to Noah and the other guys. The hot, backbreaking labor actually looked like the sort of thing he needed to distract himself.

He went to offer a hand later on, but as he shoved off the wall he saw something from the corner of his eye.

Clay.

Watching him.

Just down the street, and his gaze was . . . off.

Swallowing, Hank moved deeper into the building, meeting David halfway across the floor. "This way," he said curtly, cutting through the side door and moving down the alley.

David just shrugged, and as they strode down the alley Hank resisted the urge to look back. Until the very end.

That was when he saw Clay again. His cousin had moved down to peer down the alley, and there he was.

Up there on Main, watching Hank, the way Hank watched him. Over the distance their eyes met, and Hank felt the impact of it down to the soles of his feet and he wanted to scrub himself clean, but he couldn't. This stained him to the soul and *clean* would never happen.

A shiver raced down Hank's spine and David must have seen something because he looked back as well. The second he did, Clay spun around and disappeared.

"What's he up to?" David asked, his voice soft.

"Not sure." Hank shook his head, focusing once more on the sidewalk under his feet and what he had to do. "But lately, if I'm there, so is he. It's been going on a few days and I don't like it. I'd just as soon get this over with. I get the feeling he doesn't want me talking. To anybody."

"How are you two related?" David asked softly.

"Our moms are—were—sisters. His mom died when he was a kid. Spent most of his life bouncing around between his dad and some of the aunts on my side of the family." Hank shot David a look. "And some of the time, he lived with my grandparents."

"Fuck." David shot a look up the street as they exited the alley. "Let's take my truck. He'll probably be looking for yours."

"Yeah."

David gunned the engine and pulled out of the parking lot without another word. He could just imagine why Clay didn't want Hank talking.

The drive was a terse, quiet one. Noah hadn't said much of anything when David told him he had to leave. He'd just taken a long, silent look at Hank and then glanced at David.

As they climbed out of his truck a few minutes later, it seemed like every soul in town had their eyes locked on them. Judging by the way Hank hunched his shoulders and tucked his head low, he felt the same.

"I hate this," Hank mumbled, his voice thick, cheeks ruddy.

David had nothing to say. He'd never made this walk, never planned on doing it. He'd told a cop—once. He still had the scars left from that. In the back of his mind, he could hear the sound the whip made as it whistled through the air, the crack of it on his skin—

"—long it will take—"

David jerked his head around, stared at Hank, realizing he had been talking.

"Sorry," David mumbled with a shake of his head. An icy beat of sweat trickled down his spine and he fought the urge to shudder as memories started to slam into him.

In time, you'll be a man. . . .
Receive the honor . . .

Pain, digging into him, cutting through him. Hands, bruising and hard—

Sweat, thick and oily, was like a film on his brow and he wiped it off as the memories screamed at him. He swiped his forearm over his brow, saw that his hand was shaking.

Son of a bitch. Furious, he closed his fingers, made a fist, so tight it ached. *Shut up. Shut* up*!* The memories continued to thud and pulse inside him until he had to slam them into submission. Slam them down, or go mad from it.

Hank's reddened eyes cut into him.

David had never wanted to turn his back and run so much in his life.

But he couldn't do it.

He wasn't even here to talk. Wasn't here to do anything. If Hank could do this on his own, then fuck it all, David could stop being a pussy and stand here.

"If you don't want to be here—"

David cut him off. "I don't," he said sourly. Then he met the man's eyes dead-on, held them for a minute before he looked up at the police department, that simple brick building just ahead of them. "But you don't want to be here, either. You're here. So I'm staying."

They headed up the steps, but before David went in he stopped, turning, and looked at Hank. "I told the cops. Once. I told Chief Andrews."

Hank's eyes went wide and David laughed. The sound was ugly, broken even to his own ears. "You can imagine how well that went over. I was desperate, determined to get out. That was the beginning of the end. I told the chief, one night after a potluck at church." David closed his eyes, remembering how the man's eyes had been so kind, so understanding. *Don't you worry, son. I'll handle this.*

When David got home, his father had been waiting.

Even now, David could hear the echo of their voices and the sound of that whip, their jeers. And he'd seen the chief's face for the first time when he lifted the mask.

Betrayal isn't tolerated, son, he'd said sadly.

"I couldn't go to school for weeks," David said. "I've got scars all up and down my back. All because I told the wrong cop." He looked back at the doors and finally opened one. "I guess that's why I never tried again."

"Hank!"

Both of them turned.

David saw it first, the matte black finish of the gun in Clay's hand. Instinct had David moving even as Clay lifted his hand, and he shoved Hank down. Something fiery hot tore through David's shoulder as he hit the ground and there were screams, startled shouts, and somewhere he thought he heard a crash.

The doors flew open and people pounded past him as he sat up, staring down the road. Clay was gone.

"Are you—shit, you're hit."

He scowled up at Jensen when she jerked off her jacket and shoved it against his arm. As she made contact, he hissed and tried to jerk away. "Don't be a baby, David."

"How about you be a cop instead of a doctor and go find Clay Brumley, figure out why he was shooting at Hank?" he demanded. He grabbed the jacket from her and held it in place himself, with a little less pressure. She was damn strong for somebody who looked like she barely weighed a hundred pounds. And mean, too.

"Clay?" Her eyes sharpened on David's, then moved to Hank.

Hank had just sat up and was staring dumbly at David. At the sound of her voice, Hank shifted his gaze to her and then nodded. "Yeah. It was Clay. He's . . . he's been kinda following me for a few days," Hank said, his voice hoarse.

"Are you two okay?" she asked, rising.

"We're fine. Go be a cop," David said again as red, hot blood continued to seep out of him.

She turned and on her way down the steps she barked at one of the uniforms to call an ambulance. Then David heard her snarling instructions into a radio about Clay, his vehicle and other police bullshit. They'd find him. That was what mattered. Clay would be better off if they found him before David did.

He was now in a really, really bad mood.

Agitation twisted inside.

That hadn't just happened.

Had it?

Things should be calmer now.

So little stood in the way.

But then they were on the steps. And there was a gun. Now he was running—

The gas pedal seemed to go down on its own.

The man looked up—who was he? His face was unknown. For a moment, their eyes met through the windshield.

There was a heavy thud.

Clay shrieked when he went down. It wasn't enough, though.

Reverse. Back up. Do it again. He must die.

An eye for an eye.

He was trying to get up, pushing up on his hands, although his legs didn't want to work.

In the distance, there were sirens.

Now. I must do it now.

His eyes swung toward the truck. And he knew. As the truck lurched forward, he opened his mouth to scream.

A moment later, there was a dull, sickly crunch under the wheels.

Don't look back. It's time to leave.

There were police cars coming. *Calm. Be calm.*

The calm mask was in place. But it was just a mask.

"What do you *mean*, nobody can find him?" Jensen fought the urge to snarl and spit the words out. The uniform who'd just given her an update looked like she wanted to turn tail and run. Taking a deep breath, Jensen took another look at the woman's name. "Officer Peyton. It's been two hours. We've got Brumley's truck. He's not at home or at work. Nobody reports seeing him? There's nothing?"

"No, ma'am." The officer shifted on her feet and then licked her lips. "He's probably found a place to hide or had somebody waiting to pick him up, something."

"We won't speculate." Sighing, Jensen nodded and then waved a hand. "There are probably some witness statements we haven't collected. See if you can help."

There were two witnesses who hadn't been processed yet. Of course, one of them should have his ass in the ED, but David Sutter hadn't seen fit to go there. He'd taken one long look at the stretcher and then told the paramedic to fuck off.

Jensen hoped the bullet had just grazed David, because if it was inside him they were going to have problems. She had a feeling the man would let himself get sick before he'd willingly go to the doctor.

As she strode down the hall, she wasn't surprised when Chief Sorenson joined her. "Things sure as hell were a lot less interesting around here a few months ago, weren't they?" he asked easily.

"Yep." She pushed a hand through her hair. "All this needs to come out and be dealt with. I want every last monster locked up. Preferably forever. But I'll be damned glad when it's over and done."

"You and me both."

They paused outside the room where David waited. Hank was in the other room, although he had been edgy about going in there, with the door shut. Jensen had ended up putting Thorpe on the door, because there wasn't a cop there she trusted more. Well, other than herself and Sorenson.

Hank seemed to be happy with that, but she doubted it would last for long.

She paused briefly by the new detective, eyeing him. "You talked to them any?"

"Just to make sure they were okay. Sutter still refuses medical treatment. He did finally let one of the EMTs bandage him up, but that's it." Thorpe paused and then added, "It just grazed his shoulder, an inch or so away from the neck. But it could have been bad."

Jensen processed that and then nodded. "Yeah. Any idea why they were here?" She suspected she already knew, though. That gun hadn't been pointed at David.

"Hank came in to speak with you." Thorpe glanced back over his shoulder to the room where the man in question waited. "Sutter just came with him."

"Moral support? I don't see David being big on that." But then again, if Hank was here for the reasons she thought maybe David had decided to make an exception. Good thing he had, too. "I'm going to poke my head in with David, then go talk to Hank. Stay on the door."

Thorpe just nodded like he had absolutely no plans to go anywhere else.

She slid inside and David was slumped in the chair. His dark head was bent; his lashes lay against his cheeks like shadows. He looked relaxed, but she didn't buy it for a minute.

"Any idea when you're going to let me out of this box, Bell?" he asked a split second later. He hadn't even looked up, hadn't so much as lifted his lids to look in her direction. But he'd known who'd come into the room. Sooner or later he'd stop being so damn spooky, but she didn't know when that would be.

"I need to get statements from you both." Hooking one hand in her pocket, she left the other to hang free at her side. "I'd rather get that done and see what in the hell is going on before I let the two of you out."

He lifted his lids now, pinning those penetrating blue eyes on her. "You find Clay Brumley?"

"Not yet."

He sighed and lifted his head, staring at the door.

"That's a damn shame, Detective Bell. It would be a good idea if you found him before I did."

"David, do yourself a favor and don't say anything to incriminate yourself, okay? As fucked-up as everything is, I honestly believe you don't have anything to do with the murders in town—and that's *off*-the-record—but if you go spouting stupid shit, you'll tie my hands."

Crossing the floor, she stood in front of the table and leaned against it, planting her hands on the table as he finally focused his gaze on her. There was something in his eyes, his expression pensive, as though he wanted to ask her something. In the end, though, he just shook his head. "Just what do you want to ask me, Detective? I can't tell you much. Hank's the man you need to speak with."

"I'll get to Hank." She rubbed her hands over her face and then pulled out her recorder. "I'm putting this on-record."

She paused to give David a chance to say something, but he just stared at her. After a few seconds, she said, "You can have somebody with you. Do you want an attorney?"

"I don't need one."

Those blue eyes were peaceful, calm. He looked like he'd slept like a baby every night of his life and planned to do the same once he got out of here. He sure as hell didn't look like somebody who'd just been shot. He didn't look like a man who'd spent much of his early life in hell.

But she knew otherwise.

After a few more seconds, she reiterated she was recording their conversation, covering her ass on all fronts, before she braced her elbows on the table and leaned in. "So why did Clay Brumley try to shoot you?"

A smile tugged at his lips. "Clay didn't try to shoot me. I just happened to be in the way."

"You mean you put yourself in the way." She arched a brow.

He shrugged. "Adds up to the same. Hank wasn't hit. I was. Nobody died."

"Anybody ever tell you that you talk too much?"

"Daily." He said it without batting an eyelash.

Despite herself, she laughed. "David, I really hope you're not tied into this. Because I think I could find myself liking you." *Even if you are a scary-ass son of a bitch.*

She went at him again, from other angles, pushing at him and trying to pull more details out of him. But the man was a rock—he just didn't yield.

Since she had other ways to beat her head against a stone, she shut off the recorder and pocketed it. "Okay. I'm not done with you. I'll have one of the uniforms come in and get your statement. Can I trust you to stay put?"

He cocked his head, pondering that. Then he shrugged. "Yes."

Again, her gut said she could trust him.

Stifling a curse, she headed to the door. Once there, she paused. "Have you called Sybil yet?"

His eyes went shuttered, the first *real* reaction Jensen had seen from him since walking into the room. Although she knew it was her imagination, it seemed the temperature in the room dropped a good ten degrees. Tension wrapped around him like a shroud and the intensity of his eyes seemed to suck the air from the room.

Then he looked away. "No. No reason to." He shrugged, and if the movement caused him any pain from his injured shoulder he didn't show it.

Let it go, she advised herself.

But Jensen was something of a bulldog and she knew it. "No reason?" she echoed, resting a hand on the wall. "The way you two were the other day and you don't think she'd want to know you were shot?"

His arctic gaze came back to Jensen's face. "No. We know each other and sometimes, we fucked. That's not exactly a declaration of undying love." His mouth curled in a bitter smile. "I'm not the guy for that anyway."

His voice went dull on those words. Jensen wondered if he realized it. Softly she asked him, "You really believe in burning your bridges in spectacular style, don't you?"

CHAPTER FIFTEEN

The truck was tucked away.

There had been blood on it. Blood and gore and other . . . things.

Don't think on it. It had been necessary.

Sometimes it was necessary to do hard things.

Hard? It was a sly whisper.

"The devil. Ignore him."

That wasn't a hard *thing,* the voice crooned. *It was . . . evil.*

"No." Denial was a living, breathing thing. "Not evil. Necessary."

Oh. But it was. Evil. And you loved it. Just as you loved it then.

Because it was too hard to silence that voice when still, the one who watched left the silence and moved out into the cool, open air, breathing it in.

"A walk." That was a good idea. "A walk will clear my head."

A walk. No thinking about what had been done.

"No reason." Now there was a smile. "What's done is done."

But as clothes were changed, hair brushed and dealt with, hands shook.

Evil, the voice continued to insist. *Evil.*

"Necessary."

Grass crunched under solid, sturdy soles. Birds called in the distance. The voice went silent. For a moment.

But then it returned, even more gleeful. *Perhaps,* it acknowledged, *it was necessary. But also, evil.* You *are evil. Because you enjoyed it. Twisted, evil thing.*

A sob.

"No." It was a strangled, muted whisper.

Yes.

"How is David?"

The sound of his name was like salt being rubbed into a wound. "Ah . . ." Sybil fumbled for words as she met Taneisha's gaze. Everything had changed in the span of a few days. How could so much have changed? Sybil hadn't outright *told* Taneisha how she felt about David, but her friend knew. "We're not really talking right now. I guess he's okay. Was Drew good? He's spending a lot of time with you lately."

For a second, Taneisha just stared at her, and then she looked at the two boys still jabbering together in the living room. She reached over and caught Sybil's hand. "Porch. Now."

Sybil gaped at her and looked down at her robe, hastily pulled on over the thigh-length T-shirt she'd pulled on. "Hey, gimme a minute—"

When Taneisha didn't give her that minute—or even thirty seconds—Sybil clutched her robe closed. "What's the problem? Was Drew—"

The door shut behind them and Taneisha paced away.

"Drew was fine. This isn't about him, so be quiet." Taneisha turned around, her face set in grim lines. "You didn't hear."

Sybil's heart fluttered and then stopped. For a few seconds it just stopped and it took everything she had to stay upright. As her legs tried to melt underneath her, she sagged back against the wall. "Didn't hear what?" she asked, forcing the words out through a throat gone tight.

"He was shot." Taneisha's words were soft. Gentle.

But they cut through Sybil like a blade. Clapping a hand over her throat, she stifled the cry before it could escape. *Drew. Can't scare—*

"Hey. Hey," Taneisha said, her voice firm. Then she caught Sybil's face in her hands. Taneisha's dark face loomed, wavered in and out of focus. "Look at me, girl. You look at me. He's okay."

Shot. David was shot. Horror spiraled through her, and her heart was already lying in pieces on the floor.

"Damn it, Sybil. Listen to me!"

Taneisha shook her and the shock of that finally cut through the fog she'd fallen into. "*He is okay*," Taneisha said again, carefully enunciating each word. "He was shot, but he is okay. He didn't even have to go to the hospital."

"Fuck." Sybil sagged to the floor then. Tremors grabbed her, wracking her body so violently, she thought she might be sick. *Shot. David had been shot. But he's okay.*

He hadn't even called. . . .

Her heart sank slowly to her feet, and she swallowed around the bruising knot that had settled in her throat. Blinking back the tears, she looked up at Taneisha. "So, he's okay."

"Yeah." Taneisha sank down in front of her, folding her legs gracefully beneath her. "He didn't call you. At all."

Sybil closed her eyes as the tears started to burn.

"Like I said," she whispered thickly. "We're kinda not talking right now."

The silence was thick and heavy. After a minute, she opened her eyes to look at Taneisha and she found the other woman watching her with hot, angry eyes. "That son of a bitch."

"Neisha," she said, her voice rough.

"No." The other woman shook her head with a fury that had her curls bouncing around her pretty face. She shoved upright and started to pace. "I get that he's had a shitty life and I want to punch people around town who are treating him like a leper. I feel bad for him, but that doesn't give him the right to treat you like that."

"We . . ." Sybil fumbled for the words. *Broke up?* It wasn't like they'd ever committed. *We aren't sleeping together?* Finally, she settled on the truth. "He doesn't love me. Ten years, Neisha. That's what we had, and in the end it doesn't matter enough to him."

Just saying it brought a knot to her throat and smashed her heart into pieces all over again. "He doesn't love me," she whispered, forcing herself upright. She met Taneisha's eyes, surprised to realize her own were dry. It had been . . . what, three? No, four days since he'd walked away. Part of her had kept hoping something would change. That he'd realize this wasn't any way of solving *anything*. But she'd been an idiot. "Somewhere inside me, I was holding on, thinking maybe he'd start to miss me. Start to realize he's just being . . ." She laughed sourly. "A man. An idiot. Whatever. But this drives it home."

He'd been shot and hadn't even bothered to call her. She'd never heard. The past few days had been slow— she'd had a rehearsal dinner to shoot in Jeffersonville on Thursday night and the wedding on Friday and she'd worked from home on Saturday. The honest truth was that she'd been *hiding*, tucked up inside her house so she didn't have to worry about seeing him, but what did it matter, really?

Numb, aching cold spread through her. "When did it happen?" she asked softly.

"Friday."

Her lashes swept down and she rested her head against the porch railing behind her head. "Yesterday. And he doesn't bother to let me know. Yeah, I'd say this drives it home, all right. David really doesn't love me."

"Honey." Taneisha reached for her.

"No." Sybil held up a hand. "Don't. If you hug me now, I'll start bawling. Okay? I'd rather do it later. Once I'm alone and in the tub, with a glass of wine."

"You—" Taneisha stopped, blew out a breath. "I can take Drew with us. You can go have that bath now."

"No." She rubbed her hands down her arms. "I haven't seen him enough as it is with that wedding in Jeff. I'll be fine." She went to open the door and the sound of the boys geeking out on the video game she'd picked up made her smile, just a little, despite the misery that spread through her like some insidious disease. "Besides, listening to him is the best medicine."

Maybe she shouldn't have said that, Sybil realized thirty minutes later. She now had *two* boys in her living room while Taneisha was out doing her "running" or whatever she had to do.

The boys were yelling up a storm, too, and after another ear-shattering screech Sybil decided she couldn't handle any more. Grabbing some clothes, she locked herself in her shower. Five minutes of privacy and then they'd go down to the diner for some lunch.

No, she didn't want to be alone with herself, because if she were—

He'd been shot.

She stumbled against the shower wall. Shoving a fist against her mouth, she muffled the sob as it ripped out of her. The tears followed soon after.

You son of a bitch.

Sinking to the floor, she curled her legs against her chest and pressed her face to her knees as the misery tore and dug into her, like a rabid beast.

The pain, she thought, it just might kill her.

You son of a bitch.

Then softly she whispered, "Why do I have to love you, even now?"

"She loves you, you know that?"

The voice cut through the air, shattering the silence. David closed his eyes for a second and then opened them, focused on the work, on the pain in his shoulder.

"You hear me, you overgrown son of a bitch?"

David hefted another bag of mulch out of the back of the truck and threw it on the ground before looking down at the woman standing at the foot of his truck.

His shoulder was screaming at him, but he refused to see a doctor for it.

He'd spent the morning working on Mary's flowerbeds and he'd kept his ears peeled for the noise in town. He could hear the cars, the occasional shout. If there were sirens, he'd hear those, too. Sooner or later, Clay Brumley would show his sorry ass. It had been almost twenty-four hours. How could a man hide in a town the size of Madison?

That thought infuriated David, though. Because he knew better than most just how easy it was to hide. He'd done it, for twenty years. But Clay's truck was still here. Nothing missing from his home. He'd taken off down the sidewalk and—*bam*. Just gone.

"You going to stand up there like Paul Bunyan and act like you don't hear me talking to you?"

Sighing, he straightened and slanted a look down at the slim black woman. "Paul Bunyan. Giant, with an ox and an ax?"

"You're probably as stubborn as an ox." She curled her lip, craning her head to glare up at him. "And you're standing up there like a damn giant instead of moving your ass down here. So yeah. Paul Bunyan."

He went to shove a hand through his hair, but pain shrieked through him and the limited range of motion had him lowering his arm. Finally, he hopped down off the bed of the truck to stand in front of her. *What in the hell does she want?*

She was a nurse; he remembered that. Had taken care of Max—the name clicked a minute later. *Taneisha. Fuck.*

Running his tongue around his teeth, he turned away. "I'm busy, ma'am."

"You and your busy self can shut the hell up," she snapped, marching around and planting her body in front of him.

She was built like an amazon—nearly six feet in her tennis shoes and she was all long, lean curves. The look in her eye told him that if he wanted her to move he'd have to move her.

Pissed off as he was, he wasn't about to go that far.

"I've got things to do," he said, cutting off the sidewalk to go around her.

"You couldn't even take five minutes," she said softly. It was the sheer lack of fury in her voice that had him going still. "Five minutes out of your busy day to call her and tell her what happened. She heard it from me, and the way she looked, you'd think I'd punched her right in the gut."

Guilt grabbed him by the throat and he spun around, already snarling. "Then why the fuck did you tell her?"

"Did you think she wouldn't *hear*?"

If his fury scared or startled her, Taneisha didn't let it show. She closed the distance between them and slammed the heel of her hand against his chest. "Have you *seen* the size of this town, David? It didn't grow much in the past twenty years. What did you think would happen? You'd get shot and nobody would talk about it?"

He opened his mouth. Closed it.

"Or did you think she wouldn't care?" Taneisha's voice was softer this time and the look in her eyes had him wanting to just jerk back. Get away. Put some serious miles between him and those dark, knowing eyes. "That's it, isn't it? Some part of you thought maybe this wasn't that serious for her. If it isn't serious, it wouldn't matter that much to her, right?"

"There's nothing—"

"Don't." Taneisha shook her head. "You don't look at me and lie to me that way. Maybe on *your* part, you look at it and see nothing. But that's because you're blind. But hey . . ." She shrugged and turned away. "You got your wish, big guy. You wanted to push her away, you did it. You ripped her heart out and left her feeling like she was nothing—you made her *into* nothing." A bitter smile curved Taneisha's lips. "Goal accomplished. She's gone now, man. You win."

When he reached out and caught Taneisha's arm, he didn't know who was more surprised, her or himself. The second she looked back at him, he dropped his hand, barely able to believe he'd even touched her. He was losing his mind. That's all there was to it. He looked at his hand for a second before looking back at her.

"Don't," he said, barely resisting the urge to rub his

hand against his jeans to wipe away the feel of another person's skin on his.

"Don't what?" she challenged. "Don't tell you what you did?"

"That's not . . ." He stopped, floundering for words. "I don't want her hurt."

"Hurt?" Taneisha stared at him. Then she shook her head. "You think she's hurt? You ripped her apart. She's loved you for years and you pretty much crushed her. All by not calling."

He clenched his jaw and averted his eyes, staring out over the river. It was dark and grey, echoing the overcast sky. "What's the fucking problem? I'm not even *hurt*." Hell, he'd been hurt worse than this by the time he was thirteen.

"The problem is you didn't think about her. Not once." Taneisha shrugged. "It doesn't matter. She said you two weren't talking and I guess that's a good thing, since this is how you feel about her."

"You don't know the first thing about how I feel." The words tore out of him before he even knew they were there. But he couldn't take them back.

A black brow arched over dark, knowing eyes. "Do you?" she countered. Cocking her head, she said, "Let me ask you this: If she was the one hurt, hurt or sick or scared . . . whatever, and she didn't call you, how would it make you feel?"

Something twisted in his heart and a feeling he knew all too well started to crawl through him. Shame. But this time, he deserved it and he couldn't blame anybody but himself.

"If you two are over, then you're over." Taneisha started to walk away. "But I don't look at either of you and see somebody who is *over* anybody."

David dropped down. He hit the ground and curled his arms around his upraised knees, staring at nothing. Vaguely he heard the roar of Taneisha's engine.

Then there was silence.

The noise from town sounded like it came from a tunnel.

Something pricked against his skin, but he ignored it. It was that weird, eerie feeling he'd had a hundred times. Like somebody watched him.

But he didn't care.

All that mattered was what Taneisha had just said . . . and Sybil.

You ripped her heart out and left her feeling like she was nothing—you made her into *nothing. Goal accomplished.*

"Fuck." He shoved the heel of his hand against one eye while images swam through his head.

Sybil's eyes, wide with hurt. *The bottom line is you don't want me enough. So fine. It's over.*

Are you really going to choose the past over me?

Somewhere off in the distance, he heard a siren wail.

Slowly, he lifted his head.

A siren.

But instead of rising, he just sat there. And waited.

"Oh, shit."

Jensen thought she might just get sick.

The uniform who'd been the first on-scene was Officer Luther Gardiner, and while the black man didn't look like he was getting ready to hurl his cookies, he looked pretty tight around the mouth.

Wanly she smiled. "That is a person, right?"

"Yes, ma'am." Then he grimaced. "Or it was."

He came closer and she hated to admit it, but he had

a stronger stomach than she did. Of course, he'd worked in Louisville for about five years before transferring here. Maybe he was used to scraping people off the pavement. Kneeling down just a few inches away from the bloody mess of pulpy skin, broken bones and blood, he blew out a sigh. "And I hate to say this, but I think it might be Clay Brumley."

Swallowing back the gorge, she glanced up at Thorpe. He looked as pale as she suspected she was. "Why?"

"The hair." Gardiner looked at the smashed skull. "Not many people had that reddish mess of curls."

Jensen had to breathe shallowly as she shifted her gaze to his head. Or what was left of it. If she was careful—looking at him without thinking about *what* she was looking at—she could see wiry ginger curls.

"Okay."

Backing away, she gave herself a minute. She didn't think she was being weak, not at all. She'd never seen a body so thoroughly destroyed before, save for the four-car pileup they had one New Year's Eve a few years back. A car full of drunken idiots had left Belterra, instead of letting the casino call a cab. They killed themselves and four others. Sorting out the body parts had been something of a nighmare and Jensen still had bad dreams about that.

Hearing the shallow breathing coming from just behind her, she looked over at Thorpe. He'd been on the job for less time than she had, and she realized he hadn't been there for that New Year's crash, either. "If you need a minute," she advised, "take it."

"I'll be fine." He set his jaw, focusing on the wall.

She didn't argue with him.

Her stomach was raw when she turned back to look at the body, the ruin of it.

"Well," she murmured, shaking her head. "One thing

is certain: If he was involved in Cronus, we won't have any shortage of suspects."

Gardiner slid her a smile grim with dark humor. "That's not helping."

"Well, there are other things I want to say, but that's unprofessional."

Rubbing the back of her neck, she looked around and spied the jewelry store across the way. "Thorpe. Go talk to the manager at Beringers. I want the security tape for the past twenty-four hours. If he gives you grief, tell him I'll be over there in five seconds flat and I won't be happy."

"Yes, ma'am."

As he walked away, she stripped off the gloves and then sanitized her hands. It didn't do shit to eliminate the stink of death that filled her nose, but she'd tried.

She wasn't done here, but she had a call to make.

They'd had plans.

After punching in a number she knew by heart, she waited until he answered.

"Hello, darlin'," Dean murmured, his voice low and rich, wrapping around her. It was like a brush of velvet and silk against her skin.

For a moment she closed her eyes and lost herself to it. A sigh drifted out of her before she said, "Hello back."

There was a brief pause and then Dean said, voice a little more brisk, "That isn't the voice of a woman who's going to be rushing back home anytime soon."

"You're a man of stunning intellect."

"No." Sardonic humor colored his words. "I'm a man who knows the difference between cop Jensen and my Jensen. It's all cop Jensen I'm talking to right now."

"Even cop Jensen is yours." Every part of her belonged to him.

"I know that. But cop Jensen has other priorities besides a naked breakfast in bed with me. As it should be."

She made a face. "Yeah." Darting a glance behind her, she watched as Gardiner continued marking the scene, his face set in an unreadable mask.

"We found him. We . . . think."

"Exactly what do you mean, you think you found him? Found who? Brumley?"

"Yeah." She mentally braced herself for what she had to do next.

"You don't know for certain, though."

"No."

Dean was quiet and then he said, "That won't be pleasant, then."

He'd been a lawyer in Lexington. He knew too much about the kind of work she did. Thankful she didn't have to explain, she closed her eyes. "No."

"I'd hoped you could come back here, get a decent meal in you . . . nap. She laughed, despite herself. "You mean you wanted to feed me, then fuck me."

"Well, yes. But then I wanted you to rest. You've barely slept the past few weeks. The past few *months*."

"Doesn't matter. I'll sleep when this is over. For now, I have to deal with this—take care of Brumley, or what's left of him. If it's him."

"Somebody got to him before the cops did." Dean's voice was grim. "Fuck, I hope I'm not going to have to go after that Sutter guy. He's already been through hell."

"You're not." Jensen shook her head, her gaze on the window. "He's . . . I think he's connected to this somehow, but he's not *involved* in it."

Hearing the approach of more cars, she peered around the corner. "The ambulance is here. I think I see the ME's car, too. I have to go. I'm sorry I'm missing out on brunch and '*spend the day naked*' plans."

"So we'll do dinner, and spend all night naked instead." His voice dropped to a low, smoky drawl. "Love you."

"Hmmm. Love you, too."

Then, as the phone disconnected, she turned back to the bloody, grim death that awaited her.

The wail of sirens faded.

The misery building inside him didn't.

David kept waiting for that rush of anger, because anger won out over pain any day. He'd nurtured the anger, giving in to that red rush of rage over and over again. When the pain crept too close, he'd blocked it off and turned to anger instead.

For twenty long years, he'd fed that ravenous beast and starved the misery.

That was how he'd managed to cut off almost all the emotion in his life. How he'd choked it out of himself, or so he'd thought. He'd been wrong, a fact that he'd slowly been forced to accept over the past few weeks. Since Abraham had died, and the fact had been driven home even more vividly after David had stood at the graveside as they laid Max to rest.

Abraham gone.

Max gone.

And now, according to Sybil's friend, she was gone, too.

Not *dead* gone, but still . . . lost. Lost to him.

It was a blow more crippling than he could imagine.

Because it hurt too much to sit there and just think about it, he surged upright and started to pace.

But the wide, open yard of Max's house felt too small, so David started to move up and down the sidewalk. Before he knew it, he was striding down Main Street, but even that wasn't far enough.

Sybil.

Gone.

Fuck—

Then he was running.

That pain was one he couldn't escape, and he couldn't outrun it.

He wasn't sure he could live it with it, either.

What is wrong?

He sat there for the longest time after the black woman had left. The woman was a nurse. She was familiar. Had taken care of Maxwell Shepherd.

Is she one of them?

She'd seemed to be kind to the man sitting in the yard, but now he looked . . . sad.

Abruptly he stood.

The look on his face was one of misery and rage.

Don't let him see you. Not yet. The voice of caution was strong, drowning out that insidious, taunting whisper.

Hidden eyes watched as he started to pace, first in the yard. Then up and down the sidewalk.

By the time he was heading into town, he was so far ahead, there was no hope of catching up with him.

His face was tortured. Angry.

It was that woman's fault.

She'd have to be dealt with.

Just like all the others who'd gotten in the way.

Taneisha finished the shopping before she called Sybil.

It was that or clue her in on the fact that she'd paid a visit to that big, beautiful bastard Sibyl had, sadly, fallen for. Once she'd packed all the groceries in, Taneisha *almost* felt calm, so she made the call.

"I'm on my way home. They drive you nuts yet?"

"Oh, that ship has sailed, my friend." Sybil's voice was just this side of despondent. "We went out to lunch. Fortunately, I was smart enough to tell Drew about David's . . . accident before we did, because Meg Hampton decided to drop by the table and chat all about it. Of course, David's now being hailed as a hero, but if I hadn't told Drew—"

All over again, Taneisha got pissed. "*He* should have told you. Then you could have told Drew before this." Swallowing back everything else, she blew out a breath and shot a look at the mirror before swinging over into the right lane. "Is he okay?"

"As okay as I can expect. You going to be home soon?"

"In about three minutes. Finished up grocery shopping. Where are you?"

"Ah . . . probably three minutes behind you. Want me to just bring Darnell home?"

"Go ahead." She was tempted to invite Sybil over, but she suspected it was a waste of air. If she knew Sybil, the woman would want some time alone.

"See you soon." They disconnected and Taneisha pulled up in front of her house. To herself, she started to mutter about David Sutter all over again. "What a fricking ass."

As she climbed out of the car, she used the key fob to pop the trunk. She glanced around out of habit, her gaze bouncing off the black work truck parked in front of the house next door. The woman sliding out of it didn't look familiar, but Taneisha didn't waste more than a glance on her.

How in the hell could that son of a bitch just brush Sybil aside like that? Yeah, yeah, she should *probably* be more patient, more understanding, but what the hell ever. Sybil loved him, and as far as Taneisha knew, Sybil hadn't fallen for anybody else. Ever.

Just him.

"Stupid fucking jerk. He ain't *ever* going to find somebody like her," Taneisha said to herself, hauling a bag out.

"Excuse me, but can you help me, please?"

She turned around. The only thing she saw was a flash of hair, a reflection of light.

Then pain exploded through her head.

Sybil caught a flash of light reflecting off something near Taneisha's house and she grimaced, tugging the sunglasses off her face as she went to press on the gas.

But her heart froze, blood going to ice as she caught sight of what was going on.

Taneisha—body still, limp.

Somebody shoving her into a trunk—

Black truck—

Laying on the horn, Sybil gunned the engine. The woman's head whipped around. For one second their gazes connected, and then the woman dropped Taneisha and took off running.

Instinct screamed at Sybil to jump out of the car, but she didn't. Instead she grabbed her phone. The boys were in the back, shouting, and then Darnell saw his mother, started to scream. Sybil just barely had the presence of mind to hit the child locks.

And all the while, she watched the woman.

In the truck now, and then, with a screech of tires, she was whipping down the street in reverse.

But Sybil could still feel those eyes. Muddy brown, dead like a shark's.

"Nine-one-one. What is your emergency?"

"I need to report an attack," she said. Woodenly she repeated Taneisha's address, still looking around for that black truck. It looked to be gone, but Sybil couldn't take the chance, not with the boys.

"Witnesses report seeing a black truck near this alley." Thorpe went over the list, his eyes studiously avoiding the board in front of him and the pictures. "Meg Hampton, in particular, reports seeing a black truck, one she says she didn't recognize, and a woman driving it."

Meg owned a salon a few doors down and she spent more time just outside the door than *inside*. She claimed she liked the fresh air, but people knew she just liked poking her nose in everybody else's business.

While Thorpe continued to detail information from the local business owners, Jensen slid a disc into the DVD player and leaned against the table.

On the far side of the wall, they had numerous corkboards. Three were mounted to the wall, but easels had been brought in for the others. They'd had to get yet another board for Clay. They were running out of office supplies, she thought grimly. Small town going broke trying to solve murders.

"Let's see what we can find on Beringers' security feed," she said, hitting the remote and fast-forwarding. She stopped every so often, checking the time stamp. As it edged closer to the time of the incident between Brumley, Redding and Sutter, she put it on regular speed.

People passed back and forth in front of the screen. A few stopped in front of the door, blocking the camera.

"Is that . . ." Thorpe murmured, more to himself than anyone else.

"Brumley." She gripped her arms in front of herself, watching as the man bolted down an alley. She checked the time. Minutes after the shots had gone off. That alley was two blocks from the police station.

"Somebody had been watching," she said softly.

A truck whipped down the alley, almost plowing into a work van. The color was something pale, indeterminate thanks to the imperfect grainy image, but she recognized the logo. Delivery truck. FedEx. She could track the driver down. They probably wouldn't remember anything.

Didn't matter.

The angle of the camera wasn't great.

She could only see the tail of the truck as it tore down the alley.

Her breath hitched, caught as the truck backed up. But it didn't come *out* of the alley. She could practically hear the wheels squeal as it lurched forward again.

And again.

And again.

She looked away after the fourth time. She watched the people on the screen, saw them look on with puzzlement before shrugging and carrying on.

"Somebody really wanted him dead," she mused.

Less than ninety seconds elapsed before the truck backed out, for good this time. The driver had long hair—the color, again, was indeterminate, and when she turned her head the shape of her face was impossible to make out. Jensen had the vague impression of soft cheeks, a softly rounded nose, but nothing more.

The driver checked traffic. Carefully. "A conscientious killer," Jensen murmured, feeling sick to her stomach.

"Very much so."

Startled, she looked up, realized the chief had quietly slid in behind them. His gaze lingered on the image of the truck that Jensen had frozen on the screen. "White female. Brown hair. That's about all we're going to get from this. I bet my left nut the feds wouldn't get anything more even if they tried."

"From this? No. From *this* . . . ?" Jensen smiled, then shrugged as she waggled the report she'd conned out of Pittenger a few hours earlier. "I got all sorts of juicy goods out of this."

Sorenson's eyes sharpened on the report and he strode over to her. There was a knock on the door and Thorpe moved to answer it as Sorenson started to read.

"Son of a bitch," he whispered.

"Yeah. Pretty much." A sour smile curved her lips. "And people say *we* are the weaker sex."

"Chief. Jensen."

The taut sound of Thorpe's voice had them turning.

Jensen looked at her partner, something in her gut going tight at the look on his face. *Ah, hell.* "What?" she demanded, one hand curling into a fist.

"Attack," he said, his voice flat. "Taneisha Oakes."

"What in the *f*—"

Thorpe lifted a hand and Jensen blinked, going silent. "She's alive. Dispatch has uniforms en route and EMTs are already there. Sybil Chalmers interrupted it and the perp took off . . . in a black work truck."

Something hot and excited slammed into Jensen even as part of her exploded into fury. She knew Taneisha— adored the woman. She was funny and smart and fearless—

"No." Jensen shook her head. "Something doesn't fit. She doesn't fit *any* of the profiles."

"She has to fit in somewhere," Sorenson said, nudging Jensen's shoulder. "There's a connection. Somewhere. Get to Oakes and find me that fucking connection."

CHAPTER SIXTEEN

Sybil wasn't there.

He paced. Up and down the sidewalk, hands curled into loose fists at his sides.

Sirens wailed up and down Main, but he ignored them. Not once was he tempted to follow.

If they had another one of those sick fucks, then they had him. Bell and Sorenson would deal with him. *Maybe—*

He stopped as that thought rolled through his head. No. Not a thought. A memory.

Don't start down this trail, David. There's nothing down it but death for you if you take even the first step.

Death. Death for who?

Max had told him that, not long before somebody had stolen him. Ended his life.

"You weren't talking about me killing those sons of bitches, were you, old man?" he whispered.

Now, looking back, he realized the truth of it.

Max had already known David could—and would— kill. But Max had also realized that David's soul was so broken, it wouldn't take much to push him over.

Maybe that's what Max had meant.

If David had focused on that road, and he had—

focused on the past instead of what he *could* have. Instead of Sybil.

And now here he was, once more feeling dead inside.

He'd thought that was how he wanted it.

Slowly, he looked up at Sybil's house; then he looked around. Up on Main an ambulance went flying by, and he looked away, a harsh shudder wracking him.

He needed the quiet.

Needed to think.

What he *really* needed was Sybil, but she wasn't here.

Absently he brushed his hand along the white picket fence in front of her house, and then he started down the sidewalk, shoulders hunched against the cold wind that had started to blow in off the river.

"I was impatient."

There was no answer, but the man she spoke to had been in the ground a long while.

She already knew why it hadn't gone the way it should have gone. She didn't need to hear any explanations or pray about it or think on her mistakes.

She'd been hasty.

Anger had guided her actions and now there were going to be consequences.

A face swam into focus in her mind and she closed her eyes, smiled despite the tears that ran down her face. It was all for him. Everything had always been for him.

She'd harmed that woman, her child had seen and that was an awful thing. She'd have to suffer for it, but she would suffer gladly.

She'd harmed the woman who had *hurt* him. Nobody had a right to do that. It was a tragedy that the child had seen, but that woman had brought that tragedy upon herself, *and* her child, by interfering.

"I won't fail this time," she whispered, rising.

After all, she'd made a promise. A long time ago. She would keep it no matter what.

"You can't talk to her." The doctor stood in the hall, his arms folded over his chest.

Jensen plastered her best smile on her face despite the fact that it felt like it would crack. "Two attacks, both involving a black work truck, in the span of twenty-four hours. There's evidence that the same woman was involved in *both* incidents and we also have evidence that this woman was linked to a third crime—" Okay, that was stretching it, but a woman *was* involved in *one* crime. Who was to say it wasn't this particular woman? Still smiling at the doctor, Jensen asked, "You want to have this hospital lined with bodies?"

"No." He inclined his head. "And I know Taneisha. If she *could* talk, she'd already be yelling at me to let you in. But I said you *can't* talk to her. She lapsed into unconsciousness in the ambulance. Once she wakes up and is ready to talk, I'll let you know. Until then . . ." He just shook his greying head.

"Once." Jensen closed her eyes. Denial screamed through her and she wanted to weep. Instead, she squared her shoulders. Crying wouldn't help Taneisha. Doing her job *would*. "Is she going to wake up?"

"I don't think I know a more stubborn woman." He eyed Jensen over the rims of his glasses. "Except maybe you. If anybody can pull through it, she can. Head trauma is tricky, of course, but she's young and she's strong."

Then Jensen was left alone to pace the halls.

"The good news is . . . thanks to you, Jensen, we've got four more names." Sorenson rubbed his tired eyes, checked his phone again. They'd all been doing the same thing for the past day and a half. Taneisha Oakes hadn't woken up. It wasn't a good sign.

"That wasn't me." She shook her head. "Hank Redding came in. Gave us the names." She grimaced. "Almost got shot for his efforts."

The four cops in the room sighed.

"Now we have one man dead, crushed by a mysterious black truck. He was connected to this . . . club." Sorenson's lip curled when he said it, like the word tasted foul. "Two of the men Hank named have already rolled. Shit, Gordon Cramer practically had a breakdown when they knocked, all but pissed his pants."

"He's been sleeping with a gun," Jensen said sourly. "Thinks he's the next one to go down. Like he's going to do much better in prison."

They shared a grim look, like they'd all been thinking the very same thing.

"Think any of them will shed light on who has been hunting them down?" Luther asked.

"Those idiots couldn't shed light on anything without the help of a searchlight." Jensen shook her head and went back to studying the board in front of them, now boasting four more names. Cramer had no clue about who had been hunting them like sick dogs. Pushing that aside, she focused on the other crime—Taneisha's assault. "A black work truck is seen at the same area where Taneisha Oakes is assaulted and almost thrown in the trunk of her own car."

"She doesn't fit the profile." Thorpe leaned forward, staring at the board in front of them. "Black woman, no husband. It's not like there's a connection to the club there. Her son isn't even in the age range. He's too young."

Jensen had to bite back the words that rose as Thorpe continued to think out loud. He was being a cop, just like he was supposed to do. "She also isn't from here.

Moved to town eighteen or twenty years ago. She went to high school here, but everybody else had roots here—their families have been around for generations. We've got no connection from her family to Cronus."

"There is a connection. Has to be." Luther Gardiner leaned in; his dark, normally serene features were tight. He was one of the few whom both Jensen and Sorenson had trusted to bring in to help with the mess they had on their hands. His eyes ran over the boards as though he could find that invisible line, if only he searched hard enough, long enough. "We're just not seeing it."

Jensen got up and grabbed a pen. "Let's look at this again."

Sybil slid into the narrow space available next to Taneisha's bed. The woman had no family, save for Darnell. Her mother had left her when she was young and her father had died a few years ago, up in Indianapolis. Rules or not, Sybil shouldn't be alone in here, but Darnell couldn't come in and Taneisha wasn't spending all these hours alone, in the dark.

"You need to wake up," Sybil whispered, holding on to Taneisha's hand.

Sybil listened to the low murmurs out in the hall and kept a firm grip as she started to talk. She didn't have a lot of time. She'd left the boys with Ali and Tate, but she didn't feel right doing it for long. She just had to come, see Taneisha with her own eyes. Know the woman was still alive. Still breathing.

"Wake up and tell me who did this so I can hurt her, okay?" Sybil said softly, her voice breaking. "Bad enough I'm losing David. I don't . . . I don't need to lose you, too."

The hand in hers tightened. Just a little.

A soft sigh escaped Taneisha.

"Neisha?" Sybil whispered.

A faint smile curled the woman's lips. "'M not goin' . . . anywhere."

"Oh, shit." Tears burned Sybil's eyes and she practically leaped from the chair, but Taneisha's hand tightened. "Oh, shit. Girl, you scared us. I . . . I need to get the nurse."

"No." Seconds ticked by and then Taneisha's lids flickered open. "Damn. Head . . . hurts."

"Let me call the nurse," Sybil said.

"In a minute." Each word was rough, but her voice grew steadier and Taneisha's eyes focused on Sybil's face. "Why am I here?"

"You don't remember?"

She went to shake her head and then winced. "No. Remember . . . talking to you. The store. Seeing . . ." She licked her lips. "Seeing David."

Sybil blinked and then blew out a slow, careful breath. "You went and saw David."

"Wanted to rip him a new asshole. The jerk." Then Taneisha closed her eyes. "He does care, you know."

A knot settled in Sybil's throat, but she swallowed around it. "We'll worry about that later. Fuck, you crazy bitch. I kind of hate you for scaring us like that. I need to call the nurse—"

"Fuck the nurse. I ain't going anywhere, you know." Taneisha's lids drooped lower, a sigh escaping her. "He's scared. That's all. Just scared. Being a man."

"Well. He *is* a man." Sybil forced a smile, tried to sound like it hurt less than it did, just hearing his name. "Come on now. Let's deal with you."

She pressed the button on the pad hooked to the side of the bed, ignoring Taneisha's protests.

A truculent look crossed the woman's face. Taneisha's voice was cross as she asked, "What . . . happened?"

A nurse came rushing in and Sybil moved out of the way as she answered, "You were attacked. Do you remember anything?"

* * *

If David never saw a cop again, it would be too soon.

He had too many thoughts in his head and things he wanted, *needed,* to say, but the woman he wanted to say them to wasn't anywhere to be found.

He'd driven by her place. Three times. Once yesterday and twice today.

He'd driven by her studio. Again, three times.

Then he'd come back here.

He'd almost called—about ten times—but what he had to say needed to be said in person, so he continued to pace. And wait. Maybe she'd taken Drew to Louisville for the weekend. Or Indianapolis. Maybe they'd gone to see Layla.

Sometimes Sybil took him out for little weekend trips. She'd invited David along, more than a few times.

Heart wrenching as he thought about it, he wished he'd gone. Even once.

That was probably what she was doing, spending time with Drew. But she'd be back soon. Tomorrow was Monday and there was school. So she'd be home by nightfall. If nothing else, she'd be home by then because she always took care of Drew.

But instead of brooding over what he had to say, he was dealing with a cop.

Again.

Jensen Bell glared up at him.

He glared back, debating shutting the door in her face.

She smacked a hand against it and wedged her foot in the opening to keep him from shutting the door.

"Taneisha Oakes was here. Yesterday. Why?" she bit off.

David blinked at her. "Why?"

"Shit, do you ever leave this place? Talk to anybody?" She shook her head. "Yank your head out of your ass. Turn on the news, the radio." She bent down and grabbed one of the papers piled next to the door. "Read a damn paper. She was attacked. It sounds like it happened not long after she left here. Why was she here?"

David took the paper, slowly unfolding it to see the headline. Another one caught his eye, though, and he read it, something pulsating behind his eye as he took it in. "Brumley is dead."

"Focus on the woman who was attacked after she left here."

David shook his head. "She was fine when she left. She came to rip my ass over . . ."

Jensen cocked her head. "Sybil."

David just stared at her.

"They are friends. Their boys are pretty tight." She bared her teeth in a mockery of a smile. "Not surprising T. came to lay into you. Equally unsurprising that you're clueless about their friendship. You probably never did much to learn jack about her."

He curled his lip at Jensen. He knew more about Sybil than Jensen could dream. But let her snipe at him. He deserved that and more. "What do you want?" he said, biting the words off.

"I need details. What time she was here, when she left, whether anybody was with her."

The way Jensen snapped off each question, the weird gleam in her eyes had him biting back the instinctive *fuck you* that rose to his lips. Cocking his head, he studied her for a long moment. "Around eleven. She wasn't here any longer than ten minutes. Nobody was with her. She got out of her car, yelled at me, then got back in her car and left."

"And nobody was with her?" Jensen demanded, agitation coming through. Normally, her voice was easy and level, and although his experience with cops wasn't particularly extensive, he had a feeling this wasn't her normal.

And that light in her eyes . . .

"What's going on?" he asked.

"I wear the badge. I get to ask the questions." Something flitted across her face and then, like a curtain had dropped, her features smoothed and when she spoke her voice was controlled, once more polite and easy. "Any chance somebody drove by, walked by?"

David glanced up the street, then down before he looked back at her. "In case it's escaped your attention, Judge Max picked a fairly quiet street." Other than this house and the burned-out hull that had once been the Frampton place, the street had no other homes. "If anybody had driven by, I would have seen." He paused, then shrugged. "But . . . there was something."

"Like?"

He looked away. "I didn't see anybody. But I've had the feeling somebody has been watching me."

"Watching you."

"Yeah." He looked back at her. "Off and on, for a few weeks. People are usually staring at me and I've gotten used to that, but this was . . . different."

"But you haven't *seen* anybody."

Lifting a brow, he calmly said, "If I had *seen* anything, trust me, I'd know."

Jensen studied him, adrenaline pumping in her. Yeah, he would have seen. And if he'd seen anybody walking around, he would have noticed that, too.

"Why haven't you mentioned this?" she asked softly.

He ran his tongue across his teeth and she could see him debating whether or not to answer. Then he just shrugged. "Honestly, because there's only one reason I can think of that somebody would watch me—one of those fuckers—and I could only *hope* he'd be that stupid."

"And you would just merrily wait."

He just watched her. Crazy son of a bitch. Except he was wrong. She debated on whether or not to tell him, although if he'd bothered to read the paper, he'd already know.

What the hell, Jensen decided.

"At this point, it appears Brumley was hit by a woman driving a black work truck. Descriptions are vague, but we know she's white, long brown hair. Age is harder, but probably over thirty, under fifty."

His lids flickered and something might have sparked in his eyes. Maybe.

She angled her head and tossed out the one thing guaranteed to grab his interest. "Taneisha is alive because that attack was interrupted. Again, a black truck was at the scene. A woman was trying to shove Taneisha into the trunk of her own car. A witness arrived—described the woman as probably in her forties. Pale skinned. Very long hair. Round face. Looked right at Sybil—" His pupils flared. Widened.

Gotcha.

"Sybil," he rasped. His face went hard and his blue eyes were colder than ice.

"Yeah. She showed up to save Taneisha, just in time. Taneisha's spent eighteen hours unconscious." She rocked on her heels and studied him. "You know, I didn't see it until now. We kept missing it. But that connection? It's there. It's got nothing to do with Cronus—that's a different mess entirely, and for some reason those attacks seemed to have stopped. . . ." She paused and narrowed her eyes on his. "I wonder if you could shed any light on that. But all these attacks lately? Yeah. There's a connection there, and you know what it is."

A muscle pulsed in his jaw. "Get on with it."

"Right in front of me. Max. Louisa. Brumley—although if he hadn't accidentally caught *you* instead of Hank, he'd probably still be alive. And then Taneisha. All the people who've died were connected to you."

"Am I under arrest?" he asked caustically.

"Oh, you're not the killer." She shook her head. "Somebody is killing them . . . *for* you. Now. Why don't you help me figure out who it is?"

"No." He shook his head as a dark, ugly knowledge bloomed inside his heart like a poisoned flower. "Not yet. First, you have to do something for me."

The cop sitting outside her house had Sybil scowling.

Benjamin Thorpe smiled at her as she told Drew and Darnell to stay inside the car. She'd thought that after picking up the boys she could come home and put them in Drew's room in front of the TV with pizza and a movie and she could camp out in the living room with pizza and a stiff drink.

Later on, chocolate just might join the pity party. She figured she needed it. Was maybe even entitled, although she tried not to go that route too often.

But how often did a woman end up with her sister in rehab, get pulled in to the police station because her lover *might* have something to do with a woman's murder, get dumped by that same lover, have her best friend get attacked and then have a cop camp outside her door? All within the span of a few weeks.

And that was on top of the crazy shit happening in town that had nothing to do with her.

Brooding over the rim of her rum and Coke, she stared at the blank screen of the TV.

If anybody was entitled to enjoy a drink, she was.

Careful, careful, a mocking voice in the back of her mind taunted.

Down that road lay trouble. Layla had ended up in trouble because she thought she was entitled to lots of shit.

Then again, Layla thought busting a nail was the equivalent of a worldwide catastrophe. Sybil had pretty much had the dreams she'd been quietly harboring over a period of ten years shattered, like someone had taken a hammer to them.

"Here's to me," she whispered before taking a healthy swig.

Then she set the cup down with a decisive *thunk*. She wouldn't have more than the one and she needed to keep her head clear.

Of course, now that she had a long, lean cop out in the car outside she wasn't sure if anything was going to let her sleep.

Why the hell was he here anyway?

But the longer she thought, the more nervous she got. The more anxious.

She tried to ignore it for about the first little while, but after that she gave up and told the boys she'd be out front. She hadn't even cleared the front porch before Benjamin Thorpe was unfolding himself from the unmarked squad car.

"Why are you here?" she asked shortly.

"Ma'am?"

She jabbed him in the chest with her finger. "Don't you *ma'am* me. I changed your damn diapers, Benjamin

Thorpe." Granted, she'd been all of eight at the time, but she'd still changed him. And once he'd peed in her face.

His face reddened, but to his credit, his polite *everything is fine* smile stayed in place. "Sybil, we're just keeping an eye on things. I'll be around here tonight, that's all." Ben nodded at her and then, as she heard the door creak open behind her, he lifted a hand to wave.

She didn't have to look to know that the boys had come outside.

"Tonight?" she asked calmly.

When he didn't answer, she folded her arms across her chest and lifted a brow. Waiting.

That look was the one that had Drew shifting on his feet, drove her sister insane. It was the look that had put more than a few Franken-brides in their places and had set the diva-prone teens Sybil dealt with down a peg or two during photo sessions.

Thorpe just hooked a thumb in his front pocket and smiled at her.

Damn. He used to be easier to rattle. Jensen was really taking the shine off of him.

Pushing her hair back from her face, she asked, "Just *why* are you hanging around here tonight?"

"Standard precautions."

"Yeah. Try that on somebody who was born yesterday, Ben." She continued to wait.

He lifted his hands. "I can't tell you any more. If you want answers, you'd have to talk to Detective Bell or Chief Sorenson. Although they are both busy." He gave her a slow smile. It still held a hint of that shyness she was used to from him, but it was more confident than normal. It probably would have had a lot of women feeling bad. *Wow. He's just a hardworking cop, doing his job.*

Narrowing her eyes, she pointed out, "You should

probably be busy, too. Too busy to be babysitting me. Yet . . . here you are."

"Yes, ma'am. I've got coffee and some food. I'll be just fine out here in the car, don't you worry." Then he nodded at her and headed for the car.

What . . . the . . . hell.

"How certain are you that it's her?"

David tried not to show any sign of what he felt inside. He'd kept his ass on the porch, even though what he wanted to do was lunge past Jensen and race to the truck, climb in and tear the town apart until he found Sybil and Drew.

He didn't do that, because first he had to do this. If it was her . . .

Fuck, why?

He thought back to years ago, remembered the way she used to smile at him, the shyness, then the humor.

That had all faded and now she just looked at him with grim purpose. Purpose. Like she had a set goal in life and nothing else mattered, save that goal. She'd accomplish it and there would be no deviations.

What's your goal?

But he had no idea. No clues. Just the sheer, insane workings of a madwoman.

"I'm not certain," he said for the fifth time. "You wanted to know if I had an idea. That's the only woman I can think of that fits that description. Now, instead of pestering me, why aren't you out there talking to her?"

"We are. I've got men heading out there to question her."

"And look for the truck?" If it was her, there would be evidence on the truck somewhere. He wanted to think it was wrong. A mistake. How could any of this be true?

"If it was her, wouldn't there be . . . evidence or something?"

"We're working on it," Jensen said, her voice patient.

It snapped what remained of his control and he surged upright. "Fine," he growled, shooting her a dark look. "You do that. *You* go work on it. I can't sit here and wait and answer the same fucking questions over and *over* again while I wait to see if she is the one out there jerking people around. I'm not going to let her hurt anybody else."

"Who else do you think could be a target?" Jensen tried to cut him off, and he just went around her.

When she tried it again, he crossed his arms over his chest and pinned her with a flat stare. "I'm leaving," he said softly. "You've got exactly one way to stop me." Then he dropped his eyes to stare at the gun she wore under her jacket. "That's your one way. Are you going to do it?"

"David, let me do my job," she warned.

"I already told you, go do it. I'm doing mine."

"How is running off half-cocked doing your job?" She whirled to glare at him as he went around her, keys already in hand.

"I've got very few people that I care about, Jensen. My job is making sure she can't hurt them, and she's already hurt too many." He hauled open the door to the truck, letting some of his fury bleed out as he did his best to tear the door off its hinges. He slammed it and glared at her as she came storming over. "Your job is to find her, stop her."

"Wrong." She curled her hand over the lowered window, eyes flashing. "Your job is to help me to do *my* job."

"Yeah, well. I guess I never learned that part. Better let go, Detective. You don't want me running over your toes."

"David. Why are you so certain it's her? Why would she want to hurt *anybody*?"

He shoved the keys in the ignition, turning that thought over in his head. He thought of the dead, flat eyes he'd seen when he looked at her, thought of the odd way she'd spoken over the past few months. The anger in her voice.

Then he shook his head. "I'm not sure of that answer yet."

Then he put the truck into drive. "But she was at the funeral the day we buried Max. She saw Louisa laying into me. I thought I'd just imagined it, but looking back, it was her, standing by the truck, just watching me. Why would she have been there? She didn't even like Max."

Jensen continued to clutch at the car. "Who did she like?"

"Sarah Yoder never did really like anybody, Detective. She's the most unhappy woman I've ever met in my life. Probably as unhappy a person as I am," he said softly. Then he nodded at Jensen's hand. "Let go or get ready to run."

Then he pushed on the gas.

She let go.

CHAPTER SEVENTEEN

I can't take your call right now. Please leave a message—

The sound of Jensen's voice mail—*again*—had Sybil ready to bite something. Instead, she waited for the beep and left a message. Again.

"It's Sybil. I want to know why I have your shiny new detective sitting out on my curb instead of either getting some sleep or out there figuring out who hurt Taneisha. Call me."

She hung up and lifted up her wine.

She'd called and left three messages in the past ninety minutes.

Somehow, she didn't think she'd be getting an answer.

The bedroom had been quiet for almost forty-five minutes and now she was left alone to brood and wonder.

Black truck.

She'd spent the evening reading the paper, including a short article about how David had pushed Hank Redding out of the way when somebody pointed a gun at him. Clay Brumley. And nobody was going to know just *why* Clay had wanted to shoot Hank, either.

Somebody in a black truck had run Clay over, killing him.

Taneisha's attacker had driven a black truck.

Sighing, Sybil rose and moved to the window, staring outside. "And now I've got a cop outside my house. Just what does this have to do with me?"

She rubbed the back of her neck as she studied the car, the light reflecting on the windows. She could just barely make out the darker shadow, and when she saw Thorpe move some of the nerves crowding inside her settled a little.

But not by much.

She wasn't going to feel a lot better until she talked to Jensen and figured out just what was going on here.

Scowling, she turned.

The glass she had in her hand fell from numb fingers when she saw the silent form standing in the doorway across from her.

*   *   *

Until he saw her, David hadn't realized just how tight that knot of tension had grown.

He still wasn't ready to believe what his mind was telling him. It wasn't possible.

But the facts were adding up. In some fucked-up world, it might actually be true.

In case that fucked-up world was *this* one, he had to take matters into his hands, but first he had to see for himself that Sybil was okay. Jensen had promised she'd put a cop on Sybil's house, but that wasn't enough for David.

Not that he'd told Jensen.

She'd told him that she'd be putting a watch on Sybil's house, that she had Detective Thorpe out there for a while, then Officer Gardiner would head out to see Sarah.

While they *talked*. Okay, they'd talked. Jensen could get her ass to work on finding Sarah. David would do the same. Jensen might not like it, but she didn't know Sarah like he did.

And he had to look at her. Had to see her, had to understand *why*.

But for now, across a room gone dark, all he could see was the pale oval of Sybil's face and the glitter of her eyes and need hit him so hard, he thought he'd die from it.

The glass fell from her hand, hitting the floor with a muffled thud, and a ragged sound left her throat.

Her mouth opened as he crossed the floor to her.

Leave.

That was what his brain said.

He'd only come here for one reason, to make sure she was okay before he took care of everything else. Maybe, just maybe, when that was done he'd be ready to look at other things, all the emotion and the knowledge that had been brewing inside him before Jensen had shown up at his house.

Sybil had been right.

He'd known it all along, but the thought of letting himself feel again—feel *more*—left him feeling stripped and bare and he just shut down at the thought of it.

But that was for later. First he had to make sure Sybil was safe. Drew was safe. That they *stayed* safe.

David had seen what he needed to see.

But it wasn't enough, he realized.

Nothing had ever been enough, not with Sybil. Time hadn't been enough. Sex hadn't been enough. The few stolen hours in the night hadn't been enough. Hearing her whisper his name hadn't been enough. The closest he'd ever come to *enough* had been a few days ago, when she'd whispered she loved him and they'd spent the afternoon wrapped around each other in that miserable excuse of a bed.

The closest he'd ever come to *happy* had been the day they'd buried his grandfather.

The day she'd told David she loved him.

"What are you—"

The rest of the words were crushed under his mouth as he caught her up against him. She tasted like beauty and pain and her and he thought he'd die if he didn't have more.

Walk away . . . from this. From her . . . How am I supposed to do that?

Her fingers curled into his shirt, and for one perfect moment she clung to him.

And then pain ripped through him as she drove her foot down on his instep before tearing away from him.

"You son of a bitch," she said, her voice low and soft.

Breath coming in heavy bursts, he stared at her.

"What in the hell are you doing?"

Losing my mind.

He almost said it. Almost. Then he just shook his head. He should leave. Fuck it all, he knew he should. Instead, he took a step toward her. "I had to make sure you were okay."

Her lip curled. "Why wouldn't I be?"

Taut, heavy moments of silence passed. They hadn't told her.

Closing his eyes, he tilted his head up while the anger pulsed and pumped through him.

Floorboards creaked and he slowly lowered his head, lifting his lids enough to stare at her through his lashes. Sybil was just a foot away now, and even in the dim light he could see the flush on her cheeks, the glitter in her eyes. "*Why* wouldn't I be?" she demanded again.

"Max. Louisa. Brumley. Taneisha." He said each name softly, watched as her lids flickered. "Each of them had a connection to me."

"But—"

She stopped. "Connected how?"

"Max was my grandfather." He turned away and moved to the window. Through the slats of the shades he could see the police car, but it didn't make him feel any better. After all, he'd gotten in, hadn't he? He had a key and the locks on the back door were solid, but would they stop somebody who really wanted in?

"Max?"

He turned to look at her. "Yes."

He waited. Sure enough, she spun away and started to pace. "Your grandfather. How?"

"My mother's father. My . . . grandmother, she and Max had a few nights together, and then she up and left town. Didn't come back until my mother was three or four. Neither Max nor Mary knew until then. Max and Mary got married before he joined the army." David shrugged, restless, thinking about how different life might have been for him, for his mother, for everybody, if Max had been involved in his daughter's life. He'd offered. He'd tried. But . . .

No buts. The past was just that. Over and done.

Brooding, David hooked a hand over his neck and focused on the floor. "He was my grandfather. I've known awhile. I've got his hands. His eyes. I saw a picture in his house and you see it, you can't miss it." Without looking away from the boards of the floor, he sighed. "He's gone, because of me. Louisa is dead, because of me. Because she was pissed off and yelling at me at the funeral."

"That's bullshit." Sybil's voice, cold and dismissive, cut through the tense silence.

Sliding her a look from under his lashes, David asked softly, "Is it?" Without waiting for a response he turned away. "Brumley shot at Hank, but I pushed him out of and I got shot. A few minutes later, Brumley is dead."

"And what about Taneisha?" Behind him, he could hear Sybil pacing, her feet whisper quiet on the floor. "*She* didn't try to kill you, even if she was pissed off at you."

"She was out at my place." Out at his place, where he'd felt that weird sensation of eyes crawling all over him.

"I know that," Sybil snapped.

At her words, he turned and lifted a brow.

She met his gaze dead-on. "She was there, but it's not like she tried to kill you." Sybil's gaze raked over him. "If she had, you'd look a little more battered."

That was entirely likely. But he shrugged and said, "Max didn't try to kill me, either."

For a long second Sybil just stared at him, and then she spun away, shoving her fingers into her hair, and tangled them there, tugging like it might unravel the problem. "I don't understand, David. Maybe I'm a little slow here, but I'm not following. Exactly what is the connection here and why am *I* supposedly in danger?"

He turned to look at her, standing there framed by the dim light filtering in through the window. It gilded her body with soft light, but her face was lost in shadow. Hunger swamped him. Need battered him.

Slowly, he crossed the wooden planks of the floor, stopping in front of her so he could look into her eyes. Reaching out, he curved a hand over her neck, half-expecting her to pull away.

She just stared at him.

"Max was an old man, lying in his bed, and somebody smothered him. You're asking me to help you make sense of somebody who could do that." He edged in closer, unable to ignore the siren call of her nearness. "Louisa was a nosy old bitch. I didn't like her, but in the end, she didn't matter to me. But somebody beat the hell out of her—she was beaten to death, Sybil. It's just that simple. Taneisha came and laid into me because I hurt you. And while Brumley sure as hell deserved to die, he's dead because he missed Hank and shot me. The connection is *me*." He rubbed his thumb over her lip. "Now . . . why else do you think you have a cop sitting in front of your house?"

Sybil curled her lip. "I don't see any reason for Thorpe to be sitting in front of my house. We're over, right? You don't want that *ugliness* from your life to affect mine," she said, her voice scathing. "Put out an announcement in the paper or whatever you have to do. You dumped my ass."

She curled her hand around his wrist, tugged his hand down until he no longer touched her.

The loss of contact was like a visceral pain. "Go on, David. You don't need to worry about me, okay? Thorpe is out there, and if I hear or see anything I'll call him, flash the lights or whatever. You don't need to concern your—"

The flash in his eyes was the only warning Sybil had before she was trapped between him and the door.

His hard body crushed up against hers, one big hand framing her face while the other was braced over her head on the door. "Shut up," he muttered.

She blinked, caught off-guard by the sheer fury in his tone.

Well, for about two seconds.

Then she shoved up against his chest. He didn't move. "Excuse me?" she snarled, remembering at the very last second to keep her voice down. "Did you just tell me to shut up?"

He boosted her up, one heavy, solid arm wrapping around her waist and hauling her up until they were nose to nose. "Yes. I said *shut up*, Sybil. Do I need to spell it out?"

"Put me down." She spoke the words through clenched teeth, something hot and heavy pumping through her. She wasn't sure if it was hunger . . . or rage. But under it all was misery. A knot formed deep in her chest and she curled her hands into fists to keep from reaching for him. "Do you hear me? Put me down."

He didn't listen and she balled up a fist and swung it out. He caught it in one hand, but since he had his other arm wrapped around her waist he couldn't block her other punch. In the end, he spun around and took her down on the couch, catching her wrists and pinning them over her head. "You son of a bitch," she hissed, bucking against him. "Get off of me and the hell out of my house. You don't get to do this! You . . ."

Hurt, angry words built inside her and she bit her inner lip to keep them from spilling out.

But then he touched his lips to the corner of her mouth. "Sybil . . ."

Squeezing her eyes closed, she thought, *No*—

In desperation she jerked her knee up, but he just rolled, moving off the couch and taking her with him until she sprawled across his chest. He still held her wrists. "You don't get to do this," she said again, her voice hitching. "You can't just walk away, break me like that, and then try to come back."

"You're not broken," he murmured against the hollow of her throat.

"What in the hell do you know?"

He turned his face toward hers and she heard it as he breathed in, like he was trying to breathe *her* in.

"You're too strong for that. For me."

Shows what you know.

She twisted against his wrists again. If she didn't get away from him soon—

He moved again, and this time she ended up on her back with him splayed between her thighs—and he'd let her wrists go. Groaning, she reached up, catching the heavily muscled torso as he settled his weight down on hers.

"Tell me to go." He said the words against her collarbone.

"I've already done that."

He flicked open one of the buttons on her sleep shirt. "Say it again. I should go. We can't keep doing this. It's not good for you."

That familiar ache spread through her. "I don't see why you get to decide that," she whispered, her voice sounding hollow, even to her own ears. "I decide what's good for me. Not you."

His lips brushed against hers. "You should be with somebody who makes you happy."

"I didn't spend ten years with you because you made me miserable, David." She sniffed, the ache in her chest expanding. "Well, not until recently. Recently, you've made me really miserable."

His thigh pushed between hers.

She shuddered at the feel of it.

He was right.

They shouldn't do this again. Because he wouldn't stay. If he couldn't *be* with her, all this was going to do was hurt her again. Break her.

But when he flicked open a button on her nightshirt,

and then another, all she did was open her eyes and watch him. When he pressed his lips to the skin he'd bared, she curled her hands into his hair and pressed him closer.

And when he stripped her nightshirt away, she was the one to urge him to his back and mount him.

If they'd have another night, she'd make the most of it.

She didn't tell him she loved him, though.

She'd done it once, stripped herself bare and watched as the shutter fell over his eyes.

No more.

He bucked underneath her and his fingers tightened on her hips, leaving bruises as he shuddered and came, her own orgasm crushing her in its grip. Tears burned in her eyes, and in her chest there was a bittersweet ache.

He lay on his stomach, face turned to stare out the window. He didn't remember when he'd picked her up and carried her into her bedroom, but he'd done it.

Now Sybil lay tucked up against him, one arm across his lower back as she slept. That he could take her touch was one of those little miracles he'd never taken for granted, one of those little miracles he didn't know if he could live without.

And now, as her body tensed, he had to brace himself.

She woke quickly, going from a soft, sleepy woman to alert and ready in the blink of an eye.

She sat up and he turned his head without moving anything else. Once he moved, this ended and he had to decide. Not just where to go, what to do next. But about everything. It hadn't been fair of him to come back here.

He shouldn't have done this and he knew it.

Lying there, staring into her wide, unreadable eyes,

he had to admit the truth. He'd never been able to think past the moment, not when it came to her.

She reached up and he tensed, breath locking in his lungs as she touched a mark, up high on his shoulder. It was an ugly raised ridge of flesh. He could remember, vividly, when it had been put there. The stink of scorched flesh flooding the air, his screams muffled behind cruel hands.

It was a brand. In the shape of a sickle, it was the mark of Cronus. *Their* fucking mark.

They'd put it on him the first night they'd dragged him down there.

"They still have you."

Stiffening, David went to pull away.

But, before he could, her eyes caught his.

She didn't say anything, didn't do anything to stop him.

Instead of pulling away, he fisted one hand in the pillow and just stared at her.

"How long has it been since one of them touched you?"

Shutting his eyes, he rolled away into a sitting position and sat up, his back to her. When the light, soft touch of her fingers ghosted over the mark, he tensed. She didn't stop. "Twenty years? More?"

Silent seconds ticked by. He opened his mouth to tell her, once more, to stop, but to his surprise, it was something else.

An answer.

"More."

The assaults had stopped right before his sixteenth birthday. The beatings hadn't stopped. If anything, *those* had gotten worse, but they'd started to talk to him, tell him how he was growing up. Getting older. Bigger. Stronger. Soon it would be *his* turn.

His turn—

Clenching his fist in the sheets, he thought about how often he'd thought about killing them. One by one. Himself. Doing both. But he'd been too scared, then. As a boy, he couldn't have done it. Once he was older, he could have, but Max had already done that job.

"Twenty years." David stared into the darkness as he spoke. "The last time my father raped me was the day before I turned sixteen."

Sybil stopped tracing the scar—the *brand*—on his back.

Her hand moved to rest on his shoulder and he reached up, covered her hand with his as he continued to stare outside. There was nothing to see, just the bright white paint of the fence he'd put up for her a few years ago. "It didn't end there. But that was the last time one of them—"

She moved then, sliding around to curl up in his lap. "I don't need to know this. Not unless you want to tell me."

Closing his eyes, he buried his face in her hair.

The curls blocked out the light, the room, the world.

Want to tell her . . . of the shame, the horror. They'd done their job well, teaching him to expect the pain, to almost need it—*hell. Almost*? He needed pain now. It was the one thing that centered him, and they'd done that to him, taught him to function on pain, to function *through* it.

No. He didn't *want* to talk about it.

"No." The word came slowly, through a throat gone tight and rusty. "I don't want to talk about this, not any of it. But they broke me down there."

"You're only broken if you let them *keep* you down there." Her hand smoothed down his shoulder. "You're still trapped, David. Still barely living. Don't let them do this to you."

He barely even heard the words. "They expected me to be just like them."

She stiffened in his arms then.

Looking down at her, he told her what he'd told no other soul. Oh, he knew the cops probably suspected, but he'd never told anybody. It was too ugly, too evil, to think about it. Saying it was even harder. "That's what it was. Their fucked-up, sick little boys' club was a family thing. They passed it down from father to son, uncle to nephew, grandfather to grandson. My father expected me to join—to be another one of the monsters. And if I had a son, they'd expect me to be one of them."

Her low intake of breath told him that she hadn't figured it out. A lot of people probably hadn't. When the trials started, more people would begin to understand, but for now there was speculation. There were lies and rumors and gossip.

But nobody really had the faintest clue.

Brushing her hair back, he met her eyes.

"My father was brought in when he was the same age I was. And I suspect the same thing of his father. It was one long, ugly cycle."

The sheer, utter horror of what he was telling her just froze her.

She couldn't think past it. She didn't want to think at *all*, but she couldn't shut this out of her head.

It hurt and it sickened and it infuriated.

His gaze, always so direct and unflinching, cut into her and she wanted to look away.

But she couldn't. If ever there was a time to meet that hard, blunt gaze, it was now.

"But you ended the cycle." He'd fisted a hand in her hair and she reached up, curled her fingers around his wrist. "You made it stop. That matters. Now finish the job. Get out of the hell where they tried to break you."

"I *am* broken," he said, his voice soft. "And I ruin everything around me."

Then he eased her off his lap and rose, moving to pace the bedroom.

His voice, so final, so steady and sure, was a slice against her already raw heart. "You're not broken," she said, fighting the urge to go to him. *Again*. She couldn't make him accept her love. She couldn't make him accept this.

And if he walked away . . . again . . .

If he couldn't break the chains of a past that was strangling him . . .

Tears choked her. She needed him. So much. She knew he needed her. But sex without anything more would slowly kill her. She needed more. And she knew he'd never let himself give anything more. That he was even here now was a shock.

Sighing, she sat up, reaching for the blanket, chilled to the bone.

"Why are you here?" she asked. It had been hours since he'd shown up and she knew he was convinced that she was in trouble somehow, but she still wasn't following. With her body aching from hard, bone-melting sex, her brain spinning from what he'd told her and her heart one giant bruise, she didn't know how she'd process what he had to say, but he needed to say it.

So she could make him leave.

But he continued to pace, like he hadn't even heard her speak.

"David." She said his name again, watched as this

time he came to a halt, turning to look at her. "Why are you here?"

Why are you here?

The soft question cut through the noise in his mind, but the thunderous torrent that followed wasn't really a welcome distraction.

Black truck.

Max . . .

Taneisha Oakes was attacked—

Without saying anything, he turned and moved out of the bedroom, looking around until he spied his jeans in a tangle a few feet away from the door. He snagged them and gathered up the rest of his clothes before retreating back into the bedroom. It was past midnight. If he could, he'd spend the rest of the night here, wrapped around Sybil. He could hope that she'd turn to him, again, and that he could hear her voice break as he made her come again.

Or maybe, those softly whispered words.

Words she hadn't given him again.

Not even once.

Could he have said them to her while she'd slept? It had been decades, maybe even a lifetime, since he'd given those words to anybody.

If he'd ever harbored any feelings of love for his mother, that emotion had died long before she had. *May the bitch rot in hell.* Some part of him wished she were still rotting down in that cellar, but the discovery of her miserable corpse had set in motion a series of events that would eventually be the downfall of Cronus, for good. So he couldn't really regret it.

He'd never told his father, but his father had been a monster.

His father . . .

Closing his eyes, he thought about that evil bastard.

It had been twenty years since David had seen him, climbing out of the car on the winding road leading out of Madison.

Max had seen the car, pulled over. It had started to rain. Blood had been pumping out of him.

Peter had that good ol' boy grin on his face. *I don't know what my boy has told you. . . .*

And Max had lifted the gun.

Peter had gone white.

After that, David's memory had gone black, fuzzing in and out as blood loss and shock settled in.

He didn't remember much of anything after that.

The first clear memory he had after Max had leveled that gun after his father had been when he'd been lying in a bed, staring up at a wooden roof.

"David?"

Fighting the urge to just go to her, he dragged his clothes on and started to speak.

"It's all about me," he said softly. "Whoever killed Max, Louisa, Brumley. Whoever attacked Taneisha, it's about me. I'm not just broken, Sybil. I'm poison." *But I'm going to fix it. I'm going to purge it. Just—*

He clenched his jaw. *Just what?* he thought, half-wild. *Give me time?*

She'd given him ten years. How much more time did he need to purge that poison, to cut out the diseased parts of himself?

"*You* are not poison," she said, her voice stark. Then she sighed. "But I can't make you believe otherwise, and I'm tired of trying."

The defeat in her voice ripped at his soul. *Give me time . . .* but he didn't have the right to ask. He had to find a way to make himself whole. To make himself better. If he couldn't do that, he didn't deserve her. *Fuck that.* He already *didn't,* but he sure as hell needed her.

"There. . . ." He cleared his throat. "We can't do this now. I came to make sure you were safe. I think I know who is doing this and I've already talked to the cops. But for now, I just—"

When he cut himself off, Sybil started to laugh. It was a sad, cynical sound. "Even when you try to open up, you can't."

The words cut deep gouges into his heart, but they were no more than the truth. "I can't do this right now," he said quietly. "I can't be here, around you, because being around me isn't safe."

He pulled his T-shirt on and then looked at her through the darkness of the room. "I won't risk you. Not for anything." He glanced up, as if he could somehow see Drew sleeping overhead. "You and Drew are all that matter— the only things in my life that really do. I won't risk it."

When he looked back at her, her eyes were sad.

"So go on then." She shrugged and tucked the blanket around her tighter. Her shoulders were naked, vulnerable in the moonlight, and he wanted to go to her, sink down and pull the blanket away, press a kiss to each shoulder, then lower, down along the swells of her breasts, tug at her nipples with his teeth and then go lower, lower . . . until the distance between them faded away and nothing but sighs and breathless need remained.

But Sybil kept her gaze downcast on the sheets.

And somewhere out in the dark night, somebody searched for him.

He could all but feel her, out there, slinking through the dark. *I never saw you,* he thought. *Why didn't I see you?*

"I have to go," he said, his voice rough. *Before she finds me here.*

"I already told you to go." Sybil looked up then and her eyes, sharp and cutting, met his. "I need to tell you something, though."

She slid from the bed and David felt the hair on the back of his neck stand on end. Her feet made no sound as she came to him, wrapped in white, her hair a dark mass down her shoulders. The shadows wrapped around her and her eyes glinted at him as she came to a stop just inches away.

"When you leave here," she said, her voice soft and sad, "I want you to understand something."

He reached for her hand, twined her fingers with his.

She squeezed and lifted his hand to her mouth and kissed it, her lips soft on his rough skin.

Then she looked at him, her eyes honest, direct. And so full of pain, he would have done anything to take it away.

"Don't come back," she said quietly.

He tensed.

She pulled her hand away and turned her back. "I love you," she said, the words spoken to the darkened room around them. She didn't look at *him* this time. It hurt more than he'd thought possible. "When you leave, just stay away. I don't care what the reason is and I don't care how much trouble you think I might be in. Tell Jensen, tell Noah, skywrite it, I don't care. Let somebody else get the message to me. I'll take care of Drew, and myself. But if you can't come back to *stay*," she said, turning to look at him over her shoulder, "then don't come back at all."

"Sybil . . ." Her name fell from his lips on a rasp and he had to fight the urge to go to her, haul her back against him. *Not now!* He wanted to snarl it, wanted to shake her. He understood now. He couldn't be without her. He needed her, and fuck it all, he *did* love her. But now this, none of this could be discussed when he stood there with a target all but vibrating on his back.

He shouldn't have come at all, and if he hadn't panicked he would have figured that out already.

She looked at him over her shoulder, that white blanket falling around her like a queen's robes. "I understand you. Better than you think. You want to protect me, despite the fact that I don't *need* your protection. My sister is a junkie—both Drew and I are used to talk. We know how to handle it. He's heard it since he was a baby. He's already come home asking me what a whore is, because that's what his mama is—or so he's been told. Drew knows what *rough* is. *I* know what *rough* is—we were the town trash, in case you don't remember." She looked around the house she'd been slowly fixing up, remember how it had been all but falling down around their ears when their father had died, leaving Mom alone with two young girls.

"If you think you're protecting him or *me* by staying away, you don't know shit." She shook her head and moved to stare outside. "What you're doing is just taking the easy way out. That's fine. You've had it rough and maybe you need easy. But don't think we can keep this up. I won't keep waiting."

Easy—none of this was easy.

Just give me time . . . he almost said it. Then and there.

But he couldn't. He had to have something to give her. Something solid. Something real. He wasn't there yet. Since he couldn't offer her anything, he just continued to stand, head bowed, feet on the floor.

Her silence nearly sent him to the floor.

The odd, shaking sigh all but gutted him.

"Sybil," he whispered, his resolve trembling. "You know I care about you."

"Care?" She laughed, the word bitter and ragged.

"David, you are a stupid ass. You love me, every bit as much as I love you. You just aren't willing to take the risk. And I'm not going to wait around for a coward."

She turned to look at him then and he held still as she came to him.

Yes, I love you. The words were right there. He could say them. Almost did. He could nod, pull her against him, show her in a dozen ways. But not until he knew he'd done what he could to keep her and Drew safe. That wouldn't happen until he'd stopped things, found answers.

So instead of reaching for her, he held still as Sybil stopped in front of him. He held still as she pressed her lips to the corner of his mouth.

"I hope you find it somewhere, David," she whispered.

It wasn't until she was halfway to the bathroom that he asked, "Find what?"

"Whatever it is you're looking for."

I will. He watched as the door shut behind her. One hand clenched in a fist and he had to fight not to pummel something. Anything.

I'll find it. Then I'm coming back here, damn it.

This wasn't done. It wasn't over.

He'd come back, and even if he didn't come back *whole* he'd at least have enough pieces of himself that he could try to make them fit. It was the only acceptable outcome.

The silence in the room echoed through him like a death knell and he hunted down the rest of his things, shoes, socks, keys. In under five minutes he was ready, but at the door he lingered.

You saw for yourself.

You know she's safe.

It wasn't enough, though. Without thinking it through, he moved upstairs, avoiding all the little spots that made the stairs squeak. The door to Drew's room was open and David lingered there, a hand on the doorjamb, his gaze on the boy in the bed close to the door.

A quick look inside told David that the boy slept. Sprawled across a blow-up mattress was the skinny form of Taneisha's son, his face half-shoved under a pillow. The slow, quiet cadence of the boys' breathing filled the room and David stood there nearly an entire minute before he pulled away.

He wanted to go in there, he realized.

Wanted to wrap his arm around Drew and hug him. Just once.

Before he left.

Instead, he just moved downstairs. As he did, he saw the door to the library open, caught a glimpse of Sybil. But he just kept right on walking, out the back, down and across the yard.

It was dark. It was cold. But he'd spent plenty of nights in the cold.

He'd didn't leave yet. He didn't leave for hours. He settled himself in a corner, on the ground, braced against the cold. From there, he could see the back windows— exposed panes of glass, the most vulnerable area in the house, he thought.

He stayed there, kept watch.

Once the sun kissed the horizon and he could see Sybil moving around, he unfolded his stiff, aching form. That was when he left. Dawn. The perfect time to find the woman he needed to see anyway.

CHAPTER EIGHTEEN

The farm was . . . quiet.

Almost neglected.

David walked around, the work boots he hadn't fully broken in crunching on leaves that hadn't been raked away. The gardens were overgrown. It was mid-November. Winter was breathing down their necks and Sarah hadn't even cleaned up the dead vegetation, much less started preparing the gardens for winter.

That alone sent a weird little chill down his spine.

But then he went inside and saw the layers of dust.

He could see where she'd been here recently, cooking, yes. There were dishes in the sink from a recent meal, but she hadn't even cleaned them.

That was just about unheard of.

There had never been a day in this house when it was less than spotless, not that he could recall.

The gardens had never gone untended.

And even though it was early and there were morning chores to be tended to, animals to be cared for, Sarah wasn't there. An air of melancholy hung around the place. He could hear the chickens outside and horses from the pasture closest to the house, but that was it.

There wasn't a soul nearby.

Prowling through the house, he searched for some sign as to where she was.

A note would have been nice.

David/Caine:
  I'm in town. I'm looking for you. I killed Max and Louisa and Clay Brumley and I'll tell you why. Just find me at . . .

Disgusted with himself, he left the big room near the front of the house and checked Sarah's bedroom, frowning as he moved around. It looked even more abandoned than the rest of the house, the layers of dust so thick, it was like she hadn't been in here in weeks.

He checked the room where Abraham had slept, but to his surprise it was cleaner than the rest, almost dust-free.

Something tugged at his gut, and unable to ignore that nagging sensation, he headed outside. The house he'd lived in was about a twenty-minute walk up the hill. Twenty minutes he couldn't spare, and it would take longer to drive. So he didn't bother. He hopped the fence and moved up to Bill, the horse he used the most when he had to ride. Bill nudged him in the chest and he stroked a hand down the black-and-white gelding. "Come on, boy. I need a ride."

He didn't bother with a saddle, just mounted up bareback, glad that was one thing he'd learned over the years. The ride to the quiet little house where he'd lived took just a few minutes.

That creeping sensation of dread got worse as he opened the door.

Here there were signs of life.

"Son of a bitch," he whispered, moving inside and turning in a slow circle.

The place was pristine. No dust. Nothing out of place.

Blood roared in his ears and he moved down the short hall to stand in the doorway of his room. The headboard and frame he'd built along with Abraham was still there.

And the quilt Sarah had made a few years ago was spread out along top of the mattress.

Closing one hand into a fist, David stared at that quilt for a long, long moment before moving deeper into the room. Her dresses hung where he'd once kept his clothes. His gut twisted a little tighter when he saw a pair of jeans and a small stack of T-shirts. "What are you doing, Sarah?" he whispered.

He went to turn away, but something on the shelf caught his eye and he reached up, grabbed the box.

It was hand carved, but he didn't think Abraham had made it. It didn't look like the old man's work. Flipping open the lid, David found himself staring at a stack of old photos, a couple of newspaper articles that were yellowed, worn with age. Reaching in, he pulled the stack of items out, and closed the box. Tucking it under his arm, he started to go through everything as he left the room.

The first picture was of a man—his eyes were familiar, but David didn't know him. He had a girl in the picture with him. Both of them wore the plain clothes typical to the Amish. The picture wasn't posed. The Amish didn't own cameras. David didn't know if somebody had snapped the Polaroid and given it to the man or what. Flipping it over, David saw spidery print down at the bottom: *Jacob Miller and daughter Sarah—*.

"What the fuck?" David flipped the picture over again, staring at it. Hard.

Maybe. The eyes? He looked at the man, but it was hard to say.

Dumping everything on the counter by the sink, David tossed that picture down and reached for another. It was Sarah, just her, a few years older, walking through Madison. The back of the picture this time just read: *Sarah*.

The newspaper article had been torn out of a paper. David couldn't guess at the *exact* time, but considering what was mentioned, he had a guess.

Soldiers return home from Vietnam.

His eyes narrowed on two of the names mentioned.

One of them wasn't a surprise. Max . . . David had always known that Max had been in the army. But the second name—

"Caine."

He turned at the sound of the familiar voice. Thom Yoder stood there, his eyes solemn, his face unsmiling.

"What is this?" David demanded, ignoring the name Thom had used as he strode over and shoved the article in the younger man's face.

Thom flicked a glance to it and then looked back at David. There was a flicker of resignation on Thom's face, but no shock. No surprise.

"What is this?" David demanded again.

"It's an article about Uncle Abraham. Before he came back to us."

David closed his eyes, rubbed a hand over them and then opened them, looking back down at the article again, reading it over a second, then a third time. "Before he came home. What in the hell are you talking about?"

Thom's face spasmed and he looked away. A long, tense moment passed and then he sighed. "He was born here, raised here . . . until he was nine years old. But then his father decided to leave, with him. They left and nobody saw him, heard from him. Twenty-five years passed before he returned here. He'd fought in the war, killed people." A shadow passed over Thom's face before a sad smile softened his grim features. "But they also taught him to save people. He was trained to be a medic, and he met Max Shepherd. Which is how he was able to help you."

Thom lapsed into silence then and David turned away, a thousand questions storming inside him. His chest burned and he realized he hadn't been breathing. "This . . . none of this makes sense."

"He needed peace. His father had been a troubled, sick man. Then, once he was old enough to leave that behind, he was forced into a war that went against what he'd learned as a young child—he remembered those lessons—and there was he was, surrounded by death, blood, violence."

Turning, David looked at Thom. Thom stared out the window into the cold, grey morning. "He came back here, wanting this life, wanting that peace."

That was something David could understand. But too many questions remained. "He met Max in Vietnam?"

"Yes." Thom sighed and reached up, stroking a hand along his beard. "He'd been living in Louisville before he was drafted. He didn't like to speak of it, but he did, a few times, because people talked about how he'd lived much of his life away from us. I had questions. We all did."

Memory flickered, formed. "Max has medals in his house. I saw them. Others talked. . . . He was in the Special Forces. Are you telling me that *Abraham* was in the same unit? That he was in the Special Forces?"

"He had a great need for peace, Ca—David. I can imagine you would understand that better than anybody." Thom's voice was soft, so soft David could barely make out the words.

At first, David didn't think that was any answer at all.

But then he realized, perhaps it was. A man like Abraham would need a great deal of peace if he'd lived the life that David suspected Max had lived before he'd left the military behind.

Max had found the answer in the law, in the laws, in helping others.

Abraham had looked elsewhere. Back here, to the place where he'd been born.

Reaching down, David picked up the picture of Sarah and turned it around, showing it to Thom. "And this? How does she fit in?"

"That is a much more complicated story." Thom looked around, moving through the house with more than a little trepidation. "The box. You found it here?"

"Yeah. It was in . . ." He hesitated and then finally said, "My room. It looks like Sarah has been staying here."

Thom stopped in his tracks and looked back at David, troubled. "Staying here."

"Yeah. Where does Sarah fit in? Is this her? Why does it say *Miller* on it?"

Thom looked down at his boots for a long moment before he finally looked up. When he did, his eyes were full of sorrow. "Because that is who Sarah was before Abraham took her. Sarah's father and his father were cousins. He once told me they both had a . . ." He passed a hand over his head, shaking it. "He said they were unwell. Here."

"Unwell." David curled his lip. "You mean *crazy*."

Thom inclined his head. "Don't be unkind. We don't understand what was wrong."

"*You* don't." David shook his head, staring off into nothing as he recalled the way Abraham had spoken to him, late into the night. *You must understand, son, what they did to you wasn't your fault. You must . . .*

The words had run together after a while.

But Abraham had all but drilled those words into David's head.

"You may not understand," he said, his voice gruff. "But Abraham did. He knew more about the evil, the shit that can go wrong inside a man's head. How messed up a person can get and how cruel and evil they can be."

For a long moment Thom was quiet, and then he nodded. "You're right. We don't understand, although I think, because of Abraham, we understand better than others. Jacob was unwell. Many people suffered because of it, but they all turned their backs, turned a blind eye. Sarah suffered for it—that is why Abraham left."

Why Abraham left—

Pieces clicked together.

Abraham Yoder and twelve other families had broken off from the larger community that made up most of the Amish population in this small county. That had been years ago, before David had come here. They'd formed their own district. A new bishop was chosen. A few new families drifted in, from either the other district or other states, and they had grown. David had never known what exactly caused the rift.

Until now. "That was all about *Sarah*?"

"No." Thom shook his head. "It was about her father. About Abraham's father. About things they had done . . . and how the other families just turned a blind eye. Abraham saw it—his uncle, his father's brother, had struck her so hard, she fell down, broke an arm. Abraham intervened, but they would have allowed her to go back home to him. Abraham wouldn't allow it. He took her to get her arm set. There were questions and he answered them. Police came. I don't know what happened—this all happened before I was born, but he told me once I was old enough. The police spoke with those who had seen, spoke with Sarah's father, Jacob. Eventually, they decided it was an accident."

"An accident." David clenched a hand into a fist. "How could—"

Then he stopped, looking away. Who knew that answer better than he did? People will often find a way to rationalize the things they didn't like to look at. "What happened?"

"Abraham took Sarah. He just walked into the house and carried her out. When Jacob tried to stop him, Abraham put her down, turned around and struck him. Others tried to stop him, but he warned them he'd put just as many on the ground. He wouldn't leave a child there to be abused, and he wouldn't be stopped." Thom paused for a long moment, and then he sighed, shaking his head. "Nobody attempted to stop him and he picked up Sarah. He told them that there was discipline and then there was cruelty. He wouldn't stand by and watch a child be abused. It was time for things to change."

"Change doesn't come easily." David could picture it, so easily. It was something he could see Abraham doing, even striking a man to defend a child. He'd try other ways, first. Abraham was a man of peace, but he was also one who would do much to protect the innocent. David had seen that with his own eyes. "They wouldn't change."

"No." A sad, bitter smile canted up Thom's mouth. "I heard from one of the men who came to us later—he said Jacob seemed possessed, raged like he would kill Abraham, and they had to physically restrain him to stop him. He . . ."

Thom stopped talking for a long, quiet moment, and then, as if the words were dragged from some dark, ugly place, he said tightly, "He killed his wife. That is not what they say, but it is what happened. She was found facedown in the pond behind their house a few weeks later and there were bruises around her neck. Jacob killed himself. If they hadn't protected him, his wife would be alive. Several families left with Abraham and others followed in later weeks. You know much of the rest."

David nodded, lowering his gaze to study the picture of Sarah. "And he raised Sarah as his own."

"Yes. He loved her like she was his own—to Abraham and Ruth, Sarah *was* their child. She would have been seven, I think. My older brother said she was odd in the first few years and then it was like she became a different child. She talked more. Played."

Thom moved to stand by David, going through pictures and newspaper articles. "I don't know where she found much of this. I didn't know she'd even remembered."

"How do you know about it? About any of this?"

Thom slid David a wry look. "You might not be curious about things and you might not like to talk. But I ask many questions."

She wouldn't have forgotten all of it, David suspected. Some part of you always remembered that cruelty. That pain. That misery. Slowly, he put the picture back inside the box, tucking it away. Then he covered it up with the other pictures and articles. One small square floated free and he picked it up, went to toss it in the box, but as he did it flipped over and he found himself staring at his face.

It was a close-up. A recent one. He even knew when— those dark clothes weren't anything he'd worn out around town. He'd only worn them once in fact.

The day of Max's funeral.

She'd taken a picture of him, put it in her box of secrets.

It flooded him with foreboding.

My older brother said she was odd in the first few years.

He said they were unwell.

Alarm screamed inside David's head. Looking up, he met Thom's eyes.

"Where is she?"

Thom looked away, his voice grim and flat. "I was hoping that perhaps you could tell me."

The first time she saw him, she loved him.

Nobody could understand him, his pain, his suffering or his trials, the way she did.

He'd come to her bleeding and broken and she'd helped ease his misery.

He was still broken and he'd come to her . . . soon. She'd help him, like she always did. She'd make sure he understood this time. *I should have told him*, she thought. Always she'd kept those secrets hidden within her heart, and that was her failure. She'd never let him know, but she wouldn't hide it anymore.

Not now.

But first . . .

But first she had to cut all the ties that tried to pull him away from her.

Because she'd been so impatient, so rash, she had to be more careful now.

She'd left the truck, parked inside one of the older barns. There was no way she could drive it, not now. People had seen her, seen the truck. She'd cleaned it. She knew how to take care of that. It gleamed now, but she couldn't risk anybody seeing the truck again.

She had to wash the clothes, hide them away until she needed them again. But she'd do it later. Other things were more important now.

In her simple dress, with her hair pinned up, she felt

more focused. Felt like herself. If people looked at her now, their gazes would just bounce away like they always did.

It had been different wearing the other clothes, wandering around with her hair hanging free down her back. *Wicked.* It had felt wicked and thrilling, but it had been for a purpose and it wouldn't do any good to appear in public that way now.

Not after seeing the paper. She'd seen a copy on the way into town when she stopped to fill up the gas tank. With a dry mouth and shaking hands, she'd read the article about Clay Brumley's death, Taneisha Oakes' attack. People were looking for her. Nobody had really *seen* her. A blond woman, between thirty and fifty years old, a black truck. *If you have information, please call the Madison Police Department.*

The police. They wanted people to call the police?

She was just doing what needed to be done. But people might not understand that, so she'd have to be careful. She understood that. It wasn't safe to pretend to be anything other than who she was now. Just Sarah.

She'd finish everything up now, but she'd do it as who she was.

Just Sarah.

It is more dangerous. She tried to push the fear away, tried to quell that whisper, because she knew it didn't matter how dangerous it was. She'd do it all over again to protect him, to get him away from those who would come between them.

He'd understand. Once they spoke. She knew she could make him see.

I had to do it. Sometimes even the very meek must turn into the lion. Abraham had done that for her. Now it was her turn.

Abraham . . . something bitter burned in her heart and

tears stung her eyes. *He was your lion. You became his Judas.*

"No!" She shook her head, wishing she could cover her ears to block that voice. But she was driving—driving because her beautiful Caine had taught her. Even though the others wouldn't have approved, he'd taught her, given her this measure of freedom.

She'd done it for him, for Caine. She'd done everything for him.

Abraham was gone because he'd tried to stand between them. Because he hadn't understood.

"I didn't want to do it. But he made me."

Forcing herself to stop thinking about it, she looked around, startled to realize she was already there. It seemed like she'd just turned the massive old car onto the road.

Her hands shook as she climbed out of the old car, easing the door shut. It was mid-morning, but this street was quiet. She left her car there, two streets away from her destination. She couldn't park any closer, not if people were looking for her. They might recognize the car or somebody could notice the license plate. All these people did was gossip and talk about one another.

Since she couldn't expect people *not* to gossip, she didn't want to risk having her car closer.

It was an older car but clean and well cared for. The strip of buildings on this side of the street heading down toward the hospital had once been homes, but they'd been converted into offices, many of them for doctors. Her car shouldn't gain much attention here.

Her hands shook as she shut the car door and moved to the sidewalk. Blood crashed, roared in her ears. This was the very last thing. The very last.

Then we can be together.

The longing she'd held inside, the answer to every

prayer she'd prayed for years. Her heart knotted in her chest, just to imagine it all coming to pass. She clasped her hands in front of her as she crossed the street. Sarah casually checked up one sidewalk, then down the other. Somewhere close by a door opened and she heard voices, but she didn't look back.

There was nobody in front of her and that was all that mattered.

One more street.

And then she was there, closing in on the house where Caine's whore lived. It was a pretty house, old, with two stories and windows that needed to be washed. *Lazy, then, as well as immoral.*

You deserve so much better, she thought, the ache spreading through her heart as she moved slowly down the street. There were no cars. She saw nobody as she closed in. Sybil's car wasn't in the driveway. Sarah had been watching her, learning when she left the house, when she returned.

Right now, the woman would be at the office where she worked, instead of being here and caring for the boy who lived with her, caring for the house.

Sarah's heart thudded in her chest and she moved up the narrow path to the driveway, around to the privacy of the backyard, certain that somebody would say something.

But the air remained quiet. Nobody came rushing to look for her.

She waited there, a full twenty minutes, her back pressed up against the small garage. From there, she could see the driveway, see the windows of Sybil's house, but none of the other houses. If she couldn't see those houses, they wouldn't be able to see her.

When those twenty minutes had passed, she breathed out a sigh. If somebody had seen her, they would have already called the police. Still, even though she knew that, her belly was twisted into knots as she moved up closer. She hadn't seen any of those signs that might indicate an alarm system. She knew about those. Nothing like that was needed at home. Nobody *there* would need them. They respected one another too much to ever need such a thing. But here, with the English, who knew what to expect?

She held her breath as she turned the doorknob. It was locked. She expected it to be, so she moved over to the window. She didn't want to break anything if she didn't have to, but she would. All the kitchen windows were locked. Frustration mounted as she backed away and looked again.

There—

She saw the basement window and hope flared back inside her heart. The first one was locked. So was the second.

But the third . . .

She breathed out a sigh of relief as it gave under her hands. *Thank You*, she said silently as she eased back to study the window. She needed to go through feet first. She poked her head in first, waited, listened. There wasn't any sound, nothing to indicate a dog, anybody inside the house. She whistled softly, waited. There wasn't so much as the clatters of nails against the steps. *A dog would be very bad*.

Her heart hammered so hard she thought she might be sick, as she started to wiggle through the window. It was a tight fit, her dress catching as she worked through, having to force her hips and then twist to get her breasts and shoulders through.

Panting by the time she got her feet on the floor, she struggled to fix her hair, straighten her *kapp*. Blood roared in her ears, making it hard to listen to the silence of the house. Hurriedly she moved across the floor and pressed herself to the wall, eying the steps, half-expecting to see a shadow.

It was mid-day. Nobody should be here.

But what if somebody was?

The steps were silent; the lights remained off. Slowly, her heart rate returned to normal and she smiled, peace spreading through her like a river. *A sign. Another sign.* Every time she'd taken a step to bring Caine back to her, she'd feared getting caught, feared somebody would see her, bring things to a stop. But it hadn't happened. God smiled on her. He knew that Caine should be with her—He *wanted* it. Nothing could come against her, not now.

Closing her eyes, she lifted them to the ceiling, imagined she was standing behind her home, with the endless expanse of sky spread overhead, the trees off in the distance and the sound of birds and the voices of her family the only thing to disturb the peace. *Soon.*

Soon they could both go back to that peace they'd known only there. When they were together. *Before* he'd started spending so much time here, where all that evil had broken him, nearly destroyed him. She'd escaped such evil before, had all but hidden inside herself and died. He'd been like that, half-dead inside, going through the motions of life, but inside, his soul was withered and grey.

He'd come back to life because they found each other. If he left, he'd lose that. Sarah loved him too much for that to happen.

"Give me strength."

"Sarah hasn't been home much." Thom glanced down the hill, his gaze lingering on the quiet farm. "As you can tell. We're doing what we can, but we have so much to do with our place and nobody seems to know where she has been."

Thom grimaced as he looked back at the little cabin, studying the clean counters, the dishes. "Until now." His shrewd gaze settled on David. "What is going on?"

David didn't tell him. How could he tell the younger man that his cousin might be a killer?

Not might. Is. One who had probably been warped as a child, if Thom had been even remotely on-target on the man who'd raised Sarah when she was younger. David couldn't call the unknown man Sarah's father. Abraham had been Sarah's father, in all ways that counted. But the man who'd donated the sperm had likely done too much damage.

Had bred a killer.

You're not broken, Sybil's voice echoed from the back of his mind. Clenching a hand into a fist, he gave one last, lingering glance around the cabin and then he turned away.

Maybe she'd been right. Maybe he wasn't as broken as he'd thought. Sarah was broken. And he'd been blind, because he'd never seen it.

Tension knotted at the base of his neck as he headed out. Bill waited for him and he swung up, eyeing the other horse. Not everybody rode, but Abraham had loved horses and had taught Sarah and his many nieces and nephews to ride early on. When David came here, he'd been taught as well.

Thom's dappled grey stood there patiently and the younger man swung up into the saddle before looking over at David. "You haven't answered me."

"No. I haven't." Clicking to Bill, David nudged him around, and they started down the hill. But instead of heading toward the house, he headed for the barn. The empty barn—Abraham's car should be there. One of the bigger differences between this smaller community and the larger one that Abraham and the others left behind was the acceptance of technology.

Only half of the families had been farmers. The rest had been carpenters, and it was easier to move back and forth if they had transportation. It had been voted to allow automobiles for that purpose, although once David had started helping the group out he'd done most of the driving, a fact that seemed to rest easier with everybody. He wasn't part of the church—it wasn't an issue if he drove.

He'd also been the one to teach Sarah to drive. Few people knew that, and one of the men who had known was gone.

David hauled the doors open, looking inside the empty barn. "The car is gone. The truck."

"They are hers now," Thom said, although a dark frown creased his face.

"Have you seen her driving the old truck?" David asked instead of responding to the comment. He turned to meet Thom's eyes as he asked and watched as Thom's eyes slid away.

"Thomas, don't play dumb. You know she drives and it's not like I'm going to go tattle on her." He took one step forward, hands clenching into fists. In the rational part of his mind, he knew why Thomas didn't want to say anything—he was protecting his cousin. The rules they had on technology were strict and the use of automobiles was limited to work only. Sarah didn't work. David personally didn't give a damn, but Thom did. *Too fucking bad.* "Have you seen her using the old truck or not?"

Finally, the younger man looked at him and nodded. "She's been using it, quite a bit. It's parked. In the barn in the pasture near my home." Thomas had built a home for him and his new wife a year ago, on a patch of land he'd bought from Abraham.

"The old one."

Thomas didn't bother to clarify. There was an old barn out there where some of the children liked to play, even when they weren't supposed to. Derelict, it needed to be torn down, something they'd meant to do this summer, but then Abraham had taken ill.

"Is there a road that leads to it?" David demanded. It had been years since he had been out there and he hadn't driven. He'd gone through the woods, cut across fields—something he didn't have any time for now.

"Yes." Thomas inclined his head, wariness entering his gaze. "Ca—David, what is going on?"

David jerked his chin toward his own truck and pulled out his keys. "You need to take me there."

"I'm working. I have a—"

"Thom, people are in danger," David said, taking one slow step toward the quiet, soft-spoken young man.

His gentle brown eyes narrowed, Thom studied David. Thom wasn't afraid, but that wariness, the uncertainty, on his face lingered. He didn't believe David. David didn't care. He didn't need Thom's belief—he needed fucking directions.

After a few more seconds, Thom gave a slow nod. "You will follow me. If there is something urgent, you'll need to return to town quickly, not waste time bringing me back here."

Without saying anything else, David turned and headed away, the keys to his own truck clutched tight in his fist. He didn't want to think about what he was going to do if they found Sarah. She was the only daughter of a man who had been like a father to him.

But the icy finger of dread running down his spine wasn't one he could ignore.

* * *

Sunlight shone like silvery splinters through clouds, falling down in a narrow column on the old barn. Maybe some people would find it picturesque, but as he rounded the final bend in the dirt road and stopped next to Thomas the only thing David felt was cold, and more cold.

"Her car isn't here," Thomas pointed out needlessly.

"Yeah. I see that," David muttered, striding past the other man, his focus on the barn.

Through the gaps in the weathered old doors, he could see flashes of black paint.

The truck.

The doors creaked as he pulled them open and one look inside told him that they really, really needed to get on with those plans for tearing this place down. But that was a worry for another day.

His heart thudded in his ears as he rounded the truck, and then it stopped altogether as he came to the front. The damage to the metal was minimal.

But the damage was there. David crouched down, staring at it hard. Then he looked at Thom. "I've got a flashlight in the glove box. Can you get it?"

Wordlessly Thom left and a moment later returned, handing over the Maglite. David went to his back on the dirt floor, working his way under the truck, trying not to touch it. It was clean. Too clean. She'd washed it. Otherwise, there would be dust on it. The road leading up here was dirt, and there was no way she could have kept the truck this clean.

Swearing, he slid out from under the truck and crouched in front of it, shining the light on the grill, all but crawling over it as he stared. This close, he could even faintly smell the scent of the soap she'd used. *Son of a—*

Wait.

There.

Eyes narrowing, he leaned in until he literally couldn't get any closer. It wasn't on the outside of the truck, but there. In the grill, wedged in tight, was a tiny little scrap of cloth. Faded blue, like the shirt Clay Brumley had worn. And there was a rusty red smear near it. Now that David had seen it, it was easier to see a few others.

His stomach shuddered, heaved, as his mind pieced it all together. Sarah had sat behind the wheel of this truck—Abraham's truck—and run a man over. Not once, but several times, if the rumors in town were true. David had picked up all those little whispers, things people wouldn't say to him, but he heard them all the same.

He'd taught her to drive using this truck.

And she'd use it to kill.

Because of me.

Something started to scream in his veins, a feeling he barely recognized. It had been too long since anything had horrified him. After a man has experienced some of the worst things that can be done to another, not much *could* horrify him.

But now, as David stared at the faint splatters of blood, he realized it was all true. He no longer had suspicions about Sarah. He knew it was the truth.

She'd killed Brumley. She'd likely killed Max and Louisa and had tried to kill Taneisha.

If the cops didn't find Sarah, she'd kill again.

David's fingers hovered over the grill, but he stopped himself.

Evidence, he thought. They'd need the evidence.

"Where is she, Thom?"

Thomas was staring at the fender, his brow puckered. Slowly, he looked up. "Looks like she hit something. A deer, maybe?"

"Not a deer," David said, rising to his feet as he moved

around the truck to the driver's side door. "Where is she?"

"I don't *know*." Exasperation came through clearly in his voice. "I've seen her heading into town. I thought maybe she was going to talk to you, or maybe try to find a job . . . or maybe she was even thinking about leaving. She's not happy. But I don't know where she is."

David processed that, taking it all in. "Has she attended church?"

"She was there when we held it at my home." Thom rubbed his brow. "But . . . she didn't stay for the meal."

The meal after church was important in this world. David had stopped going years ago. The pretense, the way people kept trying to make him feel part of a world where he could never belong—didn't *want* to belong— had grated on his nerves and only fanned the anger that lived inside him.

But Sarah wouldn't miss those meals.

His hand was steady as he pulled open the truck door and very slowly started to search. He didn't know exactly why, not until he reached under the bench seat and pulled out a small bundle of neatly folded clothes.

They were clothes that Sarah never would wear.

Not unless she was trying to hide.

Blue jeans. A blue T-shirt.

"What is—" Thomas stopped as he saw the clothes, a line appearing between his eyebrows.

David threw them down and slammed the door shut. Over his shoulder, he said, "Go home. Call Madison Police Department—you need to get a message to Detective Jensen Bell. It's urgent. You'll get there before my cell phone will work out here. Tell her there's a black truck out here with some damage to the front of it and what could be blood. Make sure she knows Sarah is *not* out here, though. At least not that we've seen."

"What's going on?" Thom demanded, a thread of steel coming through the peaceful, easy manner.

David stopped and turned to look at him. "Somebody shot me the other day." He jerked the collar of his shirt open, baring the bandaged wound. "Minutes later, the man who shot me was run down by a woman, driving a truck of this make and model. She had long blond hair and witnesses place her between thirty and fifty years of age. She was wearing a blue T-shirt. A woman fitting that description also attacked a woman I'd had words with a few days ago. Witnesses saw a black truck on the scene."

"You can't mean to say . . ." The words trailed off and Thom just stared at him.

"I don't want to think it." David met the gaze of the man across from him. Thomas had only been four years old when David had come here. The boy had been one of the first people David had spoken with, aside from Abraham and Sarah. No. He didn't *want* to think Sarah could hurt anybody.

But that flat, opaque look he'd seen in her eyes haunted him. As did bits and pieces of conversations that stretched back years. She had anger inside her. He'd recognized it before, but hadn't realized just how deep that anger ran.

It had been strongest when he told them he was leaving here.

Go back to the English? Why?
How can you leave me now?
Nothing but trouble will be there.

"Call the cops," he said again, his voice soft now.

Then he turned and walked away. Thom would make

that call, if for no other reason than because he wouldn't risk harm coming to another person. But he'd hurt over it. David regretted that.

Just another ember to the fire of the rage building inside him.

CHAPTER NINETEEN

The endless chatter of the two boys in the backseat had Sybil longing for a tub of hot water, her earbuds and a book. She wanted to block out the world. Just for a little while.

Block it out, pretend the past few days—the past few *weeks*—hadn't happened.

And all of that was unlikely. Dealing with two boys didn't *double* the workload the way one would think. It tripled it. Maybe even quadrupled it. The mess was three times bigger, the homework seemed three times more complicated, and the two of them went through more food than she would have thought possible.

Taneisha was still in the hospital, under observation for another twenty-four hours before the doctors felt it would be safe for her to leave.

When she *did* leave, Sybil wanted Taneisha to come home with her for a while. She couldn't entirely buy this bit that somebody had attacked Taneisha because of some weird connection to David, but if that *was* what was going on then it was better if they all stayed together, right?

Safety in numbers, Sybil thought as she turned down her street. Weariness crashed through her at the sight of the squad car, but after David's late-night visit—and the heaviness of his words—she could understand.

Maybe.

She had a feeling his gloom-and-doom outlook was coloring his view on everything, and not just their never-gonna-happen relationship, but she wouldn't risk the safety of the boys.

She waved at Thorpe as she turned in and then looked up at the house. It was quiet, the windows staring blankly back at her. Nothing looked any different. "Okay, boys. Round up the backpacks. Grab lunch boxes, jackets, et cetera, et cetera. I don't want five trips out to the car to get whatever you forgot."

"What did I forget?" Drew asked, his voice guileless.

"What haven't you forgotten?" She winked at him in the mirror as she pushed the door open. Tension gathered at the base of her neck and she decided some Tylenol was one thing she'd be getting, even if she couldn't get that bath, that twenty minutes away from the world. Tylenol and five minutes on the couch. Maybe even twenty. She'd break her cardinal rule and let the kids play video games during the week.

Blowing out a breath, she eyed her house with more than a little trepidation. It was nothing new. Ever since Taneisha's attack, Sybil had jumped at every little noise, every weird shadow. The other day, she'd left her closet door open and she'd woken up, seen something fluttering and almost screamed. By the time she worked up the courage to turn on the light, she'd been a sweating, nervous wreck—all because the robe she kept hanging on the inside of the door had been fluttering in the breeze caused by her ceiling fan.

Another reason I'll be glad when all this crazy shit is done with, she thought sourly. *I can stop feeling like some ninny who jumps at every damn thing.*

"Come on, guys," she said, climbing out and heading up the sidewalk. "Don't forget anything." She waited until the doors shut behind her before she thumbed the lock on her key fob.

They were halfway up the steps when Darnell said it, his voice charming: "Ah, Ms. Chalmers?"

"What did you forget?" she asked, sighing.

"My water bottle. Need to wash it out."

She unlocked the car with a shake of her head. Shifting the weight of her laptop bag on her shoulder, she glanced at Drew out of the corner of her eye. "You two are going to drive me nuts."

Drew just grinned. "I guess now is a good time to tell you I left my inhaler in the car."

"Go."

The door creaked as it opened.

Sarah's hand was sweaty. The gun felt like it weighed a hundred pounds. *Strong. I have to be strong.* She'd used the gun before. Once. She hadn't even known what she was doing when she'd used it, but she'd been determined and the Lord had guided her.

He would guide her again.

A boy's voice floated through the air.

Her heart clenched.

But she steeled herself against it.

There can be nothing between us.

Behind her, Sybil heard the boys talking. Their voices seemed to come at a distance as she pushed the door open. Had it always creaked so loudly?

She pushed it open, clutching at her keys. Something skittered down her spine and she clutched the door tightly instead of pushing it open for the kids she could hear pounding up the steps of the porch.

From the corner of her eye, she saw somebody move. Everything inside her tensed. Stilled.

Whirling around, she braced herself between the kids and the house. "Why don't you two go for a walk?" she said brightly.

Something clicked in her ear. A voice, almost soundless, said, "Come inside. Make the boys come inside with you."

"You two go for a walk," Sybil said, her voice firm, flat. Not shaking. That was good. She couldn't panic. "And when you're done, you can talk to your friend, Ben." As she said it, she lifted her gaze, and only her gaze, to the parked police car.

Darnell reached out, his eyes wide, something that might have been fear and understanding flickering in his gaze. He had old eyes, Sybil realized in that moment. Taneisha's kid had old eyes. He reached out and caught Drew's hand. "Come on, Drew. I don't wanna do homework yet."

"Make them come inside," the voice insisted, still so very quiet.

"Aunt Sybil—"

"Come on." Darnell started to back away, his eyes straying to the door Sybil held clutched in her hand.

She heard something click, and at the same time a hard, blunt object shoved into her side. She kept the grunt behind her teeth through sheer force of will.

Something in her eyes finally came across and Drew backed away, still frowning. But he followed Darnell, shooting a look at her over his shoulder as they headed down the stairs.

"Get them back here!"

Slowly, Sybil backed into the house, lifting her hand to wave casually at Ben. He eyed her through the window. The smile on her face felt forced, but she wasn't doing a damn thing until there was more distance between her and those boys. Once they were out of sight, all bets were off.

Carefully, she shut the door. "Ma'am, I don't know what you want. I've got money in my purse," she said, surprised to hear that her voice was still steady.

"Get the boys." Her voice was still a whisper.

Slowly, Sybil turned. "No. Did you see the cop car? If I go out there, yelling for them after I just sent them away, that will attract more attention."

She was blond, Sybil noted. The papers had been too vague in their description, too. She'd place this woman in her early forties, maybe a bit younger, but the harsh set of her face could be making her seem older.

She was also Amish—or she played the part very well.

Something told Sybil that it wasn't a part she played. Which made her blood run cold.

The gun the woman carried looked all too real, and despite the plain clothes the woman wore, despite the little white bonnet that covered her blond hair, she held the gun like she meant to use it.

Sybil felt a familiar tightening in her chest as panic started to flood through her. *Breathe. Just breathe.* Somehow, she didn't see this woman letting her go digging through her purse for the inhaler she only rarely used, but going into a full-fledged asthma attack because she was scared wasn't going to help things, either.

"I have money," she said softly. "I don't have a lot, but I'll give you—"

"So typical. The English and their greed." The woman's eyes, a flat, muddy brown, raked over Sybil. "I don't want money."

"Then what do you want?"

That utter *lack* of emotion scared Sybil to her very
core.

Please . . . God. Tell me Darnell called the cops.

Darnell and Drew rounded the block. "Don't look back,"
Darnell whispered. He'd said it every five seconds since
they walked away, smiling so wide his cheeks hurt.

"Don't look back."

Once the house was out of view, though, he looked
at Drew. "Can you run?"

Drew reached into his pocket and pulled out the inhaler he'd grabbed from the car. He stuck it in his mouth,
and a minute later he nodded. "Not for long, but I can.
What's wrong?"

Darnell's eyes, wide and dark, moved back to his. "I
don't know. But something is. She looked the same way
Mom looked the day somebody broke into my aunt's
house when we went to visit for Thanksgiving." He swallowed and then added, "I think somebody might be inside. She wants us to tell Detective Ben. Let's run."

They dumped their backpacks—maybe he wouldn't
have to do his math homework. He hated math. As they
started to run, he tried to figure out what was going on.
Layla. He bet it was all Layla's fault, whatever it was.
That girl was nothing but trouble.

Miss Sybil oughta just—

Automatically he cut the thought off, feeling bad because he knew even *thinking* that would make Mama
mad and she was in the hospital and hurt and she didn't
need to be mad.

"You breathing—" He stopped as he heard a car. He
jerked his head up, everything inside him tensing.

Up ahead, he saw another cop car, going around the
block just up ahead. "We should tell him. If somebody

is in the house and looks outside and we're talking to Detective Ben, he could hurt your aunt."

"What do you want?" Sybil asked again. She flicked her eyes to the woman's face, something about her niggling at the back of Sybil's head, but she couldn't figure out what. She knew faces, though. She'd figure out—if she had *time*.

"If you'd stayed away from him," the woman said, her voice almost sad, the first sign of emotion she'd shown, "I wouldn't have bothered you. But you came between us. You might even be why he left. That's why this has to happen."

Ice gripped her heart. "Who?" she asked, keeping the fear out of her voice. She already *knew* the answer, though. He'd told her. Warned her.

"You *know* who." Venom flooded her voice as she eyed Sybil.

"I don't," she said, shaking her head. Had the boys made it around the block? Had they told Ben? Fuck, the woman was still standing too close to the window. What if she looked outside and saw them?

Sybil had to get her away from the window. Had to get the gun.

"Caine. He belongs with *me*." The words were spoken through clenched teeth.

David . . . Her heart thudded, hard, against her ribs and misery spread through her. If this bitch hurt her, that would be another bruise, another wound, that he'd carry with him. Sybil knew it as well as her own name. It wouldn't be his fault, but nothing she did or said would change it so that he'd see it otherwise.

So don't let her hurt you. Easier said than done.

"Lady, he's all yours." Sybil shrugged, pasting a smile

on her face. "Didn't you hear? He dumped me. I guess he's already figured that *yours* thing out."

The woman blinked, caught off-guard. "Dumped you?"

"Yeah. We're not seeing each other anymore. He doesn't want anything to do with me." Forcing a casualness into her voice that she didn't feel, she moved a little, circling around so that the woman had to turn away from the window.

That's it. Watch me. Keep watching. . . .

Wariness edged across the woman's face. "You lie. Whores always lie."

"Please. No woman is going to lie about a man dumping her. I get that you might not understand that kind of thing—I imagine it's different with men and women where you come from. But with us? It's humiliating."

"You bring the humiliation on yourself."

This time, the smile stretching her face was so brittle, it felt like it might crack. "I guess so. I mean, I dunno what I was thinking with him, but trust me, I'm not going down that road again. He's not my type, anyway. I guess he's happier back on that farm."

"You wouldn't understand," the woman whispered, her voice low, ugly with malice.

"I guess I wouldn't. I like it here, where I've got a house with air-conditioning, where I can wear jeans and makeup and work a job and date whoever—"

"Whore." The word was flung out, like a stone, her voice louder.

Sybil shrugged. "If you want to view it like that, hey. Go ahead. Just . . . put the gun down. I don't have any designs on Caine. He's done with me. I'm happy with that."

She tried to judge the distance between them. Two feet.

Would she be quick enough?

If she judged wrong and got shot, then she ended up shot. And David would suffer, and Drew would end up back with Layla. But if she didn't do something, she was dead anyway.

I'll only have one chance. . . .

Edged fury lit inside David's gut as he caught sight of a familiar coat of paint.

Abraham's car.

Whipping his truck around, David turned off Main. Horns blasted behind him. He ignored them. It was harder to ignore the cop up ahead, one who lifted his head and eyed David narrowly as he came to a stop in front of him.

"Mr. Sutter." Officer Gardiner nodded at him. "Going mighty fast up there."

"Where is she?" David demanded, ignoring the officer's comment.

"Who?" Gardiner asked, greying brow cocking up.

"The woman who owns the—"

"Help!"

David and the cop both jerked their heads up. Dread twisted in David's gut, vicious and cold, as he saw Drew and a taller, skinny black boy pounding down the sidewalk toward them.

Drew's breath was tight, alarmingly so, and he couldn't speak as he struggled to breathe. But the taller boy could—and did—talk. *Darnell,* David thought absently. His name was Darnell—Taneisha's son. His eyes were huge and wide as he looked from David to the cop.

"Something's wrong. Miss Sybil . . . I think somebody might be in her house."

That slow, red drift of rage crept across David's vision. The officer moved to Darnell, but David didn't hear anything. Shifting, he stared through the houses. Just barely, he could make out the back right edge of Sybil's place.

Sarah.

She was at Sybil's.

For him, the rest of the world ceased to exist.

He didn't hear the cop's startled shout, didn't even realize he'd tried to chase him. An Olympic runner could have caught him, but that was probably it, and anybody who tried to stop him was going to go down in a sprawl of pain and blood.

Sybil . . .

He was in the yard, staring at the back of the house with no memory of running through the yards, of the fences he'd climbed or hurtled to get there. Harsh breaths panted out of him and the emotions that he'd locked awayfor so long were drowning him. Fear. Panic. Rage.

Not now. Have to think.

Sybil.

She was in there.

It was that thought that let him finally yank it all under control.

Finally.

And his steps were calm, measured, as he started across the grass. He reached into his pocket, almost surprised to realize he had his keys. He didn't remember pulling them out of the ignition when he'd stopped his truck, but he must have. He'd never returned Sybil's, though he'd told himself over and over he needed to. But of course, he never would. That string, that connection, was one he couldn't live without.

The boards of the porch squeaked under his feet as he mounted the steps.

The panes of the glass reflected his own image back at him as he crossed the porch and for a few, terrified seconds he stood there, off to the side, staring through the window to see if he could see them. Or anything else.

But he saw nothing.

The children.

Where were they?

She'd seen them, climbing out of the car. Two boys, one shorter and pale, the other tall and dark, both of them smiling. *Bring them unto me. . . .*

The scripture spun wildly through her head.

Then the whore blocked the door and sent them off. Part of Sarah had been relieved. Children. Innocent. She didn't want to hurt a child, but the one was connected to Caine. She'd seen it. She'd been watching him for so long and she'd seen how he looked at the boy, seen how he watched him. Once, she'd even stood at the window of this very house and peered inside. They'd watched the TV—Caine was watching a movie. With this family, and he'd watched the boy with a look that made Sarah's heart hurt.

He loves the boy. You can't bring him home and expect him to stay if you don't sever that connection. . . .

She'd have to kill the boy.

But the whore sent them away.

Maybe it was a sign.

The cold part of Sarah's heart that had ached so badly at the thought eased and breathing, thinking, wasn't so painful. Maybe what she was supposed to do was bring the boy *with* her, like Abraham had done. She was too old now to bear a child for Caine, but he'd want a son. All men wanted sons.

Yes. That was what she should do.

The boy wasn't responsible for what the woman had done after all. He was an innocent. Probably scared, too, of all the things she'd probably subjected him to. Innocent . . . scared. Like she'd been. Like Caine had been.

Tears burned and the gun in her hand seemed heavier, harder to hold.

There was a faint sound and she narrowed her eyes, glaring at the woman in front of her. "It's because of you that this happens. You never should have *touched* him," she said, her voice shaking.

"No arguing there." The woman lifted her hands, shifting yet again, and Sarah braced herself.

But all she did was inch around, backing away. Trying to escape. She couldn't, though. Nobody could escape judgment.

"You aren't going to come between us, ever again." Sarah steadied the gun.

Sybil caught her breath. Those muddy eyes had started to burn. Death stared back at her. Time slowed to a crawl and she lunged.

The woman was strong, solid. Sybil had a few inches on her, but the woman had several pounds and lot of muscle. Sybil's weight drove them into the coffee table and she slammed the woman's weapon hand down into the floor.

A fist slammed into Sybil's side and she grunted, pain exploding through her. She gritted her teeth, fought harder.

If she didn't get that gun, nothing else mattered. Fisting one hand in a coil of neatly pinned-up hair, Sybil yanked.

The furious yowl was like music to her ears and she yanked again, harder, more savagely.

With the other hand, she still gripped the woman's gun hand, keeping it away. Useless, Sybil hoped.

A second later, a fist slammed into her cheek.

Panting, Sybil blinked away the tears. "Wow. And I thought . . . you were a peaceful bunch of people."

"Shut *up*." The woman tried to shove up, continuing to jerk her weapon hand from Sybil.

Sybil let her jerk away, some. Then Sybil drove her fist upward into the woman's chin. Her eyes went glassy, and for a split second Sybil thought she'd be able to wrest the gun away.

But then, with a savage strength, the woman tore back and rolled to her feet.

Sybil couldn't roll herself into a ball in time to defend herself from the vicious kick to her gut. Breath exploding out of her, she fought to see past the pain. Rolling onto her knees, she looked up, certain she'd see the gun . . . and then the end of her life.

Instead, she saw the woman, standing in the hall.

Frozen.

And the look in her eyes was one that froze Sybil to the core.

CHAPTER TWENTY

"Put it down."

He'd never wanted to shove a knife into anybody so badly in all his life. Not even the one time he'd found himself standing in his father's room when he was fourteen and a nightmare had sent him sleepwalking out of his bed.

He'd woken up, standing at the foot of his parents' bed, holding a butcher knife, and he'd been that close, *that* close to using it. They'd slept on, blissfully unaware, and he'd taken the knife and stood in the bathroom instead. For nearly an hour, he'd stood there, thought about using it on himself.

But it was nothing like this.

The filleting knife had been in the dish rack and he'd grabbed it blindly. If it weren't for the fact that the gun was pointed directly into Sybil's face, he might have already sliced it across Sarah's throat. He could kill a woman. He could easily kill a woman who threatened Sybil. Nobody knew better than him just how monstrous the so-called *weaker* sex could be. After all, his mother had left him to the hands of a monster because it suited her purposes.

But the gun, shaky was it was, continued to point at Sybil.

"Put it down," David said again, keeping his voice soft as that dangerous, deadly red started to flood through him. He moved closer and she just watched him, her eyes wide and shining. That look made him want to scrub himself clean.

"You don't understand," Sarah said gently, turning her head to look at Sybil. "She's coming between us. Nobody can do that."

Sarah darted him a look, and when she did the gun lowered, just enough. Shooting out a hand, he caught her wrists and jerked up. *Boom!* His ears were still echoing as his gaze flew to Sybil. She'd flung herself away and was already to rising to her feet, watching him with stark eyes.

At that same moment, a voice boomed from outside: "This is the Madison Police Department!"

Sarah tried to tear away from him. Wrenching the gun out of her hands, he held it out to Sybil. "You better open the door before they do."

Sybil moved to the door.

He didn't follow.

Two seconds later, Sarah was slammed against the door and a startled shriek escaped her.

He didn't care.

"Why?"

"She was coming between us."

The words made no sense. "There is no *us*, Sarah."

From the corner of his eye, he saw cops fanning into the room. "Mr. Sutter, let the woman go."

He ignored them. "There is no *us*, Sarah," he said again. He stared into her eyes, watched as that flat, emotionless surface started to fracture, then break. It was like watching a glass window break, in slow motion, tiny little lines spreading out, out, out, until the entire surface gave way and collapsed.

"There *is*." A sob ripped out of Sarah.

He let her go, half-expecting the police to come rushing in, but everybody seemed frozen as she went to her knees. "There always was, even though nobody could see it. So I waited. I tried to make my father see, but he couldn't. And then he seemed to understand that you had to leave, and I couldn't have that."

"Couldn't have . . ." The words trailed off as she lifted her head.

"He was in the way. I couldn't lose you and he wanted to take you away," she whispered, her voice pleading.

"Abraham," he whispered. "You killed Abraham."

"It was for you. It was always for you." Her eyes were rapt on his face, a tremulous smile forming on her lips. "You understand that, don't you, Caine?"

"You killed him." Somebody moved up, standing closer. He heard his name, but it came to him as though from across a canyon, echoing before fading into nothing. "Who else?"

Sarah's eyes glittered with tears. "They were all in the way. You couldn't see how much you needed me because they were always there. Max knew how much you needed me, at first. He brought you to me, but then he seemed to forget. He stayed in this evil town and he just forgot. That awful woman—she had alcohol and drugs in her home and you were there late at night. How could you turn to her, Caine?"

"*Who?*"

"David, step—"

Jensen laid a hand on the chief's arm.

The woman wasn't a threat to David, and right

now she was spilling out information they just might need.

As long as she kept spilling, Jensen wanted to listen. Sybil had already turned over the gun and she stood there in rapt fascination.

Training told Jensen that she needed to get the civilian out of there. But her instincts told her that the woman hovered on the edge. Any small thing would push her over, and if she shut down on them now they might never get those answers.

Sorenson shot her a glittering look but held still and quiet, his weapon lowered, clutched in a two-handed grip.

"That *woman*," Sarah insisted. "She dyed her hair and drank too much and cried on your shoulder about her father. I'd come into town to try and get you to come back home—you were staying away more and more and I needed you."

Rita.

David seemed to realize it at the same moment. "Rita Troyer. You made it look like she'd killed herself. She was grieving and you killed her."

"She didn't *need* you. *I* did!"

David's face was like stone. "Who else?"

"Why do they matter?" The woman, still sprawled on the floor, lifted a hand to him. "I'm the one who loves you. I'm who needs you, who cried and prayed and begged for you to come home."

David slowly backed away.

That subtle rejection made the woman's face crumple. "You drove the truck that killed Brumley, Sarah. You killed Louisa, the lady in the coffee shop. You attacked Taneisha, too."

Sarah. Jensen filed that name away, just like she mentally filed away everything else.

"I only tried to remove those who stood between us."
She gave David a watery smile, the blind adulation in
her eyes something that made Jensen's blood run cold.
"Once your whore is gone, you'll be free. You'll come
back to me."

David had faced evil before.

He hadn't realized, until that moment, though, just
how much *evil* and *insane* could walk so far apart. His
father had been evil, his head so fucked-up and his mor-
als so twisted, they didn't resemble anything normal. But
now, looking into Sarah's blue-grey eyes, brimming with
tears, he realized he'd never once met anybody who was
truly, truly crazy.

They were unwell.

Had her father passed something on to Sarah? Had
his brain been so fucked-up that he'd passed his mad-
ness on to his child? Or had the abuse twisted her?

David didn't know.

"David."

He didn't turn away.

"Let the cops do their job now."

Sybil's voice was closer now. He tightened his fist on
the knife he held, tucked against his thigh.

"She can't hurt me. They aren't going to just let her
merrily walk away. It's over." There was a pause and then
Sybil said gently, "Come to me, okay?"

At that, Sarah lurched upward and the cops rushed
them.

David held still, watching as she was subdued and
then handcuffed.

She watched him with accusing eyes and he
turned, put the knife down on the coffee table. Jensen
lowered her gaze to it, stared at it for one second before she looked back at him.

He looked back, unblinking.

Then he looked at Sybil.

She stood there, hand outstretched.

Staring into her eyes for a long moment, he said softly, "She would have killed you. If Drew had come in here, she might have killed him. Maybe even Darnell. But she wanted you, probably even Drew, dead. You're the only ones who matter."

She continued to wait. "Then come to me."

He took another step, then another. "You told me to stay away."

"Only if you're not going to stay."

Slowly, he reached out and closed his hands over hers.

She moved in and tucked herself against his chest, her head settling into the curve where his neck met his shoulder.

I'm staying.

He couldn't say it yet. Couldn't say a lot of things yet. But he would.

Soon.

"I think," she said, her voice muffled against his chest, "after this, we really should have a good long talk about our relationship—you know, that one you think we don't really have."

His hand came up, curling over the back of her neck. His sigh teased the curls at her temple and he nuzzled her.

His response was lost in a fury of screams.

"No. No!"

Both of them looked up, watched as a woman in a simple blue dress and a prim white cap tried to tear away from three uniformed officers. Her face was red, her eyes full of a fury that made them almost inhuman. "Mine! You were meant to be mine. I'd kill you before I let you go."

Sybil leaned against David as the cops finished hustling the enraged woman outside. "I guess that's the difference," Sybil mused.

David's hand tangled in her hair. "What do you mean?"

"Both of us were desperate. I love you. She's clearly obsessed. But I'd die before I'd force you to be with me if you didn't want me. She'd kill before giving you a chance to choose otherwise."

Something shifted in his heart.

He'd felt a wrenching inside him when he saw the gun aimed at Sybil's face. He'd seen the women fighting and fierce pride had surged through him.

Now, as things slid back into place, he realized some of the jagged edges weren't so jagged.

They fit together. *Really* fit.

Even the broken bits and pieces that seemed to make up the entirety of his being were no longer quite so jagged. The raw pieces weren't quite so raw. And maybe, if he'd let himself really look, he would have realized it sooner.

Lowering his head, he pressed his brow to hers. "I think that talk might not be a bad idea."

Sybil's eyes widened.

He opened his mouth to tell her.

He'd held it trapped inside, hidden even from him, for so long.

But then the door banged open.

A skinny form lunged at them and David automatically found himself hugging a scared, nervous boy. It wasn't even awkward.

"Aunt Sybil!"

Without even thinking about it, David hauled the boy up. He was too big at nine to be held like this, maybe. But just then, maybe they all needed it.

* * *

"None of it will serve as a confession," Sorenson said grimly, staring through the window at the woman who'd gone still and quiet after they'd shut the squad car door shut, with her locked inside.

Their suspect had been identified by David Sutter.

Her name was Sarah Yoder and she was forty-one years old.

As yet, she hadn't spoken a single word. She'd been sitting on the same seat for more than two hours and she hadn't taken a sip of water, hadn't accepted a single offer to use the restroom and had refused the offer of a phone call.

She moved like an automaton when they brought her inside, and after they'd guided her into the interview room she'd sat down, folded her hands neatly in her lap and then just stared.

At absolutely nothing.

The look in her eyes said, *The lights are on, but nobody's home.*

Jensen sighed and rubbed her forehead. "I don't think it matters if we get a confession or not, Chief. That woman is insane."

"Insane as in planning to plead that way, or insane as in bat-shit crazy?" Sorenson asked, although he already had his own suspicions.

Jensen folded her arms across her middle. "Beyond bat-shit crazy."

"If that's not a medical term, it should be." Thorpe stood a little farther away, sipping from a cup of coffee that could double as motor oil.

"There is some good news in all of this," Sorenson said as they continued to watch Sarah sitting there, quiet as could be, hands folded and gaze locked on the wall. The simple dress she wore fell in neat folds around her, and the white bonnet covered much of her hair.

She looked so completely out of place in there.

"What's the good news?" Jensen asked softly.

"Two more men turned themselves in. They were older members, too. One of them gave me a very, and I mean *very,* comprehensive list of men who'd been involved with Cronus over the years. Of that list, the majority of them are either dead—passed away dead, not murdered—or already on our list. They're done, Jensen. We've only got a few more to bring in, and we've got enough evidence to lock them in a dark, deep hole."

A breath gusted out of her. "Done. As in . . ." She turned her head to look at him.

"Done." He smiled tiredly. "Done as in done. They are broken. Your lawyer—"

She flushed at the reference to her boyfriend, Dean, the district attorney.

Sorenson's grin didn't look so tired and an amused glint appeared in his eyes. "Your lawyer has been fielding a lot of phone calls lately, from those who are defending these scum buckets. I'd say half are already looking to make a deal."

"A deal." She narrowed her eyes. "No way."

"They aren't going to walk. Not over this. They'll all do time. That's already been made clear. It just goes to show how far they've fallen. They are at the end of the rope and they know it."

Jensen closed her eyes. "The men who hurt Caleb. And Glenn Blue's son. They'll do serious time, right?" Dirk Sims—Jeb's brother. He'd raped his own son, allowed others to do the same. And Glenn—a *cop.* Just like Jeb had been. Bile churned inside her and she turned to look at the chief. "Tell me we're not going to let them plead to some small minor little thing and they get out in a year."

A thin, mean smile settled on the chief's face and he looked at her, his eyes going hard. "No. We've got the evidence from Caleb; we've got others willing to testify. People will burn for this. It's done. You did it, Jensen."

Done. She blew out a shaky breath, thinking of the broken boy who'd sat in a hospital bed months ago. It didn't feel like enough. They hadn't *stopped* those kids from being hurt.

But maybe, now, they could start to heal. "We can find out who else they hurt. Make sure they get help. So this doesn't start again."

"Yes." Sorenson nodded.

It wasn't enough. But it was all they had.

Moments passed by, and then, slowly, she shifted her attention on the woman waiting just beyond the window. So quiet. So still. If it weren't for the occasional blink of her eyes, Jensen would almost think she weren't even alive, weren't even real.

"We need to talk to her," Jensen said flatly. Dread crept through her at the thought. There was something broken inside that woman. Very, very broken. "So. Who wants to do it?"

Sorenson snorted. Jensen slid her attention to her young, handsome partner; then, mustering up her best smile, she said, "Thorpe, I think you should do the honors."

Both Sorenson and Thorpe gave her looks with varying degrees of doubt. She didn't let her smile waver. "Didn't you hear her ranting? That's not a woman who cares much for other females." Jensen shifted her gaze to the chief and nodded. "She might open up to you. I suspect older men would yield more respect. But

Thorpe . . ." Jensen eyed the younger man with his open, innocent face and those all-American, handsome features. "Let's face it. If he puts his mean on and tries, he can be intimidating. Otherwise, people look at him and half-expect him to be a grown-up version of Opie."

Thorpe's mouth flattened. "Gee. Thanks."

"Hey, know your weaknesses and strengths. People look at me and think *fluffy, silly girl wearing a badge* more often than not. I let them think that and then sucker punch them when they aren't expecting it. It's thrown more than a few people off-balance."

Sorenson pondered it for a minute, his hangdog expression going pensive. Then he nodded, stroking his chin absently. "Play it up, Thorpe. *Sorry, Miss Yoder. Can I get you water, Miss Yoder? Should I call your family? . . .* all that shit. Nobody else has gotten her to talk. See if you can."

It took Thorpe roughly twenty minutes.

His tone was soothing, his expression gentle, and his eyes, big, dark and brown, stayed on Sarah Yoder's face like he thought she just might break.

And she did, but not in the way one might think with those gentle features.

Her eyes were hard, brittle as glass, when she finally turned her head and looked at him.

"No."

That was all she said.

Thorpe angled his head and his voice was puzzled as he asked, "No?"

"I don't want my family. None of them will understand. They never did. Call Caine."

Thorpe didn't glance toward the window, but Jensen and Sorenson saw the confusion and frustration dance through his eyes. *Now what?* They could practically see it dancing on his tongue.

"Mr. Sutter can't come see you just yet."

A fist slammed into the table.

Thorpe was still.

Jensen was impressed. She'd flinched at the violence of the action, her heart lurching in her chest.

"That's not his name," Sarah said, her voice flat. "His name is Caine. Caine Yoder. And I want to speak with him."

Thorpe just inclined his head. "Very well. I'll call him Caine, then. But regardless of what you want me to call him, it's against procedure for you to speak with him."

"Procedure." She spat the word. "Ask him. He should decide. Not you and your *laws.*"

Outside in the hallways, Jensen whistled. "Wow. She's . . . something else."

"Detective Bell. Chief."

Turning her head, she saw one of the uniforms standing there. Lifting a brow, she waited. He came forward, a glint of excitement in his eyes. "You aren't going to believe this."

"Try me." She had an Amish woman in the interview room, likely guilty of four, or was it five murders? Jensen doubted she'd be surprised by anything.

"We just finished running the weapon." He shoved the paperwork at her. "You aren't going to believe who it's registered to."

Her eyes went flat.

The door swung open.

The woman who came in was familiar. Sarah had seen her around, had even seen her talking to Caine, but she'd understood. This woman, like the man at the table, was with the police. The police had failed Caine before, but these were different people and they seemed to try harder this time around.

Except the man was coming between them now.

As the woman—her name . . . *What was her name? Something pretty,* Sarah thought. *Bell.* That was it. She was Detective Bell. As Detective Bell put something in front of Detective Thorpe, she slid Sarah a look. That look was sharper than steel and something cold danced down Sarah's spine. For a moment. Just a moment.

Caine. His face danced through her mind and just that was enough to give her strength.

"Where is Caine?" she asked politely, keeping her hands folded in her lap.

"Oh, we'll get to him later," Detective Bell promised breezily.

"I'll see him soon?" Sarah asked, excitement pulsing through her blood. She'd get to talk to him. Without that other woman. She could *finally* make him understand. Maybe he already did. Was that why he wasn't here? Maybe he was getting ready. It wouldn't be unusual. Maybe he felt like there were people he needed to say good-bye to. She didn't think it was wise, but if he was coming home that was what mattered.

Hands twisted in her lap, she pasted a smile on her face. *Be patient. Be graceful. It will be over soon.* Meeting the detective's steady gaze, Sarah inclined her head. "When may I leave?"

"Oh, there are questions yet to be asked." Detective Bell lifted a brow and moved to the table. Without her speaking a word, the male detective rose, his gaze smooth, blank as a mirror.

Sarah continued to stare at him, though, even when she could feel Detective Bell's gaze drilling into her. "I'd rather talk with him," Sarah said softly.

"Yeah, well, here's a sad fact, Sarah. We don't always get what we want in life."

From the corner of her eye, Sarah saw the detective put a slim yellow file on the table in front of her. "I'm really curious about something. I'm hoping you can shed some light on the subject." She paused and then asked, "You sure you don't want a lawyer?"

Sarah didn't look at her. She wouldn't. There was no reason. She focused on the door instead, waiting. Caine would be there. Sooner or later. She'd waited her entire life for him, and she'd always known that sooner or later he'd be there.

Now wasn't the time to give up on that hope.

"Here's what I'm really curious about."

A piece of paper was slid in front of her. Despite her vow not to look, her gaze slid toward it. And her blood went cold at the image on it. A shiver raced up her spine.

"Do you know him?"

Blood roared in her ears. The bitter taste of fear climbing up the back of her throat almost made her ill. She curled her hands into fists until her nails bit into her palms. But she was pleased when she managed a polite, calm response. "I have little reason to know people in town."

"Really." The detective's voice was dry, almost derisive. "That only leaves me with more questions, then. And that means we'll just be at this so much longer."

Sarah's heart thudded in her chest, knocking against her ribs, heavy and slow. *Longer . . . ?* "You can't keep me from leaving here."

"Oh, we could have a long discussion about that. I guess you're not overly familiar with laws and stuff. We can go into detail about that later. But for now, this question. Very important. If you don't know him, then how do you explain this?"

The next piece of paper didn't make much sense to Sarah. Puzzled, she continued to read it, licking her lips.

"What . . ."

"It's the registration information for the gun you attempted to use on Sybil Chalmers." Detective Bell smiled easily. "You know, the one you wanted to kill her with?"

Sybil. Fury lit inside Sarah's heart, a fury that burned hot and bright and hard. "She was in the way," Sarah said, her voice harder, sharper. "She doesn't understand Caine, our ways. He doesn't belong here. He needs to come *home*."

"Yeah, yeah. So you keep saying. Just explain this to me, okay? Make me understand. Just *why* do you have Peter Sutter's gun? The man's been missing for more than twenty years."

Peter.

The beast.

Slowly, she lifted her head and stared at Bell. A smile spread across Sarah's face before she could stop it. She opened her mouth, but even as the words started to form, the door opened.

A tall man, his skin dark and smooth, stood in the doorway. "Detective Bell, in the hall, if you would."

"Not now, Dean. Answer the question, Miss Yoder."

"Do not answer that question." The man came forward, scooped up the papers. "A public defender has been called. He'll be in to speak with you shortly."

"Dean, what the *fuck*?"

He spun around on Jensen, his eyes flashing. "Don't."

"I'm going to fucking kick your ass over this," she growled, storming over to him and shoving her face into his.

"Save the kinky stuff for bed, darlin'." A muscle

pulsed in his cheek, his dark eyes glittering. "Do you have *any* idea what we're dealing with here? *Any* idea?"

"Yes!" She practically shouted it. "And you just stopped me from getting a confession."

"If you'd gone forward, I could have gotten that case thrown out." Dean said it in a flat, level tone. Crossing his arms over his chest, he leaned back against the desk, glad everybody else had decided to vacate the small conference room. "Now I'm good—I'm damn good—and frankly, Jefferson County doesn't have any PDs as good as I am, and anything they throw up at this point I can handle. But if you'd kept going, we could have had problems."

She opened her mouth, then shut it. A few seconds later, she said, her voice soft and lethal, "I know how to fucking do my job."

"When was the last time you had to investigate an Amish woman of questionable sanity for *multiple* murders, baby?" he asked. Shoving off the desk, he came closer. He reached up.

She caught her breath, almost pulled away, but in the end she held still as he curved his hand over her neck. "Everybody's tempers are running high. There are men people liked, respected, in jail or out on bond, getting ready to go to trial for the systematic sexual abuse of boys that has gone back for generations. We're now looking at a woman who murdered her own father, two women and a man half this town adored and the other half feared . . . all because she couldn't get the man she loved to love her back. We're all on-edge. You were getting ready to push, too hard. And if you think it through, you'll see that."

Jensen rose up on her toes. His lids drooped as he lowered his mouth to meet hers.

Then he yelped as she bit him.

"I don't like how often you're right," she said, turning away.

"You're a brat," Dean said, gingerly touching his tongue to his throbbing lower lip.

"Damn straight." Then she blew out a frustrated breath. Opening the door, she stared down the hall to the brightly lit window. On the other side sat Sarah Yoder.

"Do you think she killed Peter Sutter?"

Dean rested a hand on Jensen's shoulder, keeping a polite distance between them now that they were out of the privacy of a closed room. "I don't know. But that woman has dead eyes. I suspect she's capable of almost anything."

CHAPTER TWENTY-ONE

Twilight slid slowly across Madison.

A taut, hushed air had clung to the town most of the day, almost like they waited.

Now, as the sun disappeared behind the horizon, a gentle, chilly breeze swept in off the river, almost like a sigh. One of relief.

Adam stood behind the counter at Shakers, taking drink orders in one after the other, so fast they all blurred together in his mind. Lana sat at the far end of the bar, earbuds in, gaze locked on the iPad in front of her. Every so often, she'd look up and find him. She'd smile and he'd feel a warmth spread through him.

Noah and Trinity were at a table, tucked in at the back. They'd been there for over an hour, and although they'd long since finished the burgers and fries, they didn't look like they were in any hurry to move.

Adam glanced up and saw Noah looking at him. He nodded shortly and went back to work on the next batch of orders—a pitcher of beer, a sweet and sour, a Manhattan, a rum and Coke.

It was a nice realization to know he didn't crave a one of them and hadn't for a while. Not even now, after he'd spent most of the day waiting.

A lull came and he moved to stand at the bar.

Lana brushed her fingers across the back of his hand. Because she was there, because he could, he leaned over and kissed her. It had taken her twenty years to come back, but it was twenty years he'd wait all over again as long as she came back. And she was his now.

"You okay?" she asked softly. "You seem tense."

He shrugged. "Waiting."

"Aren't we all?" She glanced over her shoulder toward Noah, and as though he felt the weight of that look, his head lifted.

Adam wasn't surprised when the couple moved to join Lana at the bar. "Anybody heard anything else?" he asked once Noah had settled between the two women. It had started that way. Noah. Lana. Only David was missing.

Full circle.

"He's not at the police station," Noah said softly. He shrugged. "I went by there, looking for him."

"Maybe . . ." Lana's voice trailed off. "Maybe he's at Sybil's."

They lapsed into silence and then Noah sighed. "I don't know. He was off the other day when we were working. Saw her, and it was like he went to stone. I didn't ask, but when I went to check on Taneisha after she'd woken up, she mentioned she'd gone out to talk to him. David ended things."

"Well. He's a dumbass," Lana said grimly.

"I'm still trying to wrap my mind around what people are saying happened. I mean . . . this Sarah, she was practically like his sister, right?" Trinity said, looking down the bar at Lana, then at Noah before glancing at Adam. "And she attacked Sybil."

"Obsession." Adam swiped his rag down the bar. "It

does crazy things to your head." Then he slid his gaze to Lana. "Trust me, I know."

He'd spent twenty years obsessing, hadn't he?

"It's not just obsession." Noah looked up. "There was more there. If that's what happened, if she did try to hurt Sybil because of David, then there was more than obsession. She wasn't . . . whole . . ."—he reached up and tapped his brow—"up here to begin with. She obsessed. Wanted what she couldn't have. Saw things that weren't there. And something pushed her over."

"Like what?" Lana put the iPad down with a *thunk*. "I mean, David *left*. It's pretty obvious that he wasn't going to settle down and be a happy little Amish guy. That isn't who he is."

"Exactly," Noah said softly. "And there she was, feeling abandoned and confused, because everything she had painted in her head was falling apart. He'd rather come back home to this place where people had treated him like hell than be there with her."

Silence fell between them.

Somebody yelled for Adam and he turned away with a muttered curse.

The other three remained silent.

Waiting.

Jensen needed a drink. A drink. Then bed. Then sex. Or maybe sex, then drink, then bed. No. Drink. Sex. Bed.

But Dean was still at the station, arguing about warrants and arguing with judges, and he wasn't going to be home for a little while. But she was done.

Sarah, for now, was locked behind bars. Bail would be high.

The PD had arrived and practically glued her mouth

shut, not that it was necessary. Once Jensen had left the room, Sarah had refused to say anything, but that weird little smile hadn't left her face.

She had something to do with Peter's disappearance. Jensen knew it as well as she knew her own name.

Maybe she'd—

"Stop it!" She groaned and pressed the heels of her hands to the sides of her head. Up ahead a car was pulling out of a spot in front of Shakers, and on instinct she nosed into it. She needed a drink. She'd just leave her car there. Have a drink. Walk home. It was only two blocks away, and she seriously doubted anybody would tow *her* car.

"Abuse of authority," she muttered, rubbing the tension gathering at the back of her neck. "Damn straight."

She'd been working ten to twelve hours a day for the past few months, and now she finally saw the light at the end of the tunnel. She could be lazy for one damn night.

Of course, she should have realized that if she was in the mood for a drink so was half the damn town. Brooding, she stood in the doorway of Shakers a few minutes later, aware of the odd stillness that had fallen across the crowd. The noise had dropped by half since she'd walked in, and as she took one step, then another, she could feel people staring at her.

Her brother, Tate, stood slumped against the bar and he grinned at her, tipping a bottle in her direction. She smirked, and as she passed him she said, "Man, you'd think these people never saw a cop before."

A few people laughed and some of the conversations resumed.

She breathed a little easier as she made her way down the bar, looking for an open seat.

She just about swore and turned around when she

found one. It was the only one, too. Right next to the one group of people she had no desire to talk to.

Planting her feet, she crossed her arms over her chest and eyed them. Noah looked up first, glancing over his shoulder. A golden-blond brow slid up and then his new wife, Trinity, glanced up. Lana barely spared Jensen a look, but she wasn't fooled by the casual lack of interest. "If I didn't know better, I'd get a little paranoid, coming in here to find the three of you."

"Well, technically, it's four." Noah nodded toward the bar.

She swung her head around and sighed as she saw Adam. He was mixing up drinks, but his gaze slid her way, a glint in his eyes.

"Of course." Head pounding, she took the stool and stared at the bottles lining the back of the bar. Have a drink and relax or get hammered and tell Dean to be ready to save her from herself? *Decisions, decisions.* "You know, everything comes back to you guys."

"No." Lana leaned forward, her elbows braced on the scarred surface as she stared down the bar at Jensen. "It comes back to me and David. The others were just caught in the mess of it. But if we wanted to be fair, it all goes back to the sons of bitches who started Cronus. Let's lay the blame where it belongs."

Jensen smiled sadly. "I'm not blaming you. It's just a weird circle that might finally come to its weird little end." Because she knew why they were here, she waved Adam down. "Wine. Something red and sweet—I hate that dry stuff. And then five minutes of your time."

Adam looked out at the bar, an amused grin lighting his face. He was ridiculously handsome, and half the female population had probably lost their panties because of that grin. Now, of course, he had focused all of that heat on one woman. It didn't surprise Jensen. She'd always known Adam ran from demons. That the past was tied up in Lana wasn't much of a surprise, looking back.

"Oh, I can spare five minutes," he drawled, looking back at Jensen. "I'll spend thirty minutes catching up, but anything to help out the law."

"Just smile at the ladies, Casanova," she said dryly. "They'll forgive you if the drinks come a little late."

He snorted. "Clearly, you haven't seen how impatient people get when they wanna get their drink on."

Adam took the five minutes, and he took them away from the bar.

The break room was quieter—marginally. He stood with the door shut, his back to it.

Lana stood next to him and she refused to think about how her stomach jumped and lurched. David was fine. She knew that. He had to be, because if he weren't *somebody* would have heard about it and that meant Noah would have heard.

That was just how things worked in this town.

So David was fine—

"I can't tell you what happened earlier, because we're still investigating," Jensen said, interrupting the ramble of Lana's thoughts. "But . . ." She stopped, cocking her head as though she was picking her words carefully. Finally, she focused her gaze on Lana.

Lana felt the impact of that look to the soles of her feet.

"I understand what the two of you tried to do. And I understand why you came back, why he decided to make his presence known. You realized it wasn't done and you couldn't leave it like that." Taking a deep breath, Jensen finished the rest in a rush: "It's done. It's really done."

She looked from each of them, a sad smile on her face.

"All of you ended up tangled in this mess and you're connected to it. It's not *over* yet, but they are done."

A knot in Lana's chest loosened and her eyes started to burn. But she fought it all back. She hadn't heard what she needed to hear. Not yet. "What about David?"

Lifting a brow, Jensen asked levelly, "What do you mean?"

"Don't give me that." Lana tucked her hands in her back pockets, staring at the detective, smiling coolly despite the knot in her throat. "You know how this town works. Everybody and their brother knows something went down at Sybil's today. And if Sybil was involved, David was."

"Where she is, there you'll find him," Jensen murmured, tipping her head back and staring up at the ceiling. "Yeah. He was involved. Again, I can't go into detail. I'm not surprised you haven't heard from him. But he's fine. I suppose all of it will come out soon. But he's fine."

She moved toward the door, pausing when Adam didn't step aside. "May I go?" She looked down at the glass she'd brought back into the break room with her. "Oddly enough, I seem to have drunk my wine already."

Adam stepped aside, but Lana put her hand on the door. "Where is he?"

"David?" A smile curved Jensen's face. "The last I heard, he was over at Sybil's."

Lana's eyes widened.

Jensen grinned. "A couple of uniforms dropped them off. All three of them, at Sybil's place. And David followed her inside. I guess maybe he wasn't burning his bridges quite as spectacularly as I'd thought he was."

Lana moved away from the door and Jensen paused before she headed out. "Full circle for all of you, huh?"

Just before Jensen shut the door, she heard a phone

ringing. Noah's, she thought. The ring was "The Imperial March"—he was always getting phone calls.

In the doorway, her head propped against the doorjamb, Sybil watched the two boys.

Darnell had spent nearly an hour on the phone with his mom. That was *after* they'd spent nearly an hour up at the hospital, too. Sybil had told Taneisha the boys were her heroes.

She'd meant it.

Somewhere off in the quiet of the house was another one, although he'd never believe that.

He'd come back, but she still wasn't sure if he meant to *stay* this time.

If he didn't, she was done.

She'd already decided what she'd do.

She was going to talk to the Realtor, see about putting her mother's house up for sale. And she'd leave. She was also going to talk to a lawyer about getting custody of Drew, if it came to that. Layla might not fight her on it, but if she had to, she'd do it. He belonged with her and all three of them knew it. Drew did; Layla did. Sybil knew it as well.

If David would let it happen, the three of them could have a family, be happy, right here.

But if he wouldn't, then she was done chasing after him.

Hearing a soft sound at the end of the hall, she looked up.

He stood there, hands loose at his sides, watching her. Most of his face was lost to the shadows, but the light streaming through the small window high up on the wall fell across his eyes, and only his eyes. The intensity of that gaze stole the breath from her lungs. So much that she felt her chest growing tight.

Looking back into the room where the boys slept, she gripped the doorknob in a death grip. "You said you had to make some calls earlier. Did you?"

That had been nearly three hours ago. Weird time to think of it, but she was fumbling, reaching for anything to occupy her mind now that the boys were tucked in bed and she had nothing else to keep her from turning to him, reaching for him.

Begging him.

She hadn't stooped that low before.

She wasn't going to now.

She hoped.

"Yes," he murmured, his voice so low she barely heard it.

The boards creaked under his feet as he came closer. "Come downstairs."

She closed her eyes, swallowed hard.

She'd have to do that, eventually. She couldn't just linger in the hallway and stare at the kids all night.

After a minute, she pried her fingers away from the door and then turned toward him. His hand moved to the small of her back as she started down the hall, and she was almost painfully aware of his touch, aware of the way his palm lay flat against her skin.

She was quiet, waiting for him to start in on one of his *I should leave. I should go.* But he was oddly silent, even after she tucked herself in her chair, arms folded over her chest. He moved to the window, staring outside. Moonlight shone in on him.

Something's different, Sybil thought. She didn't know what. Couldn't explain it. But it was different.

Then he turned his head to look at her. A fist slammed into her heart. There was a faint smile on his face.

A real one. Not that bitter slant, not the mockery of a smile. A faint smile, like he'd thought of something that amused him. Swallowing, she shifted up, sat a little straight as he pushed off the wall and started toward her. She almost asked him what he was smiling about but decided she didn't want to know.

"What will happen with Sarah?"

That stopped him in his tracks and the smile faded. Now his face was stark, set in those harsh, familiar lines. "I don't know." He looked down, stared at the floor. "She killed Louisa, Brumley, Max. She killed Abraham."

David lifted his head, staring at Sybil from under his lashes. "Abraham wasn't her father. I didn't know that until today. Her father . . ." He let the words trail off as he looked away, staring at something she couldn't see. "Her father hurt her. I was told that he'd knocked her down once so hard she broke her arm when she fell. Abraham rescued her from that. And she killed him. Because he was in the way."

Sybil came off the couch, shaking her head. "That isn't *your* fault."

"No." He nodded. "Logically, I understand. It feels like it is, but logically . . . I know that. She was sick. She must have been that way all her life and none of us saw it. *I* never saw it. And I still wanted to kill her when I came in here and saw her holding a gun to you. I *could* have killed her."

His gaze came back to Sybil. Her heart lurched, then started to bang against her ribs so hard, she had to struggle just to breathe. As he moved closer, the air in the room dwindled down to nothing. He reached up, touched her lips. "I don't know what I would have done if she'd hurt you. If she'd taken you from me."

Mouth dry, Sybil stood there, frozen.

He was even closer now. When had he gotten that close?

She didn't know, but he seemed to surround her, arms

locked over her shoulders, bracketing her in, his face filling her vision and the warm, dark scent of him flooding her senses. "David, I—"

"You told me to leave," he said, cutting her off.

She swallowed. *Yes.*

He backed away, looked around. "I don't feel like I know how to belong to anybody. To a family."

"David, there's no rule book. Families don't come with instructions," she said, forcing the words out. "We figure it out. We make it work."

He turned and walked away.

Her heart ripped open and despite her intentions not to beg, she found herself following him. He didn't head toward the door, though.

He went down the hall.

Toward her . . . bedroom?

He stood there. Looking inside. "I know where I feel like I belong," he said, his voice gruff. "It's with you."

She scowled at his back. "With me . . . in my bedroom?"

He looked back at her. "With you. Anywhere." Then he looked back, stared hard at her bed. "I hate the bed, though."

And once more, he started to walk, edging around her and heading into the living room.

She found him staring outside.

"David, would you—"

He moved to the door at the exact time she heard a knock.

She shot a look at the clock. It was past eleven. "Who in the hell . . ."

Noah stood there.

Behind Noah was Adam.

And there was a third man, younger than the others. Narrowing her eyes, she moved in, frowning as she took in the simple blue shirt, the brown trousers, the hat that covered the dark bowl of his hair. He was familiar. *Wait*—

Thomas. That was Thomas. He worked with David on a lot of the projects when some of the Amish builders got involved.

"What's going on?" she asked flatly.

David took her hand and tugged her outside. She was too confused to stop him, and then fifteen seconds later she yelped as her feet hit the cold concrete. "Damn it, it's *cold*," she said, jerking against his hand.

David just picked her up.

A sharp breath of air gusted out of her in shock. "Put me down. I can go get—"

He came to a stop at the foot of his truck and then he put her down, settling her so that she stood on his shoes. He wrapped his arms around her, his larger body warming hers.

She said nothing, staring into the back of the truck, puzzling through what lay in front of her.

"Abraham helped me build it. It was the first thing I ever made with my hands," David said softly.

Sybil licked her lips as her gaze landed on the headboard. It was simple, the lines clean, masculine. "A bed." She smiled. "This is your bed."

"I don't like yours."

Wiggling around, she managed to work her arms around his neck. She stared into his eyes, resting her brow against his. "You don't like my bed, so I get to keep yours? What else do I get?"

He reached up and caught one of her hands, guided it back down until he could press it to his heart. "You can't have the bed unless I get to stay, too. You told me not to come back. Unless I came to stay."

Her heart trembled. Sybil could feel it and everything else inside her was shaking, too.

"David?"

"You were right. And I've been an ass. I'm sorry," he whispered, pressing a kiss to her eyelids, her cheeks, ghosting one along her mouth before he moved to murmur in her ear, "I don't feel like I'm good enough for you. I don't feel like I ever will be. But I know I love you. I love you too much to let you go, so I'm going to just have to spend the rest of my life making myself good enough."

"David . . ."

She was crying.

"Sybil." Cupping her face in his hands, he brushed the tears away. "Don't cry. Please don't. Please don't. . . ." He kissed another tear away, closing his eyes as he pressed his forehead to hers. "If it's too late, I understand. If you need time, just tell me. I'll—"

She clutched his shirt in her hands and her mouth slanted over his.

That kiss tasted of tears. And smiles. A second later, she broke away to look up at him. "Shut up. Just shut up a minute."

Then she leaned back against him, laid her mouth to his. Softer than the last time, and he groaned, dipping a hand into her hair, twining the curls around his fist. Her curves molded to him. Through their clothes, he felt the softness of her, felt the cool air teasing his skin.

"Sybil," he rasped, drawing back a moment later to stare into her eyes.

She laid a hand on his cheek. "For almost ten years, I waited for you. Ten years, David."

He covered her hand with his, throat too tight to speak, and the words wouldn't come anyway.

Sybil leaned in, twining her free arm around his neck. "You realize, though, now that I got you, the last thing I'm going to do is let you get away . . . ever."

"I can live with that." He turned his face into her hair and breathed in the scent of her. "I was coming back. Even before today. I'd already figured it out, Sybil. I was coming back."

"Hey!" Adam's voice was a bark in the night. "You dragged me out of a perfectly warm bar to trot out to no-man's-land for this bed. Are you going to help us get it set up or what?"

David lifted his head, opening his mouth.

Sybil clapped a hand over his lips before he could speak. "Damn straight he's going to help." Then she leaned in and whispered, "The way I see it, we've got a lot of time to make up for anyway. I'd rather not waste it out here in the cold."

ALSO BY SHILOH WALKER

SECRETS & SHADOWS E-NOVELLAS

Burn For Me

Break For Me

Long For Me

SECRETS & SHADOWS SERIES

Deeper Than Need

Sweeter Than Sin

AVAILABLE FROM ST. MARTIN'S PRESS